Praise for *The Winter Palace*

"Stachniak's meticulous research helps to authenticate her vivid depiction of the period and place. . . . This novel has breathed new life into a page of history."
—*Winnipeg Free Press*

"The book roars along, with all the backstabbing, forced marriages, shifting alliances and drama that make up this royal household. . . . A very entertaining book."
—*Montreal Gazette*

"Stachniak has uncovered a treasure trove of rich material. . . .[Her] vision casts light over recent Russian history too, which is exactly what a piece of historical fiction should do."
—*The Globe and Mail*

"A wonderful novel, riven with intrigue and startling details, the sort to savour on a long winter evening."
—*Daily Telegraph* (UK)

"[*The Winter Palace*] showcases Stachniak's flair for blending biography and fact with sumptuous detail. . . . A beautiful piece of escapism rooted in fact."
—*Star Tribune* (Minnesota)

"Extraordinarily absorbing. . . . Will have you on the edge of your seat."
—*Daily Mail* (UK)

"Brilliant, bold. . . . This superb biographical epic proves the Tudors don't have a monopoly on marital scandal, royal intrigue or feminine triumph."
—*Booklist*

"At the same time baroque and intimate, worldly and domestic, wildly strange and soulfully familiar, *The Winter Palace* offers a flickering glimpse of history through the gauze of a deft entertainment."
—*The Washington Post*

"In *The Winter Palace*, Stachniak creates a story filled with political intrigue, secret affairs and dread diseases. . . . Stachniak has faithfully reproduced the historical story of Catherine."
—*The Vancouver Sun*

Praise for *Empress of the Night*

"The book's structure is ambitious and sometimes moving. . . . Stachniak's writing is distinct . . . especially in vivid descriptions of sensory details: perfume, sweat and the click of heels on polished floorboards."

—*Quill & Quire*

"Stachniak's latest novel is an intimate look at the private life of Catherine the Great, and readers of the genre who like lush and richly detailed historical fiction will likely approve." —*Winnipeg Free Press*

"*Empress of the Night* . . . casts light on Catherine's life with unflinching honesty and intimacy. This fun novel of lovers, intrigue and malicious and manipulative nobility keeps readers enthralled with every page."

—*Virtuoso Life Magazine*

"Stachniak's absorbing novel opens readers' hearts to an extraordinary and misunderstood woman. . . . Wonderfully written, Stachniak's story vibrates with passion, drama and intrigue. This is a feast for fans."

—*Romantic Times Magazine*

"Historical fiction fans will appreciate this personal account of a formidable and, indeed, infamous ruler." —*Library Journal*

"Stachniak's grasp of the 'why' is illuminating, and Catherine herself would have nodded approvingly."

—*Washington Independent Review of Books*

THE
CHOSEN
MAIDEN

BY EVA STACHNIAK

Empress of the Night

The Winter Palace

Garden of Venus

Necessary Lies

THE CHOSEN MAIDEN

EVA STACHNIAK

DOUBLEDAY
CANADA

Library and Archives Canada Cataloguing in Publication

Stachniak, Eva, 1952-, author
The chosen maiden / Eva Stachniak.

Issued in print and electronic formats.
ISBN 978-0-385-67856-8 (paperback).--ISBN 978-0-385-67855-1 (epub)

I. Title.

PS8587.T234C56 2016 C813'.6 C2016-902917-4
C2016-902918-2

Jacket and Text Design: Leah Springate
Jacket Images: Woman: Josephine Cardin/Arcangel Images; Pattern: DrObjektiff/
Shutterstock.com; Gold background: pondkungz/Shutterstock.com
Printed and bound in the USA

Published in Canada by Doubleday Canada,
a division of Penguin Random House Canada Limited

www.penguinrandomhouse.ca

10 9 8 7 6 5 4 3 2

For Hugh and Brady

Art and dance foretell the future.

They are like intuition . . .

Bronislava Nijinska

THE
CHOSEN
MAIDEN

October 9, 1939

R*oom 11, Berth 3, SS American Trader.*

My last address?

For this ship may well become my coffin, sinking here, somewhere between Europe and America, as did SS Athenia on her way to Montreal last month. Now we, too, are a tiny speck on the grey waters of the Atlantic. If we make it, New York will greet us with its skyscrapers, those towering giant lizards, scaly and beautiful. And a new life that might not be that new after all. We make vows in moments of danger then slip back into old habits.

My London contract was cancelled the day Britain declared war on Germany. With all the theatres closed and the clock ticking on our British visas, I signed with Wassily de Basil's company for their Australian tour. If we do go to Australia, that is. We make plans, my mother would remind me, and God laughs.

If the protracted visa interview at the American embassy in London was any indication, I'll have to steel myself for questions, account for the contradictions of history. My imperial Russian passport declares that Бронисла́ва Фоми́нична Нижи́нская*—Bronislava Fominitchna Nijinskaya—was born in Minsk, in 1891. My Polish passport insists that Bronisława Niżyńska is a Polish citizen, born in Warsaw in 1890. My Nansen passport argues that I am stateless. Mercifully they all agree that my face is oblong, my complexion fair and my hair blond, although my eyes are described variously as green or blue.*

Mine, I will defend myself, is not a simple story.

Sleep is still fleeting, its hazy consolations too brief to soothe. I wake up shaking, gutted by grief, and wait for darkness to lift. The instant the sun begins pushing against the edge of the ocean, I get out of bed, wrap a shawl around my shoulders and leave our stuffy cabin without the slightest noise. I was Diaghilev's ballerina long enough: No sound when you land, not even the softest of *thuds.*

On the upper deck I do a few pliés *by the railing, stretch my arms, my legs, taking note of the newest restrictions, tensions, points of stiffness. At forty-nine my body, my instrument, perfected and polished for years, is tarnished and dulled. And yet, my muscles still hold the perfect memory of dances I long ago mastered: the movements of Papillon, Ta-Hor, the Sixth Nymph, the Chosen Maiden.*

Stretching done, I lean on the railing, light a cigarette and wait for the dolphins. My husband assures me they can hear a U-boat approaching and would vanish if a torpedo were on its way. Since they never swim alone, I think of them as a smiling corps de ballet, *executing their intricate, smooth dives in well-rehearsed harmony. As soon as they appear—and lately they always do—I look for a place where I can write. On a clear day even a coil of ship ropes on the deck will do; when it is cold, windy or wet, I head for the smoking room inside.*

Where does it come from, this lifelong compulsion to fill up notebook after notebook: Childhood Sorrows, The Diary of a Young Dancer, Notebook of Unnecessary Upsets, About Vaslav, About Feodor, About Levushka. *Lined or squared, cheap or expensive, with soft or hard covers, but always small enough to slip into my purse. Is it because I've lived for so long in the shadow of giants? Always needing to prepare my case, argue for what I hold dear?*

My brother Vaslav lives in a small hotel in the Swiss mountain village of Adelboden, a puppet in his wife's hands. Dressed, fed, taken for walks. Depending on whom you believe, he is shy and childlike or irritable and agitated. Mute or talking to himself. Motionless or thrashing around the room in rage. The God of the Dance, too, is no stranger to contradictions.

Take only what is essential, *Vaslav's voice still urges me.* Discard the rest.

I open my notebook and begin to write.

PART ONE:

1894–1900

1.

THEY ARE BLACK. They are from America.

I've spotted them among the guests Father brought home with him from the theatre. They are the only ones I don't know. All the others are artists from our parents' troupe, the ones who always ask me if I've been a good girl, obeyed Mamusia and Father and played nicely with my brothers. When I say yes, they give me sweets and remind me to share them with Vaslav and Stassik.

The two black men, dressed in white tailcoats with black lapels, move about the crowded room with catlike, fluid ease, helping themselves to Mamusia's *kanapki* or to a shot of vodka from the tray Father carries around the room. I watch them for a while until they notice my presence and beckon to me. When I approach, I get a whiff of sharp, musky cologne and cigar smoke.

Their names are Jackson and Johnson.

"Ja and Jo," they tell me, pointing at one another and turning sideways in perfect harmony as if they were facing an invisible audience. Then they turn back to me, bend forward and put their hands on their knees, moving them so fast that the knees seem to pass through each other. The rings on their little fingers glitter against their black skin like stars.

I applaud so hard that my hands smart.

They do not ask me if I've been a good girl. Instead they show me a glossy photograph of the two of them onstage, standing one behind the other, canes in hand. In addition to the white tailcoats with black lapels, they are wearing top hats, shiny and most elegant. Behind them the set depicts exploding fireworks and tall buildings that touch the clouds. They have danced in New York. They have danced in Paris and London. They are on their way to Moscow.

My Russian is as good as my Polish, but when Ja and Jo speak it, familiar words crack, waver in unexpected places. "What do you call this?" they ask me, pointing at the birch-bark box in which Mamusia keeps charcoal for the samovar.

"*Nabirushka*," I say, and when they repeat it the word sounds both unusual and funny.

An idea comes to me then. "Can you say *Mama myla Milu mylom. Mila mylo ne ljubila*?"

Jo tries right away. "*Mama . . . myla . . . Mama mylo . . .*"

I shake my head and repeat the tongue twister again, slower this time. They close their eyes and listen. Then, after just one more try, both of them remember it word for word.

A moment later I hear them say it to a cheering round of applause. Father pats Ja on the shoulder. Mamusia brings more food from the kitchen and I, accustomed to the fleeting attention of adults, find a spot in the corner of the room from where I can watch without being in the way.

But Ja and Jo come back. "Do you want to learn our dance, Bronia?" they ask, and when I jump up, they motion to me to follow them to the adjacent room, where they have already put a plank on the floor and sprinkled it with sand.

"Watch!"

First they show me a few simple steps—a tap on the plank, a drop of the heel, a sweep of the foot—and nod as I repeat them with ease. Soon single taps are replaced by double and triple ones, and I follow my wonderful teachers into a roll that sounds like a horse galloping with neck-breaking speed, my feet flying, my heart swelling with joy and pride. The three of us are dancing together, brushing and flapping to the rhythm tapped by our shoes, in what Ja and Jo call a "Shim Sham Shimmy."

When we finish, it is their turn to applaud. "You are a girl prodigy, Bronia," they say. A marvel. A genius. If only my parents would agree, they would hire me on the spot to dance with them onstage. We would be a runaway sensation: "Jackson, Johnson and Nijinska!" The world would be ours. Moscow, St. Petersburg. Paris. London. America. "What do you say, Bronia? Will you come to New York with us?"

"Oh, yes!" I exclaim. I can already see myself on that faraway stage, lit with glittering fireworks. I'm wearing a black dress with a white collar, and I, too, have a shiny top hat and a cane with a silver handle.

Vaslav interrupts this thrilling vision. "You are still such a baby, Bronia." My older brother is leaning on the door frame. His voice is stern and grown-up and doesn't sound like his at all. "They are only joking," he adds in Polish. "They won't take you anywhere."

I wonder how long he has been there. I wonder if he has seen me dance.

"What do you say, Bronia?" Ja asks. "Shall we do it once again?"

Ja and Jo are clapping, swaying their hips, humming the melody that makes my feet itch to move. There is laughter in their eyes. "Don't mind your brother. He's just jealous. He'll come around. Let's show him what you can do!"

"Me? Jealous?" Vaslav sneers. "Of her?"

He is five years old. I'm not quite three. He can do all I can and more.

Fingers snap, heels click. The beat is there for me to slide right into. Dancing is like breathing. It is in me, woven into my body. All I need to do is to let it out.

I have no doubts. No hesitations. None.

I dance, fast, agile. My legs fly back, my hands swing. With Ja and Jo beside me, I turn sideways and around, with precision and wildness that delight me. There is nothing else I want or need.

When we finish, Ja rests his hand on my right shoulder, Jo on my left. Their eyes sparkle. "Excellent, Bronia," they say. "You are a true artist."

And then, in a smooth, practised gesture, they bow in front of me.

I look at Vaslav, still leaning on the door frame, his right leg bent, resting on his toes. He narrows his eyes, considering what he has just seen. He is not applauding.

"This," he says, curling his upper lip, "is acrobatics. This is vaudeville. Good practice—but not art."

Both my brothers take proper dance lessons. Father teaches them every day except Sunday. I'm still too young for lessons, but I'm allowed to watch, which I do, committing each step, each correction Father gives Vaslav and Stassik to memory. Then I practise their moves in front of a wardrobe mirror. This year, at Easter, in Odessa, my brothers will dance in a children's performance. "A classic Cossack dance," Father calls it, making the word *classic* ring with pride. Stassik will be a Cossack brave and Vaslav will be his girl. He will circle Stassik three times and then jump up in the air.

"Why have you been watching us then, Vaslav?" I ask. "Why have you not gone away?" Behind me I hear Ja and Jo tap and brush in rhythm with my words.

"Because!" Vaslav says, the answer my brother resorts to when he doesn't know what to say. It usually means that I have caught him at a lie, but he will never admit it. I know that this must be enough of a victory. For now.

2.

STANISŁAW, WACŁAW, BRONISŁAWA. We are the Nijinsky children. Our parents are the only Polish dancers with the Lukovitch troupe, which performs in Russian towns and cities. From Odessa to Kiev. From Kiev to Moscow. From Moscow to St. Petersburg. The repertoire consists of ballets, *divertissements*, amazing acts of entertainment and—every Easter and Christmas—children's performances.

The Polish word *sława* is in all our names. It means "fame and glory." Which is what our parents want for us, even though they call us "Stassik," "Vatsa" and "Bronia."

We are children of the stage. We know how to pack at a moment's notice. How to tie books together with a piece of string in such a way that it will be easy to untie. How to flatten a suitcase by sitting on it and then secure it with a belt so it doesn't burst. We love arriving in a new place, exploring our new apartment. Claiming beds, shelves; helping Mamusia place our rugs on the floor; making a room "ours" with framed photographs, a flower vase that travels wrapped up in newspapers, gifts Father has received in appreciation of his dancing. We have a bronze statuette of a ballerina, which I think beautiful but which Vaslav doesn't like because she dances alone. We have a picture of a clown with big black tears painted on his cheeks. And a painting of a Russian street market in which the birch baskets on the stalls are filled with mushrooms, apples and pears, and a little dog in the right corner is licking the greasy wheels of a carriage.

The Lukovitch troupe travels from one engagement to another in a caravan of ten carriages. Mamusia makes us hold moist handkerchiefs over our mouths when the roads get too dusty. When we get bored, she points to the fields of watermelons, which resemble giant green balls, or to barges floating on the river from which bearded boatmen wave to us. "I'll join them when I grow up," Vaslav announces. "Me, too," Stassik says, and I feel a pang of jealousy, for there are no boat women I could join. The women in the villages we pass busy themselves in front of the whitewashed houses with sunflowers growing in their gardens, clay pots drying on wicker fences, but there is no glory in being one of them when I grow up. Barefoot children feed geese, ducks and chickens. Towns have gates where bearded Cossacks stop us for questioning and tolls.

Inside our carriage Mamusia reads to us from Polish books. *Dawno dawno temu* . . . A long time ago . . . far, far away. Vaslav's favourite story is about giant knights asleep inside a big mountain, awaiting the moment when a mysterious voice will tell them, "The time has come." Stassik and I love the one about Pan Twardowski, who has tricked the devil and deftly landed on the moon, where—if we strain our eyes at night—we can almost see him, riding a rooster.

Father prefers songs to stories. About an *uhlan*, a cavalry soldier, who asks a pretty girl for a kiss. About a sun that doesn't want to set. About *zielony mosteczek*, a green bridge, my favourite. When Father sings, he makes funny faces, miming the fear with which a girl walks on wavering boards of the green bridge, or the cocky smiles of her relentless suitor, who comes up with clever schemes to make her like him.

We were all born on the road. Stassik in Tiflis, and two years later, Vaslav in Kiev. I was born in Minsk, one hour after my parents danced together in Glinka's *A Life for the Tsar*. Mamusia was still able to dance the polonaise at the beginning of the opera, but then the labour pains started and Mamusia hurried to the hospital in a *droshky* sleigh. A substitute took her place at Father's side for the mazurka and the *cracovienne* in the Polish act.

I didn't take long. By the time the curtain fell a messenger had been sent from the hospital to tell my father that, after two sons, he had a daughter.

Vaslav and Stassik both have claims to miracles. "Vaslav was born in a shirt," Mamusia says, which is a sign of distinction, a promise of greatness. I imagine him arriving from the other world in the gauze robe of an angel. Embroidered, perhaps, with stars and planets and flowers and flying birds. I wonder where this beautiful shirt is now and why Vaslav is not wearing it. Mamusia laughs and tells me that the shirt was not made of fabric. "It has dissolved," she says with a mysterious smile, and this makes it even more intriguing and gives Vaslav more reason to say, "I'm the chosen one."

We believe him, for it is not just the shirt. On the day Vaslav was born, Father was dancing at a charity ball in Kiev. Since at the end of the ball there were still prizes left over from the lottery, the organizers threw them in the air for everyone to try to catch. Father, leaping highest of all, caught a beautiful silver chalice, and brought it home as a lucky gift for his newborn son. Now Mamusia polishes it with toothpowder and places it on the highest shelf in every apartment we move into, and Vaslav warns us never to touch it. "I'll know if you do," he tells Stassik and me. He says the chalice, if sullied with our unworthy fingers, would emit messages of outrage he would hear no matter how far away he was. Only, this is a lie, for I touch it when Vaslav isn't around and he never knows.

Stassik's miracle is even more astounding than Vaslav's. Stassik has come back from the dead.

In this story I am not yet born and Vaslav is a tiny baby. Our parents are in Moscow for the season, staying in a third-floor apartment. It is sunny, with big windows that are clean and sparkling, for the hired girl has just washed them with ammonia and polished the glass with newspapers. Stassik has a nanny who looks after him all the time. But at this very moment she goes to the kitchen, for Stassik is thirsty and wants a glass of milk. While she is away, a military band passes by, and Stassik, who has a passion for music, wants to see it. He pushes a chair to the wall, climbs onto the windowsill and presses his hands on the panes. The nanny returns in time to see the window opening and Stassik falling out. She screams. Father—who is in another room—dashes downstairs to the cobbled street, where Stassik lies motionless, blood seeping through his nose and ears, his mouth covered with pinky foam.

In the hospital Stassik remains unconscious for three days, his soul already in the other world. Mamusia doesn't leave his side. She doesn't eat or sleep. She prays to Matka Boska, begging the Mother of God for help. And then, on the fourth day, Stassik sits up in his hospital bed and, seeing his favourite drum, which Father has placed by his bedside, extends his hands and laughs. "A miracle," Mamusia says, and every time we are in church, she reminds us to thank God and Matka Boska for Stassik's return from Heaven.

We give our thanks, as asked, but Vaslav and I never tell her of our grave disappointment. For when we ask Stassik about his three days in Heaven—was he floating on clouds, was he able to fly, what did the angels give him to eat—Stassik tells us that he doesn't remember anything at all.

When they are at home, our parents talk about dancing. No matter how wonderful the reviews, how long and ardent the applause, something has always gone wrong. Steps were too fast or too slow; a movement lost its tempo or has become stale and is calling for a new variation. Breath should've been held longer; an exhale was too abrupt.

For a long while this is what I understand from these conversations: Artists are never satisfied. Art is always difficult. Art demands constant vigilance. Whatever you accomplish, you could always do better.

Later I will also learn that muscles and tendons have moods. That sometimes they pull at the bones, demand longer warming up; sometimes they snap painfully and beg for a hot compress, a massage, a rest. That the mirror is a severe critic, pointing out the smallest of imperfections, teasing the dancer with a shadowy glimpse of what a step should have been but wasn't. That the audience, the black invisible presence beyond the lights of the stage, is the stern, unforgiving judge, the source of not just bliss but fear.

In this memory it is the beginning of winter and we have just arrived in Moscow. In the room I share with my brothers the wallpaper has stripes of tiny red rosebuds. "Ugly," Vaslav says, and Stassik starts pulling at the corners until strips tear off. They roll them into tight tubes then pretend these are cigarettes. "Have you ever seen a girl smoke?" my brothers ask when I want one, too.

Father walks into the room in a heavy, fur-lined coat and a Cossack hat, holding out his hand with the first snowball of the season. "Take it, Bronia," he says. "It's for you."

"What about me!" Vaslav screams, running toward us. Stassik is right behind him, his cheeks flushed with exertion, and yet Vaslav is always first. It is not just that he is quicker but that he always finds the shortest route, jumping over any obstacle on his way.

"No," Father says. "This one is for your sister. You two valiant cavaliers can get your own."

Gingerly I take the melting snowball in my hands, aware of water dripping on the floor. The new hired girl, whom we like already for she has let us touch her false teeth, is clucking with disapproval. Mamusia is just about to join her, call for rags to mop up the puddle, wax the spot, when Father touches her cheeks with his cold hands.

"Oh, stop it, Thomas!" Mamusia shrieks. "I should've known you would never grow up."

But she is laughing, too. And we are all putting on our heavy coats, and Mamusia smears our faces with goose fat to protect them from the cold. We slip on galoshes, which we hate, for it is impossible to bend our knees in them and we have to walk on straight legs. But nothing can spoil the joy of being outside and playing in the first snow. "Packing snow," Father calls it, as he makes a small ball, rolls it on the ground and shows us how it grows by taking on layer after sticky layer. Together we build a snowman, with a wilted carrot for a nose, two coals for eyes and an old bucket for a hat. We make snow angels. And run around chasing one another, a game of tag at which I'm getting better, even though I'm the youngest and a girl. Vaslav is too fast for me, but if I try hard, I can get Stassik and sometimes Father, though I suspect that he is making it easy for me, for Vaslav can never catch him.

Later that day, before leaving for the theatre, Father tells us about a snow maiden, a daughter of Winter and Frost, whose heart is made of ice. She falls in love with a shepherd, but love heats up her heart and she melts.

"This isn't fair," Vaslav moans. "You have to change the ending."

"I can't," Father says.

"But I want you to," Vaslav demands.

"But I want you to," Stassik echoes.

"If I change it, it'll be a lie," Father insists. "Snow always melts in the end. You don't want me to lie, do you?"

Now Stassik is crying. Vaslav, too, looks ready to burst into tears, and I know how Father dislikes when his sons cry, so I announce that the story does not need to be changed, because it is not yet finished. Yes, a snow maiden melts and turns into a puddle, but when the sun comes back, the water evaporates and travels all over the world as a cloud. And when the cloud is blown back over Russia, it is winter and the cloud turns into snow that falls on the ground and the children make it into a snow maiden again.

Vaslav and Stassik frown at me, not sure where this is leading, and I realize my predicament. For even though I have given my snow maiden a second chance, her fate has not changed. She will still fall in love and melt. I persist in my optimism, however, repeating the sequences of falling in love and melting and turning back into snow.

Vaslav and Stassik grow bored with my eternal procession of snow maidens and begin to yawn. Father winks at me. "Good night," he says, then adds in Polish in his funny, murmuring voice, "*Dobranoc, pchły na noc, karaluchy pod poduchy.*" Which I understand and do not understand at the same time. "Fleas for the night," I repeat to myself long after Father is gone. "Cockroaches under your pillows."

"What does it mean, Vaslav?" I ask him, my older brother who should know such things, but he is asleep and cannot hear me.

A few months later the three of us dance the "Sailor Dance" in the Lukovitch children's show. Our costumes are identical: bell-bottom trousers, blouses with wide collars, round sailor hats. Vaslav and Stassik dance their variation first. When they finish, they click their heels and raise their hands to point at the wings. This is when I appear, and the three of us repeat the variation together.

We have practised for weeks. With Father first then alone, perfecting each move. Onstage we keep straight lines, every gesture, every step reflected threefold, matching to the smallest detail. Our dance mimes rowing a boat, lowering and raising the sails, pulling the mooring line.

When the music ends, three pairs of heels click in unison; three palms raise to, but do not quite touch, our right temples, saluting the audience. We are a sensation.

3.

"ONE FOR ANOTHER through fire and water," Mamusia tells us. This is both an admonishment and the most serious of her requests.

We have to be each other's best friends.

"Just like me and my two sisters," Mamusia says, and we settle to hear again how she arrived in Russia to become a dancer in the Kiev Opera.

In truth it was only the middle sister, Stefa, who at fourteen had a job. A Kiev impresario had gone to Warsaw to scout for talent, spotted her in the *corps* at the Teatr Wielki and offered her an engagement. Stefa took Mamusia—Eleanora—and Aunt Thetya with her, on the flimsy but tantalizing promise that Mamusia, still a ballet student, would be hired in December, as soon as she turned twelve. In the meantime, one salary would be enough for the three of them. Must be. "One for another through fire and water," Mamusia repeats. Besides, there was nothing for them in Warsaw. They were orphans and their two older brothers were barely making ends meet.

I picture the sisters arriving at the Kiev Station. Beside them, in a neat line, stand their second-hand suitcases. Thetya had bought them at a Warsaw bazaar from a woman who swore they came all the way from Paris. The suitcases looked so elegant in their Warsaw apartment, but here on the Kiev pavement the scuffed brown leather is shabby and cracked and the handles are frayed and threatening to break.

Thetya, who is sixteen, thinks herself grown-up and thus responsible for her younger sisters. She is holding a piece of cardboard with the address of their Kiev lodgings, which they have been assured are just a short and pleasant walk from the Opera. Holding it so tightly that the writing gets smudged, a fact they discover when they approach a *droshky* driver and ask him in their broken, uncertain Russian if he could please take them to this address. The driver cannot read the Polish letters but knows the street when they pronounce it—Pushkinskaya.

The *droshky* plods past the University Building, past St. Volodymyr's Cathedral, but only Thetya pays attention to the sights. Mamusia and Stefa think of nothing but their appearance at the Opera the following morning. They don't have to speak to know each other's thoughts. Will they be good enough? Will Russian dancers accept two Polish girls, one barely a dancer and another still a student? Or will they be made to feel like imposters, interlopers? They squeeze each other's hands and feel a bit better.

Thetya gives a big sigh. By then she has seen not only the famous sights but also the Kiev beauties. Thetya is not a dancer. She is here to keep house for her sisters. To make sure they take proper care of themselves and do not squander their future.

There is a smile on Mamusia's lips as she recalls Thetya's words: "My sisters cannot show up at the Opera tomorrow in these Warsaw rags. What we all need here is a proper artistic appearance." Words followed by the rushed visit to the Opera offices for an advance on Stefa's wages, a trip to the drapers. Thetya spent a long sleepless night at the sewing machine borrowed from their landlady. "You two get your beauty sleep," she tells Mamusia and Stefa, chasing them to bed at midnight. "Tomorrow, I'll get my rest, but you need to dazzle them with your dancing."

I always greet this part of Mamusia's story with a thrilling shudder of pleasure. Mamusia and Stefa waking up in the morning, gasping with delight over the dresses. For Thetya has not merely matched the smart outfits of the Kiev beauties but surpassed them in elegance and flair. Three dresses have been cut to emphasize their slim waists; ruffles and pleats add substance to their skirts. All three are pearly blue, for the merchant who sold them the fabric gave them a good deal on it. It is just as well, for blue sets off their blond hair and matches their only decent pairs of walking shoes. "You should've seen us walking to the Opera. Heads up. Looking straight ahead. Heals clicking on the pavement. All eyes were on us."

There are more stories from these Kiev days. The day Mamusia proudly brought thirty-five rubles home, her first pay, proof that she, the youngest, was no longer a burden. The time she was called "Gazelle," of the long neck and tiny feet, graceful and beautiful yet serious and thoughtful, too. The time she danced in Setov's Opera alongside Italian ballerinas Virginia Zucchi and Carlotta Brianza, not just in Odessa and Kiev but also in Moscow and in the summer theatres of St. Petersburg, where she was applauded and praised for the superb rendering of her characters. "Subtle and yet masterful," one of the critics wrote. And the day Thomas Nijinsky, a dashing Polish dancer seven years her junior, declared himself smitten. Besotted. When he promised that he would stand by her in happiness and in sorrow. That he would never leave her.

She had seen him leap on the stage, soar over it like a proud eagle. Or fall to his knees only to jump up quickly in *lezginka* like a Chechen mountaineer, or throw his legs out in *prissadk*a like a Cossack warrior. She had heard the roaring applause he received, that Pole who rendered the Russian and Ukrainian dances like no other. He was not a big man, but passion filled his body and gave him strength beyond the confines of his muscles and tendons. Passion that did not leave him when he was off-stage, either. You could not miss his presence anywhere or mistake his voice for anyone else's. No party truly began until he arrived.

She refused him four times. "*Narwany*," she and her sisters called Thomas Nijinsky in Polish. Too passionate, too unstable. Does he not care that he could offer his future bride little more than provincial theatre stages and the life of a nomad? Or that one accident, one false step, could end his livelihood? When he came to her dressing room to propose for the fifth time, he pulled a real gun from his pocket and put it to his temple, threatening to die right there in front of her if she refused to become his wife.

4.

WE ARE IN ODESSA. I am five years old. It is a warm spring day, and I settle myself down on the wooden steps in the front of the house, waiting for Father to come home from the theatre, fixing my eyes on the street corner where he will appear. Vaslav and Stassik are playing in the backyard. I don't like going there because of the pigpen. Not only is it smelly, but on the day we arrived, a boar was pulled out of it for slaughter, and its terrible squeals still ring in my ears. There is a piglet in the pigpen now, small and thin, and I'm hoping we will be gone by the time it fattens enough to be killed.

When Father appears at last, I run toward him, throw myself in his arms, shrieking with joy. "My faithful little girl," he says, and tickles my cheek with his stubbly chin. He smells of cigarettes and citrusy cologne and of what I know is the theatre. The dusty, chalky whiff of sweat and glue.

"Have you done all your homework today?" he asks.

The troupe is on the road most of the year, so after our dance lessons Mamusia teaches us to read and write in Polish. In addition, Stassik and Vaslav have a Russian tutor.

"Yes," I say, and tell him that Mamusia said my range of movement has improved and that I read a story all by myself. It was about a Polish princess who chose to die rather than marry a German prince.

Father beams with pleasure, lifts me up and holds me so tight to his chest that the buttons of his coat dig into my cheek. Then he places me down and pats my head. We walk to our apartment hand in hand. Past the dark hall smelling not just of sour pickles and mushroom stew but also of coal dust and urine, the smell that always makes Father swear in Russian under his breath, "*Svoloch!*"

I walk in with Father as if he were my cherished prize, never leaving his side. I watch him take off his coat and hang it carefully on a peg in the hall, remove his shoes and put shoe trees inside them to keep their shape. Before supper Father always sits in his favourite armchair and drinks a glass of the beer Mamusia keeps cool for him—outside on the windowsill on cooler days or in a bucket of well water on a day like this one. He makes room for me beside him and I snuggle there, resting my head on his chest. Until he takes my hand and slides it into his pocket, from which I extract his silver cigarette case, engraved with greetings from his admirers. It opens with a *click*.

I take one cigarette out and give it to him. He taps it on the armrest before lighting it. "To tighten it inside," he has told me once. "Make it burn evenly."

Mamusia is inspecting the setting of the table, picking up this or that fork or spoon and polishing it or straightening the tablecloth so that the embroidered centre is not obscured by plates, while Father tells her about a meeting after the rehearsal she missed because she hurried home to be with us.

The meeting was a waste of time. Mamusia is lucky she didn't have to sit through it. Dancers are a sorry bunch. "Vipers," Father calls them. Jealous of everything. Ready to bite you when you are not looking.

"It's never that bad, Thomas," Mamusia protests.

"You are not there as much as I am," Father says, blowing out smoke in the circles he knows I've been waiting for. They rise into the air like halos from holy pictures of saints.

I'm waiting for Father to start talking about dancing. Ask Mamusia about the changes he has imagined and is planning to make in his latest variations. "A *tendu* then preparation and a quick *sissonne battue sans changer en arrière . . . arabesque, chassé* . . . a turn then a double pirouette . . . What do you think?" And Mamusia will stop whatever she is doing, think for a moment then nod and say, "Oh, yes, Thomas. This will work so well."

No matter how much I wish to slow the time, Father's cigarette is soon burnt to a stub, the beer glass emptied and we are all summoned to the table. Vaslav and Stassik come in sweaty, with reddened cheeks, and have to spit into a handkerchief with which Mamusia cleans their faces before sending them off to wash their hands.

Mamusia is an excellent cook and our dinners are a delicious mixture of Polish and Russian dishes—steaming plates of beet broth, pancakes rolled with mushroom filling and smothered with sour cream—all carefully set on a linen tablecloth decorated with a cross-stitch pattern. My favourite dish is fruit dumplings drizzled with very sweet melted butter with a dash of cinnamon in it. Vaslav and Stassik prefer the meat cutlets that Mamusia calls *bitki*, pounded thin with a wooden hammer and then fried.

"Stop fidgeting, Stassik . . . Vaslav, don't speak with your mouth full . . . chew your food, Bronia . . ."

There are so many admonitions. The Nijinsky children should be known by their good manners. No slouching, no slurping, elbows off the table, no interrupting adults when they speak. Obvious, I think them, unnecessary. I'd much rather hear about *Ekaterina, or The Bandit's Daughter*, in which Father is dancing Diavolino, a robber in love with his boss's daughter, who leaps across a wrecked bridge above a waterfall. Father is so proud of this leap!

The story of Diavolino and Ekaterina fascinates me. I've asked Vaslav what happens to them in the end, but he told me it was a secret. Only, when I refused to believe him, he admitted he didn't know, either.

"Does Diavolino marry the bandit's daughter?" my brother asks now.

"Why are you asking, Vaslav?" Father's voice has a sharp note in it.

"I just want to know."

"Which is of greater importance?" Father continues. "Who marries whom or the dancing itself?"

Vaslav lifts his eyes from the plate. He is about to say something—tell Father that it was I who wanted to know, perhaps—but doesn't.

Father is not really expecting an answer. He is not truly angry, either. I know it from the care with which he describes the new steps he has devised for Diavolino. How he added an *arabesque* and two pirouettes where there have been none and thus made the last dance more dynamic. "It has all come together at the rehearsals," he concludes. "Now I shall await the verdict of the public."

Mamusia smiles and nods, each smile and nod carefully timed to confirm Father's words. He is the best, her smile says, the most talented, the hardest working of the whole Lukovitch troupe. Thomas Nijinsky is a true artist, even if he has to dance on the provincial stages. A lot he has chosen willingly because of us, his children. So that one day, once we graduate from the Imperial Ballet School, he can say, "I'm the father of Stanislav and Vaslav Nijinsky, each a *premier danseur*, and Bronislava Nijinska, *prima ballerina assoluta*. Artists of the Imperial Theatres, their future assured beyond their dancing years, never having to sacrifice their art for bread."

It is important to make Father proud of us. Just like another Polish dancer, Felix Kschessinsky, is proud of his daughter Mathilda, whom the tsar himself called the "glory and adornment of Russian ballet."

I'm a meticulous and slow eater, cutting morsels of precise size, tasting them with my tongue before chewing. Stassik eats with abandon, always finishing first, asking for more. Mamusia says that that is because he is the oldest and is growing fast, which is true. Vaslav also eats slowly and always saves his best pieces for last. He likes to tease Stassik. This is why he holds his fork with a piece of meat in the air, and smacks his lips until Mamusia tells him to stop.

"Stop what?" Vaslav asks, as if no one could guess his intentions. "Stop eating? Do you want me to starve?"

"You know, I wonder," Mamusia says with a mischievous little grin, "if I should pray to St. Simon or St. Jude? The patron of patience or the patron of lost causes?"

Vaslav puts the morsel in his mouth and begins to chew.

"Lost causes," Father says, and laughs. "Definitely lost causes."

There is cake for dessert, and warm compote made from sliced apples and plums. There is talk of the next engagement, in Mykolaiv, which Mamusia doesn't like because the lodgings there are always really cramped but where we might be able to swim in the Buh River.

When dinner is over, I help Mamusia and the hired girl clear the table and tidy up the kitchen, while Father orders Stassik and Vaslav to stay in the dining room and account for their day. "The Russian tutor has complained again," Mamusia whispers to me. I don't take Russian lessons yet, but since I'm in the same room when Vaslav and Stassik take theirs, I've already learnt to read and write Russian letters, and I cannot understand why my brothers find them difficult.

"Speak up, Vaslav," I hear. "Answer my question. I didn't ask what Stassik has done. I want to know why *you* are wasting the teacher's time and my money. In case you've forgotten, the Imperial Ballet School exams are not just about dancing!"

There is real harshness in Father's voice now, an impatience tinged with anger. "Don't grin, Stassik. Hands on the table. And you, Vaslav, look me in the eye when you speak."

The kitchen is warm, smelling of wet ashes and doused fire. There is also a sharp sting of singed feathers; the hired girl has just swept the stove with a brush made of a hen's wing.

I hear Vaslav promising to pay attention and obey the tutor, his voice strong, serious, in just the right tone to make Father say the awaited words: "*Żeby mi to było ostatni raz!* I want it to be the last time."

Chairs rumble, feet shuffle, and Father, no longer angry, is telling my brothers to run along.

There is still time to play. Vaslav and Stassik are calling me to come and join them. Mamusia nods and takes a dishcloth from my hands.

"Go with them, Bronia," she says. "I can manage."

5.

WHEN DO I REALIZE that there is something different about Stassik?

Vaslav gets impatient with him when we stage our theatre show because Stassik cannot remember his lines. Accuses him of wanting to spoil our fun, until Stassik retreats into a corner and refuses to play altogether. Clasps his hands to his head and repeats: "How bad it smells . . . how bad it smells."

The odd moments become more frequent. During dance lessons Stassik throws himself to the floor and bangs his fists. He stoops and shuffles his feet as he walks. Screams when someone moves a chair from its usual place or when Mamusia gives him milk in the wrong cup. Or he just sits motionless, staring at the wall. When I ask him what he sees there, he shakes himself like a wet dog and says, "Nothing."

We all take Russian lessons by then, even though I am only six and could wait another year. I love them, especially since I'm beating both my brothers in all spelling bees and storytelling contests. Vaslav reminds me that he is far more advanced in dancing, which is what really matters. And that Father—speaking to Mamusia when he thought we couldn't hear him—has called him "uncommonly gifted." Stassik, however, declares all lessons stupid. When the tutor arrives, he always complains of a sudden, terrible headache. "As if someone stuck a knife there," he says to Mamusia, pointing at his right temple. Mamusia puts a cold compress on his forehead and tells him to lie down, rest a bit and join us later.

He never does. Instead he tears pages from his notebooks to make paper birds. Or spills ink on them and says that he, too, is writing but that his writing is different. "See," he says, "I've written *castle*." But all he shows us is an ink shape he has smeared on the page. Once, I come across Stassik staring at a book, his finger following the letters, tongue protruding as he labours through them. "I can read the book for you," I offer, but he snaps it shut and shakes his head.

Soon Father stops correcting Stassik's dance steps and asks me to partner with Vaslav during his daily lessons. When he turns nine, Vaslav will take the entrance examination to the Imperial Ballet School. He is almost eight already, so there is no time to waste. "You, Bronia," Father reminds me, as if I could forget, "will be next."

Do I show my happiness too much? I must, but Stassik never says he minds. He just sits in the corner watching us practise. Sometimes he says he is bored, and then Father tells him to play outside.

"I don't want to."

"Why not?"

"Because children laugh at me," he answers. Or, "Because they call me 'stupid.'"

Vaslav refuses to talk about Stassik. Pretends he doesn't hear when I wonder what has gone wrong, or—if I insist—hurries away. There is always something else that demands his total absorption. A ball he bounces with his right and then left hand, jumping in perfect harmony with each bounce; or a sleight-of-hand card trick he needs to practise. As if he believes that if we don't speak of what is happening to Stassik, it won't be real.

6.

HUNDREDS OF CHILDREN APPLY to the Imperial Ballet School, but only a few are chosen.

"It's not enough to be good at dancing," Mamusia reminds the three of us every day, even though she looks mostly at Vaslav, who is forever in trouble with the tutors. "You have to excel in everything you learn. Reading and writing, history, geography, arithmetic."

Father, too, is concerned about what he calls Vaslav's *stan wiedzy*, his general knowledge. The ever-changing tutors, I hear him tell Mamusia, are a waste of money. If we, his children, are ever to amount to anything, we need to attend a proper school.

There is a new urgency to these words. In March Vaslav turned eight and is now only a year away from his exams. Besides a proper school he needs advanced dancing lessons from the Mariinsky teachers. He needs what our parents call *protekcja*, which means having someone important from the school on his side.

For a while there is nothing in such statements that worries me. Not even when I hear Father say that we cannot continue living like Gypsies, travelling from one town to another. That there is only one solution: St. Petersburg.

Although I have two more years than Vaslav to prepare for the exams, the thought of them makes my mouth go dry. What if I fail? Never become a *prima ballerina assoluta*? I seek comfort in my strengthening muscles, in Mamusia's assurances that I am getting better with each day, but fear always sneaks in.

"Look at me, Bronia," Vaslav says when I confess to it. "Am I afraid?"

Even if he doesn't study at all, not even one single hour, he will be admitted to the Imperial School. "You'll see, Bronia," he says. And then he makes a solemn promise: by the time my turn comes, he will teach me what I need to do to pass.

We have been on the road all our lives, but the move to St. Petersburg has something different about it. In my memory there is a heaviness to the summer months before our departure, interrupted by bursts of Father's impatience and followed by Mamusia's teary silence. The door to our parents' bedroom closes with a *thud*, and when I place my ear to it, I hear Mamusia's sobs and Father's steps as he circles the room in agitation. So much angers Father, I think. The maid banging her pots when Father is trying to add up household accounts. Stassik's clumsiness. Mamusia's asking where he has been for so long and with whom.

Even during the morning dancing lessons when I think Vaslav is doing exceptionally well, all Father ever says is, "Once again . . . from the beginning . . . lift your chin higher . . . higher . . . you are a Nijinsky, so pay attention, for God's sake!"

I am spared most of Father's outbursts, but this only makes Vaslav angry at me. As soon as all our lessons are over, he takes off. "Nowhere," he says when I ask where he is going. Or, as in a fairy tale, "Where my eyes take me."

I plead in vain to go with him. I'm too young. I'm a girl. I'm not strong enough. I would only stop him from doing what he wants to do.

There is one afternoon I still return to in my mind. It is sunny, with motes dancing in the air. I'm sitting at the dining room table on a cushioned chair. Next to me Stassik is eating a thick slice of buttered bread sprinkled with sugar. A green fly is buzzing loudly, circling over it. A sunflower head, half eaten, is close enough for me to pick seeds from. I take them one by one, bite off the end and suck at the inside, until the hulls, black with white stripes, flatten out.

I am trying to finish a drawing I have been working on for a while. A horse pulling a carriage. The carriage, with its big window and wheels, has been easy to draw, but my horse looks awkward. Its legs are too short, its back too long, crooked. I try to erase the lines I've just drawn, but no matter how hard I try the old shape is still there.

Mamusia is sitting with us, darning our socks. I can tell she is nervous, for she stops often to glance at the clock, until finally she stands up and walks to the open window. "Where has he gone this time, Bronia?" she asks, leaning out, hoping to spot Vaslav among the boys playing in the street. "Why didn't you stop him?"

I don't know what to say. Vaslav never tells me where he is going, only where he has been, and every time it is a different story, each more exciting than the other. A stable boy allowed him to ride horses bareback to the river and showed him a magpie nest. He danced the *hopak* for some boatmen and they gave him a whole ruble and invited him onto their barge. He has proof, too: a shiny coin, a scarf, a bluish spotted egg he has emptied by making holes at both ends and blowing the contents out. Sometimes he brings presents. For me, pieces of driftwood that resemble a mermaid's tail or a snake. For Stassik, a horseshoe. For Mamusia, a blue almond-shaped bead, its surface cracked like a tortoise shell.

Mamusia leans farther out the window, as if she spotted him down in the street, but it must be another boy she sees, not "our Vaslav," for she says, "Where could he be this late? What if something has happened to him?"

"*Przestań, na miłość boską*. Stop it, for the love of God," Father interrupts. He is in the bedroom, dressing for the theatre, but he has left the door open. "You are making a sissy out of him with your fretting."

Something falls to the floor and rolls. A stomp of the foot stops it in its tracks.

Next to me Stassik shudders and grabs my hand so hard that muscles twinge deep inside my belly. It's the same feeling as when I go very high on a swing or when a carousel starts too abruptly.

Before Mamusia has time to say anything, the front door opens and Vaslav bursts in, panting, sweaty, his face smeared with mud. "I'm back," he announces in a cheerful voice.

Mamusia sighs with relief, her shoulders softening. "Where have you been? I was so worried!"

"To the river. Look what I've brought you!"

Vaslav is extracting something from his pocket, when Father emerges from the bedroom, his cheeks and throat covered with red blotches, his shirt buttons undone. The necktie in his hand is limp like a dead fish. "Enough of this inquisition! Why can't I even dress for the theatre in peace!"

Vaslav straightens himself up, puts his right leg forward, as if ready to start his *hopak* steps. Beside me Stassik, who has let go of my hand, begins rocking back and forth. "Stop this. Stop this. Stop this," he murmurs.

Father doesn't stop. "Don't you know that it's dangerous to play by the river? Are you an idiot? Don't you have any sense in your thick head?"

Words fly, explode, each of them sharp, blinding, each of them a blow.

"I know how to swim. And why do you care where I go?"

"How dare you speak to me like that?"

"I say what I like."

"Not in my house! Not to me!"

Each sentence is louder than the previous one. Mamusia covers Stassik's ears with the heels of her hands. My eyes are sliding from Father to Vaslav. The words are harsh: *urchin . . . tramp . . . good-for-nothing . . . fool . . . traitor.*

"Go to your bedroom, Vaslav, right now. You will stay there until you apologize!"

"To you? Never!"

Father raises his hand as if to slap Vaslav's cheek, but then he lets it fall. Mamusia is still holding Stassik. She is biting her lip and this is when I notice how red her eyes are, how swollen.

"Go to your room, Vaslav! Right this minute!"

Vaslav moves, slowly, ever so slowly. One step, two, three. Silent like a cat, until the door slams behind him.

"Stop it . . . stop it . . . stop it," Stassik moans.

"Why are *you* staring at me now?" Father roars. He is looking at Stassik, not me, but my heart is pounding. A warm flush of pee is seeping into the cushioned chair underneath me.

Father turns on his heel and runs out of the apartment, his necktie still in his hand. The doors slam shut, doors I can barely see through a shimmering veil of tears. Outside, Father is yelling at our nosy neighbour, telling her to mind her own bloody business.

"It's all right, Bronia," Mamusia mutters when I confess to wetting the chair cushion. "It was an accident."

In the room below someone is banging on the ceiling, our floor. In the corridor the nosy neighbour is denouncing all Poles. We are all the same. Thinking ourselves better than Russians. Putting on airs as if we were royalty, while underneath we are uncouth traitors, waiting for a chance to stab Russians in the back.

Later, cleaned and smelling of Mamusia's best soap, I open the door to the room we children share.

Vaslav has thrown himself on his bed, face down. I sit beside him, put my hand on his head. His hair is soft, but it smells cheesy and a few strands are sticky with tar.

"Why are you so angry with Father, Vaslav?" I ask.

My brother does not shake me off, as I fear he might. He mutters something into the pillow.

"I can't hear you." My voice is breaking, but I manage not to cry.

Vaslav raises himself on one elbow and turns toward me. His forehead is smeared with soot. There is a bruise on his right temple. "Do you really want to know?"

"Yes."

"Her name is Rumiantseva."

He pronounces the name as if it were a curse. It is a curse. We are going to St. Petersburg with Mamusia alone. All this talk about school and dancing lessons is one big lie. "Rumiantseva," my brother tells me, "stole Father away from us."

How could someone steal Father? As if he were an apple on a market stall. Or a shirt drying out in the sun.

Vaslav pulls at the scab on his chin, loosening it. A tomcat scratched him, he told me. The skin underneath it is pink and wrinkled. Haven't I heard how bears are caught? Lured inside a barrel smeared with honey.

"Let's steal him back, then. The two of us."

A smile appears on Vaslav's lips. A grown-up smile, which means that the valiant plan I'm just about to come up with—one involving secrets, climbing fences, and disguises fashioned from the Lukovitch costumes—is but one of my fairy tales. No match for the stark, jagged knowledge that Father is no longer ours.

7.

RUMIANTSEVA. MARIA NIKOLAYEVNA. For the next days I repeat the name often, probe it with my tongue like a rotting tooth.

She is not a stranger. I know her in that vague way I know most adults from the Lukovitch troupe—dancers, musicians, mimes, vaudeville artists—who can always tell how I slept, what books I'm reading, what I like to eat and what I said to Mamusia or Father just the other day. I recall the worn heel of a polished shoe, a laddered run in a black stocking, the lace hem of a skirt and finally a slim wrist with a watch strapped to it. The hand that pats my head is slender and white, with long, red nails. There is a smudge of ink on the inside of her middle finger, right above a glittering ring with a red stone. When I raise my eyes to look at her face, I see the gentle arch of her eyebrows, her red lips, the careful way she drapes the fox collar over her coat.

"Let me look at you, pretty girl!"

I'm strong, but I know I'm not pretty. My hair is thin and limp. My teeth are crooked.

She dips her hand in her handbag and fishes in it for a while before offering me chocolate bonbons with pretty pictures on the wrappers. "Take three, Bronia," she says. "For yourself and for your brothers."

I do.

I hold the bonbons tightly in my closed fist while she asks me questions: Do I play with dolls? Does Mama ever cry? Is she ever angry with Father? Did I really learn how to tap-dance after just one lesson?

I don't recall my answers, but I remember her smiles as if my every word confirmed something she already knew. And I remember the scent of her perfume, sweet, thick, talcum powder mixed with vanilla. And how, just before she leaves, she notices the run on her stocking, licks her finger and presses it to the end of the run, as if to seal it. "Never mind," she mutters, and gives me one last long look before walking away.

The morning after Father rushes out in such anger, I wake up shivering, unable to warm up. My neck and my arms are covered with red, itchy spots. My tongue, coated with slime, feels thick and wormwood bitter. Mamusia gives me sweet raspberry tea to drink and piles eiderdowns and woollen blankets over me to make me sweat, but this well-tried remedy doesn't work.

The doctor who visits says I have scarlet fever.

I don't want to think why Father does not come into my room or why I do not hear his voice or his steps. When the sweating is over, I lie in fresh bedding in a crisp starched nightgown, my mind still soft with fever, finding it hard to distinguish my dreams from what really happens. The world expands and recedes. Inside a giant circus tent, a pig is being strapped to a balloon gondola. A moment later it crashes to the ground with a *thud*. A clown weeps. A fire engine arrives with a giant ladder that extends up to the sky. Vaslav is climbing it, his grip fast and sure, but when I want to go after him, he tells me I'm too young. "Just watch me, Bronia," he says. I watch, but he disappears into the thick white clouds, and I see a mad woman whose name is Giselle dance her pain.

For the next few days I lie curled in bed, cold and hot in turn. Mamusia takes care of me alone. Vaslav and Stassik have been banned from my room. Scarlet fever is contagious. Sometimes Vaslav scratches at the door. "Can you still hear me, Bronia?" he asks. "Or are you deaf already, like the doctor said?"

When I say that I can hear him, he tells me that he has learnt a new trick. "I can walk up the wall like a fly. Touch the ceiling."

"How?" I ask.

"I'll show you when you get better," he promises, and wants to know if I believe him. Yes, I say, though I am not at all sure.

Mostly I'm alone, sleeping or drifting through feverish landscapes, haunted by what Vaslav has told me after he and Father quarrelled so bitterly. Hurtful, incomprehensible things: Father has been lying to Mamusia for a long time. The woman who stole him, this Rumiantseva, has given birth to a child, a daughter, Marina. Now she wants Father to leave us and live with her.

We are going to St. Petersburg because Father has betrayed us. Chosen *them* over *us*.

Everything else is a lie.

A ray of sun finds a slit between the curtains Mamusia has drawn so tight. My eyes hurt and smart. I don't want to think of any of that, but knowledge cannot be undone.

Father has another daughter. I have a sister, a half-sister. There is anger in this thought, mixed with pain, and jealousy, but there is something else, also, something treacherous yet tempting.

I love my brothers, but I often wonder how it would feel to have a sister, as well. A sister like Aunt Stefa or Aunt Thetya, with whom, like Mamusia, I would lock myself in a room and whisper for hours, sharing secrets.

Marina, I repeat. A baby in a white bonnet trimmed with lace, her face looming in and out of focus. A little girl, pretty like her mother? Prettier than me? Is this why Father chose them and not us?

One evening, when my fever is almost gone, but I'm still too weak to get out of bed, Father comes in and sits beside me. "Isn't it too bright? Shall I switch it off?" he asks, pointing at the small lamp on the nightstand.

I fix my eyes on the ceiling where shadows flicker. I shake my head.

"Speak to me, Bronia," he says. "Please."

"What about?" There is a crack in the ceiling, and a brown, rusty stain from some water leak. My lips are parched. I lick them, worry the flecks of dry skin.

"Parents may stop living together, Bronia," Father says. "But they never stop loving their children. I'll always be your father."

"You'll be far away," I say, my voice shaky.

"I would have to be anyway," Father says. "You children need to go to a proper school. I cannot drag you with me from one theatre to another. And I cannot stop dancing, for we all need money to live."

I've never heard Father speak in such a solemn voice, like a priest in church. Never seen his eyes bloodshot like that. His hands are trembling when he touches my forehead.

"If you've stopped loving Mamusia, you can stop loving me and Vaslav and Stassik."

"I haven't stopped loving Mamusia. I just don't love her the same way that I used to."

What other ways are there to love? This is grown-up talk. Meant to baffle. Its ending always the same: when you grow up, you'll understand.

"Is it true that you have another daughter?" I ask.

I need to hear it from Father's own lips.

"Yes," he says.

"Is she prettier than me?"

"No."

"Can she dance?"

"I don't know yet. She is just a baby."

He puts his hand on my forehead, and keeps it there for a while. He says he will write letters. And come back to stay with us in St. Petersburg when he gets a break between dancing engagements. And that I should do my practice every single day and learn as much as I can from Mamusia, for he will check my progress when he returns. He wants to be proud of me. He makes it sound like the most ordinary thing. He will be away. He will come back.

"Will you promise to write to me, Bronia?" he asks.

I fix my feverish gaze on Father, his high forehead, wide cheekbones, trimmed moustache. His eyes are pleading, insistent. Shaped like almonds, I think, just like Vaslav's and mine.

Father shifts his body sideways, forces his shoulders down. Instead of his usual citrusy cologne, I smell another scent, earthy, musky, yet almost sweet.

"Will you promise, Bronia?"

I nod.

Before the end of the summer Father helps us move to St. Petersburg, to an apartment on Mokhovaya Ulitza. Small but bright and—as Father repeats many times—close both to our preparatory school and to a trolley stop from which Vaslav can take a ride for his lessons with Maestro Cecchetti.

Cecchetti, one of the Imperial School teachers who accepts private pupils, is Italian. Before coming to Russia he danced at La Scala. Both Father and Mamusia took master classes from the Maestro a few times themselves. So did Mathilda Kschessinska. And Olga Preobrajenska. Vaslav will be in excellent hands.

"I have seen to your needs the best I can," Father says before leaving. "Everything else is up to you now." Then in a grave but steady voice he makes us promise we will be good children and make him proud of us. Stassik and I promise right away, but Vaslav stares at the tips of his shoes and refuses to say anything. To my surprise Father does not insist.

And then he is gone.

8.

FOR THE FIRST WEEKS IN St. Petersburg I cry often. I cannot find a place for myself in the unfamiliar rooms. Sometimes I think I hear Father's steps outside the apartment and I run to the front door, convinced that he has come back, but the steps continue right past. My brothers urge me to play outside, but I am still weak after my illness so I often stay with Mamusia. I help her paper the wardrobe shelves for our linen and unpack the last few boxes of books. To cheer me up, she makes me my favourite treat: *kogiel-mogiel*, a smooth paste of raw egg yolk and sugar we children love. But then the school year starts and I have no more time for tears.

Since the Imperial Ballet School exams take place in August, Vaslav has a full year to get ready. We all fall into a routine. Mornings start with a dance practice. Then the three of us go to a regular Russian school. In the afternoon while I continue my dancing lessons with Mamusia, Vaslav takes a trolley to his advanced classes with the Maestro and Stassik has his lesson with a music tutor who—Mamusia hopes—can teach him to one day accompany dancers onstage.

Father does write every month, a letter addressed to Mamusia and his "beloved children." The Lukovitch troupe remembers us fondly and everyone sends us warm greetings. He describes the ballets he has devised, new steps he has woven into old dances, gifts he has received from grateful balletomanes not just in Kiev, Minsk and Odessa but also in Moscow. Sometimes he encloses snippets from reviews praising his *ballon*, his high jump and the lively steps of his mazurka.

"Astonishing force," I read. "Thomas Nijinsky is a man of fire."

At the end of each letter Father inquires about our progress. For a dancer the body is an instrument that has to be honed and polished, he writes. The exercises we do every day assure that we develop the right muscles, in the right order. That's why they should never be altered, shortened or skipped. We—especially Vaslav—must always listen to Mamusia, be good children to her, never cause her trouble.

And he always sends money.

I sniff the letters for a whiff of that Rumiantseva woman and my half-sister, Marina, but all I can ever detect is cigarette smoke.

Every time the postman brings a letter from Father, Vaslav turns to Mamusia. Brushes her hand, plants a quick kiss on her cheek. Or makes her touch him, presenting a smudged forehead to be cleaned or insisting that she inspect his eye for some invisible mote. Ever since he began his lessons with Maestro Cecchetti, he looks taller, more grown-up. During our morning practice his movements are deliberate and precise. He has infinite patience with each muscle he wants to strengthen or stretch. Mamusia is pleased with Vaslav's dedication. She regards it as a promise that—if he doesn't squander his gift—he might become a true artist.

I know not to ask Vaslav to add even one line to my letters to Father. "You've promised him, Bronia. I haven't," he has said, so I alone write:

> *St. Petersburg is beautiful. I like my new school. I can do an* arabesque. *Vaslav can do a* grand jeté *and he says he is not nervous about the exams at all. Stassik's tutor is now teaching him to play the accordion. On Sundays, after we finish our homework, we all walk to the Summer Garden. We love the Krylov monument best. My favourite figure is the monkey with spectacles, even though someone broke them off. Vaslav likes the big bear holding a cello, and Stassik likes the bear, too.*

Not knowing what else to write, I sit, biting the tip of my pen. I feel that I have to cover the whole page, for if I don't, it'll look as if I wished to say something else, something hurtful, but had no courage to write it. So I dip my pen in an inkwell and continue, my letters growing slightly bigger with each line to take more space:

> *On our way back I stayed behind for a moment to look at the shop window with beautiful tins of chocolates and then I couldn't see Mamusia or Vaslav or Stassik anywhere. I was afraid at first, but only for a moment. There was no use trying to find them in the crowd, so I decided to go back home on my own. I remembered many buildings on the way and I followed them until I got home. Since no one was there, I sat on the steps and waited. All that time Mamusia, Vaslav and Stassik were looking for me and they were very frightened. Mamusia even asked a real policeman to help, but he couldn't find me anywhere, either.*

When Mamusia and Vaslav and Stassik finally came back and saw me waiting for them, they were very happy. Vaslav didn't believe me when I said I found my way back to Mokhovaya Ulitza all by myself. He was sure I had to ask someone to take me home. But when I described to him every building I remembered on the way back, he had to admit I did not lie.

I look at what I've written, pleased that I've filled up the whole page, with just enough space left for signing my name. Then I take a clean piece of blotting paper and carefully place it over the letter so that the ink won't smudge.

9.

Do not marry a poor man of ill health.
Do not marry a dancer.
Do not become the mistress of a powerful man.

This is what I learn in Aunt Stefa's spacious bedroom in her house on the outskirts of Vilno, where we arrive with Mamusia for Christmas, our first without Father. Aunt Thetya, a widow by then, lives with ailing Stefa, keeping house for her. Stefa, the most beautiful and talented of them all, is wasting away after the man for whom she abandoned the stage and a respectable life left her to marry "one of his own class."

Once the celebrations are over and the presents have been opened and marvelled at—ours especially sumptuous to cheer us up—my brothers venture into the snow-covered fields. When they come back, Vaslav tells me they have been trapping hares and building a snow fortress with really thick walls and a tower, but Stassik confesses to much less thrilling activities: riding downhill on a discarded plank, or putting an old bucket on a fence and trying to knock it down with snowballs.

In my memory that darkened Vilno bedroom smells of birch sap and mint. Thick, burgundy velvet curtains are always half drawn to keep even the pale winter sunlight out. A painted portrait of Stefa's beloved general hangs over her carved bed. He's a handsome man, resembling the tsar himself with his oval face, moustache and carefully trimmed beard. Standing by a marble column in his splendid dress uniform, a row of medals on his chest, he looks ahead with confidence. Beneath him, buried under white linen, Stefa lies, thin, diminished, almost ugly with sorrow.

I pick up a book or a pad of drawing paper and sit silently until my presence is forgotten. I don't want to miss a single word.

They never stop talking, Mamusia and her sisters. Of the old dreams and most current betrayals, of who said what and how and when, each minute detail dissected and weighted. The ardent promises of a besotted man, the brief joy of loving and being loved in return, the inevitable discovery that not all has been as it seemed. They remind themselves of premonitions and signs, ignored or overlooked. Or recalled too late.

Thetya's husband laughed at her fear of a hooting owl, only to clutch at his throat and fall lifeless to the ground a month later. Stefa—whose mirror broke in her hands—ignored her lover's prolonged silences and increasingly rare visits until, over her morning coffee, she opened the Vilno newspaper and saw the announcement of his marriage. And Mamusia? She took the trouble to teach that Rumiantseva woman the polonaise, blind to the knowing looks of the other dancers in the Lukovitch troupe.

This is what happens. You make one bad choice and nothing can undo it. Time robs you of good looks and grace. Birch sap tonic is too weak to keep your skin fresh. Hair thins in spite of kerosene oil. Children come, disfigure your body, and their needs are more important than yours. Your husband looks at you with unseeing eyes. Your lover decides that a rich wife is better than an artist who has sacrificed her art for him.

There are no second chances. All you can do is to warn your daughter or your niece not to follow in your footsteps.

They sigh. They dab their eyes with Stefa's embroidered handkerchiefs. Until Thetya chastises them for giving in to gloom. "Eat," she says, bringing in her winter consolations. *Bigos* flavoured with dried wild mushrooms. Cheesecake smothered with cherry sauce. The dishes they remember from their Warsaw home conjure up memories of my grandfather, who made such beautiful cupboards and bookcases, with stained-glass inserts and inlaid columns. Or my grandmother, who decorated her hat with peacock feathers. The grandmother who—when her husband dropped dead on his workshop floor—retired to her bedroom, turned her face to the wall and, deaf to her children's pleas, to their cries, refused to eat, until death took her, too.

There is a whole world in their stories.

Mamusia at five playing with her dolls inside their mother's wardrobe and falling asleep. Waking up to the sound of wailing, everyone fearing she had been kidnapped by Gypsies.

Stefa at ten sneaking into the Teatr Wielki, where the dancers are rehearsing *Swan Lake*. Watching from behind a column, as Odette whirls onto the stage. Beautiful, fragile and so graceful that all Stefa wants is to be like her.

"And so you were," Mamusia and Thetya assure Stefa.

"If only I had not given it all up." Stefa laments. For that faithless man who broke his promises and left her. It never pays to give up one's talent. For lovers or husbands. Men appreciate only what they cannot have. "I should've been like Kschessinska," Stefa says. "Bold. Ruthless."

When Mamusia and Thetya protest, Stefa asks them bitterly, "And why not? Have talent and hard work ever been enough?"

I have seen Mathilda Kschessinska only once, in *Les Saisons*, when Mamusia got two gallery tickets to a matinee. At first just being at the Mariinsky Theatre thrilled me. The crimson curtain decorated with gold imperial eagles, the fringed bronze chandelier, the blue drapings on the proscenium arch. A man was sitting in the imperial box and I wondered if he might be the tsar himself. But all these thoughts vanished when Kschessinska burst onstage— fiery, sparkling with jewels—her thirty-two *fouettés en tournant* sending the audience into a frenzy that wouldn't end. The skin of my neck crawled and I gripped Mamusia's hand.

For days afterwards I turn Stefa's words in my head. Weigh them against Mamusia's doubts, Thetya's admonitions. Squirrel these thoughts for the time when I grow up and when—as adults always promise—all will finally become clear.

10.

IT IS AUGUST 20, 1898, the day of Vaslav's exams. I wake up to the muted sound of Mamusia's prayers. "Matka Boska, Mother of God, help Vaslav. Keep him in Your care."

Vaslav, who likes to sleep late, is up already. I can hear him in the bathroom, washing up and brushing his teeth. The very first selection, Mamusia has said, will be based on physical appearance. As you are seen, so you are judged.

This is why Vaslav has a new dark blue suit that perfectly matches the kid gloves he got for Christmas. And a sailor's hat, on which the word *Russia* is embroidered in gold letters in the middle of a dark blue ribbon band. He tries the hat on every which way, always making sure that the letters are positioned perfectly in the centre. Mamusia has taught him to bow properly: draw his feet together, lower his head without bending his back, hold his arms in line with the seam of his trousers.

When I get out of bed, I see my brother in front of a wardrobe mirror, smiling at his reflection. How handsome he is, with his dark brown hair, long thick eyelashes and high cheekbones. Everything about him gleams: his slanted dark brown eyes; his even, white teeth.

Like Father's, I think, though do not say.

"Nothing but tea for me," Vaslav says when Mamusia serves us breakfast. I am not hungry, either, and only eat half my buttered bun. I have asked Mamusia to let me go with them to Theatre Street and she agreed. It will be good for me to watch and learn.

"Watch me now, Bronia!" Vaslav says, lifting his glass with tea as if it were a precious chalice. "Learn from the master!"

I kick him under the table, and he pretends to be mortally wounded and slumps in his chair until Mamusia tells us to stop.

Stassik has refused to sit with us. He is crouching in a corner of the room, pulling at the flap of skin between his thumb and his index finger. "Why can't I go?" he asks.

Mamusia doesn't tell him that she is afraid he may start screaming or run away. "Look what I've found," she says, instead, and hands him a box with his favourite strawberry pastry. "It's all for you," she says, and Stassik smiles.

Before we leave, Mamusia crosses herself and blesses Vaslav, and I can see how tense she is—her jaw is clenched, her hands tremble.

Vaslav sees it, too. "Don't worry, Mamusia. I'll be accepted." He clasps her hands in his. "I'll be a great artist," he says, holding her hands to his chest. "The tsar will come to see me dance! I'll be so rich that I'll buy you a big house with a garden. And you can plant all your favourite flowers there. And then I'll buy you a silver fox coat for the winter. And elegant dresses with matching hats. For you, too, Bronia, and for Stassik."

"I don't care for furs or dresses," Mamusia says with a laugh, freeing herself from Vaslav's grasp. "All I want for my son is to be a great artist."

"How great?" Vaslav asks, and does a perfect pirouette. Then another one with his arms bent over his head, fluttering like wings of a giant bird.

"I don't care for dresses, either," I say, although it is not quite true. Now that we are going to a regular school I see how shabby my "good" clothes are. Mamusia makes most of my dresses herself, from her old ones, and the colours are always washed out and old seams are sometimes visible.

Vaslav, his pirouettes completed, bows. "Let's go," he says. He is ready. He doesn't want to be late.

When we arrive at the Imperial Ballet School, I see boys crowded in front of the examination hall. Some are pacing back and forth; others attempt a few quick stretches. Vaslav stands with us, sailor's hat in hands, patiently bearing Mamusia's last-minute admonitions: "Think before you say anything . . . listen to instructions . . . bow when you are finished." When the clerk calls his name, he springs forward, his eyes clouding only when he is told to leave the sailor's hat with his mother.

I take Mamusia's hand and squeeze it. In his last letter Father promised to pay for my advanced dancing lessons. "But ask yourself, Bronia, if you really want to dance for a living." I read this sentence over and over again, poking at the words, bewildered. Father never asked if Vaslav wanted to dance. Why is he asking me? Doesn't he trust me? Or is his new daughter already a better dancer than I am?

We wait, tense and silent. From behind the closed doors of the examination hall come the sounds of the piano, the patter of running feet, the staccato of jumps. I glance repeatedly at the hands of a big clock on the wall, but they barely move. For a while I manage to get absorbed in the portraits of the imperial family that hang on one wall. The tsar's grey uniform, his beautifully trimmed beard; the tsarina's oblong face, her glittering tiara. If Vaslav is accepted, a few months from now he might be dancing on the school's stage and the tsar might come to see him. Not just him, I correct myself; other students, too. But still!

There are other paintings on the wall, of famous dancers I recognize from stories I have read. Brilliant Auguste Vestris, his face delicate like a girl's, soaring above the stage without touching the ground. Marie Taglioni, the incomparable Giselle, the ballerina who first made dancing *en pointe* into art.

When the doors to the examination hall open and the first group of boys come out, Vaslav is not among them. I am about to ask Mamusia if this is a good sign, but she has folded her hands and is murmuring a prayer. Two hundred eighty boys are here today, she has said, all hoping to be admitted. Many with greater *protekcja* than Maestro Cecchetti. All with families who want the best for them, too.

The boys who have come out are immediately surrounded by a small crowd, eager to learn what is happening inside the examination hall, but when I make a step toward them, Mamusia stops praying and catches my hand. "Stay right here, Bronia," she whispers, and I do.

The doors open again and more boys come out. They are all standing in groups now, whispering, looking at the big clock. A few have buried their faces in their hands. A clerk calls for silence. In a loud voice that can be heard in the farthest corners of the corridor, he announces that the boys who are still inside have been retained for a medical examination. Everyone else should consider himself not admitted to the school.

There is a ripple in the crowd. Voices rise. Some mothers cry; some clutch their sons' hands and leave in great haste. Many of them give Mamusia and me sharp, resentful looks.

Mamusia draws me closer to her, and I picture *our* Vaslav inside that examination room, executing his perfect bow.

Finally the last twenty boys come out of the examination hall. Unlike the others who jump with joy, throw themselves into their parents' arms, Vaslav merely lets Mamusia hug him and kiss him on both cheeks. Didn't he tell her not to worry? Wasn't he right all along? When I catch his eyes, he winks and makes a funny face.

A few moments later the official list of those admitted to the Imperial Ballet School for the first, probationary, year is posted on the door of the examination hall. The boys rush toward it. A few turn away, their faces grim and pained. Vaslav takes one glance at the list and returns to where Mamusia and I stand.

"Can we go home, now?" he asks, grinning. "I'm really hungry."

11.

"VASLAV'S SCHOOL," WE CALL IT, for it is still his only. That first year, when he is a day student on probation, coming home when classes end; and the second, when he is a boarder, turning into the much-awaited guest we see only on weekends.

It is all new. Vaslav's school uniform of black pants and light blue jacket with an embroidered lyre on the collar, which I like to touch to feel the tightness of the embroidery. His formal black coat, his shiny leather walking shoes, two pairs of pyjamas, a dressing gown and five pairs of underwear, one set for summer and one for winter months. Once Vaslav has become a resident student, there is nothing he needs that Mamusia has to buy for him. No dancing shoes, no books, no notebooks, not even pens and pencils. All is provided. All is paid for because Imperial School dancers are the wards of the tsar.

Two more years, I think, before my turn comes, and in my mind time stretches and multiplies. Two years equals twenty-four months. Not 730 days, though, but 731, for 1900 is a leap year, which strikes me as particularly unfair.

I pester Vaslav with questions. Who teaches him and what he has learnt. Who his friends are and what they talk about. Is it true that the Mariinsky artists come to the school for rehearsals? Has he seen Kschessinska up close? Preobrajenska? What do they do for practice? How do they stretch?

Vaslav's answers come clipped, bare of the details I crave. Mikhail Fokine, who teaches technique, is his favourite teacher. Why? Because he is much younger than the others. Yes, there are other classes: mime, posture, music and ballroom. Yes, he has friends, boys he refers to by their last names only: Bourman, Rosai, Babitch. Bourman's father didn't want him to become a dancer. Rosai can play the piano blindfolded. Babitch can spit farther than Rosai and Vaslav, but none of them can really jump.

With Mamusia he is more forthcoming. At her request he demonstrates what he has learnt each week, admits to praises and distinctions. Fokine has picked him again to lead dance exercises. Cecchetti has called on him to demonstrate how to perform a new move to the whole class. And he always assures her that the food at school is nowhere near as good as at home. No one makes *bitki* the way Mamusia does.

With Vaslav at the school, praised by his teachers, it is Stassik Mamusia worries about most. At the Russian school Stassik never moved up to the higher grade. The teachers began to summon Mamusia, complaining about his behaviour, so she let him stay home with her. Yet in my memories from this time my eldest brother is mostly calm, playing his accordion or helping Mamusia around the kitchen, sweeping the floor, peeling potatoes for dinner. Only when Vaslav appears does Stassik become agitated, poking his tongue out at Vaslav or shaking his fist at him. When Mamusia asks him to stop, he covers his ears. "Don't touch me," he screams if Vaslav takes even a tiny step toward him. Sometimes he murmurs a strange melody that reminds me of the rattling sound *droshky* wheels make on the wooden pavement.

"*Nie to nie*," Vaslav says in Polish every time, for Stassik has never really learnt Russian well enough to understand more than a few words.

Just as you wish.

As soon as Vaslav became a boarder at school, Mamusia moved my bed into her room, so Stassik now sleeps alone. It is like having a sister, I think, as I lie there at the end of the day, the darkness of the evening diffused by a small lamp, and listen to the sounds of her hairbrush clacking on the dresser top, her hairpins dropping into the glass jar, the tinkling of rosary beads as she retrieves them from the sandalwood box she keeps on her night table. Tired after dancing, I always fall asleep long before her, but sometimes her sobs awake me. "What will happen to Stassik when I die, Bronia?" she asked me once. I got out of my bed to embrace her and tell her that Vaslav and I would always take care of Stassik, but she only shook her head. "You two have to have your own lives," she said, and ordered me back to sleep.

Letters appear under our door. Mamusia throws them into the fire. "It's nothing," she lies, but once I get a glimpse of big awkward letters: "Your son is a monster . . . an abomination . . . he should be put down."

When I ask her who could hate Stassik that much, she flinches. "*Homo homini lupus*, Bronia," she says. Men are wolves to each other. It is her cross to bear. And then she makes me promise never to tell Vaslav what I have read. Vaslav is *narwany*, just like Father. Unpredictable. Especially when he gets angry. Acting first, thinking later. There is no telling what he might do, whom he might confront. We are Polish. Always more suspect than Russians. One denunciation and Vaslav might be suspended from the school. And how would that help anyone?

"Will you promise me, Bronia?" Mamusia asks, and I do.

12.

FOR ME THESE TWO YEARS are filled from morning to late evening. I wake up when it is still dark and do the practice Mamusia designed for me, with special exercises for each day of the week to develop different muscles. After a quick breakfast I go to the Russian school, where the lessons are easy since I am really good at reading and writing. Then homework and an early-afternoon dancing lesson with Mamusia.

My mother is a patient, exacting teacher, able to explain where I'm wrong and what I need to work on. My turnout is increasing. My muscles are getting stronger; my joints are becoming suppler, but we both know that it is not enough. Like Vaslav before me, I, too, need advanced training and *protekcja,* the pull of someone at the school who is firmly on my side.

This is why every evening of these two years I take a trolley to a class with Maestro Cecchetti. Father, assured that I still want to become a true ballerina, "just as I always have," pays for them every month. He calls it his "investment," and demands detailed reports of my progress. This is not an onerous request. Listing the exercises I do at the barre, describing the Maestro's routines, fills up the page much faster than accounts of what we all did on the weekend.

I share the class with five other girls, but Frossia is the one I really like. She looks like a ballerina. Her face is perfectly oval, her hair thick and shiny. She is also taller than I am, more willowy, and I can easily imagine her onstage, graceful in a tutu, her legs straight like arrows. When I despair over my own stocky body or thin hair, Frossia shakes me by the shoulders in mock anger. "Stop it, Bronia," she says, and reminds me that Cecchetti doesn't teach just anyone. In a year's time we will both be Imperial School students.

"Look at me, Bronia. Repeat what I've just said."

"We'll both be accepted."

"And we'll always be best friends."

"Always."

We are best friends already. We exchange *knijonky*, little books we buy for ten *kopeks*. Frossia likes the adventures of the Kiev knights best. I like the story of a Siberian girl who walks on foot all the way to St. Petersburg to plead for her wrongly imprisoned father. But most of all we talk about dancing. Is grace more important onstage or is vitality? Who is greater—Mathilda Kschessinska or Olga Preobrajenska, who has just been made prima ballerina? "She dances like a breeze," Frossia, who has seen her twice already, says, imitating for me, who has not, the way Preobrajenska floats through the air and vanishes, leaving her earthly lover overcome with longing.

I agree that there is beauty in fragility, but I still argue for the fiery volcano, maybe because I have felt Kschessinska's unstoppable power on my own skin. But I also agree with Frossia that before I can make such an important choice, I need to see Preobrajenska myself. Until then we have other questions to discuss: like who is a true artist and who is still a mere dancer.

Frossia straightens herself and raises her finger in the air. "Listen to me, girls," she announces, her voice thickening in the imitation of Maestro Cecchetti's Italian accent. "With a true ballerina, you know. She is a star. She shines."

Cecchetti is a strict teacher, noticing every mistake, every hesitation. He corrects me far more than anyone else, makes me repeat steps he would've considered good enough in others. When he repositions my legs or guides my spine into a deeper bend, his fingers leave bruises on my skin. "There,

Brooonia," he says, in his floundering Russian. "For now, just remember how it feels."

I'm making progress. This is what I overhear Cecchetti tell Mamusia when he thinks I cannot hear him, for the Maestro doesn't believe in spoiling his pupils with praise. But three months before the entrance exam, in addition to my regular class, he tells me to join his ballerina master class. It is a great honour. I'm only nine years old, merely hoping to be admitted to the school, and I'll practise alongside Kschessinska and Preobrajenska. Anna Pavlova, too, who has just graduated from the school and who, I hear, might surpass them both.

"Remember everything," Frossia urges. She wants to know what the prima ballerinas wear for practice and who comes to pick Kschessinska up at the end of class. Is it Grand Duke Sergey Mikhailovitch, in the imperial carriage?

Frossia smiles when she says all this, even though she has not been chosen. "I knew it would happen," she assures me, squeezing my hand. Other girls in the class—she calls them "sparrow brains"—can say all they want, but she knows *I* deserve it. Bronia Nijinska is her best friend.

The master class is in the same room where I take the evening "baby" class, but in the spring daylight the room looks bigger and grander. I've come early and stretch, in the corner, the only place I am sure is no one's favourite.

The mirrors have just been polished; the acrid scent of ammonia is still in the air. The floor is still wet in places. I can feel my tights dampen when I sit down to stretch my hips.

The accompanist is the first to arrive, followed by the ballerinas, some of whom cast a surprised glance in my direction. Dance bags land in another corner, some with a careless *thump*, others softly. I don't know all the ballerinas, but I recognize Olga Preobrajenska right away, for I have seen her picture on a Mariinsky poster. She goes up to the pianist and asks him something I cannot hear. He lets her play a few notes and then nods vigorously.

Anna Pavlova I recognize, as well. She walks in, fingertips on her lips, and announces that she has just seen the first snowdrops of this spring. A whiff of perfume trails after her. Three other dancers follow in her footsteps, chattering. "The days are still cold. But getting longer. White nights are not far away."

Their woollen practice tights are black, just like mine.

I keep stretching and looking, eager not to miss anything. Before they take their places at the barre, the ballerinas adjust their pointe shoes, tighten the ribbons, dip the tops in a rosin box. Pavlova's narrow ankles may appear fragile, but she grinds her toes into the powdered rosin with great strength.

Kschessinska is the last to arrive, right before Maestro Cecchetti makes his entrance, barely on time. Her maid—or at least I think she is a maid—takes her dance bag and her street clothes and hurries out of the room. I make sure I'm not staring at her, but I take note of pink silk tights. She is shorter than she looks onstage, and I recall her nickname, "Mała," which is Polish for small.

Before the *prima ballerina assoluta* takes her place at the barre, her eyes sweep over the room. Quickly, like a flick of a whip, but long enough to strip all disguises, expose all faults. In one moment I, too, am assessed.

You are not a threat, her eyes tell me. Not with how you look. You can be ignored.

The burning pain of this dismissal! The shame of it! Luckily I have no time to dwell on it, for the doors open and Cecchetti walks in, thumping his cane on the floor. With a graceful bow, he greets the ballerinas and motions to the pianist to get ready. His classes always begin on time.

"Take your place, Broonia," the Maestro summons me from my corner. "Fast." He is impatient, snapping his fingers, pointing at the only empty place, at the end of the barre. There is no time to waste. *Port de bras* is what he will stress today.

"Everyone ready. Let's begin!"

I take my spot, grip the barre. Too tight, for I can feel its shape imprint itself on my hand. The prima ballerinas are in first position, listening to Maestro Cecchetti's instructions. It's absolute precision he is after. Quality not quantity. They may all be great artists onstage, but in his class they are, and always will be, merely students.

The music starts. The class begins with simple *pliés* and *tendus*, the same for everyone, the same that I've done thousands of times. I recall Mamusia's encouragement: "You should be proud of yourself, Bronia."

But the polished, mirrored walls are harsh and relentless. There is another voice in my head now, louder than hers or Frossia's. Kschessinska was right in her dismissal. The ballerinas beside me are not only so much more assured and wonderfully fluid but also beautiful, while my own face is too round, my hair too thin. They have short torsos and long legs, while my body is stocky, unsuitable for the lightness of tulle.

Doubt ensnares like the sticky threads of a spider's web. It brings me to stillness in that mirrored hall. My hands and legs grow heavy, impossible to move. Blood rings in my ears.

The music races ahead of me.

This is when I feel a lash across my shin, a sharp pain yanking me out of despair. Maestro Cecchetti has struck me with his cane.

The music stops. Everyone is looking at me, the clumsy horse, the girl who has lost her place, who cannot move. Kschessinska's lips lift in a sneer and I see the edge of her impossibly even teeth.

"Pull yourself together, Brooonia," Maestro's voice explodes right behind my ear. "Spine straight! Chin up! And once again, from the beginning."

The harshness in this voice is worse than the pain from the lashing. But his tone works. My fears scurry away. When the music returns to the beginning, obedient, pliant, my legs and my arms follow.

Attitude croisé devant . . . attitude éffacé derrière . . . palms forward . . . palms down . . .

Thoughts leave; muscles take over. There it is, that moment when the body is one with the music and nothing else matters.

"Better . . . better . . . once again . . ."

Maestro Cecchetti walks up to me and pats me on the head. "Well done, Broonia," he says. And then he bends toward me and whispers, "Don't ever look at others, Broonia. Listen to the music and dance."

When the class ends, I do not join the circle that has formed around Cecchetti, but I don't leave, either. I wait until the room is empty again and then I walk over to where Kschessinska has stood. The upper barre is too high, but I grip it nevertheless and then let go. Watching my reflection in the mirror, I move my arms the way the Maestro has taught us, mindful of balance and timing, of line and strength.

—

Three months later, in August of 1900, Mamusia and I again walk to Theatre Street together, past the same porter, to the same corridor where Vaslav stood waiting two years before. I know that 214 girls applied this year. I know that only twelve will be chosen.

The day prior, in our kitchen, Mamusia made sure that my pointe shoes were properly broken in and the ribbons firmly sewn. Then she darned the tops so that I would not slip. In the other room Stassik was pounding his fist on the wall. His last music tutor had left threatening to report us to the police. "He'll kill you one day," he shouted at Mamusia. "And whose fault will that be?"

"Bronislava Fominitchna Nijinskaya!" The clerk calls my full Russian name and I leave Mamusia's side and join a group of about thirty girls who are to follow him inside. To my great joy Frossia is there, too, and I slide toward her so that we can walk in together.

The exam room is big and bright, the unwaxed floor even. The barres are positioned at two levels so that all of us, taller and shorter girls, can get a comfortable grip.

The judges, Mathilda Kschessinska and Olga Preobrajenska among them, sit at a table covered by a white tablecloth, open notebooks in front of them. Maestro Cecchetti is not there.

Preobrajenska smiles at me when our eyes meet, but Kschessinska turns her gaze away, toward the bearded judge on her right. At home Vaslav mocks Kschessinska's forced smiles and imperial gestures, making us laugh loudly. For the tsar's "special little dancer" comes to the school often on the lookout for future partners or rivals. Vaslav is an excellent mime. His hands linger over his neck, pretending that he is caressing the necklace of imperial jewels. His chin goes up; his lips form a beak. The voice he summons is thin and high-pitched, sweetened by sugary notes: "Oh, do show me how you prepare for your jump, Vaslav Fomitch Nijinsky! Are you sure there are no springs in your shoes? Will you *kindly* permit me to inspect them?"

The exam begins. The instructions are simple: stand still, run, stop, heels together. The judges make notes on their writing pads and most of the girls are dismissed right then. Frossia flashes me a smile of triumph, for both of us are told to move on, to another room, where we step on the big scale to be weighed and measured. The school doctor then listens to our heart and lungs, asks us to cough and bend down while he traces the line of our spines. A nurse then checks our sight and hearing, we are asked to sing a scale and—finally—we follow the governess to another room for a general examination in reading, writing and arithmetic.

In the end only twenty of us are invited back to the judges' room for the final demonstration of our skills at the barre.

The movements we are asked to perform to the music are not much of a challenge, either: leg forward, leg back, arm up, arm down, *plié.* My shoes, the ones Mamusia darned so carefully the day before, do not slip. My legs do not shake or buckle. My arms never lose the perfect arc I wish them to follow.

By the time I'm allowed to leave, I know I'm one of the chosen twelve, eight years away from becoming an Artist of the Imperial Theatres, just like Vaslav. And so is Frossia, who is shaking her fists over her head with joy.

But as I run into Mamusia's outstretched arms with my glorious news, I see one of the girls who has been let go at the last round. Her mother is encircling her in her arms. Her father is pacing around her and her mother, shaking his head. He says something I cannot hear. Then I see him lift his daughter up, carry her out of the building into the street.

I burst into tears.

October 11, 1939

Soon after we left Southampton, a giant grey tarpaulin was spread on the upper deck to make SS American Trader less visible to German planes. Additional passengers were taken on at the last minute and the ship is overcrowded. We are sharing our cabin with an Irish grandmother and her nine-year-old granddaughter. At night the two of them sleep curled together on a folding bed. Being hard of hearing shields me from the worst of their nocturnal whimperings but not from the loudest of groans.

In our last telephone conversation Romola, my sister-in-law, insisted that Vaslav shuddered when he saw the headlines announcing the pact between Hitler and Stalin. "Act II begins," he said.

I want to believe that he understands that much.

"I hated being there, at the school, Bronia," Vaslav told me once. We were already dancing for Ballets Russes then: he, Diaghilev's golden star and still my most demanding teacher, and I, a dancer in the corps *and an eager student. "It was like living in a glass bowl. Everyone watching you. Evaluating everything you did and said. If you picked up a book, it was because you didn't wish to talk to others. If you didn't hear the teacher's question, it was because you were an idiot incapable of understanding what they were telling you."*

"A trained monkey," other students called him. "A little Jap. A Tatar bastard. A Pole."

At the school, Vaslav said, he was always bored and lonely, confined and imprisoned. "Only when I was dancing, Bronia, did I feel free."

PART TWO:

1900–1908

1.

I LOVE EVERYTHING ABOUT the school I dreamt of attending for so long. I love my uniform, a long blue serge dress with a tight bodice and a low waist, covered by a starched pinafore apron, black for weekdays, white for Sundays. My dance dress is made of the grey Holland cloth. It is all paid for. The only thing Mamusia buys for me is a pencil box to hold all my pens and nibs. "Choose the one you like best," she says, and I pick the one with a lid decorated with a string of little birds.

Every morning Mamusia walks me to the school and I climb the wide marble stairs that lead to the Girls' Division on the first floor. The Boys' Division is above it and all contact between boys and girls is strictly forbidden.

Being a day student means that I am not admitted to the dormitory, and do not join the morning walk all resident students take before classes begin. Even at lunch—on tables with white tablecloths, with older girls serving food to younger ones—resident girls get full meals, while we day students get only hot tea and have to bring our own sandwiches. Frossia, who hates the blue serge dress because it is itchy, whispers that she can always tell a resident girl by her stuck-up manners: "Inky fingers but nose in the air."

The school, we are reminded daily, is a place of hard work in pursuit of excellence. The tsar, whose wards we have become, expects us to apply ourselves in all areas of study and to show perfect manners at all times. In the corridors imperial servants in livery, governors, governesses and caretakers are always on the lookout for any misbehaviour. Those who break the school rules will be reprimanded at first, and if they continue with their transgressions, suspended or expelled.

I cannot yet imagine such foolishness. Mistakes, yes, but wilful transgressions? As if anything, a whim, a temptation, could be more important than learning to dance?

School days start with dance classes in one of the spacious rehearsal rooms, or now and then, when the Mariinsky artists do not need it for their own practice, in the dance hall with a gallery where visitors sometimes come to watch the students below. Technique is my favourite class, especially after I figure out all the French dance terms my new teachers use. I like ballroom, too, the only class boys and girls take together. At first I hope for a chance to exchange a few words with Vaslav, but the governess reminds us that boys and girls are forbidden to talk even if they dance together. "All boys and all girls," she says, looking sternly in my direction.

I don't mind. There is a grown-up thrill in dancing with my brother as if we were strangers. As if we were already onstage.

Two months after I begin at the Imperial Ballet School Father announces his visit. I cannot sleep from excitement, hoping that he has changed his mind and we can be a family again. Mamusia must be wishing for the same. She has changed her hairstyle, ordered a new dress from her dressmaker, and our kitchen has filled up with delicious smells.

On Saturday afternoon just after Vaslav returns from the school, Father arrives with gifts: chocolates and French wine for Mamusia, an elegant lace dress for me, a Jules Verne book for Vaslav and a ukulele for Stassik. "Just for two days," Father says when I ask how long he will be with us. He is "not at liberty to stay longer."

"Is this what *she* said?" Vaslav asks. Mamusia quickly leaves for the kitchen and Father acts as if he hasn't heard and begins showing Stassik how to tune his ukulele.

There are more such moments: Father talking of how he has left the Lukovitch troupe, how he now works at the opera house in Nijni Novgorod, how he has danced in Paris at the Folies Bergère, all without looking at Mamusia or even praising her cooking; Vaslav and I putting on our uniforms, hoping Father might offer to come to the school to watch us dance, only to hear him say, "Remember that many are called but few arrive."

Most of all I recall Father arguing with Mamusia, trying to persuade her to let Stassik stay with him. A watchmaker Father knows in Nijni Novgorod is looking for an apprentice and Stassik needs to learn some useful trade. "For goodness' sake, I will be there to keep an eye on him," I overhear Father counter Mamusia's objections. And then Mamusia: "What makes you think that *she* will let you. That she would suddenly care about *my* child."

In my memory, the bitterness in our parents' voices ebbs and wanes, Stassik is absorbed in his new ukulele, Vaslav declares that one day he will dance at the Paris Opera and not some vaudeville theatre no one has heard of.

And I?

I declare myself too tired to keep awake. No, not sick, I tell Mamusia, who checks my forehead for fever; just tired. She sighs but asks no more questions and sends me off to bed.

"Do you still love us?" I ask Father when he comes to say good-night, as I was hoping he would.

"Can't you tell, Bronia? Don't I take good care of my children?"

The terse note in his voice hurts. To stop myself from crying I wrap my arms around his neck and press my head to his chest.

A moment later I feel Father's warm hand smoothing my hair. "When you grow up," he whispers the words I hate by now, "you will understand."

I may not be able to talk to Vaslav during the week, but I hear of him often. Of his astounding leaps, his flawless carriage, his exemplary dedication to dancing. His rare gift.

The best students from the graduating class, five years ahead of him, demand him as their partner. Master Fokine—not just an esteemed teacher at the school but also a Mariinsky choreographer—is assigning my brother to yet another school gala, ahead of more senior students. Every day resident girls stop me in the corridor or wait for me outside the practice room. Some are straightforward enough and ask about Vaslav, but many feign interest in me. They say they like the simple way I tie my hair. They ask the old question I detest by then: whether I prefer

Kschessinska or Preobrajenska. A few have invited me to visit them at home. For tea. For supper. For a whole day of playing or dancing.

Mamusia, who waits for me on the ground floor every day at the end of classes, calls them "false friends." I have to be vigilant. Polite but firm in my refusal of invitations that are extended only in hope of being reciprocated to ensnare Vaslav. And I must never, under any circumstances, promise to pass on a message to him. Ballet is a nest of vipers, she reminds me. Some students would do everything to see Vaslav expelled.

Having relented and sent Stassik to Nijni Novgorod to live with Father, Mamusia worries about Vaslav again.

"He doesn't have your judgment, Bronia," she tells me. "He acts first, thinks later . . . he is too trusting . . . he will do anything if his friends egg him on."

She reminds me that Vaslav has already been officially reprimanded for "bad conduct" a few times, caught sliding down banisters, climbing on doorknobs to open and close the swinging doors with his legs.

I defend him to Mamusia the best I can. Boys get such reprimands every day. The teachers are always more severe with them than they are with girls. Once to strengthen my position I even confess to being caught climbing up a narrow corridor using just the strength of my legs. All I got was a finger wag and a warning. Any boy doing the same would get an official reprimand.

But I do end up worrying about Vaslav, as well, for my brother is falling behind in academic subjects. "Everyone wants Vaslav to dance, so he has no time for homework, Bronia. And then they blame him for not studying hard enough."

On our walks home Mamusia confesses to other worries. Father may be sending money, but it is barely enough. Now our landlord has objected to her taking on even an occasional dancing student and has raised our rent, forcing her to search for another apartment. At the end of the school year we will have to start packing again.

"Don't mention it to Vaslav, Bronia," Mamusia always says as she ends her accounts. "He'll only do something rash."

For Vaslav can be as reckless as Father. Didn't he storm out of the Polish church at Easter, right from the confessional? "Our Motherland is enslaved," the priest told him. "And you prance onstage in tights? With our oppressors?" Refused to go back, even when Mamusia pointed out that the school demanded a certificate of confession at Easter, that Vaslav wouldn't be allowed to continue his studies without it. It never occurred to him that Mamusia had to find another Polish priest and beg on Vaslav's behalf, blaming herself, her failure to bring up her son properly. Allowing her child to put his art before his patriotic duties.

When Vaslav comes home on the weekends, there is no talk of troubles. Mamusia cooks our favourite dishes and we demonstrate what we have learnt that week. Or entertain Mamusia with our accounts of evening performances at the opera, where students are often employed as extras. Vaslav and I take as many of these engagements as we can. They not only pay fifty *kopeks* per evening but also allow us to be backstage. We sing our favourite arias for Mamusia, recall the funniest bits of gossip: torn costumes that had to be held together with one hand, makeup ruined by sweat, the wrong ballerina carried away—to the surprise of her partner.

There is always homework to do for Monday—passages to read and summarize, history dates to learn by heart, compositions to write—so every Sunday, after we return from Mass, Mamusia makes us take out our school books. Vaslav always moans and tries to argue with her for more rest time, but she clears the dining table, folds the tablecloth away and tells us to get going.

Recalling Mamusia's words about Vaslav not having time to study during the week, I insist on reviewing the past week's material together. To get Vaslav to pay attention, I read the appropriate passages aloud and ask him to explain them to me as if I didn't understand. Sometimes I propose contests: who can draw the most accurate shapes of the Oka, the Volga, the Dnieper. Who can memorize more of the dates assigned for the week:

1709: Peter the Great defeats Swedes at Poltava
1762: Catherine the Great becomes empress
1812: Aleksander I defeats Napoleon
1861: Serfdom is abolished

Vaslav has an excellent memory, and so do I, but if anything gives us trouble, I have come up with a helpful trick. I make up funny sentences in which first letters of each word stand for whatever we have to memorize: names of planets or colours of the rainbow or lines of a Pushkin poem.

My strategy works and soon Vaslav's marks improve, with one exception: writing compositions for his Russian class. An empty page makes my brother fidget, nibble his pen, shake his head in such a comic way that I have to laugh. I help by asking him questions and making him write down his own answers, until they form a paragraph of sorts, awkward and flawed but long enough to get him a passing grade.

One day, however, Vaslav remembers his Russian composition at the last moment, when we are just about to finish studying. Or pretends to remember. He mimes astonishment, slapping his forehead with his flat palm, declaring, "How silly of me, Bronia. It slipped my mind."

"What do you have to write about?" I ask.

Vaslav opens his notebook and reads what he has copied from the blackboard: "Describe the most memorable moment from your last summer holiday."

"That's easy," I say.

"No, it isn't," he groans, rubbing his nose.

"Try," I say, and he scribbles a few words on a piece of draft paper, stops, bites the tip of his pencil, erases a word, writes another one in its stead. He rolls his eyes, stands up, does a pirouette and sits down again.

After a few good minutes of that I relent and look at what he has managed to write: "I went fishing. In the morning I woke up early to go fishing. I like fishing very much."

Vaslav gives me a pleading look. The teacher has asked for a whole page. He has no idea what else he could possibly write about.

I should do what I always do—ask him a few questions, make him take notes. But it's getting late. We have been studying for four hours. Vaslav is yawning. Once or twice he has already put his head down on folded arms. From the kitchen where Mamusia is preparing our supper comes the smell of baked apples.

I take a fresh piece of paper and write:

During my last holiday the moment I remember the most happened during the morning when I went fishing. I woke up at dawn and, after a simple breakfast of a buttered roll and a glass of milk, I set off toward the river. I walked down the road between the fields of ripening rye, immersed in thoughts about the future. Mist covered the ground, so it felt like walking on a cloud. By the time I got to the river, the sun came out, and I saw strange figures gather on the river shore. In them I recognized the creatures of fairy tales and poems we have been reading in our Russian class: a hunchback horse, a village fool with a golden heart who can speak with birds, Petrushka at the Maslenitsa fair, a snow maiden who melts each spring.

Vaslav is standing behind me as I write, reading and grunting his approval. As soon as I get to the bottom of the page, he snatches it with a loud whistle.

"This is *so* good, Bronia," he says. "The teacher will love it."

I smile, pleased with myself. Vaslav may be still ahead of me in his dancing, but there are things in which I, his younger sister, am already better. Vaslav may not admit it, but he knows it, too. This is as important as knowing I've just diminished Mamusia's troubles.

2.

I SEE HIM FOR THE first time backstage on my way to the wardrobe mistress to pick up my costume. It is January 1901, two weeks after my tenth birthday, and I'm one of the extras in Gounod's *Faust* at the Mariinsky. Feodor Chaliapin, Russia's greatest opera singer, will be playing Mephisto. Tall, dressed in an elegant black frock coat, a white scarf around his neck, he is holding a woman's hand, pressing it to his heart. Another woman, her curled hair pinned up, rises onto her toes and whispers into his ear. Yet another, a fur coat sliding down her white round shoulders, is holding a large basket of white roses. Chaliapin's broad face lights up as he laughs.

A dandy, I think, with a pang of disappointment, Mamusia's word, one that dismisses any man "too handsome for his own good."

Chaliapin takes a step; everyone follows in his wake. I move to the side and let them pass.

An hour later, when the curtain rises, I'm standing at the side of the stage, dressed in my village-girl costume, an ill-fitting brown ensemble that smells of pickles and someone else's sweat, when I see Chaliapin come out from the wings.

He is no dandy. He is Mephisto, the Prince of Darkness, invincible in his malice. In front of my eyes he plots the downfall of an innocent girl who is still singing her chaste prayers.

"'Hell,'" Mephisto sings to Marguerite, "'is calling you. Eternal anguish, eternal night.'" I feel Chaliapin's voice in my skull, in my chest. It makes my whole body vibrate. As I listen, transfixed, I am no longer just a student, an extra. I am someone else. Someone I do not yet recognize but can sense already.

That night when I leave the Mariinsky I ignore Mamusia's warnings to walk straight home. Chaliapin's rich, thick voice is still inside me and I'm clinging to it with all my might. The thought that I will hear him for two more nights floods me with joy.

I walk along Bolshaya Morskaya all the way to the Nevsky Prospekt, past the palaces and sparkling hotels from which guests in evening dress spill into the street. In the window of a confectionary store I see boxes of "caramel Chaliapin" stacked in a pyramid, with pictures of Mephisto on the lid. I pull at the heavy carved door, but it doesn't give. The store is closed. I vow to return the following day.

The night is warm. I can smell the briny waters of the Moyka. "Vote for indivisible Russia, one with the tsar," a poster on the wall urges. "Do not turn our mighty country into a pile of autonomous and weaker regions." Another one warns: "If you want to steal someone else's property, go to the socialists, for such is the paradise they promise you."

The beam of light from the Admiralty tower makes the Nevsky look like an elaborate theatre set.

"Want your fortune told, pretty girl?" a Gypsy calls out, lifting the lace hem of her dress, silver bangles rattling on her wrist.

I fish a five-*kopek* coin from my pocket. "This is all I have," I say.

She grins and reaches for my right hand.

"Long life," she mutters, flattening my palm, tracing the lines with her finger. Her nails are painted bright red, but some are broken, jagged. She mumbles something about a long journey, a great pain. "I cannot see him clearly," she says. "The man who is hurting you."

Not much for five *kopeks*, I think, and pull my hand away. How foolish to have been tempted. No one can foretell a life. I'm old enough to know that.

I turn away to leave, when the Gypsy stops me. "Wait," she says, and gives me back my coin. "For good luck," she mutters. "You will need it."

I feel a chill over my shoulders. I want to say something, ask her what else she has seen, but the Gypsy is no longer looking at me. A few steps away a young officer is leaning forward, probing the air like an ant on a path yet untried.

When I get home that evening, I find Mamusia in tears. Her suitcase is opened, lying on her bed. She is packing our black dresses, petticoats, shawls. A black hat with a veil is lying on the dresser top.

"Father?" I ask, my heart thumping, wild from fear.

She shakes her head and hands me a telegram:

> Stefa died peacefully at night STOP Funeral on Saturday STOP Dress warmly STOP Thetya STOP

It is Thursday night. We will leave early Friday morning, come back on Sunday. Alone, without Vaslav, who is again behind in Russian and mathematics. Unlike me, my brother cannot afford to miss two days of school.

Chaliapin's voice weaves itself inside me, echo to all my thoughts. On the train to Vilno as Mamusia blames Stefa's foolish love for making her sick. During the funeral at St. Anne's Church, to which the general doesn't come but does send a wreath: "From grateful balletomanes." At the reception when Thetya takes me aside to tell me how disciplined I am, how sensible, how much comfort to my mother.

But most of all in my strange and feverish dreams, which are filled with swirls of fluttering ribbons, blue, crimson, yellow, and peacock green.

3.

MASTER FOKINE COMES TO watch me at the barre. Mostly he observes in silence, but sometimes he asks me to step forward and extend my arm or do a turn or *plié.* He does not praise me, but I am often picked to demonstrate a move to other students. Maestro Cecchetti also corrects me far more than others. "Higher, Brooonia, from the hip!" he commands, coming up to me, and I feel his cane on my shin, prodding me to a greater effort. Or his fingers digging into my ribs, making me shift my weight even further.

"Mamusia says these are all excellent signs," I write in my weekly report to Father, wishing with all my heart that Vaslav could have seen me in all these moments. I want him to confirm what matters to me the most: I have something far more precious and unpredictable. True talent!

With Vaslav there is no need to looks for signs. In my letters to Father I write how Fokine applauds him in class as if Vaslav were onstage. How for the upcoming Annual Student Performance, my brother is already selected for a *pas de deux* with Ludmila Schollar, who is a senior student of great promise, and he will dance his own solo from the *Nutcracker*. To entice Father to come, I add that the Student Performance will take place on March 13, which is one day after Vaslav's twelfth birthday.

In the last few lines, I write about Mamusia, still sad about Stefa's death but pleased that she, too, has a dancing engagement in a Christmas pantomime. And I always ask about Stassik: Is he happy? Can he repair a clock already?

Every month Father sends money for our rent and expenses and a letter addressed to Mamusia, Vaslav and Bronia from "your faithful correspondent." He is happy to learn his children are such excellent students. Stassik's apprenticeship with the watchmaker is going reasonably well. He can pick a clock apart, although he is still learning how to put it back together. The letters end with Father's most recent reviews, the name Thomas Nijinsky underlined in red ink and a reminder for us to obey Mamusia in everything, "for she has nothing but your happiness in mind."

I put all Father's letters into an empty tin chocolate box with another of Chaliapin's pictures on the lid. They are tied with a green ribbon I have smoothed over a boiling kettle, the way Mamusia has taught me.

Father's other daughter—for this is how I think of Marina—is now almost five years old. Her name is never mentioned in our house, but I do wonder what Stassik—who must have met her—will tell me when he comes back.

—

When we return to the school after the Christmas break, Cecchetti tells Frossia and me to see him after class. "I have chosen both of you to dance in the Student Performance," he says, pounding his cane on the floor. "You have three months to prepare. Will you be ready?"

The Student Performance is a display of the best, most promising students, a chance not to be squandered. Someone from the imperial family is always in the audience and at the reception afterwards. So are all the teachers and parents. We both nod, barely able to contain our happiness. Day students on probation? Chosen ahead of residents?

But this is not the end of the good news. Cecchetti is giving us our own dance in a tableau called "The Kingdom of Ice."

The dance is simple and clean. We are to advance from the wings *pas de bourrée en pointe*, meet in the middle, turn to the audience and then, still on pointe, separate and disappear into the wings. Frossia to the left and I to the right.

A very short dance, I remind myself, not to get too ecstatic, but I'm giddy that finally Vaslav will see me dance onstage. Not just to admire how far I have developed—even though this is a thrilling thought—but to guide me to go even further.

For the next three months I work on my solo at every opportunity, not just with Frossia but also alone, in front of a mirror, which—I have learnt by then—is the most unforgiving of teachers.

My hair is still thin and limp, my teeth uneven and too big for my mouth. I look even more boyish and stocky than I used to. But I'm constantly getting stronger, more agile. At home Mamusia often checks the shape of my legs, their flexibility, the angle of my hips. She shakes my ankles and wrists loose, massages my feet. My thigh muscles are thickening, she assures me; my feet are alive. When I fret over my new dance, she tells me to picture every step in my mind, in its perfection, right before I fall asleep. "Until you do it without thinking," she says.

I picture more than the dance—I envision the hours leading up to it. At the end of the lessons Mamusia will pick me up and we'll hurry home. I'll wash and change and eat a little bit, just enough not to faint: a slice of roasted chicken breast, an orange, a piece of dark chocolate. I'll drink a glass of sweet tea. Then I'll return to the school right away, with plenty of time to put on my costume and makeup, and begin my preparations. I have already chosen a spot at the end of the corridor where no one will bother me. This is where I will do my stretches and warm-ups. Just before I have to go backstage, I will close my eyes and empty my head of anything that is not my dance.

"Wait here for your mother," a school maid says on the day of the performance as I am on my way to the lobby, where Mamusia should be waiting to take me home.

The maid has such a stern face as she points at the row of chairs in front of the inspector's office that I know something bad has happened. Has Vaslav done something foolish again? Talked to some girl, perhaps? Or been caught smuggling in forbidden treats? This seems to me most probable. Yesterday was his birthday and Vaslav—*narwany*, as Mamusia still calls him—must have decided not to wait with a celebration until the weekend.

At first I'm angry at my brother. Why is he so careless? Does he ever think what would happen if he were expelled? How much pain it would bring us? What shame? But then I recall the composition I wrote for him for his Russian class. It was a few months ago, but what if the Russian teacher just found out? What if both of us get expelled?

My hands grow cold. My forehead erupts with sweat.

I take a deep breath and close my eyes, swatting away each terrifying thought the way we used to swat the deer flies that swooped on us as we played in the yard. Quickly, before they could bite.

Then the door squeaks, and I open my eyes to see Mamusia coming out of the inspector's office.

"What happened?" I ask, running up to her. "Has Vaslav done something bad?"

Mamusia looks at me and shakes her head. Her eyes are full of tears.

Vaslav hasn't done anything. Vaslav is dying.

On our way from school to the hospital, in the *droshky* someone kindly called for us—black, like a funeral hearse—Mamusia tells me the little she knows. During recess the students organized a contest. Vaslav was jumping over a music stand, somehow fell, and crashed to the floor so hard that he lost consciousness. Only when classes resumed did the teachers start asking where he was, begin looking for him. He was found lying on the floor, blood streaming from his mouth.

Like Stassik?

Mamusia must have thought that, too, for her hand clasps mine so hard that I feel the hardness of her bones.

As we walk along the gleaming hospital corridor, I recall that I was in the rehearsal room during recess, practising my solo. Then Frossia and I practised together until the governess came by and told us to stop and get some rest. Why didn't someone inform me then that my brother had been hurt?

The doors to Vaslav's hospital room are white, painted over many times, for streaks of paint have thickened in uneven coats. They are closed. We are forbidden to see him. His condition is serious, if not hopeless, the doctor says. He repeats the words "internal hemorrhage" three times. Invisible wound, he also says, blood seeping somewhere deep inside.

"I must see my son," Mamusia insists.

The doctor shakes his head. The time is critical. Vaslav's organism is gathering all its strength. He is not to be disturbed.

"I must see my child," Mamusia repeats.

There is no hesitation in her voice, no pleading. Just the sheer force of her demand: "My presence won't weaken him! My son has to know I'm here, beside him."

"A few minutes, then," the doctor relents, and opens the door to Vaslav's room. But when I, too, stand up to follow, he puts his hand on my shoulder and tells me to wait.

I sit down, stand up and then sit down again. I stare at the white tiled corridor walls, at the big clock, its face covered by a convex glass, the minute hand quivering before skipping forward. Underneath it there is a portrait of the tsar, in a grey uniform decorated with medals, his beard and moustache carefully trimmed and combed. The imperial family is with him. Empress Aleksandra, seated, is holding baby Anastasia on her lap. Their three older daughters, Olga, Tatiana and Maria, are perched at their mother's feet.

A nurse walks by in her starched white apron and a nun's wimple. Behind her a peasant woman, head wrapped in a black kerchief, follows on bow-shaped legs.

I close my eyes. I try to pray for my brother, but the words I mouth silently come out flaky and brittle. Dark flecks float on the inside of my eyelids. The very thought of losing Vaslav freezes the core of my being. I chase it away before it lodges itself in my mind.

Finally the door opens and Mamusia comes out. A new, deep line divides her forehead. Her eyes are rimmed with red. "We have to go, Bronia," she says, crossing herself. "It's all in God's hands now."

In a *droshky* that takes us home Mamusia tells me that Vaslav looks peaceful. Pale but quiet, she says. As if he were asleep.

It is a good sign, she insists.

"Bourman, Rosai." Mamusia turns to me and asks, "Have you seen them at school, Bronia?"

I nod. I've seen Vaslav with these friends of his. Pushing one another, making each other laugh with a loud belch or a sharp whistle. "Copycats," Frossia has called them for the way they imitate Vaslav's gait.

"Vaslav is never alone," I say. "Everyone wants to be his friend."

"From such good families," Mamusia mutters, puzzled. "Why would they run away? Leave him for so long? Alone, without help? And on the very day of the Student Performance? Of all days?"

We both grow silent. The answers that suggest themselves are too cruel to contemplate.

Back at the school, where Mamusia drops me off, nothing seems real any more. As I walk toward the dressing rooms, eyes follow me, grave and serious. There are whispers, too, subdued murmurs that die when I turn in their direction. In my dressing room an attendant helps me change into a tutu, rouges my cheeks and darkens my eyebrows. "You don't have to say anything, Bronia," she whispers.

I squeeze her hand with gratitude.

In the wings Frossia runs to embrace me. I can tell she has been crying, but she, too, is considerate and asks no questions. Instead she chatters about the performance. Fokine is in the audience, in the first row, and so is Cecchetti, with his wife and sons. If I lean a bit from the wings, I will see him. "Mathilda the Great," as Frossia calls Kschessinska, is there, also, wearing her sapphire necklace. Any heavier and she would fall on her face. Grand Duke Sergey Mikhailovitch gave it to her. The tsar has not come. The uniformed man who sits in the imperial seat is Grand Duke Andrei, the tsar's first cousin. He will give out the imperial gifts to us at the reception. Frossia has seen them already, boxes beautifully wrapped in golden cloth.

I don't ask who will dance Vaslav's roles.

When the time comes for "In the Kingdom of Ice," I take my place in the wings, feeling numb, detached from my own body, aware of a black hole behind the haze of the floodlights where the audience sits. I don't believe I will be able do a single step. I see nothing but the closed hospital door and the mute horror in Mamusia's eyes.

But bones and muscles carry their own memory, and their own remedies for pain. When the music begins, at the cue I have practised to for so long, I *bourrée* toward the centre of the stage where I'm to turn toward the audience. The music unfurls; my arms and legs move on their own.

I dance, forgetting everything else, until the applause returns me to the place where pain and worry have settled and will not lift.

4.

FOR THE NEXT FIVE DAYS Mamusia and I talk of nothing but Vaslav, unconscious, on the edge of death. "He is only twelve. He is so strong," we say to silence fear. "He will pull through."

Mamusia rushes to the hospital every morning to wait for news. I suffer through lessons and dance practice until I can join her. We sit together in the same spot in the corridor, outside Vaslav's room, awaiting the doctor who does the final evening round. Every day Vaslav stays alive, he tells us, is a promise, every peaceful night a sign of healing. We take great comfort in these words until one of the nurses tells Mamusia that the other patient in Vaslav's room, a young Imperial Horse Guard badly kicked by a horse, has just died from internal bleeding.

At the school everyone is quieter, subdued. Vaslav's name is repeated with great reverence. "Russia's pride," our teachers say. "The most talented dancer I have ever taught." I cringe at these praises, for they sound too much like funeral orations. To disarm them I evoke ordinary moments of joy. Vaslav doing a pirouette when Mamusia buys him his first pair of long trousers. Vaslav walking on his hands around the room when Thetya hands him a new balalaika after his old one broke.

On the sixth day Vaslav opens his eyes. He can move his fingers and toes. He knows who he is. This is what Mamusia tells me when I arrive at the hospital. She is smiling and crying at the same time. "He made this funny face when I kissed him," she whispers. "Moved his nose like a rabbit."

I am finally allowed to see my brother for a few minutes.

Vaslav is lying on his back on an iron bed, covered by a white quilt. I note the crisp, freshly starched linen, its edges still smooth and shiny. On his side table is a vase of elegant-looking flowers. Orchids, roses and lilies, tied with a silver-rimmed ribbon. Beside them lies Mamusia's favourite rosary, of dark blue beads.

"Get well," I whisper.

Vaslav is looking at me, his eyes focused and clear. And then he nods, winks at me and tries to lift himself up.

"Don't move," I warn him, and he obeys.

The nurse taps me on the shoulder, urging me to leave. Vaslav's eyes close. He sighs and swallows hard. I want to bend and kiss him on the cheek, but I'm afraid to hurt him, so all I do is pat his shoulder and follow the nurse out to the corridor, where Mamusia is waiting.

"Vaslav will live," we tell each other. Everything else will arrange itself. In time. With patience. With effort. We do not confess to fears that the fall may have injured Vaslav's spine. We refuse to think that he might never be able to dance again.

"I have been late with my letter," I write Father, "for we were waiting for news. Now we know that the worst is behind us."

Cards, best wishes, baskets with delicacies arrive daily. From the school, from other dancers, from Vaslav's teachers. Nothing is too good for him. Caviar, smoked sturgeon, quail eggs. Boxes with dried fruit and chocolates. Books. A music box that plays the opening from *Giselle*. Father has also written, but Vaslav refuses to show me the letter. "He is not coming, if you want to know," he says, making me regret I've asked.

I visit Vaslav every free moment I have. I read to him from his favourite books: Krylov's fables, *Tales of the Thousand and One Nights*, Pushkin's

Onegin and Tolstoy's *Childhood.* We play games and I let him beat me in chess—which is not easy, for Vaslav makes many rash moves I do not anticipate. I repeat to him all the praises I've heard about his dancing, of his lightness, his force, his dedication to perfecting every move. "Who said that?" he asks. Fokine? Cecchetti? Soon he is allowed to sit up then walk, and the doctors confirm that—in a month or two—he will be allowed to dance.

"Tell me what really happened?" I ask him a few times, but Vaslav shrugs off my question and says he doesn't remember. Or that it is not important. Or that I wouldn't understand anyway. When once I repeat the rumours that Bourman and Rosai smeared the floor with soap and then raised the music stand too high the moment he wasn't looking, Vaslav's cheeks turn white with rage.

"That's a vicious lie, Bronia," he screams. "It's only stupid people who say such things."

"How can you be so sure?"

But Vaslav doesn't want to listen. He fixes me with his eyes and says, "I forbid you to ever mention it again."

They come to see him, in their school uniforms, shuffling their feet. They pretend not to see me. Bourman has brought Vaslav a tin box of chocolates. Rosai has come with a book: *The Mysterious Island* by Jules Verne, with rugged rocks and a tiny raft on the cover. It is the same one Father gave him during his last visit. Don't say anything, Vaslav's look warns me as he puts the book on his night table. Fresh flowers are there—as always—but Mamusia's rosary is nowhere to be seen.

"Where is Babitch?" Vaslav asks.

They do not answer. "Get well s-soon, Vaslav," Bourman stammers. He has freckles under his eyes, and a red pimple on the side of his nose.

"Yes," Rosai echoes, staring at the tips of his shoes.

They stand by Vaslav's bed, refuse his offer to pull up the chairs and sit down. They are smaller than I remember, tense in the shoulders. Their voices rise; they speak too fast.

Vaslav opens the box of chocolates, offers them around. I take one, a square wrapped in golden foil. Bourman and Rosai shake their heads. The chocolates are for you, Vaslav, they say.

When Vaslav insists, they choose the smallest ones. Bourman's fingernails are bitten to the quick, the ends of his fingers reddened, with strips of skin peeling off. His index finger is stained with ink. Rosai is squinting as if the light coming through the window—pale as it is—blinded him.

They tell Vaslav they are practising pirouettes now. Yesterday Fokine called them "talentless idiots with legs of clay," and said, "If only Nijinsky were here."

"Will you visit me at home when you get well, Vaslav?" Bourman asks. He wants my brother to spend a whole Sunday with him. His mother has promised to bake her special marble cake with marzipan. His father has offered to take them for a boat trip on the Neva. To the islands to watch the Gypsies dance.

Rosai nods vigorously, as if he, too, has been invited.

Sheepish, I think them, scared. Calculating, assessing how much they can trust my brother to keep silent. The investigation is still going on. The inspector told Mamusia that they will be questioned again "to clarify the inconsistencies." If they are caught lying, they will be expelled from the school.

It hurts me to see how eager Vaslav is to please them, opening the drawer of his stand to reveal the stashed delicacies. Bonbons, the candied cherries he loves, small cakes wrapped in cellophane. Showing them his new harmonica, which the doctor doesn't yet allow him to play.

"Guess what goes up and down but does not move?" he asks.

"Don't know," they both answer, shaking their heads.

"Really?" Vaslav asks, his eyes sparkling with triumph. "Stairs!"

They laugh too loud, clapping for emphasis. "Stairs—of course!" Bourman repeats, and shakes his head anew. "Stairs!" Rosai echoes.

I'm relieved when they finally go away after assuring Vaslav that they will be back tomorrow right after school. With some good jokes.

When we are again alone, my brother turns to me. "They are my friends, Bronia."

From somewhere thick, brackish, I dredge a smile. I'm only ten and a half, but I know that Vaslav, my brilliant genius brother, is wrong. Talent breeds resentment; brilliance attracts envy. Lesser souls seek comfort in bringing down those who are admitted into the company of gods. Envy rules the human heart. Only the strong can hope to survive.

—

My memories of the time that follows are filled with joyful relief as Vaslav makes his first tentative, wobbly steps and, a few weeks later, is permitted to dance again. Then comes a long, lazy summer with Thetya, in the countryside, where Mamusia sends us for a proper vacation. And—upon our return to St. Petersburg—the unexpected delight of seeing Stassik again, even though our elder brother bursts into tears for no reason or covers his head with his arm whenever anything startles him.

What Mamusia finally confesses to us is that while Vaslav was still in hospital, Father broke his leg really badly and was not able to earn any money. Unable to pay for Stassik's apprenticeship, Father entrusted him to some friends of his who had promised to teach him folk dancing. By the time Mamusia learned of the arrangement and went to visit Stassik, she found him locked in a woodshed, filthy, bruised and hungry.

How easy it was, in the excitement of my first resident year at the school when I, like Vaslav, became Mamusia's weekend guest, to believe that everything would turn out for the best. Until one Saturday in October, when Vaslav and I arrive home, our brother is no longer there.

"The doctor took him," Mamusia says, blinking back tears. And then, in a voice I can still feel on my skin, she tells us that the sanatorium where Stassik lives now has a beautiful park and we can visit our brother whenever we want.

5.

IN THE YEARS THAT FOLLOW there is little beside dance. The school challenges and urges me on. Nothing can equal the thrill of performing with the *corps de ballet* in *Swan Lake*, *The Sleeping Beauty*, *The Magic Mirror* on the stages of the Mariinsky, or the only slightly lesser stages of the Aleksandinsky and the Hermitage. Or the delight of dancing in *The Fairy Doll* in a costume designed by Lev Samuilovitch Bakst, the costume I can still recall in minute detail: pink socks over white tights; ruffled pantalettes showing beneath a white muslin skirt; a wide pink ribbon over one shoulder, tied in a bow below the waist.

School awards mount up, moments of recognition. The pink dress of distinction is followed by the white. Marius Petipa, the great choreographer, puts his hand on my head after I execute a *pas* of his and says, "*Bien.*"

With each year I am better, stronger, more assured, and ready to reach higher than before.

In January 1906, when I am in my sixth year at the school, the Mariinsky Theatre stages *Don Juan*, in which my brother, a year away from his graduation, dances alongside the prima ballerinas Preobrajenska, Vaganova, Egorova and Trefilova. Mamusia is there on the opening night, Friday, the sixth, in the first row, among the invited guests. I, like all resident students of the school, have to satisfy myself with stories.

On Saturday when I come home, the maimed papers lie on the table. Mamusia has already cut out all the reviews and set aside a pile of them, ready to be pasted into a scrapbook with Vaslav Nijinsky spelled out in gold letters on the cover.

"'An enchanted being, exceptional talent,'" I read aloud. "'All lightness and elevation. Such fluid and beautiful movements. At sixteen, the student Nijinsky is already an undisputed genius of dance.'"

Am I proud?

Yes.

Vaslav walks into the room soundlessly as I read these words. Grace and agility are in all his movements, even the most mundane ones. As he bends over to pick up something from the floor. As he turns around when I call him.

Am I jealous?

Yes.

Not because I dance with the *corps de ballet* when my brother is already a star. I am jealous because he has a boy's body and growth holds few dangers for him. Yes, his voice has thickened. But he is also leaner, sharper, stronger than before. And no breasts will ever spoil the shape of his torso.

This is not a new feeling, but at fifteen I can no longer push it aside. I have seen girls leave the school because their widening hips diminished their turnout, changed their centre of balance, destroyed their talent.

My brother sits down beside me, his right leg stretched out. He pushes the reviews away.

"Have you read them?" I ask.

"I don't care what they say."

"Careful—don't mix them up," Mamusia says before hurrying into the kitchen. A hissing sound means that some of the Sunday broth has spilled over the stove.

It pains me not to have seen Vaslav in *Don Juan*. At the school we are rarely taken to outside performances, especially now, when Russia is at war with Japan. Every day brings news of assassinations, riots, demonstrations. A year before, on the Embankment during the Blessing of the Waters, a live cannon shot barely missed the tsar. A few days later in front of the Winter Palace the Imperial Guards fired at workers who tried to deliver a petition demanding the end of the war and improvements in their living conditions. Hundreds died, maybe even thousands. Since then the unrest has not stopped. Strikes are constantly erupting at factories around the city; crushed, they erupt again. Electricity is cut off so often that candles are in short supply. At the school the residence windows are always shut, and we are strictly forbidden to even look at the street. We can still hear shots, though, fired close enough to shake the glass.

In Helsinki, Moscow, St. Petersburg, terrorist bombs kill grand dukes, generals and government officials. The tsar—still our absolute ruler—has wavered and allowed the creation of a Duma, a parliament to advise him. Elected, not appointed, we hear.

"Politics," our teachers say when we ask what it all means. Too complex for us students to understand. Dangerous, too, like the demonstrations during which so many youths have disappeared that parents and friends are still searching through hospitals and morgues for their bodies.

At home Mamusia adds her own warnings. We are Polish, watched far more closely than the Russians. We cannot afford the slightest suspicion. Especially Vaslav, already a young man, not a boy. "All it takes is one blow to your head with a Cossack sabre," she says. "Even if you do not die . . ."

There is no need to finish this sentence; evoke Stassik's rages, his broken life.

I arrange the *Don Juan* reviews on the pages of the scrapbook while Vaslav concentrates on extending his legs. Then he retrieves a small rubber ball from his pocket and squeezes it in one hand then in the other. There is a half-smile on his lips. Of boredom? Derision? I don't know what he thinks anymore. He has never spoken about the school much, but now he refuses to speak about it at all.

"I don't want to . . . I don't care . . ."

So hard, growing up, I think now. So lonely. So beset with fears.

6.

IN MARCH OF THAT YEAR Vaslav and I are both dancing at the Annual Student Performance. Vaslav in *A Midsummer's Night Dream,* for which Fokine has mounted a special *pas de deux*, and I in *The Prince Gardener*.

After five long years Father has finally promised a visit.

In the two months before the performance, worried that the unrest might prevent Father from coming, I often examine the large maps hanging on the walls of our geography classroom, comparing the vast expanses of Russia with the small islands of Japan. This is a reassuring sight.

On the performance day, before the carriages arrive to take the students to the Mariinsky Theatre, there is an elegant reception for parents in the large dance hall at the school. I'm sitting with Mamusia beneath the portrait of the tsar, waiting for Father.

"Have you eaten?" she asks.

I say yes, even though I've only had half of my usual buttered bun for breakfast and a glass of sweetened tea. Why is Father late? I think, as the time we could be together shrinks. Has anything happened?

"There he is," Mamusia says, her voice quiet but tense.

I see Father, too, by the door, looking around, elegant in a black tuxedo, diamond studs glittering in the front of his dress shirt. He waves as soon as he spots us, glides through the room in his black patent leather shoes with such easy grace, all eyes upon him.

I've promised myself nothing will spoil my joy at seeing Father again. Not the shrug of Vaslav's shoulders every time I mention Father, not even

Mamusia's remark that Father hasn't come to St. Petersburg just to see his children dance. He is here to audition for a role in Moscow's production of *The Merry Widow.*

"Count Danilo Danilovitsch, first secretary of the Pontevedrin embassy, at your feet," I hear him say in his low, familiar voice. "The audition has only just ended. I haven't had time to change. Overdressed, am I?" he asks, looking around at the other fathers.

He is the only one in a tuxedo, but why would I mind? I throw my arms around his neck, breathe in the familiar citrusy scent of his cologne, my heart thumping from joy. He lifts me up and turns me around, and it feels as if nothing has changed, that I'm still a little girl and he has just come home from the theatre. A moment later he is admiring my dress; praising my posture, the strength of my back muscles, which he carefully feels with his fingers. Earlier that day in the washroom I overheard two senior girls gossiping about me. "Have you seen the sister of you-know-who," one of them said. "Doesn't she look like a grasshopper with those thick thighs?" Now their malice seems merely silly.

"And where is Vaslav, Bronia?" Father asks, as if I tracked all my brother's moves.

I hope Vaslav has a good reason to stay away. Fokine's last-minute correction of his steps, perhaps. Or a request from another student. My brother is always besieged with pleas for help.

"Did you get the part?" Mamusia asks Father. If she feels any strain at his presence, she has hidden it well.

"I sincerely hope so," Father replies, sitting down with a look of satisfaction, humming "I'm off to Chez Maxim's." I, too, sit down, beside him, feeling shy all of a sudden. The carriages are waiting on Theatre Street, the governesses are already gathering the students, and I know that I should join them, but I don't want to.

"Are you nervous, Bronia?" Mamusia asks.

"No," I say.

"Time to go, then," she says, and I stand up and straighten my skirt, still reluctant to leave.

Mamusia taps me on the shoulder. "Off you go," she murmurs, and I obey.

—

As I enter the theatre, my head is spinning and I stumble a few times. If not for Frossia, who spots my unease, I would've fainted. She—my true friend—makes me eat an orange and gives me reviving salts to sniff. Then she helps me arrange the lilac sprigs in my hair.

From the wings I watch Vaslav dance his *pas de deux* with Ludmila Schollar, whose legs are slim and straight as arrows, and then his solo. There is applause at both times, but the solo is followed by a standing ovation and I think I hear Father's voice cheering Vaslav on. When my turn comes, I don't dance as well as I had wished to. Even though I, too, am applauded, I know that my jumps were too subdued, too restrained.

During the break Vaslav and I are standing together in the wings when Father comes backstage, grinning. He pats Vaslav on the back, hugs me. "You were very good, Bronia," he says. "But you are strong enough to go higher. Don't stop yourself. Don't be afraid to—"

"Bronia is not afraid," Vaslav interrupts. "She didn't eat enough all day. They told me she almost fainted."

My heart quickens. Vaslav's voice is so harsh, I think, so challenging. It douses all the joy his veiled approval might have brought.

Father turns to him. "And you, Vaslav," he says, his voice light, playful almost, merely teasing. "You don't have to show yourself off as an *adroit porteur*."

My brother's face pales; his jaw tightens. "I don't show myself off," he says. "I just give myself up to the dance."

The unspoken words hover in the air: a father who leaves his children has no right to give them advice! All he can do is to admire how well they have grown up without him.

I've never been more grateful for the bell-ring that announces the end of the break.

Father doesn't stay with us this time, but he comes by our apartment early next morning and asks us to show him the school. I fear Vaslav will refuse, but his eyes light up at the thought and he agrees right away.

Since it is the Easter break, the school is empty. We go in through the artists' entrance and Vaslav takes us straight to the second floor, to the Boys' Division, which I, too, am seeing for the first time as it is empty for the holidays. He shows us the library, the practice rooms, the dorm where he sleeps on a bed that is even narrower than mine.

Father runs his hands along the wooden banisters, touches the spines of library books. Asks about Fokine and how his lessons differ from those of other teachers, like Cecchetti, who by now has left the school and gives private lessons only. "Does Fokine, too, have you do the same set of exercises that cannot be altered?"

"No," Vaslav says. "He is not a slave to routine."

For the next while Father listens attentively to Vaslav's explanations, interrupting only to ask a question or to bring up the praises he has heard. "Is this where the teachers applauded you, Vaslav, at the end of the exam? What did Fokine say about your three *tours en l'air* and your *entrechat dix*? Like a bird in the air? Did he really say that the school should come up with a new highest grade, just for you?"

Vaslav nods.

I want to leap from joy.

In the large rehearsal hall Father takes off his jacket and hands it to me. "Let me show you two some of *my* dances now," he says.

He walks to the middle of the hall, stops and clicks his heels. And then, without music, in his street clothes and walking shoes, Father begins to dance.

Prissadka . . . *lezginka* . . . the *hopak* . . . mazurka . . . and then his own dances, from which I recognize some moves, seeing that he has altered them in ways that are his alone. It is impossible to determine where a step starts and ends because all blend so smoothly together, with such clear-cut precision. He glides on the inside edge of his shoes as if they were skates. In the pirouettes, outlines of his body blur like the blades of a rotating fan. His jumps linger in the air, higher than it seems possible. And when he drops, even the drop differs at each landing, soft and gentle or hard and fast as a stone.

I cannot take my eyes off him.

When he finishes, he bows and then straightens himself, awaiting our reaction. I'm holding my breath, sear what I have just seen to memory.

Then I applaud. Alone. For Vaslav, when I turn to look at him, is staring at the floor. He hasn't even raised his hands.

Father is still breathing hard from the dance, his cheeks glowing, flushed red. Pools of sweat have gathered under his arms, wetting his shirt. He takes a few steps toward us, extending his hands to me, to retrieve his jacket. How alike we are, the three of us, I think. The same shape of legs and feet. Even our hands look the same, little fingers curved inwards, with almond shaped nails.

"What do you say, Vaslav?" Father asks.

"Dancing tricks," Vaslav snorts like a horse ready to take off. "I have no use for them. This is acrobatics, not art."

I feel the jacket yanked out of my hands. Father's eyes have hardened. "Is that what you think, son?"

"That's what I think."

"Then you are not as smart as I thought you were."

They both turn toward me now, their authority, their judge. Choose your side, two pairs of eyes insist. Both almond-shaped. Both lit with impatience. Hurry up, Bronia. Declare yourself. There is only one truth. One right way.

I turn and run out of the dancing hall, wiping away tears. I don't want either of them to see how weak their anger has made me, how hollow.

The following day Father goes alone to the sanatorium to visit Stassik. Afterwards he comes back to say goodbye. Vaslav refuses to leave his room. Only when Mamusia asks him to behave in a civil manner—the way *she* has always taught him to behave—does he emerge, and mutters a clipped "Goodbye, Father."

"I can't stay," Father says when I ask him to sit with us for a while.

"Can I walk with you to the station, then?" I ask.

"Only if your mother agrees," he says. "And only if you take the *droshky* back. I don't want my daughter alone in the streets."

Mamusia nods her permission, and I put on my black school coat, button it up and wrap a scarf around my neck. I follow Father out of our apartment, down the stairs, into the street. He walks fast and we are both silent for a while. The spring snow is melting and it is easy to slip and fall.

"Did you get the part in *The Merry Widow*?" I finally ask, unable to bear this silence.

"Yes," he says. "It'll be Moscow for me for a while."

I want to ask him so many questions: Does Marina, my stepsister, want to become a dancer, too? Is she preparing for the school entrance exams? Did Stassik recognize him at all? Was he still proud of the new gloves and woollen sweater Mamusia had knitted for him? I want to tell Father how much it hurts me every time Vaslav refuses to visit Stassik with us, saying that it makes no difference to Stassik anymore. But I don't know how to say any of it without making Father angry or hurt, so I decide to talk of dancing.

"Is it true," I ask him, "that Moscow dancers sacrifice tradition for cheap effects?"

"Where did you hear that?" he asks.

"At the school."

No, he does not agree. He thinks the Mariinsky style too academic, too stale. He prefers the Moscow way: less correct, sometimes untidy, but more vigorous. Not afraid to admit to the effort behind the poses, while St. Petersburg dancers always try to make every step seem easy. "Does it make sense to you, Bronia?" Father asks.

"I don't know enough yet," I say.

"That's a wise answer," Father says, and smiles the way I love so much. A wide grin that reveals his teeth. "You are a born diplomat."

Outside the train station Father finds a *droshky* to take me back home. He questions the driver first, asking which streets he intends to use. Before paying my fare, he demands an extra blanket for me to put on my knees. And then, when I finally settle in the *droshky* seat and wrap my legs with two horsehair blankets, Father asks, "Remember the "Sailor Dance" the three of you danced? You and Vaslav and Stassik?"

I nod.

"It all has gone so wrong, hasn't it?" he says, and turns away quickly. Too quickly for me to catch one last glimpse of his face.

7.

"NO MORE IMPERIAL BALLET SCHOOL," Vaslav says on the day of his graduation. "Ever. Glory be to God."

Mamusia is so happy. All her efforts, all her worries, are finally paying off. Vaslav does not graduate with an award—because of the academic subjects—but he receives the highest mark in dancing: a 12. And the New Testament in Polish. And the complete works of Lev Nikolaevitch Tolstoy.

On the day of his graduation Vaslav also submits his application to become an Artist of the Imperial Theatres. Four days later an official letter confirms that Vaslav Fomitch Nijinsky has been accepted as a *coryphé*—which is already an exception, as everyone else starts in the *corps de ballet*—at 780 rubles a year.

Father has sent a hundred rubles for his expenses and has invited Vaslav to visit him: "I'm not asking for much, just one week of your vacation, Vaslav. My friends in Nijni Novgorod all want to see my son dance."

Vaslav doesn't want to go, not until Mamusia says, "Your father should see how well you've turned out."

Before Vaslav leaves, I write a letter to Father. I tell him that we have started looking for a new apartment, more spacious than our current one, necessary now when Vaslav is no longer a student but an Artist of the Imperial Theatres. I write how much I, too, am awaiting my own graduation and dancing at the Mariinsky.

All of it takes only half a page, so I decide to write about last summer when Vaslav agreed to take a private pupil on the condition that his sister take lessons, as well:

Before the first class Vaslav took me to Lifshted's, where we all buy our dancing shoes. "How can you dance in these?" he asked when I reached for a pair of girls' pointe shoes. He took one in his hand, tried to bend it, and declared pointe shoes useless.

"We all dance in them at school," I protested. "There are no others."

"Try these." He handed me a pair of boys' shoes.

I liked the look of them—black, made of soft leather—but not the thought of dancing in them. "How can I dance on toe without any support?" I asked.

"As I do. I cannot teach you anything in shoes that are as hard as boxes."

Vaslav didn't like the way I was taught to jump at school, either: from demi-plié, taking the power from my knees. He made me and the other pupil watch his technique. He said it was all in the preparation, and taught us to feel the floor not just with the soles of our feet but also with our toes. He taught us to quickly stretch the body, to let the power of the arch and the instep throw us upward.

These lessons seemed so hard then, so demanding. The soft shoes were not supporting my toes. I often cried, doubting I could ever satisfy Vaslav's expectations, but when the summer ended and I returned to the school, my teachers were amazed how much my arches, insteps and toes had strengthened, how elastic they had become. Now I can do sixteen fouettés sur pointe all in soft men's shoes!

I look at what I've written. My letters are even and neat. I check all the sentences for spelling mistakes and awkward phrases but do not find any, so I lick the envelope flap and seal it. Since Vaslav will take the letter with him, instead of Father's address I put *Wielmożny Pan Tomasz Niżyński łaskawie odebrać raczy*. For the Honourable Thomas Nijinsky, into his own hands.

It is such a formal phrase, but it sounds both elegant and very proper.

I'll never know if Father has read my letter.

"Nothing will force me to see *him* again," Vaslav says when he returns from Nijni Novgorod after only one day there. His face is set, rigid, his voice firm. "And I don't want to speak of him, either."

Later, to me in whispers, Mamusia hints at what has happened. Father wanted Vaslav to meet Rumiantseva. "That woman," she calls her. I don't like the way she turns her wedding ring around her finger as if it were a rosary bead. Or the pained gaze she tries to hide.

"Is it true, Vaslav?" I ask him later when he is standing on a stool, wrestling with a warped dining room window that won't open, cursing this rat-trap apartment we've had to live in for so long. It is a double-paned window, sealed with putty, its inside littered with dead flies and spiders.

"I told you I don't want to speak of him again," he says.

Tears flow down my cheeks. The window frame creaks, shedding flecks of old paint.

"Give me a hand, Bronia," Vaslav says, his voice softer. Not quite an apology, but a plea. "Bring me a screwdriver."

I go to the kitchen where Mamusia keeps Father's old tools in a wooden box under the sink. I get the biggest of the screwdrivers and take it to Vaslav, who uses it to pry the edges of the frame from the last layers of paint. Then he pulls on the handle once again, and the frame cracks as it finally lets go.

8.

VASLAV IS DANCING the Bluebird in *L'Oiseau d'Or* at the Mariinsky. He is only eighteen, but he has managed the impossible. The administration—not prone to such extravagance—has let him abandon the traditional costume and design his own.

This is why instead of an elaborate full-skirted coat he is wearing a short blue tunic and tights. There is no supporting wire frame for his wings, either. Unlike all who have danced the Bluebird before him, Vaslav is free to move his body and his shoulders the way he wishes. Be a bird. Fly in the air.

And he does fly. Up and down and sideways. He soars, glides, leaps. His wrists flitter and the wings follow.

I cannot take my eyes off him. In the air his arm wings open wide. Again and again. He lingers in these flights, comes down for a fleeting moment to touch the ground with half toe and soar again. My brother has become a bird, flying low over a swift current of a river, skimming the surface of the water, bathing in the spray, only to fly upward and soar when he has had enough.

He is in his own world. He follows his own visions, his own rules. He is free.

I watch him pirouette, ten, eleven, twelve times. At top speed. Until he stops and gives us, the witnesses of his genius, a look of amused bewilderment, as if he danced for himself alone. As if only his innate grace, his consideration of less fortunate mortals, made him acknowledge our eyes, our applause, our ecstasy at seeing a god dance.

The light that shines on my brother, so richly deserved. For a long while there is nothing in these thoughts but pride and joy.

—

After the triumph of the Bluebird, Vaslav's impatience grows more noticeable. With a misplaced dress shirt, a crease that has not been ironed out properly, a necktie that won't come out straight.

"Stand still, Vaslav," I tell him, laughing. "Let me try it."

We both laugh, Mamusia and I. "Our Vaslav," we say with exaggerated sighs, so touchy, so set on perfection in everything he does. When he finally leaves for his evening out, the floor of his room is littered with discarded clothes. We pick them up, noting the fine cloth, the fashionable cut, the elegant musky scent of his new cologne. We put his shoe trees back into his smart leather shoes. His wardrobe is an investment, not vanity. An artist needs good clothes, has to maintain an "artistic appearance." We wonder who invited Vaslav this time and where. Whose chauffeured car will drive him back home at night.

Vaslav has to make proper connections. Vaslav needs to build his career.

From time to time Mamusia hints at my brother's girlfriends—*sympatje*, as she calls them in Polish. A mention of a certain Nina, who took Maestro Cecchetti's class, has made Vaslav blush. Then there is this Maria G., with whom he has gone out a few times, until—as Mamusia has predicted—she asked him to get her a dancing part at the Mariinsky. Now he invents excuses not to see her again.

Which is good riddance, isn't it?

Mamusia's greatest worry? Some ruthless girl who will snatch *our* Vaslav, saddle him with "mouths to feed," make him smaller. "Why can't he spend more time with someone like Maroussia?" she asks me. She means Maria Piltz, who comes from a family of artists and whose mother is Mamusia's friend. How nice it would be if Vaslav married someone just like Maroussia. Not now, not when his young heart is hot and foolish and one rash mistake is enough to make him pay for it all his life. But one day, in a few years, when his career is well established.

Mamusia's endless warnings, I think, making light of the fact that I'm listening to them, not my brother.

For Vaslav is no longer just her son. He is the new master of the house. A man with expectations and demands who sets his own rules, whose money pays for this new beautiful apartment where we live now:

"Vaslav is resting, Bronia . . . He needs his morning sleep, so we'll go to Mass alone . . .

"Thetya wants us to come for a visit, but Vaslav won't go. He says he has nothing in common with her. We can go to Vilno if we want to, but without him.

"He cannot come with us to see Stassik. Not this time.

"Vaslav is working. Teaching a class. Preparing for his role. You know how he is, Bronia. A true artist. Dedicated. Absorbed in his work."

The door to Vaslav's room squeaks as I sneak inside. Jars with silver lids stand in an even row on top of his dresser. Beside them a pair of white leather gloves, stained on the fingers.

I open the jars one by one for a whiff of sandalwood and lemon balm, Vaslav's favourite, then dab a tiny bit of thick cream on my face. His brushes, I note, have lovely tortoiseshell handles; his new glove stretchers are of ivory, not cheap wood.

I open Vaslav's wardrobe, finger the fabric of his dress shirts.

My skirt slides to the floor with a *shush*. Unbuttoned, my blouse follows.

Vaslav's fine evening clothes fit me well; we share the same basic mould. We are both rather short, with powerful thighs and small feet. My breasts break the line of his shirt, though, so I leave it open. Dressed up, feet snug in Vaslav's leather shoes, hair hidden under his top hat, I could be his twin.

I turn around, glance over my shoulder. I picture men looking at me. Not a man but men, who emerge from vagueness in thrilling fragments. A thick line of a brow, a cleft chin darkening with stubble, a mouth sucking in the flesh of oysters, a muscled arm lifting me up for a shoulder sit.

The skin along my collarbone flushes. My arms are strong; my feet are alive. I step forward, toe to heel. I turn. Faster than a swooping hawk—

"Where are you, Bronia?" Mamusia's voice summons from the other room. "Can you help me?"

"Coming!"

Quickly I take Vaslav's clothes off. Fold his trousers with careful regard to the crease. Smooth his dress shirt flat before folding it, unpin the collar, remove the necktie. Everything has its place, on the shelves, hangers or inside drawers Mamusia has lined with parchment paper.

I make no mistakes. Vaslav will never know.

9.

"VASLAV'S NEW FRIEND," Mamusia calls Prince Lvov, Pavel Dmitrievitch. Older than Vaslav, mature. He is so considerate, so generous. Sending us gifts of marzipan, *petits fours*, caviar, salmon, cheeses, baskets of fruit and excellent French wine.

A generous patron of sports and arts who calls our Vaslav a "divine artist."

A friend who wishes to spare us from any hardships. Who once took a pile of court summonses caused by old unpaid bills—from the time of Father's accident—and told Mamusia not to give them another thought. "But we owe that landlord . . ." she started explaining, before Pavel Dmitrievitch put a finger on his lips and said, gallantly, that it was nothing. That his own lawyer would sort it all out in no time. That she had done enough for her children. That now when Vaslav is an Artist of the Imperial Theatres, she, the mother who raised him, deserves some rest. And if she still has any misgivings, she should consider Vaslav's feelings. How can her son who brings so much pleasure to so many in this increasingly fractured world devote himself to his art if he has to worry about his mother having to pay old debts?

Or live without a decent piano of his own.

Or go about the town on a trolley.

Or give lessons in ballroom dancing to bored debutantes? Waste his time on trifles when he himself should be taking advanced classes with Cecchetti, like all the other great dancers. Master classes for which he, Prince Lvov, will gladly pay himself.

"Madame Nijinska, when Vaslav becomes famous, I'll let him pay me back."

Prince Lvov, tall and slim, seated in Mamusia's favourite armchair, the palms of his hands resting on the ivory top of his silver cane. I admire his erect bearing, the diamond studs in his cuffs, the way he extracts his pocket watch and flips it open to check how much time there still is before they have to leave.

"*Our* friend," Vaslav insists, "not just mine."

True, there are car rides to see the imperial palaces of Peterhof and Tsarskoye Selo for all of us. There are invitations to concerts, races, restaurant dinners and at Prince Lvov's sprawling palace on Bolshaya Morskaya, where, in the marble vestibule, footmen in grey tailcoats fall to their knees to remove our outer boots. In the dining room other footmen, in black tailcoats and white gloves, serve us sturgeon and Beluga caviar. Not just Vaslav but his mother and sister, too, are Prince Lvov's cherished guests.

During one of our car rides, on a cold spring day, seeing that I'm freezing, Prince Lvov takes off his fur coat and wraps it around me. It is light and soft, and when I curl underneath it, I get a whiff of cigar smoke. "Feeling better, Bronia?" he asks, and I say yes, but he sees that I don't stop shivering and orders the driver to take us to the nearest restaurant. There he makes me eat a bowl of lip-scalding borscht and then drink sips of brandy, which singe my throat. Until beads of sweat appear on my forehead. Until he feels my hand and says, "Good, Bronia, even the tips of your fingers have warmed up."

In the kitchen Mamusia is having tea with her old friend from the dancing days, Madame Sarik, who was once wardrobe mistress for the Lukovitch troupe. They ran into each other in the street, quite by chance, and cannot get over the fact that both are living in St. Petersburg now. "The Nijinsky children!" Madame Sarik exclaims at the sight of us. "And to think I still recall you in that 'Sailor Dance'! Look at you now. The things I hear of you, Vaslav."

"All good I hope," Vaslav says, withdrawing quickly, pulling me after him out of the kitchen, where Madame Sarik insists she wants to help Mamusia prepare tea. He is getting ready to attend a symphony concert with Prince Lvov. It's a Saturday, so I'm home from school.

"Do you want to go with us, Bronia?" he asks me. "Rachmaninov is playing tonight."

"Yes," I say. Too eagerly, perhaps, but I'm anticipating Frossia's envious sighs on Monday morning. Her complaint that all she gets to do is visit some old aunt and listen to fascinating tales of invincible gout. I'm so lucky, am I not?

There is so much I envy my brother. The ease with which he comes and goes, the half-smile with which he dismisses Mamusia's questions. Even the way he has dodged Madame Sarik's praises and now rolls his eyes every time her merry laughter erupts from the kitchen, followed by the murmur of her voice.

"Women and their gossip," he says, and what I hear is: true artists have no time to waste on trifles.

I iron my navy-blue skirt and my white batiste blouse. My hair does not look so limp after I braid it and tie it with a blue ribbon. I spray a little of Mamusia's perfume on my wrists and behind my ears. "Here," Vaslav said when he handed it to her with great pride, a gift bought with his first salary from the Mariinsky, and she protested his extravagance but with such a warm smile. Jasmin de Corse, it says on the bottle, and it does smell of jasmine blooms.

Prince Lvov picks us up in his car. "Come on, children," he commands us, stepping into the hall. "Hurry up."

Vaslav puts his finger on his lips and points at the kitchen.

It is all playful and light. "Ripping fun," Prince Lvov calls it. The smiles the two of them exchange, the hushed admonitions. The way Vaslav tiptoes out of the apartment, motioning me to follow.

As soon as we reach the theatre, we go to Prince Lvov's private box, where I take a corner seat. Vaslav plants himself in the middle and makes room for Prince Lvov beside him. Madame Sarik forgotten, they laugh about something I don't know about. "Your fault," my brother teases Prince Lvov. And then comes Prince Lvov's protest: "No, Vaslav, yours alone!"

Like little boys, I think.

Below us, the concert hall glitters and hums with excitement. Women in fashionable evening gowns, hair pinned high, jewels sparkling, take their seats. Their companions, many in parade uniforms with the golden insignia, ribbons and medals of imperial orders, follow.

There it is again, that easy banter between my brother and his new best friend. The playful slapping of hands reaching for opera glasses. The jokes, the laughter. Flaring cheeks. The talk of some party they are both going to later that night, after they escort me home. Rachmaninov will be there. And Karsavina. Is this why Fokine begged to be invited? Still in love with her, isn't he?

"Cheer up, Bronia. We haven't forgotten you. We have lots of chocolates!"

"From Maxim's, the ones you love best, with cherry liqueur."

Our arrival has been noted. From the parterre a woman casts a curious look in our direction and then quickly turns to her companion. A man in the third row trains his opera glasses on our box and doesn't turn away even when the music begins.

They are all looking at Vaslav.

No wonder. Mathilda Kschessinska herself has publicly called Nijinsky her favourite partner. In the *Petersburg Gazette*, the most prominent critic, Svetlov, described Vaslav's elevation, *ballon* and brilliancy as "truly astonishing." This is what fame is, I think. Drawing all eyes to you, not just onstage but everywhere you go.

Prince Lvov whispers something in Vaslav's ear and points toward the parterre. Vaslav laughs. Only this time there is something about his laugh that makes me uneasy. It is too loud, too harsh. A challenge, not joy.

I want to think more about it, but just then Rachmaninov walks onstage. His gait is cautious, slightly awkward, but as soon as he settles at the piano, all awkwardness disappears. With the very first chords of Chopin's sonata I know I'm listening to one of the finest pianists of my time. Precise, clear, even in the most complex of configurations.

So why do my thoughts drift?

During the interval the looks in our direction persist, though no one but me pays attention to them. A few of Prince Lvov's friends stop by, or are they my brother's friends, too? One—an older, stout man someone has addressed as count—comes up to me and sniffs the air in an ostentatious way. "Young girls should smell of nothing but soap and water," he says. "Hasn't your mother taught you that?"

Anger swoops like a hawk. "My mother has taught me to be polite," I shoot back, but even the flash of astonishment in the count's blinking eyes doesn't soothe me.

Vaslav doesn't notice the count or my anger, caught as he is in a conversation that ranges from his pressing need for a tailcoat, as his dinner jacket will simply not do, to praises of Rachmaninov's exquisite touch and the music that still awaits us. Rachmaninov's own pieces! The same ones Sergey Pavlovitch Diaghilev has already played in Paris, to a stunning reception!

"Parisians don't have enough of Russia." Prince Lvov's voice rises above all others. "You, too, should go to Paris, Vaslav."

"Is that what you want?" My brother laughs, raising his arms above his head and tilting his head as if he has just finished a pirouette. "To keep me far away from your tennis rackets? Or your champagne?"

How much Vaslav reminds me of Father. In this easy elegance, his suave gestures, the unwavering certainty in his eyes. And that tinge of raw arrogance, which suits him so well.

"What do you think, Bronia?" Prince Lvov turns to me. "Am I wrong to say that Vaslav Nijinsky will throw Parisians on their knees?"

"You are not wrong, Pavel Dmitrievitch," I say, and stop, for he is not looking at me. He is looking at my brother.

The old count is staring at me with disapproval, muttering something I cannot hear. Am I blushing? I wonder. I must be. My cheeks are burning. For suddenly everything feels wrong, awkward, out of place.

It's possible to know and not know. To hear and not understand. To build knowledge of layers, like hills of sand, their shapes shifting with every wind.

Nijinsky is an *invert*. He *has his grammar wrong*. He is *incapable of loving a woman*. Such words are pronounced in a rising voice, with a wink, a tone of superiority. Disgusting? Wrong? Merely embarrassing? Or just funny?

There are other words, too, other whispers.

Vaslav Nijinsky is not ready to advance so fast in the ballet roles. His ascent is all due to Prince Lvov's money. Fokine needs it so badly that he is ready to promote "Nijinsky's acrobatics" over the merits of established dancers.

Vaslav has sold himself to the highest bidder. It is greed and lust for fame that move him, not art. He takes what he can grab, with both hands.

Not just him but all of us, gleaning after his harvest. The Nijinskys are on the prowl.

Homo homini lupus. I hold on to Mamusia's words, my shield. Artists are always jealous of each other. There will always be slashed tutus, packing pins left in the folds of the costume "by mistake," legs that trip you when you are not looking. Praises meant to sting more than flatter.

Those who will never be as good as Vaslav want to sully him, smear him with their hatred. Haven't they almost killed him once with their taunting? The higher he soars, the more they will want to pull him down. And those who love him.

"The barking of dogs as the caravan passes," Vaslav calls such talk. "Art is all that matters. A true artist takes what he needs, discards what is not necessary."

He is right.

And yet, no matter how defiant my thoughts, the memory of this evening is an excruciating one. Nothing can quiet my whirling mind, the thumping of my heart. Not even the music, slipping away as I curl into my seat, nauseous and sore.

In this confusion there is only one certainty, and it is not a consolation: Where Vaslav goes, I'm not wanted. What Vaslav does, I'm not allowed to do.

10.

FROM THAT TIME ON, when Vaslav asks why I refuse his and Prince Lvov's invitations, I come up with excuses. Exams are approaching and I have homework to do. Mamusia is alone during the week, so when I'm home, I want to stay with her.

Vaslav doesn't press. I wonder if he even notices my absences, occupied as he is. St Petersburg cannot get enough of him. His *pas de deux* with Pavlova in the Bluebird variation has been called a "miracle of a divine gift . . . two musical voices responding to each other with unequalled lightness . . . at the heights of artistic perfection." He will be partnering with Kschessinska in *Nocturne*.

Until Isadora Duncan breaks my resolve.

It is February of 1908, and Duncan is in Russia for the second time, performing at the Souvorinsky Theatre, where Prince Lvov has taken a box.

At the school she is the topic of passionate disputes. Why does she call herself a dancer, not a ballerina? What does she mean by declaring that dance should be more than "being sugar plums for the eyes"? Or that she has freed herself from "the stifling poses, the prescribed moves"? No tutus? No tights? Feet released from pointe shoes? Is it art or affectation? A fad that will come and go? Or the way of the future? Even our teachers join in these discussions. "A sensationalist," some teachers say, "a dilettante." Fokine, however, tells us to remember his words: "Duncan is showing us Russians the way."

Vaslav and I are not the only guests of Prince Lvov this evening. Tamara Karsavina is here, too. She has just danced in *Swan Lake* to great applause, having substituted the expected thirty-two *fouettés* in Act III with her own variation.

"Tati," Vaslav calls her. She calls him "Vatsa" and asks him to sit beside her. "Give me your hand," she demands, and traces the lines of his life. "I see journeys," she murmurs in a tingly voice. "I hear unending ovations."

"Tati who knows the future." Vaslav laughs. "Only why you have to tickle me as you are telling me this is beyond me."

"I don't have to. I want to."

Prince Lvov is a considerate host. He has made sure I have a seat in the first row, for an unobstructed view of the stage. He has dismissed my thanks for the invitation with a nonchalant wave of his hand. I'm an artist, like my brother. A ballerina in the making. I need to be inspired. He is the happiest when he can be of use.

His eyes never leave Vaslav. There is such intensity in them, such longing. I wonder if they have quarrelled. And if they have, why.

But then the curtain rises, Isadora Duncan begins to dance, and I see no one else.

Her dress is loose, like a Greek tunic. Her movements are simple, natural—a slight run, an extension of a leg or arm—free, flexible, fluid. Her feet are bare. Her face changes from exultation to fright. Freed from corsets and tutus, she leans with the music, kneels on the floor, falls back, throws up her arms.

Her dance tells no story.

From the moment she appears to the time she disappears into the wings, as if fleeing from the intensity of our applause, she is the music we can see with our eyes.

There is no one like her, I think.

When the break comes, it takes me a moment to find my bearings, to hear what others say around me. "A historic moment . . . Another face of progress."

"Don't repeat this drivel, Pavel." Vaslav rolls his eyes. "You can't really mean it!"

My brother is standing with his back to the auditorium. His new evening suit of black broadcloth is perfectly tailored, showing the top of his single-breasted waistcoat and his white dress shirt. The diamond ring Prince Lvov gave him for his birthday glitters every time he moves his hand.

"Progress is not achieved by discarding what is old," he declares. "You want a new ballet? Invent it. Come up with new ideas. Don't tell me that these barefoot childish hoppings are the answer. Yes, Duncan is expressive. This much I can grant you. She feels and she dances what she feels, but this is not art. This is a scream. This is an exhibition of her own self."

His brows shoot up. His whole body tenses.

I listen, bewildered. I haven't heard Vaslav speak like this before. Not with so much certainty. Not with such flair. This is what fame does, I think.

"Can you teach it?" Vaslav continues. "No? So how can you call it art?"

Prince Lvov leans back in his seat, playing with his gloves. Two limp snow-white hands smacking each other.

"But, Vatsa," Karsavina interrupts. "You are too harsh. Isn't there room for both? Classical dancing and this? Free expression?"

"Free?" my brother asks. "Is freedom all that matters, Tati?"

"But what else does?"

"If there are no rules, if nothing is forbidden, nothing matters."

The doors to our box open. Guests and admirers stop by with greetings, join in the argument. Someone has sent a note to remind Vaslav that he and Prince Lvov are invited to a party Kschessinska is giving in Duncan's honour.

I'm a schoolgirl still. No one asks me what I think. But this doesn't stop me from turning what I hear around in my mind.

My brother is right when he insists that ballet should seek new ideas.

My brother is wrong when he says that free expression is not art.

This is what I tell Vaslav later that evening, when Prince Lvov's car moves slowly toward Theatre Street. The houses are shrouded in misty darkness, store windows with mountains of chocolate tins, pyramids of cakes. The river smells of rotting fish.

"You don't know what you are talking about, Bronia."

"That's not fair," I say. "Just because I disagree with you, it doesn't mean I'm wrong."

"Don't be so naïve, Bronia. Don't believe everything you hear."

"You can say what you want, Vaslav, but this is the dance of the future!"

"If this is what you believe, you have a lot to learn."

I feel a flash of anger. "Talk to me, Vaslav. Argue your point, but don't dismiss me."

"Vaslav, Bronia," Prince Lvov interrupts, opening a hamper with refreshments. Thick chunks of smoked sturgeon, a bottle of Abrau with the two-headed eagle on the seal. The champagne cork pops, releasing a bubbly stream, tiny drops landing on my cheeks. "Enough of these disputes. Stop, I beg you . . . like our great poet tells us, 'Especially since the local wine/Is duty-free and rather fine.'"

Vaslav is stern. "Bronia is still a schoolgirl. She can't have any."

"Not even a tiny sip?" Prince Lvov asks, extending his hand with a glass.

"Cut it out, Lvov," Vaslav says, pushing the glass away, spilling the wine. "They've bent the school rules already to let her come with us. I gave my word to the *inspectrice* that I'd watch over her. What do you want me to say when they smell her breath?"

"All right . . . all right," Prince Lvov concedes his defeat.

A short-lived quarrel after all, an eruption followed by a reconciliation. The party they are heading to after they drop me off at the school is in Strelna, at Kschessinska's country mansion, which she refers to as her *dacha*. There is some disagreement on which route to take there, but it is playful.

"Own up, Vaslav. You have no sense of direction."

"Look who is talking!"

"A world-famous cyclist."

"Touché."

I'm anticipating the excitement at my return. Frossia must be glued to the window already, awaiting my account of Duncan's dance. I've decided I will not say a word. I'll demonstrate what I've seen. In my nightgown, with bare feet, on the dorm floor.

This is when the car stops at the entrance of the school, and Vaslav leans toward me. "In this supposed dance of the future," he whispers in my ear, "Duncan has left no place for a man."

He pushes me out of the car before I have time to answer.

11.

FATHER DOESN'T WRITE. Not on my seventeenth birthday, not on my graduation. He doesn't send money for my trousseau, either, though he knows that all Artists of the Imperial Theatres have to buy their own costumes.

I don't speak about how sad this makes me. Mamusia has enough of her own worries and Vaslav refuses to even hear Father's name.

"We don't need him, Bronia," he says. "Not anymore."

Prince Lvov offers to buy me a graduation trousseau, but I refuse. I also refuse his present of old lace that once belonged to his grandmother and that would look beautiful on my costumes. I tell him such a treasure requires special care and that it should stay with his family.

"'Foolish Bronia,'" Vaslav calls me.

"Then let me be foolish," I say.

A few days before my graduation Mamusia takes me to Aleksandrovsky Market to help me choose my artist's wardrobe. We buy a second-hand beige outfit, two woollen skirts, three silk blouses and an opera cloak of "respectable provenance," as the merchant calls it, all for a hundred rubles. My graduation dress, however, is new. It is muslin, rose-coloured, Vaslav's gift. I think it exquisite, almost too beautiful to wear. "Nonsense," my brother says. He makes me turn around in it and praises the way the material flows along the body. And then he hands me a small, velvet-covered box. "From Lvov," he says. "Read the note before you refuse this one, too."

This small gift has no connection to my family and requires no special care. Promise me that one day you'll also wear it to your wedding and that you won't forget me when the adoring balletomanes are lining up in front of your dressing room.

Inside the box is a small pin made of tiny rubies and diamonds, shaped like a flower.

On my graduation day, before putting on my dress, I stand in front of the wardrobe mirror. There it is, my body, the instrument that I have trained and battered daily for as long as I remember, extending its flexibility, its strength, its range. My arms are supple and toned. I'm still stocky, but my legs and feet are very strong, and so is my back. I've learnt to hide my protruding teeth, cover them with my lips when I smile.

Easing myself into first position, I close my eyes and place my hand on my breast, moving it up and down, slowly, in a caress. I try to picture a man's hand touching me. The images that come are those of Albert and Giselle, Odette and Prince Siegfried. Caresses of the *pas de deux*, hands sliding down the corset, the flighty steps on pointe.

To other passions I am still blind.

I slip into my graduation dress, fasten Prince Lvov's glittering pin above my left breast and secure the clasp. I pick up a bouquet of yellow roses. Outside the door, Mamusia is already waiting, her eyes moist with tears, her hand raised in a blessing.

The Akt takes place in the large hall of the school. I am honoured with the highest First Award, one hundred rubles—which I have already spent on my outfit—and, like Vaslav, receive the New Testament in Polish and the complete works of Tolstoy.

There are seven of us in that hall, graduating from the Girls' Division that year, in our fancy dresses, with flowers, and with family and friends cheering us on. When the ceremony is over, we all visit the most beautiful of St. Petersburg's islands, as custom demands. Passersby stop us as we walk, admire our turned-out gait and congratulate us on our achievement. They ask our names and present theatre programs for autographs. One day, they say, when we have become famous ballerinas and they will have to line up for tickets to see us, they will boast of this moment.

"Remember, Bronia, when we were told to knit socks for the soldiers on the Japanese front?" Frossia whispers, chuckling with laughter. "How crooked yours turned out to be and how perfect mine were?"

"Yes . . ."

"I bribed our maid to knit them for me."

It is still there, the smooth fabric of our as yet untried friendship. Funny couplets we came up with:

I see Fokine when I am dreaming
That's why I always wake up screaming.

The time we searched in vain for the note "the lunatic Ann," a reckless girl who—older girls had told us—had eloped with an officer of Horse

Guards after having written the story of their courtship on the lining of one of the school wardrobes.

The day is beautiful, sunny, warm. The sea smells of seaweed. We laugh. We hold hands. We pose for pictures. On the one from Stone Island, I sit on a boulder, with Frossia right beside me. We look like sisters, legs stretched out, arms locked.

During all this I keep looking for Father to appear, asking forgiveness for being late. *Parents do not stop loving their children, Bronia.*

When he doesn't, I probe my memory for the exact words of my last letter to him, the one Vaslav took with him to Nijni Novgorod. I wish I had kept a copy. I wish I could read it again, see if anything in it could have offended Father that much.

The day after graduation, the custom calls for visiting family and closest of friends. I put on my beige outfit and go alone to visit Stassik.

He is sitting on his bed when I walk in, pale, silent, staring at his hands. The fold of skin between his forefinger and thumb is torn and bleeding.

"I'm no longer at school," I say, waiting for him to raise his head and look at me. "Soon I'll be earning my own money. I'll bring you gifts."

He doesn't move.

"Mamusia will come tomorrow. She will bring you a cake."

I continue my monologue until a nurse comes and gently points at the door. She is young, with unruly auburn hair that manages to evade her tight wimple. I wonder when she first knew she wanted to become a nun and a nurse. I wonder if she ever has doubts and—if she does—how she pushes them away.

As I'm leaving, I hear the nurse's cheerful voice, assuring Stassik that supper is on its way and that he will get as much buttered bread as he wants.

I don't go home right away. I walk through the Nevsky Prospekt, past the elegant displays in the windows. High school students in uniforms have gathered by the monument to Catherine the Great. One of them holds a cigarette in his cupped hand. A *droshky*, drawn by a scrawny horse, stops and then moves on.

From now on my days will consist of company classes, rehearsals and performances. My days will be spent at the theatre. I will learn new roles whether I am assigned them or not, to be ready if a replacement is called for.

I won't let the smallest opportunity slip by. Nothing will stop me, neither disappointment nor happiness.

I will devote my life to art.

12.

ALL SEVEN OF US become Artists of the Imperial Theatres that year, new girls in the troupe, which—apart from Vaslav, its rising star—includes Anna Pavlova and Tamara Karsavina. The troupe with which Mikhail Fokine, once our teacher, now our choreographer, is mounting his new ballets.

We are all *corps de ballet*, at six hundred rubles a year. Placed "by the water," as the saying goes, far backstage. To be noticed we will have to shine.

After rehearsals, we all go to a café on the Nevsky. We order tea and one sweet buttered bun, which Frossia cuts into seven pieces with apothecary precision.

We still have the school nightmares of missed exams, lost ballet shoes, tights that keep slipping down. Mine are filled with foggy emptiness as I try to recall capitals of countries the teacher points to: France, Germany, the United States, Argentina. Until I remember that I'm no longer a student and leave.

"Lucky Bronia," Frossia says. "When I try to walk away, my legs stick to the floor."

"Not just in your dreams."

"Silly goose."

It helps to laugh together, tease each other over our most daring escapades from the past. Frossia jumping from bed to bed in the dorm. Me climbing up the walls of a narrow corridor, legs spanning the space, all the way up to the ceiling. "Have you seen Nijinska?" the governess asked once as I was up there. Frossia still counts it among one of her greatest achievements that she didn't look up or giggle.

But mostly we dissect every ballet we've seen, argue its faults and merits and their importance. This is the time to make decisions that—we know—will affect our future. What will it be? Traditional ballet or the experimental one? Petipa's choreography or Fokine's? Or both? The answer determines which rehearsals to attend. Whom to ask for instructions and corrections. Which variations to study on our own.

"The witches' Sabbath," Frossia calls these heated hours.

"Why 'witches'?" I ask. And she mimes a grimace of surprise and asks, "Aren't *you* ready to pledge your soul to the Prince of Darkness, Bronia? For one good chance?"

Vaslav never had to do any of it. He was a *coryphé* right away, marked for fame. He didn't have to wait for the older dancers to take their spots at the barre before taking his, or keep respectful silence when they practised. He didn't have to fear that he might be overlooked, denied a better role, pushed to the back during a curtain call. I used to think such recognition was the best, most magnificent reward for his talent, not yet knowing that all rewards come at a price.

But I'm getting ahead of myself. In these Mariinsky days I'm young and fearless, impatient with anything that might slow me down. Jumping out of bed in the morning, swallowing big chunks of my breakfast bun, taking just a few sips of tea before I rush to the theatre.

By then we have moved again, to an elegant apartment on Bolshaya Koniushennaya Ulitza with a lift and a telephone. It is spacious enough for Vaslav to have his own two rooms, a bedroom and a study, which Prince Lvov insisted on decorating for him with antiques and rare sculptures. Vaslav's piano, a Blüthner, arrived straight from Germany.

"Exquisite, rare, unique," Prince Lvov said. Like Vaslav, like his art. Every object he has chosen is a tribute to my brother's genius, to the supreme joy his dancing brings.

Do I feel any resentment at such words? Jealousy? I answer such thoughts with questions. Why would I be jealous? Am I not an artist in my own right? Working hard at what *I* can become?

With my first Mariinsky salary, I buy a new bed, a dresser and a matching desk, all made of Karelian birch. Mamusia thinks them too simple, but I like their modern lines, free of ornate carvings. Unlike Vaslav's green velvet drapes, the window curtains I sew for myself are made of light cotton. The floor is of pale wood, and I leave it uncovered but for a small rug, a circle woven out of bright strips of colour: red, green, white, yellow.

The seven of us practically live at the theatre, from the morning class to the end of the evening performance. We practise our moves until we can move in absolute harmony. *Corps de ballet,* however, is not only about the keeping of straight lines and the even lifting of hands. It is learning any dance we might be called to substitute at rehearsals or even at performances themselves. As is the Mariinsky custom, we ask senior dancers to teach us their roles. No one refuses or stalls. For the performance to go on, we all need to be ready to step into each other's shoes at a moment's notice.

I wouldn't have it any other way.

Modern becomes my favourite word.

Marius Petipa's choreography is old and stale, Fokine tells us at rehearsals. Modern ballet is so much more than a set of variations, displays of unconnected virtuosity. Modern ballet is not a parade of egos; it is art.

In my ballets, Fokine tells us, ballerinas will not wear their best jewels and costumes as they do now, regardless of whether they are dancing an Egyptian queen or a peasant girl. There will be no stopping a performance to let a soloist bow and do an encore. No acrobatic variations will be added just to beat a rival or fulfill a balletomane's request. In my ballets each dance is part of an organic whole; each dancer a fragment of an artistic vision, enhanced by the costumes and scenery, freed from the tyranny of tradition.

Modern ballet should break boundaries, chart new paths, achieve the unity of music and movements. Modern ballet should be a feast for the eyes.

I listen, enraptured, all doubts banished. Oh, how I listen!

October 13, 1939

Crossing the Atlantic takes ten days. Today is day five, which should lift the collective mood but intensifies rumours instead. The latest one—circulating among the dancers hired for the Australian tour—is that America is refusing entry to anyone with a Nansen passport.

What utter nonsense, I tell myself. They cannot turn us back.

Today I woke with a memory of Mamusia sitting by the darkening window of our Parisian apartment, turning her wedding ring around her finger, refusing my offer to switch on the light. "Remember Vaslav's mandolin, Bronia?" she asked. "Encrusted with such beautiful flowers. And your tin box with a ballerina on top!"

This, too, troubled her in the end, the fate of objects, once so precious, now stripped of their stories, cast adrift among strangers. A small golden medal of the Black Madonna she bought for Stassik's christening. A tortoiseshell comb her sister Thetya once gave her on a whim, unpinning it from her hair and saying, "Take it, my dear. I wish to think of you wearing it."

Mamusia gave a sigh tightened with grief, a pause filled with thoughts too painful to put into words. Untended graves. Fading memories. The thinning of hope. Everything I wanted to resist knowing.

"What's gone is gone," I said, impatient, preoccupied with my dances, students, a coming performance . . .

How many of them, the sins of pride?

On the upper deck waves are spraying the grey tarpaulin with foamy water. Puddles gather in every hollow. Judging by the lingering sour smell of vomit in the corridors, not many of us will come out for breakfast or claim the tables of the common rooms.

The wind is whipping cold, blasting, the sea steel grey.

They are persistent, our ghosts. Huddling behind us, dark and sticky, ravenous for any scraps of life we can still feed them.

I extinguish my cigarette and return inside.

PART THREE:

1908–1913

1.

IT IS NOVEMBER OF 1908; Fokine is rehearsing *Le Pavillon d'Armide.* In it a lover is caught in an imaginary garden, a web of enchantment that can only be broken by death. This makes for a flimsy plot, but I don't mind. I'm not a little girl who needs to know what happens next.

The rehearsal is going smoothly in spite of a few substitutions Fokine has made since the premiere. Onstage twelve boys in gold and silver perform the "Dance of the Hours." Like everyone not immediately needed, I am sitting in the audience, watching.

A ripple goes through the room, heads turn, backs straighten to the whispers of his name. "Sergey Pavlovitch Diaghilev!"

I, too, look behind me.

Imposing? Oh, yes! Dashing in his tailored coat with an astrakhan collar, a cane with a silver handle swaying in his hand. A bit heavy, perhaps, the dancer in me notes, but taking up more space only adds to his force, making him look older than his thirty-six years.

Fokine stops the rehearsal, hurries to greet the distinguished guest and escort him to the best seat, almost tripping over a dance bag carelessly left in the aisle. His voice hovers over the din of excited whispers: "Sergey Pavlovitch . . . dear Sergey Pavlovitch . . . what an honour . . . how much awaited."

"Well, here I am." Diaghilev's voice booms. "Astonish me!"

I'm a mere few seats away. I note his broad chest, big head and the silver streak of hair cutting the raven black. "Chinchilla," they call him because of it. A bulldog, I decide. Attractive and menacing at the same time.

Fokine returns to his spot in the first row, signals for the music to start again and claps at the dancers. The rehearsal resumes.

Onstage, the Dance of the Hours is finished, and the twelve boys leave. Vaslav—Armida's Favourite Slave—takes his position, modest and subdued, a half-smile on his lips. I lean forward not to miss anything, noting how already, then, in his stillness before he begins, something about him is speaking of pain.

How does he do it? I try to crack my brother's secret. Is it his *épaulement*, the position of his shoulders, subtle and yet making him seem askew, as if he were limping? That slight imperfection of a man who possesses so much beauty, endearing and pathetic at the same time?

There is no point in asking Vaslav about his technique. He doesn't believe words can ever capture what movement does. He laughs at Fokine when he gives us— dancers—slips of paper with background stories about the characters we are to portray.

"You don't need a story, Bronia. You need to feel, not know."

"Like Duncan?" I tease him.

"No," he says, frowning. "Like Nijinsky."

What does Armida's slave feel? Love for the one who owns him, mixed with fear? Is he both powerful and vulnerable, modest and shameless? Luminous? Calm? Wild?

Does he know that if he wants to live, he has to sustain his owner's affection, not just by making Armida know his worth but by amazing her again and again?

"I'm a pearl, but for you I'll become a diamond."

Is this what Vaslav dances? The pain of chains chafing him, the desire to free himself, from his mistress's grip? To learn from my brother, I have to read all his movements, even the tiniest ones.

During the break Vaslav walks up to where Diaghilev is sitting and, seeing me, motions to me to approach. "My sister, Bronislava. Artist of the Imperial Theatres." He even pushes me forward, as if I ever wished to hide.

"Another dancer in the Nijinsky family?" Diaghilev exclaims. It is a complaint, not a question, but I answer it anyway.

"Yes!"

Taken aback by the force of my voice, he gives me another look, the long, questioning look of an examiner. His lower lip quivers slightly. He blinks. I have the distinct feeling I do not pass.

"Do you know who I am?" A thump of a cane on the floor beats the rhythm of his words.

"You are Sergey Pavlovitch Diaghilev."

"Is that all your brother told you about me?" Diaghilev asks, eyeing Vaslav now, his voice softer, on the edge of pleasure. "Might the great Nijinsky be ashamed of me?"

Vaslav hesitates as if it were a real question, before protesting this "grossly unfair accusation."

"No, no, you couldn't be ashamed, Vaslav," Diaghilev continues with a wide smile. "I'm related to Peter the Great, after all. Illegitimate, of course, the other side of the imperial blanket. But the resemblance is there."

My brother winks at me. The whole Sergey Pavlovitch, his eyes say with fond amusement.

"Do you think I resemble Peter the Great, Bronia?" Diaghilev is looking at me again.

"Perhaps," I concede.

"Only perhaps?" he repeats with a dismissive puff of his lips. "Definitely! And it's not because of my big head, which caused my poor mother's death, but the direction."

He pronounces the word *direction* with great emphasis, three fingers of his right hand bunched up, and raised, the way the Orthodox believers prepare to cross themselves.

His hands are small, I note, white, pudgy. A ring on his little finger is too big for them, too loose.

"Like Peter the Great I'm aiming at the West, opening a new window on Europe, making sure that Russia is noticed. I'm getting rid of all that is the provincial."

Vaslav nods.

I take a half-step back, still seeking an opening in the conversation where I can enter, but I don't get a chance. I can only listen to how successful the Parisian season has been and what a splash Russian opera has made. The French have been thrown to their knees by Feodor Chaliapin's supreme genius. Such is the power of pure art. Yes, opera can be great theatre and great music rolled into one. Yes, the mighty West can learn a few things from us Russians.

"I'm accustomed to telling people to go to hell," Diaghilev's booming voice continues. "Which is not easy to do, but it is almost always beneficial."

There is more in the same vein, all for my brother's benefit. Vaslav knows it, too. It amuses and pleases him to be singled out like this.

Our break is coming to an end. Vaslav, who always needs time alone to get into his role, detaches himself from us even before the *régisseur* thumps the floor with his stick. As I watch my brother walk away, I can tell when he begins to transform himself into the Favourite Slave, for his steps became both lighter and suppler. He has, I think, both the strength of a man and the grace of a woman.

Sergey Pavlovitch leans toward me and whispers, "Your brother is a genius, Bronia. Unequalled. Unsurpassed by anyone. But you know that already, don't you?"

"Yes," I say.

"What did you think, Bronia?" Vaslav asks me that evening when he finally comes home. We are in his beautiful new study, I by the window, he by a marble column on which he has placed a bronze candelabra.

"So, Bronia, what did you think of Sergey Pavlovitch?" Vaslav repeats.

There is such impatience in his voice. Hurry up, his eyes say. Tell me what I want to hear.

I stare at the pattern of my brother's antique rug, the black and yellow border, the orange and green flowers in the centre. Every time I ask Vaslav why Prince Lvov hasn't visited us for a while, he says that Pavel is travelling on business.

"Truly exceptional," I say.

The light in his eyes tells me I've chosen my words well.

2.

PTASHEK. THE LITTLE GREY THRUSH Vaslav has brought home after some late-night party. He is so mysterious about it. No, he didn't buy it, he says. No, it was not a gift.

"Let's say I rescued it," he says once when I tease him about it too much. There is a warning in these words. I'm not to pry, so I don't.

Ptashek is so tame that we never lock its cage. It flies about the room, perches on our shoulders or pecks crumbs from the table. Sometimes it flies right into our hands and lets us smooth its feathers. Mamusia calls it a "little pest," but she doesn't really mind, not even the droppings.

When Vaslav invites Diaghilev to tea, Mamusia is quite flustered. "Such a great honour," she says, and rushes in and out of the kitchen with her offerings. Plates, forks, napkins edged with crochet frill. "Not the chiffon cake again, Mama," Vaslav says in his moaning, childhood voice.

"Mama," I note, not "Mamusia."

"I thought you liked it," she says with such tragic seriousness that Vaslav laughs and swears he was just joking. Of course he likes her cake. Loves it. He bows and kisses her hand. He puts his palms together in supplication. Until she, too, begins to laugh.

Behind me I can hear Ptashek scratch at something in its cage. It is shy with visitors.

Diaghilev's eyes linger over Vaslav and Mamusia before he takes in our oak table with thick carved legs, the high-backed chairs, the blue ottoman. Over me his eyes slide with what I decide is polite indifference. Granted only because I'm Vaslav's sister and thus cannot be entirely ignored.

I vow not to mind. To excel I have to be strong, resilient, see more, understand what is hidden to others.

So I watch, and note, and remember. The eagerness with which Sergey Pavlovitch asks to see Vaslav's study, and how my brother hurries to show it to him. Pointing at the antique desk, its gleaming mahogany top. The sculpture of the two boys carrying a fish. The amber inkwell. The letter pad with a few of his drawings.

"Dance moves?" Diaghilev asks, taking the pad in his hands and examining it through his monocle.

Vaslav nods, though all I can see on the page are a few geometrical shapes, triangles and squares.

"Fascinating!"

Diaghilev inquires about every object in my brother's room. The piano is Blüthner? The rug Turkish? Tribal? The column of Carrara marble? He must see how different this room is from others. How Vaslav winces every time Mamusia mentions Prince Lvov's generosity. Or calls him "our guardian angel," or "a generous patron of the arts."

There is much laughter that afternoon. Sergey Pavlovitch calls Mamusia "Pani Nijinska," in the Polish manner; asks about her dancing, which always brings forth the best of her. Makes her recall the day her three children watched her onstage for the first time as Princess Maria in *The Fountain of Bakhchisarai,* kidnapped by a fierce-looking Tatar. "And there they were, Sergey Pavlovitch, my two sons and my daughter, in the audience, praying loudly to Matka Boska to save their mother from harm."

"Vaslav, too?" Sergey Pavlovitch chuckles.

Vaslav, too? becomes the most repeated phrase during this afternoon. For in spite of my brother's protests, Diaghilev insists on hearing everything about Vaslav's childhood pranks and triumphs. Climbing on roofs, shooting darts from the school's windows at the people below, which almost got him expelled. That first Cossack dance, when Vaslav danced a girl's part so beautifully that no one recognized him when he started. His firefighter performance during a children's pantomime. His escapes from home, to ride horses bareback into the river, to dance for the boatmen and sail with them on a barge.

"Pani Nijinska, you have raised a genius who will change the world of dance."

"Pani Nijinska, mothers are our most precious angels. You reign supreme among them all."

"A man of education and refinement," Mamusia whispers to me in the kitchen, where I am helping her, pouring scalding water from the samovar to dilute tea essence.

"A big man," I say.

I arrange slices of cake on the platter, decorate them with spirals of whipped cream. Spoon jams and preserves into small bowls. In spite of our guest's booming voice I can hear Ptashek chirping in anticipation of a treat.

How sharp Diaghilev is in this memory. The chair pushed away from the table, his right foot hooked on the rung, left one touching the floor lightly as if in preparation for *en pointe*. Leaning toward Vaslav as he empties the bowl of jam onto his plate, as he asks for another helping of Mamusia's chiffon cake.

"Nectar and ambrosia," he says. "Pani Nijinska, your food is truly fit for immortal gods."

He talks incessantly. He makes us listen.

"Here they come, Diaghilev's stories," I will say with a laugh later, but even after hearing them over and over again, I recognize their worth. Fluid. Precise. Deliberately chosen, altered at each telling to bring about whatever effect he desires. When Sergey Pavlovitch Diaghilev wants to charm, his is always a flawless performance that I—a child of the theatre—have to admire.

That afternoon, of course, these stories are all new. Diaghilev the student showing up at Tolstoy's residence, unannounced and uninvited, and yet admitted into the grand man's presence. Or my favourite: Diaghilev in Paris calming Feodor Chaliapin, who has drunk "one too many" and fallen into a melancholy mood. "Until I assured him no one in the whole of Europe is his equal!"

This is his offering to us, a whiff of a bigger, more daring, world. A promise of unexpected transformations.

Vaslav applauds with great force. Mamusia does, too.

What happens next is so unexpected. The flutter of wings; the ruffled feathers, which make our Ptashek look bigger and grander than it really is; the opened beak; the brave, desperate charge for the cake crumbs. It could be a funny story—Sergey Diaghilev jumping in his seat, shrieking, trying to wave away a tiny bird. Vaslav running to his rescue, catching Ptashek and putting it back in its cage. Locking the door.

"It must be your monocle, Sergey Pavlovitch," Mamusia says, offering her explanation. "Reflecting the sun . . . that must be what frightened the poor bird."

"But this is nothing, Pani Nijinska," Diaghilev assures her, although I can see his hands shaking as he accepts another slice of cake.

It never becomes a story. Not for Sergey Pavlovitch. Not for Mamusia. Both of them so superstitious, forever evoking endless lists of bad omens.

A hat placed on a bed, a whistle indoors, a black cat running across your path, a woman as the first visitor on New Year's Day.

3.

"SERGEY PAVLOVITCH WILL STAGE *Le Pavillon d'Armide* in France," Vaslav tells me.

It is almost noon on a Sunday, the only day Vaslav can sleep in. He comes into the sitting room wearing his silk dressing gown, the one with red facings. There is a blemish on the skin of his chest, an oblong purple bruise. His feet are bare, for he detests slippers, especially the ones with flattened heels.

"He is already on the train to Paris," Vaslav continues after a glance at the big clock.

"The whole ballet?" I ask. "Why?"

Le Pavillon d'Armide, Vaslav points out, as if I didn't know, has been a great success in St. Petersburg. Sold out, applauded, showered with praise. Parisians will love it just as well.

In the kitchen Mamusia is asking the new hired girl what she has done with the fine sieve, for the flour needs sifting. Her name is Pasha and she has already confided in me that she is engaged to a fireman. The confidence was a forced one; the fiancé sent Pasha a letter, and since she cannot read, she had to ask for my help.

Vaslav has placed his hands behind his head to stretch his arms. He has begun lifting weights and the effects are visible already. His chest muscles have expanded. I've also noticed how he uses every free moment to tone his body: lifting on his toes to strengthen his ankles, squeezing an India rubber ball in his hands to improve his grip.

"*Le Pavillon d'Armide,*" I say, "is Petipa's old choreography through and through, with dances devised to display each soloist's skills. Even with Fokine's changes, it's like going back in time. Where is the unified performance Fokine wants so badly? Where is art?"

"Whose enlightened verdict is that?" Vaslav asks, snorting his disapproval. "The gossipy *corps*? The collective wisdom of the witches?"

Upright and on my toes to make myself taller, I count off each point on my fingers: "Taking a few of the best dances to Paris, yes! Taking you, Vaslav, Armida's Favourite Slave, yes! The wonderful backdrop of the enchanted Gobelin tapestry that comes to life when the gauze lifts, yes! The costumes, yes! But taking the whole thing? No!"

I can see that my brother listens, but I also know he will never admit I might be right. He is stubborn, immovable. "So much like Father," Mamusia often says, but never in his presence.

Is this why my voice rises? My hands clench?

There is a *thump* in the kitchen, followed by Pasha's grunt. The door opens and Mamusia emerges with her hair dusted in flour, palms clasped on her ears. "Don't speak so loud, Bronia, for God's sake," she says. "You mustn't sound as if you are always ready to quarrel."

Another rule that never applies to my brother.

But this is not where this memory ends. For a few weeks later, on the day Diaghilev returns from Paris, I wait for Vaslav to come home. Exhausted after the whole day at the Mariinsky, I fall asleep at the table, head on my hands. It is well past midnight when he opens the front door. He is catlike quiet, but I've always been a light sleeper.

"Vaslav!"

I note the signs of his excitement. A snap of his fingers, a pirouette. The fiery flashes in his eyes. Ptashek wakes up, too, chirps and flies out of its cage, right onto Vaslav's hand. He doesn't even look at it. His dinner jacket smells of cigar smoke, which he once detested.

"We are going to do it, Bronia. It's all set."

I stand up, my shoulders stiff. My feet are throbbing hot. Frossia swears by her remedy: a bucket of cold water. "Icy cold," she says, with pieces of ice floating in it. "Plunge your feet right in, Bronia, and hold them in even if it seems you can't. It will be cold first, then warm, and then the pain will go away." I'm more and more tempted to try it.

"I'm going to Paris, Bronia," Vaslav says. "With Sergey Pavlovitch. As soon as the Mariinsky frees me for the summer."

He extends his hand and lets me take Ptashek, who pecks at a scab on my thumb. Not hard, just making sure it really is not a crumb. I smooth its feathers and take it back to the cage.

Vaslav does another pirouette and then mimics a *grand jeté*. The floor squeaks. "Shh . . ." I point in the direction of Mamusia's bedroom. The last remnants of my sleep evaporate. I haven't heard my brother talk with so much passion for a long time.

"Brilliant people, Bronia. Painters. Writers. Philosophers. I've been locked in ignorance for so long. I've seen so little. Heard so little. But this is going to change."

His eyes glitter, his hands tense.

His voice is like a waterfall. Pounding over boulders. Dislodging the smaller ones, weakening the bedrock.

"Serge is a genius, Bronia."

Sergey Pavlovitch Diaghilev has become "Serge." Serge, who says that the whole ballet is not worth showing to Paris. It's much better to pluck the best scenes, take a few of the dances, present them to the public like jewels from the imperial crown.

"Me, Pavlova and Karsavina."

Didn't I tell you this before, I want to ask. But that would be a complaint, useless and futile. By then I know that not everyone's words are equal. That to be heard is the same as for a dancer onstage to be watched: It cannot be claimed or forced. It has to be earned.

So I listen while my brother tells me that art and dance are matters of great significance. He does not mean fame or the adoration of the balletomanes but the true art of dance.

These are not Vaslav's words, but he has made them his: art is an anchor for human salvation. It is the only real value in a world that is churning out false gods and goddesses. But art stagnates if not stirred, loses itself in the trinkets, and has to be prodded back to the forefront. Art also has to be saved from its enemies who want to destroy it with jealousy and hatred. Mediocrity will end on history's trash heap.

There is such conviction in my brother's voice, his raised arms, the tilting back of his head. He is changing in front of my eyes. His features soften, become fluid. He can shift shapes, change in ways that I only sometimes can predict.

"I wish you could hear Serge yourself, Bronia. But he never invites women. There is only Dunia."

Dunia is Diaghilev's old nurse, who tends the samovar and makes sure there are platters of *canapés* and tidbits on the table. Vaslav doesn't have to tell me that Dunia has nothing to say about art, music or theatre.

"I told Shura how you admired his painting," Vaslav continues. "And his directing the dancers to stand in groups that matched it. The tapestry coming to life! He was very pleased."

Not Alexandre Benois but "Shura." Not Lev Samuilovitch Bakst but "Levushka."

"If only you were a man, Bronia . . ."

He never finishes this thought, and I don't finish it, either.

At the Mariinsky, where Vaslav soars, I've been told not to jump higher than other dancers. And when I argued that I cannot predict how high others will jump, I was told that if I don't, others will.

4.

MY BROTHER IS IN LOVE.

I see it in his catlike stealth when he returns home late at night, humming, eyes shining with mischievous glow. I hear it in his words: "All these years, Bronia, I haven't even known how much I've been missing."

And I see it when he dances. Even at rehearsals, when many artists hold themselves back and only go through the motions, he—in his practice costume, black pants held with a leather belt, a white sports shirt with open collar and long sleeves—dances with full force, so that everyone, even the carpenters installing the sets, stop to watch him.

I notice every new variation, every new twist of my brother's body, every new gesture of his hands. I can even tell when he is extending his dancing practice just to be left alone, to spare himself the company of Diaghilev's friends.

But not *him*. Never *him*.

Not the man who is opening new worlds to my brother, worlds I'll have to discover by myself.

Saison Russe de Serge Diaghilev. I hear it repeated in the wings, corridors, rehearsal rooms of the Mariinsky. A season in Paris with Nijinsky, Pavlova and Karsavina. At the Théâtre du Châtelet. With dances from *Le Pavillon d'Armide, Prince Igor, Cléopâtre. Chopiniana*. The best of Russia.

—

Every day Sergey Pavlovitch is approaching Artists of the Imperial Theatres, offering contracts. One thousand francs for three months, I hear, more than the Mariinsky pays for six. Not just soloists. *Corps de ballet*, too.

It's easy to tell the chosen ones. Standing together, elated, teasing each other over French pronunciation. Planning trips to the Louvre, the Paris Opera, the Bois de Boulogne, the Galeries Lafayette.

I expect Diaghilev's offer every day.

I have good reasons. Fokine has praised me. I've already danced in his *Chopiniana*, alongside Vaslav and Anna Pavlova. Yes, they were the stars then, weightless, ethereal, in perfect harmony, but I—barely out of school—was one of the *sylphides*, floating onstage in a poet's vision, my steps one with the music.

Chopiniana—I remind myself—which Diaghilev has chosen to show in Paris.

"Will you put in a word for me, Bronia?" Frossia asks. "When you are signing your contract?"

She is not the only one.

But the rehearsals for the Parisian season begin, and I see dancers hurrying out of the Mariinsky, bags in hand, for rehearsals at the Hermitage Theatre. Making little leaps as they run. Or I hear them in the wings declaring that Diaghilev—if it can be believed—is even harder to please than Fokine.

I'm not asked to join them. A test of my will, my purpose? Or Diaghilev's judgment? It is Mamusia who says, "You must speak to Sergey Pavlovitch about Bronia, Vaslav."

My brother gives her such a startled, embarrassed look. As if she had demanded he do something shameful. "Sergey Pavlovitch knows what he is doing," he says. "He needs dancers for *modern* ballets. Bronia is too set in classical dance."

"She is better than others he hires, and she can learn fast."

Vaslav tosses his head back.

I will him to look at me.

He doesn't.

"Bronia is eighteen, Vaslav," Mamusia says, not giving up. "This is the time for her to go forward. Someone has to tell Diaghilev that."

"Why me?"

"She is your sister."

I go into my room and close the door. Not fast enough to miss the irritation in my brother's voice. "And is this why she would be suitable for Paris?" he asks. "Just because she is *my* sister? Ballet is not about favouritism. It is about art."

I wipe tears off my cheeks with my thumb. In the wardrobe mirror I look at myself. I have none of Pavlova's fragile beauty or Karsavina's magnetic charm. I'm still short and stocky, with protruding teeth and a strong chin. Unfeminine.

Is that what it is, in the end? Not art, not breaking barriers, but the shape of your face? The length of your legs?

Mamusia's rising voice cuts into these thoughts. "Open your eyes, Vaslav, for God's sake. Stop living so high in the clouds. Can't you see that everyone has a protector? If you don't look out for Bronia, she will lose not because she is not good enough but because no one speaks for her when the lists are being drawn."

In the mirror my nostrils expand and contract. I think of Isadora Duncan dancing alone. Free, bold, clad in her lose tunics, listening to nothing but her own music.

"If you don't go to Diaghilev, Vaslav," Mamusia says, "I will."

He runs out of the apartment. I hear the *thump* of closed doors and go to the window. I see him in the street below, hands in his pockets. He walks fast until the end of the street, kicking a stone.

"Don't be angry with Vaslav, Bronia," Mamusia tells me later that evening. She has brought me a glass of hot tea. I shut the book I'm pretending to read. "He is still young. He doesn't know the world of dancing as well as I do."

I shrug. I take a sip of tea, the way I learnt as a child, a tiny sip that warms but doesn't scald my tongue. "I don't care what Vaslav thinks."

"He agreed, Bronia," Mamusia tells me. "He'll talk to Diaghilev first thing tomorrow. You'll go to Paris."

"I don't want to," I say. "Not anymore."

"You can stay in St. Petersburg and sulk," Mamusia says, smiling, "or you can prove to Diaghilev how wrong he has been."

—

The next day my contract for the 1909 *Saison Russe* waits on my dressing table. It is already signed. *Dvoryanin: Sergey Diaghilev.*

I read it carefully. Two pages of many warnings and few promises. For the payment of one thousand francs Bronislava Fominitchna Nijinskaya will undertake her responsibilities in good faith. Will be obliged to participate in all rehearsals at no additional compensation. Will always be on time and conduct herself properly. Will accept all changes to the repertoire, be available for any publicity required of her.

Briefly I imagine myself sending it back without a word. Instead, as I sign it, I vow that this will be the only time my brother will have to intervene on my behalf. Ever.

A vow I've kept.

5.

IN THE SPRING of 1909 Vaslav goes to Paris with Sergey Pavlovitch, ahead of everyone else. It is his first trip abroad. Mamusia frets; he needs new shirts and suits. He needs to know never to leave his hotel without the address clearly written on a piece of paper, or go alone into parts of the city he is not familiar with. He is not to trust strangers who want to show him sights or take him to a restaurant. He should avoid crowded places where his pockets can easily be picked. He should never eat foods he doesn't know or drink more than one glass of wine.

"Oh, Mamusia." Vaslav laughs off her warnings. "If I listened to you, I would never see anything."

To me he says, "Paris will be hard work, Bronia. Things will be happening there you might not understand."

"I'm not a child," I answer.

A dance company is not a place for secrets. Our bodies are our instruments. We oil them, display them, abuse them when necessary. Every time I'm tempted to forget it, I look at my feet. The callused, bleeding feet of a dancer.

In the crowded dressing rooms of the Mariinsky Theatre I hear that my brother is holding his nose high, pretending to be made of another clay.

Diaghilev's golden boy. Or his slave?

It'll all come to a crashing halt one of these days.

Everything that goes up must go down. There will be a terrible price to pay.

I push these words out of my mind. Other thoughts, too. Of the locked drawers in my brother's desk. Of the expanding silence, the line that divides what Vaslav and I can talk about and what should never be mentioned. This is a fluid border, ever changing, and I have to feel its shape, follow its surprising curves.

Serge Diaghilev, Vaslav says, is a magician. We, his dancers, never suspect what effort, what energy, what endless sleights of hands are required to keep a dance company going. It is one crisis after another. The imperial court revokes the promised funding. This is not enough? Suddenly the Hermitage Theatre is no longer available for rehearsals. Another venue has to be found the very same day.

Then there are the artists themselves. Childish. Unreasonable. Ruled by their petty jealousies. Kschessinska was invited to go to Paris *after* Pavlova and considers herself slighted. Benois is sulking because Serge chose Bakst's drawings for the Parisian posters. Dancers denounce one another just to get a better role. They never see beyond their own needs, never see the whole ballet, its art.

"And he," Vaslav says, hands raised, "has to deal with it all."

We see Vaslav off at the train station, Mamusia and I. With a farewell basket Mamusia—unfamiliar with dining cars—has prepared, covered with a kerchief sewn in Ukrainian cross-stitch patterns. There is a whole roasted chicken inside, cut into portions and garnished with baked apples. Cutlery and napkins are packed neatly in a birch bark box.

Serge Pavlovitch is waiting on the platform, his black coat unbuttoned. Seeing us, he waves. He tips the porter who has delivered Vaslav's suitcases and orders his servant, Vasily, to take them inside.

Before giving Vaslav the basket, Mamusia takes off her glove, smooths my brother's hair, removes an invisible speck from his cheek.

"Dear Pani Nijinska," Diaghilev says. "There is no need to worry. Vaslav is my most talented dancer. I'll take care of him myself."

Vaslav smiles and rolls his eyes. Impatient like a little boy fussed over too much.

"Get in, both of you," Mamusia says, glancing nervously at the station clock. "It's time."

A moment later Vaslav waves to us from the corridor, leaning from an open window. The train engine puffs, the cloud of steam rises from its chimney and the train begins to move.

A uniformed stationmaster walks by, whistle in hand, and Mamusia squeezes my hand. I know what she is thinking. We have both read in the *Petersburg Gazette* that the train robberies along the Vladikavkaz railroad were committed by railroad workers themselves.

"I was hoping we would all go to Paris together," she says.

The air smells of steam and soot. We wait on the platform until the end of the train disappears from view.

When Prince Lvov comes by, I'm alone at home, sorting out the clothes I want to take with me to Paris. I choose dresses that are easy to wash and dry in a hotel room. My most comfortable pair of walking shoes, I notice, is in dire need of new heels.

Prince Lvov glances over my open suitcase. "I just came to say goodbye," he says. "And wish you a happy journey."

There is still that sheen of unlimited means about him, but his skin is pale and sallow. I wonder if he was ill this winter.

"You must have some tea," I insist.

He sits down at the table and I bring him a glass of tea the way he likes it, with lemon and Mamusia's cherry preserves. He says he saw me dance in *Chopiniana* at the Mariinsky. "I know I'm not an expert, Bronia," he says, "but I thought you were superb."

"Not as good yet as Vaslav and Pavlova," I say.

"Quite true," he says. "As I said, I'm not an expert. But now you are going to dance in the City of Light."

We chat about Paris. Of the difficult French audience, which—unlike Russian balletomanes—thinks ballet third-class entertainment and not art. Of the need to prepare myself for catcalls and whistles. He offers a few recommendations for restaurants, oblivious to my age and finances, as one of them is Maxim's. Tells me not to rush through the

Louvre trying to see everything but to choose a few rooms I like and spend my time there, ignoring all else. Urges me to just walk in the streets, observe the crowds, have coffee in one of the outdoor cafés. "Breathe Paris, Bronia," he says.

"I will."

The clock strikes one. Ptashek chirps in its cage, in hope of a treat. We don't have many visitors. Vaslav dislikes "playing host."

Last winter had been hard for him, Prince Lvov continues, taking another sip of tea. He was personal secretary to the minister of communications, responsible for the Trans-Siberian Railroad, and travelled all over the country with him. Strikes and protests have spread far outside St. Petersburg. He saw a mob set fire to a police station. Why? Because a child was flogged for stealing a few potatoes.

He pauses, takes another sip of tea. Removes a fleck of tea leaf from his mouth, places it on the edge of the saucer.

"This is what always happens when punishment is too excessive," he continues, putting a spoonful of preserves into his mouth. "Unequal to the crime." His point is simple, straightforward: injustice brings out violence. Anyone should see it. And what has the tsar been doing so far? Wavering, stalling necessary reforms, listening to some crazy Siberian monk, as if matters of state could be solved by blind faith.

His hands are as beautiful as I remember. Manicured, slender, white. In a few years such hands will mean a death sentence, even if the rings have been hurriedly removed, but I couldn't foresee that.

I'm sorry when the tea glass is empty and Prince Lvov rises to leave. He, too, is sorry—I see that he lifts himself slowly, with reluctance. "I might not see you again for a very, very long time, if ever," he says, his voice choking. "I've always been happy in your home. Please tell your mother that."

"Will you not visit us again, then?" I ask lightly. "Or come to Paris to see us dance?"

Another pause, a clearing of his throat. "I know my limits and I don't dispute them. Vaslav needs to be with artists. My connections are with the sporting world. I do not wish to hurt his career. I gave Diaghilev my word."

I stand in silence, unsure what to say, until Prince Lvov asks me to grant him one last favour.

I think he wants me to pass on a letter to Vaslav or some small gift that I can take with me to Paris. But his request is even more modest: "Will you let me sit alone in your brother's study for just a few minutes?"

"But of course!" I exclaim.

I open the door to Vaslav's room, the one Prince Lvov has furnished with such care. We walk in together and I point at Vaslav's favourite chair, inviting the prince to sit down. On Vaslav's desk, in a thick silver frame, there is a photograph of Mamusia. A paper knife is lying on top of Tolstoy's *Childhood*.

Prince Lvov picks up that knife and holds it in his hand. "They say you should never give knives as presents. I should've remembered that."

As I close the door, I see him slump into my brother's chair and hide his face in his hands.

6.

IN PARIS I have no time for cafés, walks in the streets or even visiting the Louvre. Every morning I wake up in the small hotel room I share with Mamusia, have a croissant with jam and café au lait for breakfast and hurry to the Théâtre du Châtelet, right by the Pont au Change, for the whole day of rehearsals. All I have seen of Paris so far is a glimpse of the towers of Notre-Dame, from the bridge, and the metal lace of the Eiffel Tower. Thank God for a small square nearby where I can sometimes snatch a few breaths of fresh air during a break, or look at the flowers, since spring comes so much earlier here than in St. Petersburg.

On our first day in the city Mamusia and I—eager to see a Parisian theatre—admired the Palladian facade of le Châtelet. Now that I spend whole days here rehearsing, I see how shabby and run down it is inside. Not only are the seats faded and carpets threadbare, but the bells that summon artists for the stage often do not work. The floor of the stage is cracked, and as we rehearse, workers are covering it with loose planks, leaving nails and their tools lying about.

In France, it seems, there are no male dancers of any renown. Few men would even consider appearing in a ballet. In the Paris Opera, women are dancing male roles. Without an imperial court to support it, French ballet is a diversion, a filling in-between opera scenes.

There are other differences. In St. Petersburg the artists don't have to please the press. In Paris Vaslav has to pose for photographs. Right after rehearsal, when Vaslav should be resting, I see him in the wings, pretending to leap so that each photographer can get a good shot. All of it in his costume, which I think beautiful but also too heavy, stiff with embroidery,

He hates posing, but he doesn't complain.

Not that we talk much, if at all. Vaslav's hotel is right by the Opera, a good fifteen-minute walk from where Mamusia and I stay. As soon as my brother arrives at the theatre, always with Sergey Pavlovitch, a crowd surrounds them right away; Diaghilev's friends. Jean Cocteau, with rouged cheeks and carmine lips, is a famous poet. Misia Edwards, whom Sergey Pavlovitch loves and respects above all others, has impeccable musical taste. All Parisian *mélomanes* await her verdict. She, like us, is Polish, born in St. Petersburg. The elite of Paris. Anyone who *really* matters. Critics, artists, patrons of the arts. Those who will judge us.

On the advertising column I pass on my way to the theatre, Anna Pavlova—in an *arabesque* pose sketched in charcoal and chalk on a grey background—promises "The *Saison Russe* will amaze you!"

You swooned hearing the divine Chaliapin, Diaghilev's voice booms in my mind as I practise, polishing each step, each variation of my dances, until they etch themselves into my muscles. *You loved my Russian opera. This time, I shall also give you Russian dance, Russian music, Russian scenery. Prepare your tongues for Russian names you shall never forget, Pavlova, Karsavina, Fokine, Bakst, Benois.*

Prepare yourself for Nijinsky.

By the evening of May 19, 1909, we are all nervous. As soon as the audience begins to gather, we take turns peeping through the small hole in the curtain. Isadora Duncan, I hear, has just arrived, but I cannot see her in the audience swaying with expensive furs and glittering gowns. Mamusia is sitting in the first row, looking very distinguished in the new satin dress Vaslav insisted on buying for her. Purple, I vow to tell her when the evening ends, suits her greying hair.

In the wings the usual chaos rules. A prop has been misplaced, a dancer has strained her ankle, someone has found a loose nail on the floor. There have been last-minute changes in the cast. Pavlova won't dance at the premiere "Due to an unforeseen delay," she telegraphed, so Diaghilev has put Karsavina in her place. The latest backstage gossip holds that Pavlova is cautious. If we fail, she won't come at all, and her name will not be sullied.

When the curtain rises, I'm one of the dancers kneeling onstage with my garland of roses, part of the tapestry that slowly comes to life. We make a beautiful picture and the audience rewards us with a murmur of appreciation.

And then Vaslav bursts onto the stage, radiant and sparkling, too powerful for the eyes to keep up with him. Words also fail. Twelve pirouettes followed by a triple *tour en l'air*? He has broken the pull of gravity? He is soaring!

The audience is ecstatic. People stand up, cry for encores. Vaslav bows and leaves. The applause continues until he comes back.

He bows again and again.

My memory of the rest of the evening is one of being carried on a powerful wave that crushes everything in its wake, of an elation that frees me from myself. I must have danced well—we all have—but when I probe my recollection of a specific move or an execution, it recedes. Even my *pas de deux* from *Le Festin* with Vaslav is but a joyful blur of fire.

But I still see the never-ending shower of flowers, the admirers flooding backstage. Sergey Pavlovitch is beaming, rushing from one dancer to another, bestowing his embraces, placing kisses on our cheeks. "Wonderful, amazing," his voice rings. "My children, you've shown them true Russia!"

"Didn't I tell you, Bronia?" he gasps when he spots me. "A genius! The God of the Dance. And this is just the beginning."

A peck on my cheek, a whiff of almond blossom and cigar smoke.

I nod. My right foot is throbbing. Mamusia is waiting for me in my dressing room.

"You are not happy for Vaslav, Bronia?" Diaghilev asks.

His eyebrows knit. His upper lip raises on one side in a lopsided grimace. "Crocodile's grin," one of the dancers called it, and I think these words apt. A smile with a tinge of warning in it, a prelude to a lurch forward, the crushing power of predator's jaws.

"I'm very happy, Sergey Pavlovitch," I say. I desperately want to know what he thinks of *my* performance, but this is not a question a dancer from the *corps* can ask him. Not even Vaslav's sister. If I disappointed him, I will know soon enough. His praise I have first to earn and then—like everyone else—await the moment he thinks suitable to bestow it.

"Can I have no peace?" Diaghilev snaps. "Ever?"

I look at him with surprise, only to realize that he is not talking to me. Vasily—of whom dancers say that he is not just Diaghilev's servant but also his spy—saunters toward us, smacking his lips. When Vaslav prepares for his dance, Vasily—on Diaghilev's orders—stands guard at the door. No one can get inside, not for any reason.

"Master, please, quick," Vasily says, rolling his eyes, his hands miming a crown over his head.

Diaghilev leaves with a grunt, and as soon as he is gone, dancers unwind. Shoulders loosen, spines slouch, smiles fade from faces, eyes lose their sheen.

I take a deep breath and step away from all this unravelling, the world of torn costumes, limping legs, bloodied shoes. My own costume stinks of sweat. There is a hole in my silk stage tights, right below the knee, which I will have to darn very carefully for tomorrow. I've glued the headdress to my hair, but the French glue I used is not as strong as Russian and the headdress threatens to fall off.

Beside me rise the excited whispers of those who have been invited to the post-performance celebration at Chez Larue. The *crème* of Paris society will meet, touch and hear Nijinsky and Karsavina. Others, less lucky or less distinguished, are talking of going to a small brasserie behind Notre-Dame that serves excellent fish soup. "Pavlova must be kicking herself now," someone says with a laugh.

"Want to join us, Bronia? Come on, we deserve it!"

I don't want to go anywhere. I don't care about places where artists become ordinary people. I so prefer us onstage.

7.

WHEN I RETURN to Russia after that first Parisian season, I'm a dancer transformed.

In spite of Fokine's successes, most of the Mariinsky ballets are still ruled by Petipa's spirit. The audiences may love them, but I think them stiff and artificial. No soul in them, I tell my friends, no art. This is ballet that has outlived itself. This is the past that has to be smashed to release the true art from its shackles.

I am one of the "Diaghilevcy." This is what we call ourselves and this is what other Mariinsky dancers call us. We itch for new means, new methods, challenging, bold. We seek eruptions of energy.

Ballet needs a revolution, we say. Russian art needs a revolution. Of colour, of music, of movement. Russian art needs freedom from the past.

Our Petipa-loving enemies, "Imperialisty," think us crass and shameless. We are *not* freeing ourselves from anything; we are merely rejecting the best of Russia. Besides, we are ungrateful, biting the hand that feeds us. Where would we be without the imperial court? Begging for handouts like dancers in France?

Frossia frowns when I mention the Paris season. She still doesn't believe that I couldn't say a word on her behalf, that Vaslav's *special* friendship with Diaghilev gives me no advantages. She hasn't yet worn the silk scarf I brought her from Galeries Lafayette.

"What is so wrong with the harmony of *Swan Lake*, Bronia?" she asks. "The richness of *The Sleeping Beauty*?"

In the dressing room we share, she has moved her makeup tubes away from mine. A childish, churlish gesture, but it hurts. As do Frossia's growing silences, and her dashing out without waiting for me, even though we are going to the same café.

"She is jealous," Mamusia says to calm me when I pour out my hurt to her. "You are better than Frossia is. You danced in Paris. It's hard on her. It would be hard for you, too."

Mamusia massages my feet every night when I come home from the theatre, feet that do not have time to heal. She examines my blackened toenails, thickened calluses; smears broken skin with disinfectant. We discuss the merits and limitations of remedies she, too, knows well. Lambswool stuffed into the pointe shoes, ice-cold compresses, longer warm-up sessions.

It is not just Frossia. The friends I started with at the Mariinsky all eye me with taxing caution. Now when I arrive at our café, conversations abruptly turn to trifles: the rising cost of silk tights, the cuts of dresses and coats they are thinking of buying or having made. In St. Petersburg Parisian fashion still means dresses in pale rose or faded lilac. I do not tell them that before leaving France I saw storefronts displaying the bold colours of the *Saison Russe*: bright blues, greens, yellows.

"In a ballet company one is always alone, Bronia." Mamusia's voice echoes my thoughts.

I still believe that she is wrong. I believe that there are old ways and new ways. That art—the true art I see being born—transcends jealousy, melts resentments and hatreds. Not entirely, I am ready to concede, but enough to soften the sharpest of edges. Break up the old stiffness that the school has instilled in us so well. Make room for a new range of movements, new feelings, new joys.

The Mariinsky is our duty. We Diaghilevcy live for the summer. Sergey Pavlovitch, we hear, has already commissioned Stravinsky to write music for a new ballet. Rehearsals for the new *Saison Russe* will begin soon.

A few weeks after our return from Paris, Fokine and Bakst agree to mount *Carnaval* for a charity ball organized by the Technological Institute. With Vaslav as Harlequin, alongside Karsavina, his Columbine. Fokine has offered me Papillon.

Fokine has only three days to mount the ballet, and I am not called for a rehearsal until the day before the performance. When I arrive at the auditorium, the whole ensemble is practising the "Valse Noble," and Fokine greets me with a quick nod.

I put my dance bag in the corner.

"I need to go back to the Mariinsky," Fokine tells me when the music ends and dancers begin to leave. "Let me show you quickly what I want for tomorrow. You'll have to practise right now, alone."

My role is simple. I am a butterfly trapped in a room, fluttering my wings until they capture me. "Like this," Fokine says, circling the stage with outstretched hands in slowed-down tempo so that I can memorize the steps.

I repeat what he has just done.

Fokine nods, gathers his notes and walks toward the wings. "Just stay with Schumann's music," he adds before leaving. "*Prestissimo!*"

The pianist begins to play and I repeat the steps Fokine has just shown me. Simple, I think them, undemanding. Vaslav's voice takes me by surprise, for I did not see him come in. "No, Bronia," he says, giving a sign to the pianist to start again. "You are too slow."

I gather all my force to speed up my steps, but Vaslav is still shaking his head. "You are not breathing with it, Bronia! You are showing your effort, breaking the magic."

"Try four bars at a time. Now try eight. *Prestissimo!* Just as the music demands."

"No, not like that. Your hands are too slow. They have to be as fast as your feet."

"Stop!"

I stop, panting, sweaty.

"Look, Bronia!"

There it is, my brother's miracle, simple and pristine, each perfect movement leading into the next. Vaslav has turned into a weightless butterfly, skimming the floor with his feet, his fluttering arms holding him up in the air as he whirls faster and faster. Frightened, terrified, crazed with panic.

The pianist has left us by then, but Schumann's music is flowing in my brother's every step, and when he gestures me to join him, I follow. We circle the stage together until Vaslav stops.

"Now you've got it, Bronia," he says, his eyes shining, and I am overflowing with joy.

That is how I dance it the following day at the gala. The auditorium may be just a pale shadow of the Mariinsky, but I am wearing Bakst's beautiful ankle-length crinoline of crisp white muslin, transparent butterfly wings and colourful silk ribbons at my wrists. My body, for years so rigidly trained, is beginning to break out of its mould.

I am elated when Diaghilev announces that he will include *Carnaval* in the second Parisian season.

8.

THE 1910 PARISIAN season of Ballets Russes causes a greater sensation even than the first. *Giselle, Carnaval*, Stravinsky's *Firebird* are all declared masterpieces, but it is *Schéhérazade* that truly awes the Parisians. Or, rather, Vaslav's rendering of the Golden Slave: "Terrifying half cat, half snake," the reviewers gush, "sub-human and super-human . . . a panther in thrilling spasms."

Piles of letters and telegrams are delivered daily to my brother's room, requests for his signed photographs and invitations to fashionable parties where—should he deign to accept—he would be the cherished guest of honour. Gifts flow in: gold rings with inscriptions, holy icons, silver goblets. His restaurant bills are paid by mysterious strangers. Merchants bow when he comes into their stores and refuse payment. Any shirt Vaslav Nijinsky chooses to wear is going to start a trend.

Vaslav has conquered Paris.

Vaslav is the God of the Dance.

Vasily and two other servants guard the door to his dressing room at all times. Otherwise some admirer will sneak inside in search of mementoes. Vaslav's costumes will be torn apart, each shred later lovingly framed. His makeup tubes, his used ballet slippers, even his underwear will disappear.

When I return to Russia at the end of August 1910, with Mamusia but without Vaslav, St. Petersburg seems smaller, petty, tarnished with envy. Loneliness is what I taste, but I do not want to admit it.

At the Mariinsky I am the sister of *that* Nijinsky.

"Haughty like all Poles," I hear, "too big for his breeches."

That Nijinsky dazzles Paris but spares himself when he dances in St. Petersburg, thinking Russia not worthy of his talent. Pleads an illness to defer his return, though he is seen walking in the Lido with Diaghilev, decked in fineries: a morning coat with striped trousers, a straw hat, white spats.

"Learnt all he knows here, but now the Mariinsky is not good enough."

The lines of division are marked by averted eyes, vague smiles. Friendships I thought only maimed are now dead and rotting. Frossia walks past me without even a wave of her hand. There is no place for me at the café table where the dancers with whom I started still dream of a chance to leave the *corps*.

Vaslav is above such pettiness, I think with envy. Vaslav can live for art, for beauty. Vaslav is surrounded by like-minded spirits.

He is soaring.

Vaslav writes to Mamusia every day, even if his letters often come all at once. It is one of his promises to her he always keeps. "It's for both of us," Mamusia insists, handing me my brother's letter, asking me to read it aloud. When I finish, she wants me to read the reviews he attaches, or the inscriptions on photographs in which he stands beside his new friends: Erik Satie, Maurice Ravel, Pierre Bonnard.

Mamusia's latest scrapbook of Vaslav's triumphs is already full, and she has just started another, bound in Russia leather with gilded borders. I prefer to read of my brother's transformations:

> *At the Louvre, today, I looked at the Greek vases, the ones with black figures, some of them dancing. I try to assume the poses they depict, to the amusement of the guards. It is not that easy, believe me.*
>
> *Serge took me to see the pictures of Gauguin. "What do you think of his women?" he asked. I said they were not ordinary women, but visions of ecstasy and art. I also said that Gauguin couldn't paint like this had he not broken his own ties to the past.*
>
> *An artist does not belong to one place in the world. Art belongs to us all.*

"Is that what Diaghilev tells Vaslav?" Mamusia asks, and frowns. "That Russia is no longer enough for him?"

"Isn't it true?" I counter, flushing with impatience.

Mamusia sighs and says that appearances matter. To place oneself too much apart from others is a mistake. Russia doesn't forgive a betrayal, real or merely perceived. Vaslav is only twenty-one and has had enough temptations already. He doesn't need to be encouraged to break with those who always loved his art.

Mamusia, I think, resisting these words with all my forces. Always cautious, always expecting the worst.

—

When Vaslav finally returns to St. Petersburg, he spends as little time at the Mariinsky as possible, arriving only for his scheduled performances, leaving as soon as they end. At home he is patient with Mamusia but shrugs off my questions about Paris and his travels, though I can always get him to talk about Tolstoy, whose death the whole of Russia is mourning.

Vaslav has marked pages in his *Complete Works of Lev Nikolaevitch Tolstoy* with red ribbons. His favourites are the passages calling for the brotherhood and humanity of all men, the renunciation of privileges and the celebration of the simple faith of ordinary people who work with their hands.

"Beautiful words," my brother says.

Yes, these are beautiful words, but how can I agree with Tolstoy when he declares: "No matter what work a woman does—teaching, medicine, art—she has only one real purpose in life in sexual love."

What about Isadora Duncan, Vaslav? Anna Pavlova? What about me?

"Duncan, Bronia?" Vaslav's voice has this new, forced note of worldliness I dislike. "You know what she said to me in Paris? Why don't we have a child together? What a dancer it would be!"

"That doesn't prove anything. That is party talk. The kind you used to hate."

"Believe me, she meant it!"

Vaslav puts the book away and gives me a sideways glance as I announce that this is not the Tolstoy I love. That I prefer the Tolstoy who wrote *Anna Karenina* and *War and Peace*. Who was not telling me what to think.

"How typical of a woman!"

I am not yet angry, not until my brother's forehead creases in a frown. Not until, finger in the air, he speaks of a woman's impatience with the abstract, her lack of courage to pursue her dream, her desire to dwell on earth when the male spirit struggles to fly.

"If only you were a man, Bronia, you would understand."

I gather all my force to appear calm. "These are not even your own words, Vaslav," I say. "Is this what Diaghilev tells you?"

"I won't talk to you when you're like that," Vaslav says. "Not when you are in such a state."

"What state?"

He shrugs, irritated, and walks away. The door to his study closes. A moment later I hear him punch his fist against the wall.

I still wonder what it was my brother meant then. The force of my insistence that he had just parroted Diaghilev's words? Or was it something else, more basic, animal-like? The telltale smells of my monthly flow every dancer who lifts us up knows so well?

9.

"SERGE IS TIRED of having to borrow artists from the Imperial Theatres," Vaslav tells me a few weeks later, his voice rising in excitement. "He wants to form a permanent theatre company. His own Russian ballet. With Cecchetti as ballet master!"

We are in our living room, at the heavy mahogany table with matching chairs—Mamusia's pride, which I have long thought cumbersome and old-fashioned. It is the end of November, a dark, chilly St. Petersburg day. Wind rattles the bare branches of the ash tree in our yard. Soon we will bundle ourselves in furs and wrap our faces with scarves, drawing breaths of the warmed air through the cloth.

"Who will want to join it?" I ask, although I am tempted already. "Give up permanent employment and pension?"

"I will," my brother says. "What is money or imperial privileges beside experimentation and art? Golden shackles. Obstacles."

I think of Mamusia, all her sacrifices, her joy at knowing our future has been assured.

"That is not all," Vaslav continues. Diaghilev wants him to mount a ballet for the next Paris season. *L'Après-midi d'un Faune*. It will be set to Debussy's music. He has already been thinking about it for some time. Ancient Greece. A faun. A passing nymph.

"Sergey Pavlovitch wants you to replace Fokine?" I gasp.

"Fokine is finished."

Vaslav stands up, too restless to sit still. His voice is full of conviction. He has said these words before. "Fokine is derivative, constantly churning out the same ideas. Besides he is not modern enough. *Schéhérazade* may dazzle, but it is full of sentimental drivel. Fokine's limitations are of the worst kind."

"Why?" I ask. Not because I disagree, but because I want to make sure I understand.

"Because by tinkering with the past, Fokine stops a true revolution of movement and of colour."

I grip the edge of the table to steady myself.

Vaslav doesn't want Fokine's fluid lines, his soothing movements. His inspiration is in ancient Greece, in the black figures frozen on the old pottery he has seen at the Louvre.

He begins mimicking his own thoughts, standing up with his profile to me, not just his head but the whole torso, and walking in half steps. And then—like a flash of lightning—he turns to me and asks, "Will you work with me, Bronia?"

Lightning can kill, but it can also melt sand into glass.

My insides turn. My head spins. My brother is asking me if I have the courage to care for nothing but art.

The quiver beneath my breastbone is a tug of joy.

Faun, as Vaslav calls his new ballet, is our secret.

Fokine cannot know about it. He is already resentful of Vaslav's fame. This is why we cannot rehearse at the Mariinsky. Or talk about it with anyone.

Our secret. Oh, the taste of these words, its tingling sweetness. It is as if we were the Nijinsky children again. Without Stassik but still together. Through fire and water.

In the living room we push the couch to the side and roll up the carpet. Mamusia comes in to ask what all this racket is about, but we wave her away. She raises her hands in mock surrender and closes the door.

Vaslav is the Faun and I the nymph he startles.

At first the Faun lies on a rock, motionless. Then he raises himself partway up, kneels, sits up. He is a wild creature, jerky, angular. "Ill-shaped, repellent," some reviewers will call it later, but this is all nonsense. The world of the Faun is beyond ugliness or beauty. As is all true art.

The Faun makes a small, goat-like jump followed by a few precise steps, heel to toe. There is boldness in them, and subtlety. Energy courses through his muscles, sinking into the ground. A pause, when it comes, is delightfully unexpected.

These are, I think, ancient movements summoned back to life. My own muscles twitch in response.

Vaslav laughs. His eyes flicker. He doesn't have to ask what I feel. He knows.

"Now, this is your part, Bronia," my brother says, and turns into the nymph I will become. She, too, is a phantom from the ancient world, floating through the room, feet in profile, shoulders *en face*. As she walks in, the nymph lifts up her arms, freezes, walks again. Then comes the startled gesture, the hasty flight.

"Try," Vaslav says, and I let his voice guide me through the still-unfamiliar moves, an echo of our childhood game in which, blindfolded, I sought my way to some hidden treasure.

"Yes . . . no . . . stop . . . go on . . . once again."

This is still a sketch, a collage of fragments that will have to be reassembled and filled in, but I already know *Faun* is unlike anything I have seen. I am part of what is truly new.

This is the thought that turns inside my head and leaves its thrilling presence on my skin.

For the next month we work on *Faun* every day.

The art book with pictures of Greek vases that Vaslav has brought from Paris is always opened. This is our anchor. Not to illustrate the music but to respond to it.

"We need to see ourselves from all angles," Vaslav says.

Mamusia's pier mirror isn't enough, so I fetch the triple one from my dressing table. They help at first, but soon Vaslav is not happy. Mirrors distract. They force us to look at reflections. They take us away from the dance itself.

"Let's get rid of the mirrors. You be the Faun, Bronia. Do what I tell you to do and I will watch you."

I stand in the centre of the room, my torso turned, just the way Vaslav showed me. I make a step, heel to toe.

"No!"

Another step, more fluid this time.

"Wrong," Vaslav says. "It is all wrong."

"Once again, Bronia. Just as I showed you."

I protest. This is precisely the way he has shown me. Can't he see it?

"You are not listening . . . now bend backward . . ."

"Wrong!"

This is how these first rehearsals proceed, day after day, heated, filled with Vaslav's accusations and my tears. Every time I fail to move the way he wants I'm a dunce and a klutz.

"I cannot read your mind," I plead. "I'm only nineteen. I don't have your body and your technique."

"Cheap excuses!"

In one of my memories of these days Vaslav has just slammed the door behind him in a fury. He argues with Mamusia in the hall, telling her to leave him alone. Yes, he knows what he is doing. No, he doesn't need to rest.

Tears well in my eyes. I try to blink them back but fail.

Defeated, my cheeks wet, I sit on the floor, stretch my legs in a split, roll back and forth to loosen my aching muscles. I go over every movement I've made, looking for errors. What have I missed? Where did I go wrong?

Other thoughts come, too, heavy with resentment. Why is it always my fault? Isn't Vaslav unreasonable? Expecting instant perfection? As if my body had no limitations. As if the smallest distance separating his vision from what I'm able to do was a betrayal.

The wind howls, bangs at windowpanes. St. Petersburg winters are dark and long. Spring comes in a short, violent blast, an eruption that sweeps winter away. But spring is still months off.

The door opens. I'm so sure it is Mamusia who has come to smooth our quarrel that I do not lift my eyes.

But it is Vaslav, not Mamusia, squatting beside me, rubbing tears off my cheek with his fingers. "We are not done yet, Bronia. We have work to do."

I bite back the temptation to scream *Leave me alone, find someone better than the klutz you think me to be.* I uncurl myself from the anger and the hurt.

"Yes," I say.

—

We rehearse every day, and every day is filled with contradictions. I do exactly what Vaslav wants me to do, and it is all wrong. One minute he tells me that I am hopeless, deaf and blind, another that I am the only one who can understand his art.

It's a vicious circle. We are locked inside it, stumped, muddled. At night, no matter how tired I am, I lie awake peering into darkness. At the Mariinsky I'm distracted. "What has got into you, Bronislava Fominitchna?" Fokine snaps when I stumble three times in a row. Someone in the *corps* giggles.

And then one Sunday morning in the middle of December, when Mamusia and I are dressing for church, it all becomes simple and straightforward in my mind. My brother does not yet know what he wants. *Faun* is not yet born. I'm his model and his material to shape and reshape.

Wrong means that Vaslav no longer wants what he has imagined. My movement has made it real to him. He wants to go deeper or further. Test another inspiration. Search for other echoes.

Right means that what he sees me dance is what he wants to keep and I cannot alter it even in the tiniest of ways. For apart from being his material, I'm also his scribe. This ballet, so tight, so perfect in all its delicate refinements and so brilliantly compact, takes shape on my body.

How could I not see it right away?

10.

DIAGHILEV AND BAKST are our first audience. It is the beginning of January, and we are in Diaghilev's living room, where I'm admitted for the first time. Dunia, Sergey Pavlovitch's old nanny, has just ordered two servants to clear the space in the middle. The samovar is beginning to hiss. In the corner a Christmas tree still looks fresh, its needles firm, but it no longer smells of sap.

Sergey Pavlovitch, his jacket opened, a monocle in his hand, has claimed his place on a sofa. Lev Bakst insists on standing. "I've been sitting all day," he says, deflecting another request.

Dunia is not pleased. "Tea will go into your legs, Lev Samuilovitch," she warns Bakst in a gruff voice as she brings tea glasses in silver holders. "This is no laughing matter, *devushka*," she adds when I chuckle at the thought of our distinguished set designer walking on bloated legs.

Vaslav is at the piano, playing Debussy's prelude. Dunia, of gnarled fingers and pursed lips, knows better than to offer him tea or anything else before the performance. She must think all dancers peculiar, not quite right in the head. Ballet is yet another in a long procession of her master's follies.

"Ready, Vaslav?" Diaghilev asks, rubbing his hands.

Vaslav brings the prelude to the end, stands up and takes the first step toward me, heel to toe, bending backward. By the time he is beside me the transformation is complete. He is the Faun whose moves I know so well, every one of them written into my body.

The *Faun* we dance together that afternoon is still clipped, impoverished. The piano is silent; there are only two of us: Faun and Nymph. Faun rests, plays an imaginary pipe. Nymph enters. Quarrels forgotten, we dance their startled encounter, her flight, his bewildered retreat. Brother and sister, halves of the same whole, part of the same vision.

I see it in Vaslav's eyes. He sees it in mine.

We finish, hold hands and bow.

"Brilliant, brilliant, brilliant!" Bakst is clapping, taking a step toward us and then turning to Diaghilev. "*Faun*," he says, "is a masterpiece, a work of genius. This is new art, new dance, new world."

He is not a dancer, I think; his movements are ungainly, awkward; but he has understood everything.

Sergey Pavlovitch, however, is silent, chewing on his favourite bonbons. His head cocks from left to right. Beside me Vaslav clears his throat. His feet shuffle nervously. "Serge?" he asks in a little boy's voice.

I feel the absurd urge to hurl myself at Diaghilev, shake him out of this wavering, as if my voice could sway him.

"A masterpiece, Serge!" Bakst continues, his voice brimming with excitement. "They will write about this day in ballet books!"

Now that he has seen the dance, he can dress it. Allow the colours and the fabric be part of it. Make costumes work with the movements, anticipate them, extend them.

I know what he means. I've danced in his Papillon dress.

"I see a hill," Bakst now says, picking up a pad of drawing paper and extracting a pencil from his breast pocket. "Lush, green. The backdrop has splashes of greys, browns and yellows. Like Gauguin's paintings we saw together, Vaslav. Remember?" And then, turning to Diaghilev: "What do you think, Serge?"

Diaghilev frowns. His monocle, dropped, rests on his knees. Vaslav is staring at him with such intensity that I wonder if he has heard any of Bakst's praises.

"Like this." Bakst begins to sketch. I take a step toward him to witness how, at the touch of his fingers, pencil lines create the Faun, his costume tight like a second skin, spotted with patches of black, his headdress crowned with small horns.

"The fabric should be really tight," Bakst says, holding the finished sketch in his hands for us to see. "Even the tiniest of movements must be visible."

I look at Diaghilev again, will him to say something. We all do.

The springs of the sofa moan as he slowly raises himself up, wiping an invisible tear from his eyes. "Vatsa," he says, embracing Vaslav. "My dear, dear Vatsa! This is what I have been waiting for."

Once Diaghilev is convinced, no one will outshine him in praises.

Vaslav is a genius. Unlike Fokine, who can only repeat himself, Vaslav has trampled conventions. *Faun* is true art. *Faun* is true freedom. *Faun* is a revolution. Oh, how it will shake Paris. How it'll make everyone swoon.

Not just Paris, the whole world. Which calls for his best bottle of champagne.

The three of them are standing together. Vaslav is smiling. Diaghilev has his arm around his shoulders; his free hand delivers a mock punch to his stomach. Bakst has removed his glasses and is wiping the lenses with a checkered handkerchief, his red lashes fluttering as he blinks.

"Worse than children," Dunia grumbles as a servant fetches champagne and four crystal glasses. A few moments later Diaghilev pours the wine, lets the bubbles subside and tops the glasses before handing them to us. We drink to Vaslav, to *Faun*, to triumph.

"So tell me, Vaslav . . ."

As Vaslav answers Diaghilev's questions, I take a hungry look at this room I've imagined so often. The wallpaper is blue, the curtains heavy and dark. The walls are covered with paintings of Russian landscapes, birch trees around a pond, a mountain somewhere in the Urals. In the corner stands a giant pile of books and magazines. Beside them is a pot of glue, a jar with brushes, a half-finished portrait of a nude man. I wonder why there are no shelves for all this.

Bakst is again sketching something on his pad. Diaghilev's arm is still on Vaslav's shoulders.

The *Faun* will have to remain a secret. Not just because of Fokine. Preparation is everything. Seeds of anticipation have to be planted. Curiosity piqued. Dancers carefully selected. Ballets have only one chance to take. If they fail, there is no second coming.

No one pays attention to me, and I let their voices float by, replace them with my own thoughts.

Yes, being Vaslav Nijinsky's sister is a burden. It means being judged against the highest of standards. It means having the harshest, most demanding of teachers. But it also means rising above my own limitations.

With my brother beside me, I grow.

A month later we both resign from the Imperial Theatres to dance with Ballets Russes. Vaslav after a scandal—refusing to change what the Mariinsky *régisseur* calls his "indecent" Parisian costume from *Giselle*—I a few days later in what I call in my official letter "my gesture of support."

I don't want to be part of the world I believe to be dying. I want to be part of what is being born.

This is what I tell Mamusia when she despairs over her foolish, reckless children. We have tossed out the window everything she has wished so much for us. Security, prestige, a future that could be predicted. And for what? Diaghilev's Ballets Russes? A dance company that—in spite of all its successes—still cannot pay its debts. Always one loan away from ruin.

Why not do what others do? Dance for Diaghilev in the summer and return to St. Petersburg for the Mariinsky season? Like Karsavina. Like Pavlova.

I don't argue with her. I don't defend what I've done. Not even when Mamusia says, "Especially you, Bronia. Vaslav can dance anywhere he wants, but you? If anything happens to Ballets Russes, you'll have nowhere to go."

I just do what I know is right.

11.

LES BALLETS RUSSES de Serge Diaghilev begins its first season, in spring 1911, in Monte Carlo. Our repertoire is a mixture of the old and the new. In addition to the still-popular *Schéhérazade* or *Carnaval* we have three new ballets: *Spectre de la Rose*, *Narcisse* and *Petrushka*. A dream vision of a dancing spirit, a mortal man who falls for his own reflection and drowns and puppets brought to life by a cruel magician.

Fokine is still our choreographer. Cecchetti is our ballet master. Vaslav's *Faun* is still a secret.

"Come on, children. Back to work," Diaghilev's booming voice urges us on. It's March already. "Once again . . . from the beginning . . . sharper . . . with more force . . ."

There is no time to waste. From Monte Carlo we are going to Paris then to London. There are new variations to learn, old ones to practise and polish. Success is preceded by hard, gruelling work. Every day we despair over our limitations, chip against doubt, fatigue, pain and then find strength to go on even when it feels like we have no strength left.

When I left St. Petersburg, the ice was just breaking up on the Neva, imitating rifle shots and cannon salutes. The heaps of snow along the streets were beginning to melt, revealing the detritus of winter: rotting rags, flattened buckets, deformed wheels.

Here in mimosa-scented Monte Carlo, I wake up at dawn to the sight of lush green hills where giant agaves grow beside cypresses and pine trees. To the white jagged rocks above the azure waters of the sea that smells like an oyster ready to eat. To flowering oleanders, purple clusters of bougainvillea. A giant opera set, I think.

I wash, rub my skin with a coarse cloth and pack my dance bag. Quickly I eat what Mamusia has prepared: an orange or a grapefruit, a hard-boiled egg. She always fusses, urges me to chew my food slowly, slips a block of dark chocolate into my pocket.

I never complain, but I also never concern myself with what she does all day. I assume she keeps busy. I only half listen when she mentions another ballet mother with whom she goes for walks, to the harbour, to the old town. Or letters she has to write. Or a new dancer who has asked her to help with stretching exercises.

I'm at the theatre from early morning till midnight. These are the days of exertion, sweat, pain and fatigue. Cecchetti's daily company class is followed by the scheduled rehearsals. Before the evening performance I also have to find time to practise all my new roles. It is not easy to release my body from the iron grip of the Imperial School training. The openings, loosening in the hips or the joints, are tiny and do not come often enough.

The roles I dance are small, but in Fokine's new ballets, every role is a challenge. In rehearsals he tells us to improvise, make every dance, even the shortest one, our own. He gives us slips of paper with a little story of the character we dance:

> *A street dancer in* Petrushka *has to earn her money or her father will beat her up. She has not had anything to eat all day and if she doesn't get paid she will go to sleep hungry.*
>
> *In* Schéhérazade *the Odalisque has just seen her mistress and the Golden Slave kiss. She knows the Sultan will kill them if he finds out. This is what she is thinking of when he suddenly appears and startles her.*

We practise. Together and alone. Teach each other what we know and learn what we don't. Everyone is awaiting the afternoon rehearsals, when Diaghilev, who never wakes up before lunch if he can help it, will come to watch us.

His arrival always precipitates a flutter of movement: those who have been sitting down, stand up; we all straighten our posture and put more effort into each pose. For his stars, his beloved children, for Vaslav or Karsavina, Diaghilev has praises, smiles, expensive gifts, invitations to dinners and fashionable parties. We lesser dancers have to watch him for any sign we can pick apart, collect all his offhand remarks. Rumours have it that if he pats the silver lock of his hair when he looks at you, he is pleased. Adjusting the monocle is bad. Leaning forward is good.

"It's your damn classical technique, Bronia" is all Diaghilev has ever said to me about my dancing. "You are too stiff, too set in your ways. You don't dance with your whole body."

Still? I think. In spite of my Papillon? My Nymph?

I know there is no point in asking Vaslav how I'm doing. My brother will only tell me to work harder. Or that he and Sergey Pavlovitch have more important matters to discuss than my rendering of a fluttering Papillon, or a Street Dancer or an Odalisque. "Just dance, Bronia," Vaslav will say. "If you get better, you'll know. Nobody will have to tell you."

I'm on my way to the practice room when I hear Diaghilev's voice.

I stop. I turn around. He is waving at me to approach.

"Chaliapin saw you in *Schéhérazade*," he says.

His forehead glistens with sweat, and he is wiping it with his handkerchief. I can see where his black hair dye darkened it.

"When?" I ask. "Yesterday evening?"

Stupidly, for Diaghilev is rolling his eyes. "Does it matter when, Bronia?" he asks.

"No."

"Precisely. Will you listen now to what I have to say?"

I nod.

"Chaliapin asked me who the Odalisque was and I said, 'Nijinsky's little sister.' Apparently you have remarkable stage presence, Bronia. And your feet are alive. I'm to watch you like a hawk, for you will astonish me."

Diaghilev has paused and is waiting for what he expects to follow. My delight? My humble protestations?

I don't say anything.

"Have you heard what I said?"

Black flecks whirl in the field of my vision as I nod. I clench my hands to feel that I'm not dreaming.

"What's wrong with you, then, Bronia Nijinska? I'm telling you that the greatest opera singer in the world praised you and you have nothing to say to that?"

My heart is thumping with what I take for mere joy, but it is more than joy. It is also a relief, and a profound feeling that justice has been meted out. Someone took note of my work, my talent. Someone who is himself a great artist.

"I'm very happy, Sergey Pavlovitch," I murmur.

"Oh," he says, with an ironic half-smile. "Sorry to be so blind. Your jumps of joy are a bit hard to notice. Perhaps you could persuade Vaslav to give you a few lessons."

12.

ONE LATE AFTERNOON at the end of March, I'm leaving the opera house after rehearsal with Ludmila Schollar, who joined us a week before. I've just taught her my Street Dancer role and we are both tired. The very thought of going up the hill to Beausoleil, where we live, fills us with dread.

This is when I hear Feodor Chaliapin's unmistakable voice.

"Bronia!"

Not Bronislava Fominitchna but Bronia. A girl, not a woman.

Ludmila grasps my hand.

Elegant in his beige summer suit, he is sitting on a stone ledge of a small terrace to the left of the opera house. I watch as he lifts himself up and comes up toward us, his blue eyes twinkling with warm delight. "What an unexpected pleasure to see you offstage, Bronia," he says, tipping his homburg. He is taller than I remembered, more imposing, but his voice is as rich and sonorous as if he had sung these words to me. "One rarely sees such talent! Such dedication! Will you and your friend do me the honour and join me for tea? At Café de Paris."

I note the patterned silk of his ascot tie; the sheen of his blond hair with tiny flecks of rust in it, as if he strolled hatless in the sun for too long; his crisp white cuffs; his pinky ring. Artistic appearance, I think, defying Mamusia's voice in my head.

"Thank you for your kindness," I say. "Hearing such words from the lips of a great artist gives me strength to work even harder."

Stiff, formal words. I hate myself for them. I wish I could say something light, witty, glittering. Or repay his praise with my own story of listening to him onstage in St. Petersburg when I was just an extra at the Mariinsky, watching a great artist transform himself into Mephistopheles, teaching me the true meaning of stage presence.

Ludmila's fingers squeeze mine to the very bones.

"Is this a yes, Bronia?" Chaliapin asks, laughing.

—

Café de Paris is filled with laughter and bustle. Waiters hurry with giant platters of seafood, carry champagne in buckets of ice. The maître d', beaming with delight, leads us to the table beneath a stained-glass window. "Grand Duke Aleksander," he informs us, waving at a waiter to take care of us, "demanded the very same table only yesterday. Such a charming man, so passionate about airplanes."

"Sit right here, Bronia," Feodor Chaliapin says, and pats the banquette beside him. Ludmila takes the chair across from us. A waiter is already standing at attention, pad in hand, taking the order not just for tea but for a bottle of Veuve Clicquot and three pieces of cake.

I shouldn't be eating cake. I'm a dancer.

"Just this once," Chaliapin whispers, as if he has heard my thoughts. "What's life without little pleasures?"

It is a chocolate torte, layered with hazelnut cream, moist with rum. It melts in my mouth, trickles down to my stomach, filling it with sweetness.

"May I try, Bronia?" he asks. "Your slice looks so much better than mine."

He digs his fork into my cake, scoops a big chunk and puts it in his mouth. His hands are broad and slightly reddened, with stubby fingers. The hands of a peasant, I think, surprised by the delight this thought brings me. He blinks. Licks his lips. His eyes glisten in the sunlight coming through the stained glass.

I feel his body beside me, hotter than mine, restless. His thigh and mine touch.

Feodor Chaliapin cannot remain unnoticed for long. People around us are lowering their voices already, casting looks in our direction. At the table next to us a woman in a silver-lined black turban stands up and places her hand on her heart.

At our table Ludmila is doing all the talking. Asking how long Feodor Ivanovitch will stay in Monte Carlo and where is he heading next. Will he sing in Paris when we are there? Will he come to see us dance? And what about London, at the coronation gala?

"Yes," Feodor Chaliapin answers. "I shall follow you wonderful people everywhere you go!" He is looking at me, not Ludmila. His eyes are the loveliest shade of blue.

I laugh.

"What is so funny about that, Bronia?" he asks. "Have you had enough of me already?"

"Perhaps," I say, taking a sip of champagne.

What do we talk about? Trifles. That in Monte Carlo it is easy to spot newly arrived Russians, for they walk dazed by so much sunlight. That Diaghilev stays at Hôtel de Paris because he can spy on who goes in and out of the Casino right from his window, though he would never admit it.

"Don't you agree that we Russians are far too serious, Bronia?"

I'm afraid I agree with everything he says.

"So there you are, Feodor!" Diaghilev's voice interrupts us. "I thought I saw you come in here!"

The three of us burst out laughing.

"What's so funny?"

His cane taps the floor. He is puffing with exertion, looking around for a waiter.

He is not alone. Vaslav is right behind him, a straw hat in hand, his cheeks reddened. "What are *you* doing here, Bronia?" he asks, his eyes taking in the empty champagne flutes, the remnants of chocolate cake. Not just surprised but truly angry.

Why? What have I done? I wonder.

My brother frowns and mumbles something into Diaghilev's ear. Now both of them are looking at me with disapproval.

Dance, their expressions remind me, demands my full and absolute dedication. I am twenty years old already. My body is at the peak of its abilities. If I let this time pass without pushing myself to the limit, I will never catch up.

For the first time I don't care.

As soon as the waiter appears, Feodor Chaliapin asks him to bring more chairs and more champagne. He makes room for Diaghilev on his right, which involves moving even closer to me. Underneath the table our legs press against each other. I feel the shape of his shin. "I'm sorry, Bronia," he mutters, while his eyes tell me that he is not sorry at all. "It's Sergey Pavlovitch who pushes me toward you."

Vaslav hesitates for a moment before taking a seat on my left. I haven't answered his question and he hasn't repeated it. His silence irritates me even more than his conviction that he should decide what I can or cannot do.

More champagne arrives, and oysters. Brittany oysters, the waiter assures us. Best with grated horseradish and a few drops of lemon. The conversation that follows is loud. A series of exclamations, I think, not an exchange of views. So-and-so has won twenty thousand francs at the Casino, only to lose it all on the very same night. Stravinsky has called Fokine a "dunce deprived of any musical knowledge" and other things, which cannot be repeated in the present company. Pavlova is turning out to be another Kschessinska. Sending flowers to her rivals only on the nights they danced badly. Knows where to stick a pin, doesn't she?

Vaslav is still silent. Out of the corner of my eye I see him move his head sideways and freeze, an echo of the Faun we have worked on at home. Bakst has made sketches for the set already, but Diaghilev still hasn't given Vaslav a date for the premiere. His arguments are always the same. Timing cannot be hastily decided. New ground has to be patiently tilled first, the audience cultivated. A book or a painting can await its discovery. A ballet lives only when people come to watch it. We cannot risk showing it too early.

But I do not want to think of Vaslav, a thorn in a rose. The waiter has just refilled our glasses, on which drops of condensation form a translucent sheen. A curtain? The outer layer of a dress?

"Listen, everyone!" Feodor Chaliapin announces, clinking his champagne glass as if we were at a wedding, his hand brushing mine.

All eyes move to him.

"Look at this young dancer," he continues, turning to me. "This rare talent."

Blood raises to my cheeks; my heart flutters.

"When she jumped in fright at the sight of the Sultan, I felt her fear. When she hurried away to warn her mistress, I felt the depth of her devotion."

A pause. Long enough to make what comes next even more solemn. More forceful.

"A true artist."

If I were to dance these words, I would dance the drops of rain falling on parched earth. Soaking in, moistening the dormant seeds.

"You'll turn Bronia's head, Feodor," Diaghilev says, his voice gruff but playful. "She'll want me to double her salary, and who will lend me the money for that? You?"

I know I'm expected to protest. Say that such talk embarrasses me and then fade into the background, for apart from Ludmila, who stares at me with awe, I'm not just among my elders. I am sitting with the gods.

"If *you* were dancing the Sultan, Feodor Ivanovitch," I note with a laugh, instead, "I would be even more scared."

"Me? Dancing the Sultan? With you, Bronia? But I'm too clumsy to dance."

"It's more acting," I say. "You know how to do that!"

"If Sergey Pavlovitch would have me. And if you truly promise to be even more scared."

"I do."

There is more playful laughter, interrupted by Diaghilev, forever the impresario, offering to do a contract with Chaliapin right away. Designing the poster already, on the reverse of the menu: "*Schéhérazade* . . . with Feodor Chaliapin as the Sultan."

It is all so light, so wonderfully light. In spite of Vaslav's stormy looks and the nudges he gives me every time I laugh, his steely whispers, reminding me of my duties.

"You have a new role to prepare, Bronia," Vaslav insists. "This is what you should think about!"

The latest roster for *Narcissus* has just been posted. Vaslav will dance Narcissus; Karsavina will dance Echo, the mountain nymph; I'll dance Bacchante. I'm a last-minute replacement for a dancer who has just departed in tears. Why? Some transgression noted and duly reported. Walls have ears. One dancer's fall is another's advance.

Nothing can spoil my happiness that day. Feodor—for this is how I think of him already—is right beside me. Fidgeting like a little boy; leaning forward, backward; touching my shoulder, my leg. Waves of warmth floating from his body mix with the musky wafts of his cologne. He is talking, listening, breaking into a song, the old favourite of the boatmen on the Volga River.

We are all under his spell, but he is looking at me alone. There is a moment when his hand covers mine and gives it a gentle squeeze. "Such a little hand. Such little feet and you can tell so much with them when you dance."

Just words? No. Not for me. Not then.

Not now.

In spite of Vaslav's dark looks, Feodor walks me to the hotel. It is a slow walk—deliberate—interrupted by frequent stops. Up the hill, through the park, which is now dark already, to Beausoleil, from which we can see the lights of the harbour.

"When I was a boy, Bronia, I imagined the Winter Palace standing on a green mountain so that the tsar could see the whole of Russia."

There is a quiver to his laughter, a little melody.

We have memories in common. Like the Lukovitch troupe, Feodor has toured Russia. He, too, recalls the wicker-plaited fences of Ukrainian gardens. The clay pots drying in the sun. Rows of sunflowers in the fields. The watchman sounding his wooden clapper, unhurried if all was well, a long staccato if he saw danger.

He knows the small, provincial theatres, their smells of mice and mouldy dust. He knows the stages with roughly hewn boards for a floor, the shabby, ill-fitting costumes, tearing at the slightest exertion. He has seen his share of bad actors who—accorded the role of a lover—approach their beloved as if they were about to give her a shave, not a kiss.

One more flight of stairs that lead up the Beausoleil hill and we are in front of my hotel, by the blooming oleander bush. He plucks a flower and hands it to me with a low bow.

I take it from him slowly. "Thank you, Feodor Ivanovitch, for what you have said about my dancing," I say. Even pronouncing his name is bliss.

"Don't thank me, Bronia. It was not an empty compliment. I was speaking from the heart."

"Then I don't thank you."

"I'll just wait here until you get safely inside, Bronia," he says, kissing my hand.

Am I in love already? I don't wish to call it love. Not that fast. Elation and wonder, yes. Joy at being noticed. Isn't that enough to add spring to my steps, radiance to my skin?

—

"Was it Feodor Chaliapin you walked with?" Mamusia asks when I enter the room. She is standing by the window; the curtain is still parted.

"Yes," I say, steeling myself for the inevitable, feeling blood rising to my cheeks. And it all comes, the warnings, the pleas. Chaliapin's wife is in Moscow; his mistress is in St. Petersburg. He has children with both of them, the youngest still a baby. There is gambling, too, Bronia, and the drinking. Think shame. Think disgrace. Think Stefa's lonely death.

A woman's reputation . . . a thin line . . . either an artist or a whore . . .

Why does it always have to be like this? Why can Vaslav do what he wants? Be with whomever he wishes to be? But not me . . . ever . . .

Can only a man take what he needs? Discard everything else?

13.

THESE ARE THE MOMENTS I will always hold on to. Memories of what happened and what could have happened.

I step out of the theatre, my dance bag over my shoulder, and Feodor rises from a stone bench and hurries toward me, smiling, arms outstretched. There is a tiny nick on his smoothly shaven cheek.

"Shall we walk, Bronia?"

"Yes."

"To the beach? Not too far away for you after all that dancing?"

"No."

We walk down the hill and along the pier. Past giant cacti, cypresses, rosemary bushes. We talk, about how similar all art is. How it demands perfection and yet thrives on flaws and shortcomings. Pearls form over grains of sand. Dancing, singing—they are not things you do. Art is something you live.

On the beach Feodor rolls up his white trousers. His brown leather sandals have brass buckles. His legs are hairy, stocky. Not his best feature, I think. It is a tender thought. How could I ever have considered him a dandy?

"Won't you take your shoes off, Feodor Ivanovitch?" I ask.

He shakes his head and says he had enough of going barefoot all his childhood. Too poor to afford shoes, he says of it, but rich in wonders, so this is not a complaint. He conjures up a scene for me: A wiry little boy sneaks into a room where the village women are spinning together. The windows are closed; the room is stuffy. Motes of woolly dust float in the air. The wheels spin; wool turns into yarn. He has come here to listen to the women sing, but this time they tell stories. A young widow says that her husband's ghost visits her at night as a serpent, or as a shower of sparks, or as a sparrow sitting on the windowsill. The women fall silent. Some cry. This is true love, he thinks.

"And then?"

"I sneezed. And they called me a 'sneaky devil' and chased me away. You should've seen how fast I could run then."

Laughter, too, can be a dance. A *pas de deux*.

I take off my sandals, hold them by the heel straps. The pebbles make it hard to walk, but I don't mind. They are round and warm under my feet. I walk toward the sea, past the lounge chairs and beach baskets and children playing. A red ball rolls toward me, but I step over it. Feodor is right behind me. I can hear him breathing. He is not used to so much walking.

The cool, frothy wave touches my feet.

"Look what I can do, Bronia," Feodor says. A flat pebble skims the water five times before sinking.

"Let me try!"

"You cannot beat a Kazan boy!"

"Can't I?"

A broad smile, a look of such wonder. "Six . . . seven . . . eight!"

It's all nonsense. Words do not matter much. We speak the language of the body. I'm a woman he desires. He is the man I want with all my being.

Now I want to warm myself in this moment. We walk together along the beach to where it ends and the rugged rocks begin. We sit on a flattened spot and dip our legs in the water among floating seaweeds that are like Neptune's hair.

Talking. Joking about Fokine working his dancers like plow horses. Forgetting that art has its own internal rhythm. That inspiration often comes at these fallow moments one dismisses as leisure.

His hand taps mine, briefly, a tip of a butterfly wing. Our shoulders touch.

"May I come and watch you practise?"

"Yes."

"Will you drive to Nice with me, Bronia? On Sunday? Walk on the promenade? I want to have a photo of the two of us. In the sun."

"Yes."

"I want to know all about you, Bronia. *Po dusham.* I want our souls to talk."

Every look of his changes me. I like what he evokes, that other me, made of sea foam, bewildered skin and a long, lingering kiss.

On Sunday morning the rehearsal hall is bare, save for a few empty chairs along the wall and a grand piano. "You are late, Bronislava Fominitchna," Fokine snarls when I enter, though it is the pianist who is hurrying in, breathless, fumbling for the score. His eyes slide over my practice clothes: black woollen tights, a short tunic, soft shoes. But if he wants to say something mean about my looks, he thinks better of it.

Mine is the only rehearsal that day. Everyone else is allowed to rest. Is this a warning? Am I letting myself fall behind?

Fokine's foul mood, I tell myself, has nothing to do with me. Every day he and Diaghilev fight over casting; the number of rehearsals allowed; money for the sets, for new costumes. Once Fokine hears of Vaslav's *Faun* it'll get even worse.

"Here." He hands me a slip of paper:

Bacchante is a virgin from the hills, dressed in animal skins and vine leaves, running through the forest, tearing animals to pieces. She is mad and wild.

I have seen Bakst's costumes for *Narcissus*, open-necked, pleated tunics of light wool muslin with matching pantaloons. No animal skins or vine leaves on any of them. Bacchante will also wear a wig of long, loose hair, and a patterned shawl over her shoulders. They will be easy to move in.

"Ready?" Fokine asks, huffing a sigh. Clearly I am not his choice for Bacchante. "Watch!"

The pianist begins to play and I observe Fokine as he sketches my new dance. Bends, forward then backward. A jump with raised hands. Élancer. *Cabriole*. Three turns in a row, *autour de la salle*. All simple *pas* that take no time to learn but then will have to be filled, embroidered upon, like it was with Papillon.

I do not hear the door to the rehearsal hall open or close. It is only when Fokine snorts his surprise—"Chaliapin? Here?"—that I see him. Feodor is taking a seat in one of the chairs by the wall, clumsy with haste, finger on his lips.

"I'll be quiet. I came to watch Bronia practise. Of course only if you do not mind, Mikhail Mikhailovitch. Do you?"

Fokine shakes his head and then looks at me. This, too, is a delightful moment. Not just being desired but knowing that other men make note.

The pianist begins to play. Fokine steps aside. I draw a deep breath and leap forward.

Bacchante as I dance her is not mad—she is fearless. She is a woman who doesn't shrink from what is forbidden. She takes what she wants even if it might destroy her. Follow her, I dance, if you dare. Put your hands on her body, press your lips on hers. Come, melt into her, reach into the wildest part of her soul.

A woman, not a girl.

"You are magnificent, Bronia." I hear Feodor's voice when I freeze after my last leap, breathing hard, hands hanging loose. "What a wonderful artist you are."

Only false praises destroy. True ones give courage and strength.

"I am taking you to Nice, Bronia," Feodor says as soon as Fokine ends the rehearsal with a curt "This will do."

We laugh at these clipped words as we drive to Nice in his white Oldsmobile with a black roof. "You said yes," Feodor reminds me.

I don't need a reminder.

I am sitting beside him, my dance bag under my feet. The seat is covered in soft red leather. "This car is the only good thing I've found in America," Feodor laughs. "Hold on to your hat, Bronia!"

I wish the road to stretch into infinity. The day is sunny, beautiful, the heat dissipating as the car races up and down the hills, past cypresses, clusters of pine trees, bougainvillea blooms. Down below us, where the sea is, seagulls screech and chase one another over the cornices.

"Look!"

"Where?"

"Right here."

The muscles of his forearms tense; the car brakes screech. We stop right beside the stone ledge and get out of the car. Underneath, a flotilla of white boats sails by. I imagine my face against his arm, feeling the pulse of veins inside.

"Back to the car, Bronia. We will never get to Nice if we stand here all day."

In Nice, on the Promenade des Anglais, Feodor asks me to stand by a palm tree. "Don't move," he says, and takes a picture of me with his Kodak. Then, the camera still unfolded, he entreats a passerby to take a picture of us both. Beneath the same palm tree, me in my wide-brimmed hat, Feodor smiling, his arm around my waist.

We wander among the narrow streets of the Old Town, decide on lunch at a *taverne*. The outside table we choose has a view of the street below, where children run and play. A waitress brings us two tin platters filled with oysters, shrimp and sea snails. The needles with which we pluck the snails out of their curly shells have red wool threads tied to the eyes.

Feodor's voice flows over me like a wave of music. His hand slides over my knee.

Later when I return to this moment in my thoughts, I allow us enough time to finish the meal and ask for a room. The key the waitress gives us has a heavy wooden pear attached to the ring. The stairs are narrow and we climb them, arms touching. The door opens with a *squeak*. I pull Feodor inside, feeling the weight of his arms around me.

Sunlight pours into the room. I close my eyes.

This is what really happens. We are still eating when they appear, charging up the narrow street, Vaslav effortlessly, Diaghilev panting right behind him: two bulldogs snarling in my defence. Their eyes assess the remains of the meal: the pile of empty oyster shells, squeezed-out slivers of lemons, the melting chunks of ice.

"You are coming back with us, Bronia," my brother announces. "Right now."

"Why? What have I done?"

Diaghilev points his finger at Feodor's chest. "You've promised me, Feodor," he says. "You've given me your word of honour!"

Was it Fokine who betrayed us? *Do you know where she is now? And who with?*

"Leave me alone! You are not my father, Vaslav!"

"No. But since he has run away from us, I have no choice."

Children have gathered a few feet away, delighted by the spectacle. A skinny boy gives a sharp, loud whistle. My eyes fill with hot, burning tears. My heart tightens.

My brother's voice does not stop: "Are you blind, Bronia? Deaf? Can't you see what you are doing? You don't know anything about love. How much it costs. How much it destroys."

But the worst is still to come.

"Listen to them, Bronia," Feodor says, leaning toward me. "They are right. I'm wicked, terrible. You are a pure snowflake. You must stay this way as long as possible. I couldn't live with myself if I hurt you."

I still dance for him, for Feodor. Love. Jealousy. Betrayal. Loneliness. Loss. Terror.

The dreams are still with me: vivid, bursting with colour and music, suffused with light. Dreams in which he comes to me without fail. A serpent. A sparrow. A shower of sparks.

He tells me he is watching me. He tells me he knows me better than I know myself.

Pa dusham . . . soul to soul.

I love him for himself. I don't want anything in return.

An artist can thrive on much less, for years, for a lifetime. Forever.

14.

AFTER WE LEAVE MONTE CARLO, no one mentions Feodor's name in my presence. I prefer it that way. I prefer that he is away, in Italy. I prefer the pain of his absence to the turmoil of hoping that I might run into him in the street. To dull that pain I throw myself into work.

Bacchante is my great success. Diaghilev praises me for it in front of the whole troupe. "Superbly created. Showing true theatrical gifts."

Vaslav agrees. "You are getting more open, more flexible, stronger. Everyone has noticed it."

Sweet words? Yes. Long awaited, too, even if I don't quite trust them yet. Not until Vaslav and I begin working together on the waltz from *Les Sylphides*.

After the first lift, when Vaslav puts me back on the floor, his hand is not where I'm expecting it to be. I am so taken aback that I stumble.

"I'm not here to hold you up," Vaslav says.

"You hold Karsavina. You hold Pavlova," I protest. "Why not me?"

He doesn't listen. He urges me to keep trying, until I land on my feet without hesitation, until I learn that I do not need a *porteur*. That I am strong enough to dance alone.

A few days later, in the lobby of our Beausoleil hotel, I notice a lanky man in a heavy winter coat with a fur collar. A new dancer from Russia, I think, noting his baggy trousers, shiny at the knees. I see him lean toward the receptionist—a surly thick-lipped woman who always eyes us Russian dancers with suspicion—and ask, in surprisingly good French, if the palm outside is real.

"What else could it be?" she replies.

He murmurs something I cannot hear, something that makes her laugh.

Later that day, in the wings, I see him talking to the dancers from the *corps*. By then I know that he has come from Moscow, from the Bolshoi, that his name is Aleksander Kotchetovsky, and that he wants to be called Sasha. His practice clothes, a loose cotton shirt and black tight-fitting pants, become him. His black, brilliantined hair is parted in the middle.

I'm on the floor with Olga Khokhlova, stretching. My right foot, strained a few days before, is still swollen. "Let me see," Olga mumurs, and I let her take my shoe off. My big toe looks purplish and has a blackened nail, but I can move it. Olga shakes her head. She cannot understand why I insist on soft dancing shoes. "Isn't it harder to dance in them?"

Beside us Sasha reads from a Russian paper he has extracted from his pocket and carefully unfolded: "'Teresa Amber is a woman who looks like a man . . . has whiskers and smokes a pipe . . . fought the Germans in the siege of Paris, for which she was given a Legion of Honour.'"

His Russian is still pure, unsullied by the creeping French phrases we all have woven into our speech by then. He wants to meet this Madame Amber as soon as we get to Paris.

"Is this what passes for news from France in Moscow," I ask. "A woman with whiskers?"

Sasha's eyes slide over me, but before he has time to reply Vaslav calls.

"Bronia! I need you! Right now!"

Olga winks at me and hands me back my shoe. I put it on quickly, tie the ribbons, forgetting my hurting foot and the new dancer from Moscow.

"Come, Bronia. Come with us. Look! You haven't seen anything like it!"

In my memory of the months that follow, Sasha is always there, cheerful, joking. If it is not a woman with whiskers, then there is something else to laugh about. The clown's red nose he puts on when we take a break from rehearsing or the wobbly walk with which he follows me. The swiftness with which he avoids my hand when I try to slap him.

I don't pay him that much heed.

Not in Monte Carlo. Not in Paris. Not even in London, where Ballets Russes dances in June of 1911 for the coronation of George V and everyone marvels at how similar they look—the new British king and our Russian tsar, more like identical twins than cousins. And where I'm relieved to hear that Chaliapin has cancelled his London performances for health reasons. It is a selfish thought. The layer of calm I have spun around myself is still thin.

The Premier Hotel, on Southampton Row near the British Museum, is where we stay. Our English is poor; most of us have just a few mangled phrases from tourist books. Pronouncing *Theatre Royal* or *Covent Garden* is easy enough, but our lips cannot form around *Southampton Row* and we have all written the address down to show to the cabbies. Only Sasha can pronounce the English names well enough to be understood.

Dashing Sasha, the soul of every gathering. When he appears, the dullest conversations erupt into peals of laughter. Sasha, with his broad, toothy smile, who always knows how to break the ice, even with Vaslav. This is what I discover when I come across the two of them talking about Tolstoy's last days at the Astapovo Station.

It is such a hot summer. Heels dig deep into the melting asphalt as if it were a soft rug. Sweat stains our armpits; our shirts and blouses cling to our backs. "We could breed snakes here," we say with a sigh, walking into our dressing rooms. During every performance our faces bleed makeup.

"Cute as a monkey, quick as a squirrel," Sasha whispers to me.

"Are you talking about me?"

"Not sure. I'm just learning British idioms."

On June 26, we dance at the Royal Gala in the Covent Garden, to a full house. Inside the theatre we take turns peeking through the gap in the curtain. The lights in the auditorium aren't dimmed and I see everything clearly. Trellises and garlands of flowers; the royal box decorated with fresh roses and orchids; medals; necklaces; and tiaras. I see maharajas in their bejewelled turbans and golden robes, some wearing strings of precious pearls.

Beside me Sasha is poking my ribs. "Hurry up, Bronia. Let me see, too!"

I take a step back from the curtain and he leans forward, but the glittering audience doesn't interest him.

"Plans have been made," he whispers. "A bit of a walk but not that far. Will you come with us, Bronia? Please?"

The soles of my feet are burning and a blister is forming at the back of one heel. I long for a cool bath and Mamusia's massage. Besides which I have to break in a whole batch of pointe shoes that have just arrived.

"Come on, Bronia," Sasha insists. "There is more to life than work."

The plans, as it turns out, are Sasha's alone, even though he keeps up the pretense of the *others* who will join us *any time*. The restaurant he brings me to is one of these inexpensive places with awful food and excellent beer. We take a table by the window, to be visible to our absent friends when they finally arrive. We order fish and chips and, having pushed the potatoes aside, pick at the fried pieces of cod, sipping cold beer, talking:

"Is what Diaghilev says possible? That we will dance in Russia?"

"Let's drink to it. To Ballets Russes's triumphant return!"

"To a walk on the Nevsky."

"And on Tverskaya Ulitza."

"To a visit to the Mariinsky."

"And the Bolshoi."

The table we sit at is wooden, stained, carved with initials. The air is stale, smelling of burnt oil. I slip my feet out of my sandals and flex them gently, releasing the tension of the dance.

Sasha imitates everybody: Diaghilev's orations on the backwardness of the Russian theatre, which "reeks of mothballs." Kschessinska's imperial gestures; the kneeling grand dukes who drivel and pant at her feet: "You ask me why I need two grand dukes? I have two feet, don't I?"

The "others" are merely late at first then conspicuously absent. "I have no idea what might've happened," Sasha whispers, leaning toward me as if to share a grave secret. There is a smudge of soot on his cheek and I wonder if that, too, is contrived. "Maybe I gave them a wrong address."

The restaurant has filled up by then. Next to us an elderly couple, coronation pins on their lapels, examine the handwritten menu. The woman points at an item with her finger; the man nods.

"You are a fine actor, Monsieur Kotchetovsky," I say, pulling back. My shoulders are tensing, my eyes smarting. Fatigue is catching up with me.

"Am I?"

"You almost fooled me."

"Almost? I wonder what gave me away."

At the end of the day, when we get back to our hotel on Southampton Row, Sasha asks, "What will you do during the summer, Bronia?"

I look up to the second floor. There is light in my room. Mamusia is still up, waiting for me. "I'm going home."

"With Vaslav?"

"No, just with my mother."

"Ah," he says. "Of course."

I swallow hard. It is no secret that Vaslav cannot go back to Russia without a deferral from military service. Another consequence, Mamusia says, of his giving up his position as an Artist of the Imperial Theatres. Another consequence she will have to work hard to reverse.

"Will you write to me?" Sasha asks.

"What about?"

"You are brilliant. You'll think of something."

I do write to Sasha—once. I do not mention the frustrating rounds of meetings with imperial officials, Mamusia's petition stalled in spite of the bribes left "by chance" on yet another desk. I do not mention the weekly visits to the Psychotherapy Sanatorium, where Stassik recognizes Mamusia but not me, and covers his ears when I speak to him.

Instead I describe an evening at the Mariinsky, where I went to see *Raymonda*. In Paris the director of the Imperial Theatres had come to me with an offer: if I returned, he would give me all the leave I needed for dancing abroad. "Just let me know that you agree," he said, "and I'll take care of everything." But when I see *Raymonda*, so grey and dull after *Petrushka* or *Schéhérazade*, I know I cannot dance at the Mariinsky again.

"My mother," I write to Sasha, "thinks I'm making a terrible mistake. But I cannot devote myself to two different schools, two different ways of dancing. I want to be part of what's new and exciting, not stale and dull. I don't ever wish to steal time from what matters for what is merely safe."

15.

AFTER THE HOLIDAY I return to London alone. Mamusia has stayed behind in St. Petersburg, still hoping to arrange for Vaslav's deferral. I feel sorry for leaving her there, but I'm also pleased to be on my own. On the train I luxuriate in the long hours of staring at the passing landscapes, thinking of Feodor, reliving the walk on the Monte Carlo beach, the day in Nice from which I have wilfully erased my self-appointed chaperones. I recall his beautiful voice whispering, "You are a true artist, Bronia. I know you better than you know yourself!"

Diaghilev waits for me at Charing Cross Station, in a dark overcoat, scuffed shoes. He is leaning on a cane, his top hat slightly off-kilter.

Vaslav is not there.

My brother, Diaghilev tells me, has a scratchy throat, so he has absolutely forbidden him to go out. London's weather is foul and treacherous. In Russia summer is summer and winter is winter. Here it is all half-baked, mixed up. "And since it was on my way," Diaghilev says, "I promised Vaslav I would pick you up myself."

I don't believe any of it.

"A cab awaits us, Bronia, but if you are not too tired, let's sit for a moment." Diaghilev points at a small tea shop. A waft of his cologne is overwhelming. Vasily should know better, I think.

I travelled for two and a half days from St. Petersburg to Calais. The crossing was rough; the rattling of the London-bound train, still echoing in my ears, is giving me a splitting headache.

"I'm not tired," I say nevertheless, wondering what will come next. Has Diaghilev suddenly decided I need to hear some vile gossip about Feodor? A jab of medicine I still require to keep the fever from coming back?

We take our seats, order tea. With his right hand resting on his walking cane, Diaghilev demands his tea "really hot," challenging the surly politeness of a waitress who darkens with a muted anger she cannot afford. At the table next to us a stout woman in a black mink coat is looking at us with disapproval.

"How was St. Petersburg, Bronia?" he asks.

Assuming he wants an update on Mamusia's efforts to obtain Vaslav's military deferral, I begin to describe our fruitless summer visits to the ministry, the bungled advice from a lawyer, the bribes that did no good.

Diaghilev dismisses it all with an impatient wave of his hand. "We shall see about that," he says.

It sounds like a warning.

For a moment we sit in silence. Diaghilev must have noticed someone of interest right behind me, for he picks up his monocle to take a better look. Whoever it is must be gone, though, for he searches through his pockets for something. A box with his favourite bonbons. His hands shake as he offers the candies to me. I take one. The bonbon is sweet and surprisingly flavourful. Real raspberry.

Diaghilev sighs, worries his upper lip with his tongue and then with the tip of his index finger. "I need to talk to you, Bronia," he finally says, giving me a pleading look. "*Pa dusham*," he adds. Soul to soul. About Vaslav.

I cannot stop a smile of relief.

By then the waitress has delivered a pot of tea, two cups and a small plate with slices of lemon. "They always slice lemon too thick here," Diaghilev murmurs to me in Russian, but he does not repeat his complaint in English and she is able to walk away unscathed.

The bonbon has dissolved in my mouth. I take a sip of tea and listen to what turns out to be a long tirade. How Vaslav has always been difficult. How he, Diaghilev, never knows what Vaslav will say or do—laugh or push him away. He knows Vaslav is an artist, a genius. He has always known that. This is what he always cherished. Vaslav's gift. His dedication to this gift. But now things are happening that are impossible to fathom. Just the day before at breakfast my brother broke a glass. He was holding it while they were talking about Fokine's ballets and Vaslav squeezed it so tight that it broke. Vasily had to ease the shards out of his bloodied hand. And there is more.

Vaslav took off, alone, no one knew where. Until—in the middle of the night—Diaghilev got a call from a Chelsea shelter for vagrants. Vaslav had been brought there by a policeman. He, Vaslav, didn't know who he was. The only reason they knew where to call was that my brother had a piece of paper in his pocket with the name of the hotel. And when he, Diaghilev, took a cab and went there with Vasily to pick Vaslav up, they found him sitting on a bed, his face scratched and bruised. The attendants were holding him down, for my genius brother had been leaping over beds before they caught up with him. Twenty beds on one side and then twenty beds on the other!

"I brought him back in a cab, Bronia. Do you know how many golden sovereigns it cost me to keep everyone quiet? I asked Vaslav what had happened. 'Has anyone hurt you?' I asked. 'Attacked you in the street?' But he screamed at me that it was not my business. That he wanted to be left alone once in a while. That he could not live in a cage."

A pause. Diaghilev's eyes lock on me. "Do I keep him in a cage, Bronia?"

There is pain in his voice, and hurt, and concern. Tears flow down his cheeks. "One day I'm the only one who understands him, another I'm his enemy . . . I talk to him and he doesn't hear me. I walk in, and he jumps at the sight of me as if I were the devil."

I recall Stassik's eyes, his look of incomprehension when I entered his room. The stab I feel is of fear. Vaslav is not Stassik, I remind myself.

What does Diaghilev want from me? That I watch Vaslav even closer than he is watched? Question him? If my brother has secrets, I don't wish to tease them out of him. Besides, I'm also convinced that Sergey Pavlovitch colours his story for greater effect. My brother's letters to Mamusia were all cheerful. Vaslav wrote about *Faun*, how much he was looking forward to its premiere. How eager he was to start rehearsing. How he was thinking of other ballets, too. There had been no mentions of quarrels.

"Vaslav must be creating another ballet," I tell Diaghilev.

This is how my brother has always been, I continue. If a vision came, everything else became a distraction. When he danced in a children's pantomime, he got so absorbed in his role that Mamusia had to remind him to eat. "Even pastry," I say, laughing. "Even his favourite kind—strawberry."

Sergey Pavlovitch Diaghilev is soaking up my words like a wick. I am right. I have to be right. It is just like a winter storm moving the snow from one place to the other. Underneath it all, Vaslav is always the same. An artist and a child. "My level-headed Bronia, the only sane member of this mad troupe of mine," he says.

We finish our tea. Sergey Pavlovitch motions to the waitress and orders strawberry pastries to take out. "For Vaslav," he says, winking at me. I give him Mamusia's letter to my brother and her presents: a travel cushion she has embroidered herself, a tin of Russian tea.

Diaghilev makes me promise to keep our conversation a secret. "We must let Vaslav think about his new ballets undisturbed, mustn't we?"

As we wait for the pastry to be wrapped, Sergey Pavlovitch tells me that Karsavina has to return to Russia in November and won't be available for the upcoming stagings of *Petrushka*. "I'm thinking of letting you dance the Ballerina Doll, Bronia," he says after tossing a very small tip on the table.

"With Vaslav?" I gasp. Joy and apprehension fill me in equal measure. The Ballerina Doll was Karsavina's best role in the last season.

He nods.

I must look flustered, for Diaghilev's lips curl in a half-smile. "See, I've taken note of Chaliapin's words! The old devil was right about you. I grant him that."

I murmur my thanks, but he dismisses them. All he offers is a chance, nothing more. In this imperfect world there is either art or mediocrity. I might easily disappoint him, as countless others have.

"I won't," I say. My voice is firm, but I cannot stop my hands from trembling. As I gather my things, my hat falls to the floor, followed by one of my gloves.

Diaghilev, pleased to have stirred me so much, hums the notes from *Petrushka* and heaves himself up with a stagger. Looking at dancers doesn't make him change his bad habits. No matter how many times Vaslav and I show him how he should let his head lead, his heavy, shapeless body always drags him down.

We walk out of the tea shop to where the cab is waiting, Diaghilev's cane tapping the rhythm. London is soaked with rain. People hurry by, shielding themselves with umbrellas.

The cab takes off. The window fogs up and I touch the condensation with my finger. I draw a circle, then a bigger one, then another. I think of dancing with Vaslav in *Petrushka*.

Diaghilev turns to me and says, "I also thought Kotchetovsky might make a decent Moor. I rather like the idea of him and Petrushka bashing each other's heads over you. Just the spice we need, don't you think, Bronia?"

"Just one measly letter?" Sasha asks. "People are jumping from airplanes, Bronia. A woman flies across the English Channel. And all I get is one single page from you."

"What were you expecting?"

"Five pages at least. A confession."

"Of what!"

"Of how I impressed you."

"But you did not."

"Yes, I did. I'm the best character dancer this company has seen in years. Even Diaghilev says so."

"So you impressed Diaghilev, not me."

"You may have a point here. But it's a very small point."

Just banter. Teasing. The way Vaslav used to tease me when we were little. Making me laugh so hard that my belly hurt.

Sasha is from Moscow, from the Bolshoi. I'm from St. Petersburg, from the Mariinsky. We tease each other about that, too. St. Petersburg's restraint, Moscow's flamboyance.

He makes grand plans. We will go to see vaudevilles and variety shows. We will stroll in Hyde Park. Or look at old dance books at Beaumont's Bookshop.

If we have a free day, Stratford is not that far, either.

"*If*," I say.

Just a good friend, I think then.

So when do I notice that more is happening? When Sasha manoeuvres himself next to me during Cecchetti's company class? When his hand does not let go of mine for longer than necessary? When he watches me as I dance, as if he were seeing me for the first time? Or is it when Vaslav comes by the practice room to pick me up for a rehearsal of the *Faun*?

"You seem to have plenty of time to fool around, Kotchetovsky," my brother snarls, seeing Sasha standing beside me. "Should I tell Diaghilev to cut your pay?"

When we both lower our heads like chastised children?

16.

"DIAGHILEV'S EMPIRE," AS WE CALL Ballets Russes, is growing, expanding as empires do. This is our third season and we have over seventy dancers, some exclusively ours, some on leave from other companies. Someone is always arriving or leaving. Our *régisseur*, Grigoriev, constantly forced to revise the roster of rehearsals and castings, calls it his "revolving door." Every casting is a judgment, every posted schedule a reminder who is on the way up and whose position is slipping.

I am getting better roles, and so is Sasha. In the remaining months of 1911, as Ballets Russes tours Paris, Berlin, Vienna and Budapest, we are often cast together. In *Cléopâtre*, in *Polovtsian Dances,* in *Les Sylphides*.

In *Petrushka* we are puppets brought to life by the cruel Charlatan to better entertain the crowds. Vaslav is Petrushka, the tragic clown, a puppet longing for love and freedom. Sasha, the Moor, is a simple man who doesn't comprehend Petrushka's depth, his pain, his love. A man who grabs what he wants.

And I? I'm the Ballerina Doll. Not the Doll Karsavina danced, a pretty French one from some rich girl's room, with a white face and fancy clothes. I'm a Russian doll, sturdy, sewn from rags. If I fall to the ground, I won't break.

My Ballerina Doll has no great dreams. Petrushka frightens her with his sadness and his expectations. The Moor is more like her.

"Bronislava Fominitchna has little respect for my artistic vision" is Fokine's terse verdict when he sees my interpretation, but Diaghilev is patting his silver lock. "From now on," he says, "even when Karsavina returns, the two of you will dance on alternate nights. It's good for the audience to see how two artists can express the same role differently."

I roll these words on my tongue, let the sweetness slip inside me.

"See," Sasha whispers. "Didn't I tell you?"

After each performance Sasha sends me flowers with envelopes pinned to them. He puts funny drawings inside: Sasha on his knees in front of me; Sasha running after me as I walk away. He cannot really draw. I recognize myself by my newly bobbed hair, which has freed me from the constant effort of pinning it up, pasting it with sugar water to make it stay in place. Often he attaches cuttings from reviews: "Nijinska is a young dancer with superb expressiveness, the keen awareness of loss . . . showing rare depth of feelings . . . superb understanding of the reasons behind the actions of the human heart."

I put them all into a manila folder, which I keep at the bottom of my trunk. Keep, not hide, I think, for there is nothing to hide. From St. Petersburg Mamusia's letters urge me to concentrate on my career. "Vaslav is proud of your progress," she writes. "He thinks you can be better than Karsavina!"

"Forget Ta-Hor, Bacchante and the Ballerina Doll, Bronia," Vaslav says. "Don't lose yourself in what has been."

His voice is always with me: in the rehearsal hall, in my dressing room when I put on makeup, in the wings when I prepare for the performance.

"Am I still contemplating my old triumphs, Bronia? *Spectre de la Rose*? Or *Petrushka*? No."

I still watch him the way a student watches a master. I note how strong he has become after adding more weightlifting to his routine. How, when he rehearses his part, he applies the maximum tension to each muscle, to a far greater degree than he would ever do onstage. In that way, when he is dancing in the theatre, all that he does seems effortless—he has a reserve of strength he can draw from.

"Remember the *Faun*, Bronia. Fokine rebelled against Petipa. It is our turn to rebel against Fokine."

It always comes down to the only thing that matters: the difference between a dancer and an artist. A dancer craves security, praise, applause. A true artist doesn't look back. A true artist looks into the future.

It strikes me now how seldom we all talked of Russia then. I recall some uneasy laughter at Rasputin, the dirty *murzik*. Once or twice I saw, pinned to the walls of our dressing rooms, satirical drawings cut out from Russian papers. On one of them Rasputin was surrounded by a throng of naked bodies. On another he was a towering giant holding two puppets in his hands: the tsar and the tsarina, looking like two simpletons, their faces dotted with red, their grins revealing pointed fangs. "Like the Charlatan in *Petrushka*," someone said, suppressing a giggle.

I cannot speak for others, but all these rumours, court scandals, insinuations merely annoyed me. I didn't see how they could possibly have anything to do with my life.

We are back in Monte Carlo when Diaghilev finally makes his decision: the upcoming 1912 season will be the season of the *Faun*.

"So Nijinsky now fancies himself a choreographer." The backstage gossipers repeat what they swear are Fokine's very words. "And what does Diaghilev do? Gives in. Lets his golden boy do what he fancies."

Fokine may be mounting his new ballets and sprucing up the old favourites, but Diaghilev has given Vaslav longer rehearsal times, better rooms for practice, better dancers, new costumes and new sets. This is why Fokine storms out of Diaghilev's office, his face red with rage.

Fame, Fokine believes, has turned my brother's head and made him reach for what is not his. Made him disdainful of his true gift.

Ever since rehearsals for *Faun* have begun, Fokine speaks to Vaslav only if it is absolutely necessary. Vaslav is no longer his best dancer, his material, but his rival.

For me, Fokine has nothing but cutting remarks, no matter what I do. I'm either slavishly following his directives or am obstinate and disrespectful. "Wishing to turn yourself into a man, Bronislava Fominitchna?" he asked after suddenly noticing my bobbed hair. And a few moments later, to no one in particular but making sure I can hear him: "Why do some women insist on making themselves even uglier than they are?"

Mamusia, who has joined us by then, resigned that Vaslav's deferral will take far longer than she expected, is terrified by all that malice. She shudders at the whispers that reach her: a new broom sweeps clean, but the old one knows all the corners. Is Diaghilev really that sure? All it takes is one failure.

"Storm in a teacup, Bronia," Sasha says, dismissing it all. "Fokine is a jealous fool who lashes against you only because you are Vaslav's sister. It'll pass—you will see."

There is a small basin in our dressing room. Olga has positioned herself above it, her right leg raised straight up, resting against the wall, her foot flexed. Leaning down, she washes her face and neck. When Vaslav cast her as one of the nymphs in the *Faun*, she was ecstatic. Now she is no longer sure. "Whatever I do, Bronia, it's always wrong," she says. A lock of her red hair has escaped the pins and falls over her forehead, dripping with water. She brushes it aside.

There has been much grumbling about the *Faun*. How many rehearsals do you need for a ten-minute ballet? Forty? A hundred? No variations? No changes? None? What kind of a ballet it is? Are we all dolls without a soul? Who does Nijinsky think he is?

Whispers at first, the complaints have now become loud and clear, meant to be heard. Let Nijinsky dance and let Fokine choreograph. Why change what's working so well? "We are Russians," Sasha quips to cheer me up. "We always complain." But I am uneasy. I have danced long enough to know that the mood backstage matters. If the dancers don't believe in the vision they create, the audience won't, either. It takes so little to kill a ballet. "Will the public get it, Bronia?" Vaslav has already asked me once. And I said yes. In Paris they will.

Olga listens when I explain what I already know about *Faun.* We are all parts of a precisely carved whole. There can be no variations, no alterations of the moves. Everything we do has to match Vaslav's vision. Besides, this ballet is still evolving, because it is made on us. Vaslav extracts the moves from us. He keeps a little. He discards a lot. Even for Olga, who looks up to me and wants to please, this is the hardest part to understand.

I repeat the words I cherish: *new*, *modern*, *revolutionary*.

"Why is new always better?" Olga asks, peeling herself off the wall, stretching her shoulder now, the red lock back on her forehead.

Before I have time to answer, the door to the dressing room opens and Vaslav comes in. I'm surprised, for the rehearsal of *Daphnis* should still be going on and he is dancing in it. Has he finished already? Or quarrelled with Fokine again? His shirt has patches of sweat under his arms and along the back. A good sign, perhaps?

Olga straightens herself. There is a flash of unease in her eyes. Vaslav is like a severe teacher: hardly anyone dares to approach him or ask him a question. I wish I could talk to him about it. But if I do, he will only get angry and accuse me of taking *their* side against his.

"I have to check something," Olga says. She curls the red lock firmly behind her ear and gives me a quick smile. Vaslav is waving her away. Faster, faster, his hands say. Get out. Right now.

As soon as she is gone, Vaslav walks to the window and looks out. We are on the ground floor, at the back of the building. Dressing room windows face a brick wall and there is nothing to see. Now my brother turns to the dressing table, picking up makeup tubes, examining them one by one. He opens the yellow tube and dabs a bit of grease on his cheek. It looks like a stain and he rubs it off. Then he sweeps the surface of the dressing table with his finger, just the way Mamusia checks for dust.

"What's wrong, Vaslav? Is it Diaghilev?" Fokine is sheer envy, but Diaghilev's doubt—signs of which I note more and more often—is insidious, even if it comes disguised in praises: "Too advanced, too revolutionary . . . perhaps we should've waited another season . . ." I've seen Vaslav push Sergey Pavlovitch away, screaming, "You of all people should know better. But you are just another coward! I don't care what *you* think."

Vaslav is now arranging the tubes in one row by shade and colour, from darkest to lightest. Soldiers on parade, I think. And then he freezes, leaps to the door and opens it abruptly.

The corridor is empty.

"What is it, Vaslav?" I repeat my question, my voice terse now. It hurts me to watch my brother like this. This nervous tension, the unseeing eyes once again remind me of Stassik, but the thought is too terrifying to fully let in.

Vaslav waves his hand again in dismissal and storms out. I topple the makeup tubes and watch them roll.

Vaslav is not in the practice room when I get there. Olga is at the barre doing a very slow *plié*. The other four nymphs are standing together by the window, talking. The conversation doesn't die out at the sight of me, which is good. They are not talking about my brother. The words that reach me are a confirmation: "How do you say *show me that other hat* in French?"

The cast is changing all the time. Ida Rubinstein, who was to dance the senior nymph, resigned after the first rehearsal. The steps were too difficult for her, she said, but everyone knows she didn't want to upset Fokine. Ballet is again about taking sides. The choice now is Fokine or Nijinsky. A new dancer from Moscow, Lydia Nelidova, hired for the season, has replaced Ida. If she is still unaware of the dividing loyalties, it won't be for long. New borders are always drawn in blood.

One of the nymphs has left her dance bag in the corner. Knowing it will anger Vaslav, I quickly put it where it should be, lined up with the others at the entrance. That, too, will no doubt be noted and commented upon.

Olga is adjusting her tights. I motion to her to join me in the centre. I want us to be ready to start as soon as when Vaslav comes in.

My brother has a fresh shirt on when he walks into the practice room. He nods to the pianist to take his position and to the chatting nymphs to take their places.

The rehearsal begins. To my relief it goes surprisingly well. Lydia manages the walk in profile—flawlessly, I think—heel to toe, with her whole foot, on slightly bent knees. She is well disciplined, a dancer's daughter.

Also, she has a long Grecian nose, which makes her profile particularly suitable for *Faun*. Ida Rubinstein was much taller, though, so this substitution has forced Vaslav to make quite a few unwanted changes.

Today, however, Vaslav is satisfied with Lydia's progress and tells us to repeat what he developed the day before. We walk in a carefully spaced row then pause, every step and every pause executed not as a direct response to the music but as an afterthought.

Vaslav nods. We are ready to move on.

He describes to us briefly what he has envisaged. The senior nymph wants to bathe. The other nymphs surround her and guard her with their dance. Their hands are raised, palms opened outward. The Faun appears and sees the nymphs. Startled, they run away.

Most of the time Vaslav only marks his own part at rehearsals, but not this time. The Faun walks toward the nymphs, jumps with astonishment. The jump is nervous, quirky, but forceful, too. There is a half grin, half smile on the Faun's lips, a blend of desire and curiosity. Painted, I think—no, carved into him. The grimace of a half god, half beast, yanked out of time. Vaslav's miracle, worth every pain.

He stops, snaps back into his body, and his voice is sharp, "What's wrong with your face, Olga?"

"Am I not supposed to be scared of the Faun?" she asks.

I freeze. Again all is wrong.

"Just dance the way I showed you. Make your face blank. The whole body speaks, not your face."

What is wrong with a few kind words, Vaslav? I ask in my thoughts. It would make it so much easier for us. Why can you not see it? But I know what he would reply: Why would he want to make it easier? Breaking up old rules and old conventions always hurts, but an artist must be ruthless. "Morality," he once told me, "is the revenge of the ugly."

The nymphs walk in a row, their faces blank, silhouettes, passing in and out of the Faun's vision. Every single one of us utterly alone.

At the end of that day Sasha waits for me, as he always does. Outside the artists' entrance of the Monte Carlo Opera, sitting on the terrace banister, staring at the darkening sea below. The evening is warm and fragrant. A lemon tree in the patch of greenery is in bloom. Usually we would walk away quickly, but this evening I sit down beside him. I no longer care who might see us.

"Are you sure?" he asks, smiling.

I nod.

Sasha, too, has had a rough day. Fokine's *Daphnis and Chloe* is slow to jell. As soon as Vaslav appears, Fokine's jaws tenses. When Vaslav leaves, Fokine cannot stop himself from sarcasm: "How do you know if Nijinsky likes you? Because he is staring at your shoes and not his own."

We slowly walk down the steep stairs to the street. After the stink of the rehearsal rooms, the sea-scented air is particularly sweet. I don't remove my hand when Sasha takes it. His skin is smooth and warm.

There are two signs when we get down to the street: the left one points to the pebbled beach where I was last with Feodor; the right to the harbour, where Sasha wants to take me. He has a surprise for me there.

"What is it?"

"You'll see."

The surprise is a boat that will take us to the Old Town and pick us up when we are ready. A friend of a friend owes Sasha a favour, for he danced at his wedding, and this boat ride is a thank-you gift.

Half an hour later, filled with the sights of the rocky shore and flickering lights, we sit in a small restaurant, at the best outside table. The owner, too, is someone Sasha knows, though this time the connection is less easy to explain. There is much laughter, and kissing of fingers, and smacking of lips, until we are left alone with a platter of freshly grilled sardines and bowls of dipping sauces. And much too much wine.

I am hungry. The sardines are hot and spicy, their small bones soft enough to chew and swallow. The wine turns out to be not too strong—a perfect choice for a hot evening by the sea. With each sip the memory of the theatre recedes, and Sasha's voice becomes more and more soothing. It matters little what he says—some stories of his Moscow boyhood: falling into a stream one winter and returning home encased in ice, stealing one of his father's cigarettes and getting sick from the smoke. It is his voice that matters, thickening my thoughts about him, filling in the still-empty spaces.

"You never speak about your father, Bronia," Sasha says. "Does it hurt?"

I think for a moment before I speak. My heart flutters.

"You don't have to tell me."

I shake my head. I want to tell him about Father. I just don't know where to begin. "He lives in Nijni Novgorod," I say.

"Nice place."

"I've never been there."

In the silence that follows I lift my glass to my lips.

"I'm not like your father," Sasha says. "I'll never leave you."

There is a dark shadow above his lips and on his chin and jaw. And a soft shallow cleft on the tip of his nose.

It's not a great love, I think. It's a loving friendship. But it might be enough.

When I get home, the owner of the villa—if a rooming house deserves this grand name—is sitting in the shabby armchair in the entrance hall, reading a newspaper. He waves at me when I enter. He is a funny-looking old man, with a bold shining head perfectly oval like an egg. He likes me. He always tells me when he spots some famous Russians. Today he has seen Prince Yusupov. No, not at the Casino. In his motor car. Rolls-Royce. Inside it is silver and ivory. The door panels are of embroidered silk.

He flicks his fingers as he describes the car. He knows a beauty when he sees it. He has been a chauffeur, too. At the Casino.

Prince Yusupov's car is of no interest to me and I am tired, but I listen. He is a kind man. Turns a blind eye when dancers rent a single room and sleep three to a bed to save money. Stores luggage way beyond the time allowed. We, who are on the road for months, treasure friends like him.

"Any letters?" I ask.

He shakes his head. "But you have a visitor."

I run up the flight of stairs to our first-floor rooms. When I open the door, I see Mamusia sitting on her bed, with sobbing Olga in her arms. Trying to soothe her. Smoothing her thick auburn hair, patting her back.

"There you are, Bronia," Mamusia says as I enter, and gives me an exasperated look. She needed me and I wasn't there.

"What happened?" I ask, though I believe I know, the memory of the rehearsal still fresh. But I've softened by now, and don't blame Vaslav anymore. Tempers flare at all rehearsals, not just his. He is demanding and impatient, but so is Fokine. If Olga wants to make it as a dancer, she cannot get so easily upset.

I'm wrong. Mamusia tells me what has happened. Olga was walking home, through the park above the Casino. She saw an elderly man slumped on a bench and, thinking he had fainted, approached him to see if she could help. The man was dead. Another Casino suicide, as it turned out. The police had to be called. Olga had been questioned and had only just been released. She came by right away. She refused tea. Or Russian biscuits.

"You poor girl!" I exclaim.

Olga lifts her head from Mamusia's embrace. Her face, usually so lovely and fresh, is crumpled and stricken with tears. I brace myself for the repetition of the whole story. The walk home, the slumped man. But it doesn't come.

"His right cheek," is all Olga says. "It wasn't there."

"Be careful, Bronia," Mamusia says when Olga finally leaves. "Don't encourage Sasha. Don't make my own mistake."

"Let's not talk about it," I say.

But Mamusia won't stop: "You don't know how it is . . . another dancer . . . jealous if you do well . . . demanding you give up the best of you . . . and then blaming you for holding him down."

What does that have to do with me? Sasha and I are both artists. We understand each other. We are not going to hold each other down.

"What did Sasha tell you, Bronia? That he would kill himself if you rejected him? Is he as *narwany* as your father was? Is that what you want? Your children growing up without a father?"

"You know nothing about him," I say. I whip up all my anger to push back not just Mamusia's disapproval but the brush of ill fate, her fate.

I stand straight, feet firmly planted, head up. I look at her, her dancer's body still slim and solid after years away from the stage. I don't think of how she must miss dancing. Not just the moment of standing alone on a darkened stage, bathed in light, the audience on its feet, applauding her; but being able to speak with her body, not only with words.

"I'm twenty-one," I say. "I can marry whomever I please."

17.

BY MAY OF 1912 we are all in Paris for the new season, which begins with Fokine's *Le Dieu Bleu* and *Thamar*. The reviews are tepid. Paris is waiting for *Faun*.

On May 29, at the Théâtre du Châtelet, the first bars of the music evoke the afternoon sun, still and sultry. The Faun lies on a rock, a man-beast, all ears and eyes, all flesh, with one leg bent and a flute to his lips.

He lies down, stretches, bends, crouches. He moves forward and then, as quickly, he retreats. His gestures are slow, jerky at times, then nervous and sharp. His head turns away and turns back. His hands open and close.

The nymphs float in, an ornamental border of an ancient vase, hands raised, palms opened. They, too, are ancient, part flesh, part spirit. Their dance hovers between weight and weightlessness, between moving and freezing still.

The shawl they hold unfolds as they dance.

The nymphs don't see the Faun. He belongs to his own world. They have theirs. But the Faun sees them. He is curious about these other beings the way a wild beast is curious of anything that is not a threat. He steps toward them.

The nymphs, still oblivious, move about; the shawl in their hands flutters. The Sixth Nymph is the one the Faun watches with the greatest intensity and she is the one who notices him. Startled, she breaks the dance. Her sisters run away and the Sixth Nymph, the shawl in her hands, is alone with the Faun. He approaches her, rigid and formal. He circles her. She dances around him, hopeful, excited by his presence. The Faun jumps in bursts of energy and then their hands lock, as if they could dance together. But the Nymph knows the Faun inhabits a world she cannot enter. She freezes, legs in profile, knees bent, her body facing front, her head turned to look back.

The shawl falls to the ground; the Nymph leaves.

Alone, the Faun picks the shawl up, carries it back to the top of his rock. He fondles it, feels its shape, its flow. The Nymph may be gone, but the shawl—once part of her dance—is in his hands. It cannot flee. It cannot make demands. It will surrender to the Faun's will.

From the wings, visible to no one, the Nymph cannot take her eyes off this man-beast. She knows how fragile and vulnerable he is. How little is needed to push him back into his own world.

Carefully the Faun places the shawl on the rock and lies on top of it. His body heaves and quivers. In a convulsion? A caress?

He has triumphed? Over the Nymph? Over himself?

The curtain falls. We all wait for it to rise so that we can take our bows, but it stays down. The audience is silent. The first cautious applause is broken by a shout, a few loud whistles, a boo.

"No bows," Diaghilev announces. "Back to your places. We are doing it again."

I'm overjoyed. I don't need applause to know that we have just delivered a new ballet to the world, that art has taken on a new structure. Its angles and lines are already part of every gesture, every movement of my own body.

All I want is to live in my brother's world, even for ten more minutes.

This time when we finish, the rumble of applause is like the growl of a giant beast aroused from slumber, set loose, gloriously alive.

I'm at Vaslav's side. I hear his sigh of relief.

Next day the papers declare *Faun* either a completely new, "modern way of seeing, or a loathsome abomination." Vaslav's ballet is "a perfect rendition of an animal spirit," or comes from "the childish desire to shock."

Everyone talks of *Faun*. Everyone wants to see it for himself. Within hours of the premiere all tickets are sold out. In front of the theatre I see a young man imitate the heel-to-toe walk, the backward bend, the jump. Even this awkward rendering is a tribute.

In Diaghilev's room the telephone rings incessantly. Telegrams arrive. Flowers. Invitations. Journalists beg for interviews or at least yet another photograph session. Is it true that Debussy was sitting in his box, terrified to open his eyes at first? And then, at the end, said that no one had ever understood his music that well?

The Faun and the Nymph stand frozen in the flashes of lamps, holding on to yet another pose. Vaslav in Bakst's costume, tight as a second skin, painted in big, uneven spots, his wig interwoven with golden threads. His face is covered with sallow yellow greasepaint; the sharp tips of his ears are lengthened with plasticine. I am in a long, checkered tunic, shawl in hands, eyes rimmed with kohl. Locks of my black wig reach to my hips, coiling like snakes. My feet are bare.

"Excellent," Sergey Pavlovitch declares, his pomaded hair glinting black. "Exactly what I wanted. Forget 'Nijinsky as always.' Write 'Nijinsky as never before.'"

And then the impossible happens. When Vaslav is out of earshot, answering another round of questions, Diaghilev comes up to me.

"I doubted him, Bronia. I saw the rehearsals, and you know what I thought? That it is only ten minutes. That when it flops, it won't ruin the whole evening. That Vaslav is still too young. That a boy of twenty-one is not yet ready to shake Paris. I was wrong, Bronia."

"Vaslav is twenty-three, Sergey Pavlovitch," I point out.

Diaghilev pauses, fixes me with his eyes, and that is when I know this is not a confession but a plea to take his side.

"Do you know what will happen now? He will never listen to me again! Even if I'm right! Even if it kills him!"

"Vaslav is not a boy. He doesn't have to listen to anybody."

A tight smile of amusement follows, a pat of his silver lock. "Always contradicting me, Bronia. Always so literal. What is it about you women?"

"We can count to twenty-three."

"Touché."

A look at his face warns me that victories are transient. There will be other battles. I might need his help.

I'm the Sixth Nymph. The *Faun* was mounted on my body and my soul. I am at the peak of my abilities. I am part of my brother's art and his art is part of me. What else could I wish for?

18.

"COME WITH US TO Venice, Bronia," Vaslav says after the season ends.

Rehearsals in Monte Carlo for the 1913 season won't begin for another ten days. Sasha has gone to Prague to attend a friend's wedding, a secret to be kept from Diaghilev, who never approves of Ballets Russes romances unless they are his own. Mamusia has gone back to Russia for two months. "Stassik," she wrote," did not recognize me. The doctor tells me that if I visit him more often, he will."

Headaches keep me awake at night. My joints ache. I blame it on the tensions of the past months, even though Fokine has left Ballets Russes in a huff of accusations. Venice tempts me with solitude, long walks in the ancient streets, a gondola ride to one of the islands, perhaps.

"Ah, alone at last," Sergey Pavlovitch greets me with his lopsided crocodile smile. When I admire him, I think him a big, jousting knight, encased in polished armour, a spear in his hands, fighting for his great causes: art and beauty. When he annoys me, I think of him behind a butcher's counter, splattered with blood, feathers sticking to his hair. Or picture the rolls of fat over his belly, the hairy nest between his legs. Grey? Curly? Thinning like the top of his head? "A woman who has finally cast off her sticky shadow." He means Sasha.

Vaslav grunts his approval of Diaghilev's verdict. Again he has slipped into his older-brother role, my chaperone, my keeper, as if I merely imagined the way we worked together on the *Faun*. I turn away from both of them toward the still half-open window.

On the platform a tall young woman in white is staring in my direction, as if trying to see beyond me, into the compartment. She looks vaguely familiar, pretty, well dressed, her hat adorned with pink roses, but I cannot place her. One of Vaslav's admirers, I decide; they always find a way to stalk him. They crowd in front of his dressing room, try to touch him as he passes. They bribe their way in when he is not there to steal anything of his that is not nailed down. Vasily—Sasha heard—is making a fortune in bribes.

"Draft!" Diaghilev groans, covering his throat, stifling a cough.

I slide the window down and take my seat. The train has left the station and the pale pink houses we pass are half hidden behind flowering vines. White laundered sheets, pinned down with wooden pegs, flap in the wind.

Vaslav stretches himself out on one side of our compartment. His features seem leaner, sharper, fox-like. His hair has been short for some time now, pasted to his skull like a swimming cap. His hands, always strong, have become massive, as if carved in marble.

Diaghilev settles beside me and I'm steeling myself for more admonitions. "Why do you persist with this bluestocking look, Bronia?" he asked me a few days ago. "Why don't you dress more like a ballerina?" My reply—"How I dress offstage is my own business"—surprised him for a moment, but not enough to stop a suggestion: "And what if you dyed your hair red?"

But there are no admonitions today. "Let's go and eat something, children," he announces. "I'm starving."

In the dining car, after questioning the waiter in great detail, Diaghilev chooses a lobster bisque, and beefsteak with *pommes frites*, followed by chocolate cake with whipped cream. Wine? Red, of course. French or Spanish? "Here I leave myself in your capable hands."

The waiter scribbles the order and turns toward me, writing pad poised in the air. His face is fine chiselled but expressionless.

"A bowl of the soup du jour and a small salad, please."

"Same," Vaslav says, not even glancing at the menu.

"Don't mind them," Sergey Pavlovitch tells the waiter in theatrical whisper, motioning to him to lean closer. "They are Russian dancers. They have to starve themselves to be any good."

Vaslav leans backward. "I don't starve," he says. "I just don't stuff myself like a pig."

What did I tell you, Bronia, Diaghilev's look says. A boy, not a man.

It doesn't matter what the two of them talk about—ballet, music, a dancer who is too affected, a tour that is too gruelling. It doesn't matter if they agree or not. The tension is always there.

"I'm sure the water will be warm enough to swim."

"You can swim if you like, but don't make me watch it."

"What are you afraid of now? You are worse than my mother."

A few times I offer a comment, but neither of them listens, so I finish my soup and concentrate on the salad, putting aside a wilted leaf, biting on a green olive then on black.

"Stravinsky says Paris won't get it."

"You said that about *Faun*."

"And the dancers?"

"Then hire better ones."

I have enough of this bickering. I leave the rest of the salad and excuse myself. Back in the compartment, I lie down and close my eyes. The train rattles with soothing monotony. Before I fall asleep, I think about Sasha in Prague, thoughts wrapped up in memories of easy laughter, the warmth of being with someone who listens to what I say.

I don't open my eyes when their voices wake me up. They are no longer quarrelling, and I do not wish them to start again, as I suspect they would if they knew I was listening. They both need their audience. In Paris there is a whole crowd-in-waiting, ready to play their roles. Here there is no one but me.

The talk is of the music for a new ballet. Neither can wait until Stravinsky joins them in Venice. Barring some unforeseen slight or a quarrel, which Stravinsky always seeks, he should be there in two days.

"Stravinsky . . . so touchy . . . so caught up in his own importance . . ."

I hear a whistle, a longing note of great beauty, fingers drumming on the side table. Drops of rain?

I hear Diaghilev lower himself to his seat with a heavy *thump*. Vaslav pulls down the window to let in some air. "Russian spring . . . violent . . . the earth cracking."

He must have already been thinking about this ballet for some time. His words may be clipped, hesitant, but not the vision he evokes.

The sacred hill. The lush plain. The mystic terror. The sacrifice.

"Bronia will dance it, Serge. She is the only one who can."

There is a stirring in my chest, a crackle as if of fire catching on dry leaves. The muscles of my legs tighten. I open my eyes.

Vaslav is by the window, and something about him is different already. His body seems heavier, more angular. He bends his elbows, cocks his head. The words he uses are heavy too, ominous: *ancient . . . powerful . . . the Chosen Maiden . . . dancing herself to death.*

My new dance, I think, body and soul filled with excitement. Still woven only of words but already irresistible.

How I want it, already then.

19.

VASLAV AND I ARE BACK IN Monte Carlo, in a practice room, empty but for the piano. It hasn't been cleaned for a while. Dust balls have gathered in the corners, stuck to the places where the floor has been sprayed with sugar water to make it less slippery. A stained pointe shoe is lying under the barre.

Vaslav doesn't notice any of it. Just as he hasn't noticed how dancers in the rooms we passed cast their eyes down or looked away.

"This is your dance, Bronia," my brother says.

First Vaslav plays Stravinsky's music for me, from memory. *Le Sacre du Printemps.* Not all of it, but enough to imagine the scenes that lead to my dance: pipers piping, young men telling fortunes, a bent old woman hobbling in. Young girls with painted faces joining them. Old men interrupting these frolics to bless the spring earth. Preparing for the night games, the choosing of the virgin who will dance herself to death.

My brother walks to the centre of the room. For a long moment he just stands there, frozen, his body chained to the earth. Absorbing the weight of what is to come.

Suddenly he staggers, as if hit by a blow. Then, slowly, he stirs and begins to move with more and more force. He throws himself around the room, a dancer possessed, freed from himself, in the realm beyond ecstasy and pain, beyond endurance. Until at the height of his freedom, he falls to the ground and freezes again.

He is panting. Sweat is pouring down his forehead and his neck, soaking the folds of his white shirt. The air around him is sharp, foxy. He lifts himself up from the floor and motions to me to repeat what I've just seen.

The dance is already firm in my memory, jerky yet fluid; profoundly, inseparably, mine. Everything I have worked on for so long feeds into it. My high jumps, my solid sturdiness.

I dance it, move for move. From *Faun* I know that Vaslav demands absolute precision, that in his ballets a dancer is a small cog in a giant wheel. The Chosen Maiden doesn't need to understand what she is doing. She is performing an ancient rite. The desires that push her are those of a being far mightier than her.

I dance well—I can see it in Vaslav's eyes. There will be no praise—I'm not expecting any—but there will be no criticism, either. As he watches me, his own body mimics some of my moves, and it is like seeing myself in the mirror. I know where there will be corrections. I can tell which moments are still too light, not grounded enough.

I dance until the final collapse, the ultimate sacrifice, without which the new life cannot be born.

I stay supine on the floor, motionless, staring at the ceiling. It is cracked and stained. Inside the lamp a thick dark layer of insects has gathered, just as in the apartments we lived in a long time ago.

Vaslav bends over me. His hand reaches for mine, lifts me up.

He doesn't have to ask me what I think of this dance. My thoughts are like veins on the neck of a horse, their trembling visible under the skin. The Chosen Maiden is what I want ballet to be. That bold. That powerful. That modern.

Together we walk to the wall, slide down to rest. I stretch my legs forward and flex my aching feet. Vaslav sits beside me, our thighs touching. Clumps of grey fluffy dust stick to our practice clothes. My black tights are torn at the knee; Vaslav has lost one of his shirt buttons.

Le Sacre du Printemps, he tells me, will be like nothing he has ever done before. Nicholas Roeritch—Vaslav calls him "Professor"—has already begun painting the sets and designing costumes. They are wild, primitive, from beyond time. The world they are from is raw, not yet covered by the sheen of civilization.

Vaslav has only listened to Stravinsky play the music a few times, but it haunts him. It wakes him up at night. It springs under his steps. He thinks of it incessantly, absorbs its every note. He finds the space for movements, in it and outside of it. He feels its pull. It is toward the earth, not the sky. Down, not up.

I ask if Sergey Pavlovitch has seen *The Rite of Spring* yet.

"Yes," Vaslav replies. "A few moves. I've danced them for him."

"What did he say?"

Oh . . . Vaslav waves his hand with annoyance. Diaghilev is like a beehive, which looks simple from the outside, but inside it's filled with myriad little chambers. All smothered with honey. "I never know what he really thinks," Vaslav says. "Am I a genius or an arrogant brat? Is it art that matters or applause and money?"

"But what did he say?" I insist.

Diaghilev and Stravinsky have been unsure. Mostly because of the dancers. "They think I'll be asking them to do the impossible," Vaslav says. "But this is fear speaking. Next time I'll tell them Bronia saw my dance only once and she could do it right away."

Vaslav's lips are cracked. Little transparent flecks are peeling off. He scrapes them with his teeth. He is fidgeting, too, pulling the flap of skin between the thumb and his index finger, just like Stassik used to do. I shudder. To ward off the dread, I hold on to Sasha's teasing laughter: "Here it comes, Bronia. Your world-famous Nijinskys' gloom."

I put my hand on Vaslav's and he stops.

My brother's gaze scuds around the room as he sketches the future. Others will take much longer to learn, of course. And they'll grumble. It's to be expected. Breaking the mould is never easy. *Faun* took ninety rehearsals before it turned out right. Luckily he has until May of 1913 to get *Sacre* right. It's almost a whole year.

Vaslav still doesn't look at me when he speaks. I release his hand, and am relieved that he does not resume the pulling. Instead he is now stroking the side of his shoe, smoothing the black leather as if it were creased. It is a peaceful gesture, calm, composed. And I think that my brother is like a moulting snake, every wriggle freeing him from the old skin, revealing the bright, unsoiled colours of the new one that has been growing underneath all along.

20.

ON MONDAY, JULY 15, 1912, Sasha and I get married in an Orthodox church in London. Two dancers. Two artists. Best of friends.

Sergey Pavlovitch gives me away. His wedding gift to me is a ring, set with sapphires and diamonds. "To remind you that you are already wed to your art, Bronia," he says.

Dressed in his best tails, starched silk shirt, a navy-blue necktie with a pearl pin, he insists on putting it on my finger himself. Asks me to promise I'll wear it. When I hesitate, he whispers in my ear, "Wise nomads always wear their treasures, Bronia. We never know the day or the hour, do we?"

"To pack and go?"

"To dazzle, of course!"

His moustache tickles my ear. I laugh.

"So you promise?"

"I promise."

Vaslav is our best man. The night before, he and Sasha went out together but came back after less than an hour. They're both vague about what happened. "I made a few solemn vows," Sasha said with a laugh when I pressed. "Now we are brothers."

Olga is one of my bridesmaids, Maria Piltz—we call her "Maroussia"—is the other. Diaghilev has just hired her, but we are good friends already. Not only because we know each other slightly from St. Petersburg but because she is a serious dancer. Maestro Cecchetti has praised her to me as musical, intelligent and willing to experiment.

For the ceremony I wear my rose-coloured dress, the one from my graduation, and Prince Lvov's beautiful broach in the shape of a flower. Sasha wears his new swallowtail coat of black wool, which we chose together. I think him the most handsome man in the room.

When it is all over—the crowning, the prayers, the dance of Isaiah—Mamusia presses her own beloved icon with the miraculous Virgin of Częstochowa into my hand. "Take it," she says when I protest. "She'll look after you when I no longer can."

Mamusia doesn't have to say anything more. Her thoughts are a voice in my head: "Orthodox wedding only, Bronia?" It doesn't help that Sasha's widowed mother, for whose sake we decided on the Orthodox service, hasn't come. The letter she sent is an admonition to respect each other and live in harmony. Mamusia thinks it cold and off-putting, a sign of future troubles.

"May you be right," she says when I say that I'm marrying Sasha, not his mother.

I don't like the way Mamusia is hovering around me, always finding something to adjust. My hair, which I refused to extend with false tresses for the occasion; some invisible thread that needs to be cut. Right after the wedding she is going back to St. Petersburg. "Since you won't need me as much now," she has said. "I'll spend more time with Stassik."

The wedding reception is held at the Savoy, where Sasha and I have rented a room together, our first.

Diaghilev asks for silence. "Bronia is like a daughter to me," he says, beginning his speech. "Don't ever forget that, Sasha." Then he calls me his "contrary Bronia, who knows why I call her thus," shooting me a telling look.

Sasha squeezes my hand. We have promised each other we would be patient and forgiving.

Diaghilev reminds "all who have gathered with us here" of my artistic achievements. He calls me the "jewel" of Ballets Russes. The jewel he didn't appreciate at first but has since then been proven wrong.

"Hear, hear," Maestro Cecchetti says, and raises his glass.

The tables with refreshments are all pushed against the wall. Sasha's friends—dressed as Gypsies—are playing violins, whistling and stomping until Sasha and I have the first dance of the evening. Mamusia circles the room, pressing the guests to help themselves to more wine, another bite of bliny, another cup of steaming borscht. She won't sit down, she tells me. She needs to keep moving.

"Sasha is a *dushka,* a sweetheart," Olga whispers in my ear. "I know you two will be very happy."

Maroussia hands me a beautiful leather-bound copy of *Eugene Onegin*. She bought it on the Nevsky from the old bookseller, right near Gostiny Dvor.

By the time Sasha and I get to our room it is past midnight. Olga and Maroussia have decorated it with theatre props. Garlands of flowers and a giant papier-mâché horseshoe are hanging over the door. Flower petals, from the supply Vasily keeps to repair Vaslav's *Spectre de la Rose* costume, are strewn on the bed. On a side table a bottle of Russian champagne—Imperial Abrau—is cooling in a bucket of ice. The card propped against the bucket announces it as another of Sergey Pavlovitch's gifts. Two flute glasses stand beside it.

The air smells of perfume and soot. Among the telegrams with congratulations and good wishes, the one from Feodor says:

Your happiness is all I ever wished for STOP

I slide it inside the pages of *Onegin* before Sasha can see it. I want some of my memories to remain mine alone.

Sasha pops the champagne and fills the glasses. The wine rises to my head, makes the world spin. I kick off my shoes.

Sasha's hands are around my waist then on my breasts. He unpins the broach, puts it on the table and unbuttons my wedding dress. It *shushes* down to the floor. I open his waistcoat, his shirt.

We have danced together for so long that now, naked and alone, we have no trouble finding a common rhythm, sweet mutual dance.

I remember the first three months of my married life as a happy blur of hotel rooms that I no longer share with Mamusia but with Sasha. In the summer Ballets Russes dances in Normandy, where a new casino opens in Deauville; then—after a short holiday—we begin another European tour. This is my life, filled with work, and I cannot imagine it will ever change.

The opera house in Cologne is the last stop on our fall tour. We are getting ready for *Schéhérazade*, in which I am dancing Zobeide; Vaslav is Zobeide's Favourite Slave.

We are sold out, Sasha has told me.

It is minutes to curtain time. The orchestra is tuning the instruments. Stagehands are still adjusting scenery and lights.

As I walk toward my spot onstage, I see Vasily approaching Vaslav, a telegram in hand. Another admirer sending best wishes, I think, as my brother, resplendent in his glittering costume, opens it, glances at it and folds it again.

I close my eyes, and focus on the flow of my breath. I'm becoming Zobeide, the Sultan's favourite wife, a seductress who will betray, see her lover die and kill herself—

"I'm so sorry for your loss, Bronia," a voice interrupts my concentration. "My most sincere condolences."

This is how I learn about Father's death. From a colleague's whisper, right before I am to go onstage. Vaslav rushes toward us, berating the messenger for his stupidity: "How can she dance now?"

Tears rise to my eyes as Vaslav, his face greyish-blue with makeup, his eyebrows thickened, his eyes rimmed with kohl, tells me the little he knows.

The telegram came from St. Petersburg, from Mamusia. Father died suddenly, from a perforation of an abscess in his throat.

I feel Vaslav's arms around me. The *régisseur* is stamping the floor with his pole.

There is no time to cry.

I don't know how well we dance that night, Zobeide and her Favourite Slave, the doomed lovers. Well enough for applause and five curtain calls. Well enough for baskets of flowers, a throng of fans storming the backstage door.

Father is dead, I think. I will never see him again.

Vaslav and I accept condolences. Our backstage visitors call Father a "brilliant dancer." Aren't we proud to have been his children? Wasn't he proud of us?

"Yes," Vaslav says, and holds my hand.

That night as memories come I sob in Sasha's arms. Father making the snowman for us from packing snow. Father coming home from the theatre, wrapped in his black cloak, waving to me as I sit on the stone steps waiting for him. Father, freshly shaven; his hair wet, dripping around his ears; his sleeves rolled back, revealing the muscled arms. "I can still see you doing that clever little tap dance, Bronia," he says. "Such a tiny girl, and you were so good."

Parents don't stop loving their children.

The words my husband is soothing me with mean so little. "It was not your fault . . . he made his choice . . . he never tried to see you, did he?" My own thoughts are not of guilt or blame but of loss.

The cruelty of death is that it leaves no chance to undo what has been done.

21.

"THIS IS WHAT I WANT," Vaslav screams at the top of his voice. No one will interfere with his vision. Filled seats? Cheques from wealthy patrons who come to be charmed? "Spare me the details, Serge! Leave me alone. You've made enough money off me already."

His fist smashes the table. A telephone jumps up, clinking; its handset falls off the cradle. "I'll not change a thing. This is my ballet. I didn't expect the dancers to understand what I was doing, but I expected that you would. Only, you listen to your flatterers, not to me."

It is impossible to escape these quarrels. Day after day I see Vaslav running out of Diaghilev's office, red-faced, disfigured with anguish. He passes me without stopping. A whirl of the wind. He is a thoroughbred, pushing toward the finish line with every muscle. He won't let go.

Diaghilev may be feared, but he is also loved. Diaghilev sees every one of us. His eye makes us who we are. When he is in the audience—as he almost always is—he notices every variation, every new move. He may not approve. He may tell us to stop showing off or to pack and leave. But he may also smile and nod and then we know we've done something that has pleased him.

Nijinsky, I hear, sees no one. Nijinsky sees only the dance.

During the spring 1913 London season, where apart from our regular performances we are rehearsing *Sacre* and another ballet Vaslav is creating, *Jeux*, Diaghilev frequently seeks me out, comes to my dressing room, calls me out of a rehearsal, summons me to his office. "Talk to him, Bronia! If this doesn't stop, I'll have to let Vaslav go."

Can he really mean what he says? Ballets Russes without Nijinsky? Its biggest star everyone still lines up to see? Who will dance *Spectre*? *Petrushka*? *The Golden Slave*? Who will break the shell of old ballets to create the ones yet unseen?

Sergey Pavlovitch leans toward me, digs his fingers into his hair. "Tell Vaslav I'm thinking of asking Fokine to come back, Bronia," he mutters. "Maybe this will bring him back to his senses."

Hope flickers for a moment in his eyes but then dies. He doesn't believe what he says. I know him too well not to notice.

I promise to talk to my brother, though I can already predict what will happen. Vaslav will call Diaghilev a "coward" who has no courage to come to him himself. Why? Because Diaghilev knows he is wrong. Knows he has betrayed art. Diaghilev is an empty toad, puffed up with air. Living off artists because he is unable to create anything himself.

These rows, never resolved, followed by days of stubborn silence and studied avoidance, reverberate in the company long afterwards. Nothing is private. Every rumour is repeated for days: Vaslav has pushed Sergey Pavlovitch in the street, so hard that he almost fell. Vaslav is locking the door to his room at night. Vaslav has stopped wearing the Cartier diamond ring Diaghilev gave him after *Spectre* premiered. Someone saw

Vaslav throw it in Diaghilev's face. "Pawn it," Vaslav said. "Get your money back!"

When we arrive in Monte Carlo, after London but still before Paris, I am not surprised that my headaches return. Or that I wake up at night and stay awake for hours, falling into deep sleep just before we have to get up.

One morning when I wake up again, it is well past eight o'clock, and Sasha is still asleep. I shake him by the shoulder and point at the alarm clock neither of us has heard. Our company class starts at nine, and we are expected to warm up before. I stand up too fast and feel a whirl of lightness in my head.

I take a deep breath and sit down. The whirling stops.

"It's just a fainting spell," I tell Sasha. "It's over." I make him promise not to tell Mamusia, who has been eyeing me with concern ever since she returned from Russia.

We barely make it to Cecchetti's class that day, drawing the Maestro's terse comment that he—an old fool who should have known better—only agreed to join the Ballets Russes because Diaghilev promised he would work with professionals.

I faint a few days later, in my dressing room, before the rehearsal. The last thing I remember is the smell of rotting roots and brackish water, as if someone left flowers in a vase for too long. Maroussia makes me sit down and peels an orange for me. "What did you have for breakfast?" she asks.

"I'm just tired," I say. "I'll be fine."

Dr. Marcotte doesn't look concerned, either. "There is nothing wrong with you, Madame," he says with a tired smile. "You'll become a mother."

I shiver. My head is spinning again; my mouth fills with a metallic taste. On the wall of the doctor's office hangs a picture of two skeletons: one perfectly straight; the other with a spine bent to the side, crushing the organs. *Scoliosis,* the big black letters declare.

"I'll be careful," Sasha had promised.

"That's impossible," I tell the doctor.

"When did you last have your menses, Madame . . ." He hesitates, unsure what to call me.

"I haven't changed my name."

"Of course, Madame Nijinska," and he nods. He apologizes; he should've known. Artists follow their own rules.

I strain to recall my last bleeding, never a regular occurrence. Two months ago? Three? There was a spotting that went away after a few days. I cling to the memory of these few droplets of blood, a proof of my deliverance. The rehearsals for *Jeux* and *Sacre* are in full swing. I'm second cast in *Jeux* but first in *Sacre*. I'm the Chosen Maiden.

I lift myself off the examining table and step behind the white screen. Before I dress, I press my hand over my flat belly, feel the tight, strong muscles of a dancer.

When I emerge and have a seat in an armchair next to his desk, Dr. Marcotte hands me a glass of water. He watches as I take the first gulp. He has been treating dancers long enough to have seen it all before. He knows his share of mysterious illnesses that can only be cured at a distant spa or a visit to an aunt in the country. Ballerinas don't have children that often.

I hold on to this thought. Not to tell anyone, not Mamusia, not Sasha. Feign some explanation for a few days of weakness. A cyst? A painful boil that needs to be removed right away? One word and the life in me will slip away. Quietly. A life I will never know. A child I will never meet. Imagine, perhaps, but never see.

My mouth fills up with water. I have to swallow fast before it makes me gag. The water is cool and has a minty scent to it.

Dr. Marcotte is waiting in silence. In the past two years he has treated my strained muscles, overextended tendons, blackening toenails. He knows how well I can hide my pain.

I hand him back the glass. "When?" I ask, forcing the question through my tightening throat.

"Mid-October," he says.

I begin to count. By May, when *Sacre* premieres, I will be four months gone.

Perhaps nothing needs to change just yet. I'm strong. I can dance until the summer. Or at least until the end of the season. No one has to know for a while yet. Hadn't Mamusia danced on the very day I was born? Kschessinska, too, danced when she was pregnant with Vova. It is possible.

Dr. Marcotte must have guessed the trajectory of my thoughts, for he nods. His advice is matter-of-fact: "Eat well. Drink a lot of milk. Your body will change. You will put on weight. You will be more sluggish. Don't resist. You will need to sleep and rest more."

My body, I think with defiance, fighting an old memory of a see-saw, somewhere in a muddy yard. Going up, no matter how hard I press my feet to the ground.

Sasha is waiting for me outside the doctor's office, shifting on his feet with impatience. The floorboards creak.

"Are you . . ." he asks.

Tears gather in my eyes, roll down my cheeks, touch my lips. I nod.

"Really?"

Sasha jumps toward me, puts his hands on my belly. "I cannot believe he is in there!"

He?

It will be a boy, my husband says. A great dancer, too, for he, his father, will teach him all he knows. Kotchetovsky and son will show the world a few grand tricks.

I tap my watch. It's getting late. We are both dancing that night in *Petrushka*.

"My Bronia will have to wear a dress again!"

"Stop it!"

"What's wrong?"

My husband is looking at me with wide, bewildered eyes. This is Sasha, with his lighthearted laughter, his insistence on seeing the brighter side of everything. This is what drew me to him. This is what angers me now.

We walk to the small park nearby. I sit on a bench, staring at the gravel under my feet. The day is cool, and I have wrapped a shawl over my shoulders. The trousers I'm wearing have always been tight, but now they feel like a shell.

"You said you would be careful!"

"Are you angry with me?"

I stand up and walk away. Fast. Sasha catches up with me, grabs my hand. "Bronia, talk to me. What have *I* done?"

All I can do is to repeat my own words: "You said you would be careful. I trusted you."

"But I *was* careful."

I shrug.

"You really don't want this child, do you?" Sasha continues, but the unsaid is even more hurtful: *Is dancing more important to you than our baby?*

What a hard, unyielding thought. Not wanting a life that is already inside me. I chew on it, grind it into silence. For what can I say that Sasha doesn't know already? That my body, my instrument, is being yanked away from me? Now, when Vaslav has only just created my best dance ever? One on which I have to work harder than ever before?

"You said that you would be careful," I repeat. "That we could choose the time. That it would not be now."

Sasha takes my hands in his, covers them with kisses. "I thought I was careful, Bronia," he pleads, like a little boy caught at some mischief brought about by his thoughtlessness and not malice. There is embarrassment on his face when he lifts it, a helplessness that melts the sharpest edge of my anger.

"You do believe me, don't you?"

Sasha, with his lean, handsome face, his brilliantined hair with its scent of ripe lemons, has fixed his eyes on me, searching for something, anything, he can latch on to and hold. But the thoughts that are swooping down are sharp and hard. It is all easy for *him* to say. *He* can go on dancing. A child is always a father's accomplishment and a mother's problem.

Is it really so unnatural for a woman to be devoted to her art?

"It is not the time to quarrel," Sasha implores as we walk home, if one can call our rented rooms *home*. "It is the time of joy, the time of which we will tell our son one day."

I half listen, consoling myself with the only thought that matters: In May I'll only be four months gone; I won't even show. I hang on to this promise when we reach home, where Mamusia mutters, "I suspected as much when Maroussia told me you fainted. I hope it's a girl."

Mamusia's voice has a new, soothing forcefulness to it. October, the doctor said? We can go to St. Petersburg in September, find a private clinic with the best doctors. Once the child is born we can hire a wet nurse. "You can start dancing again as soon as you want, Bronia. When you are away, I will take care of the baby."

Mamusia is tired of the constant travel, of hotel rooms and dinners cooked by someone else. Such a simple pleasure, she says, smiling. Going to a butcher shop, buying a side of pork, bringing it home to cook it the way she likes to. With marjoram and garlic and dried plums. In her own pots. In her own kitchen.

Calming, simple words. They make me smile, embrace my mother with gratitude. Confess my plan to dance until the end of the season.

"No, Bronia," she says. "You can't."

She has seen me practise, she tells me when I remind her she danced until the day I was born. This new dance is nothing like what she did. I jump, I thump my feet, I throw myself to the floor. I cannot do it. Not now and not in May, when I will be in the fourth month. Not if I want this baby to live.

I may be strong, but my child is not.

Sasha is hovering on the edge of the room. He bends to pick up something from the floor, from the hips, on straight legs. Once a dancer always a dancer? Fear springs inside me at the thought that follows my surrender: I'll have to tell Vaslav.

That night I cry myself into a shallow sleep and dream of walking on a barely frozen river, ice cracking under my feet. An old, bent woman screams at me to turn back. When I wake up, it is still dark. I am pregnant, Vaslav. I cannot dance in *Sacre*, I picture myself saying, standing straight, grounded, weight on both feet, my voice clear.

My heart speeds up. The room inexplicably smells of burnt milk. I mop my sweaty forehead with the edge of my pillow. Beside me Sasha is asleep on his back, legs splayed, his body giving off heat. He is snoring, grinding his teeth. I shake his shoulder and he stops.

A see-saw. A plank going up, only to fall down. A curse and a promise. I dig my feet into the mud and brace myself for what is coming.

22.

IT IS SUNDAY MORNING and Mamusia is still at church when Vaslav arrives in our Beausoleil rooming house for his weekly visit. I tell Sasha to stay in our room and go to Mamusia's. Vaslav is standing by the table, holding a large basket of pink roses tied with golden ribbon.

"She'll love them," I say.

I'm pregnant. I can't dance in Sacre. I try to speak what I have rehearsed, but all my preparation comes to nothing and I mumble what I know is vague and misleading. "I might not be able to dance with full force at rehearsals, Vaslav."

My brother gives me a puzzled look.

"It might be best to have a replacement." I plod on, my voice quivering with unease. "Just in case I'm not able to dance in Paris. Perhaps," I add. "Maybe. Just to be safe."

Vaslav puts the flowers on the table, too close to the edge. "Why? What's wrong?" he asks, his eyes quickly scanning my body to confirm what he already knows. I'm not injured. I'm not sick.

"Nothing is wrong. I'm—"

Vaslav doesn't let me finish. "Don't be silly, Bronia. No one can replace you. This is your dance. You *are* the Chosen Maiden."

I brush my hair off my forehead. I fold my hands together. "I'm pregnant," I say.

"What?" There is such disbelief in this question, such bewilderment. He closes his eyes and holds them shut, as if waiting out a spell of vertigo.

"I can't dance in *Sacre*, Vaslav."

The silence that comes is only broken by voices in the streets. Women laughing, one of them urging someone to hurry up. "I'm pregnant, Vaslav," I repeat, my words a flimsy shield.

Vaslav walks toward the window. Slowly, on the balls of his feet, his hands flicking at odd angles. Outside, the sky is perfectly blue, not a cloud in sight. A sunny spring Monte Carlo day. Warm. Ordinary. When he turns to me, his face is flushed, his voice pinched with panic.

"How could you do this to me, Bronia?"

"It just happened," I mutter.

For a moment it looks that he might cry, but he laughs, instead. Laughter without joy. Crackling like fire.

I take a step toward him. Too close, I think, for I see him shudder and draw in his breath. His shoulders tense; his face convulses. I think he'll run out of the room, the way he used to when he quarrelled with Father.

Instead I see suspicion creep into his eyes.

"You've done it on purpose." Vaslav is seething, lowers his head as if he intended to ram into me. "You are like all the others. A traitor."

My brother says other things about me. That I've stabbed him in the back, for I know that without me *Sacre* won't work. That I've wilfully destroyed what matters to him the most: his creation. Why? Because I'm jealous of him. Like everyone else.

These are words of rage, I think, of a passing madness. Vaslav doesn't really believe any of it. This new ballet, so complex, so different from anything anyone has ever done, is draining the last drop of his strength. I am caught in a storm. Violent but short. It will soon end.

But it doesn't.

"I thought you were like me, Bronia," Vaslav screams. "That for you, too, art mattered more than anything. I thought you, too, were a true artist. But you are not."

His words rattle in my ears, sink into the deepest reaches of my heart. I want to sprint through the door, run into the street. To defend myself, all I have are Sasha's excuses, "I don't know how it happened . . . I thought we were careful . . ."

Vaslav doesn't hear any of it. "You, Bronia Nijinska, who could've been better than Karsavina, better than Pavlova? Don't you know that a dancer has only a few good years? That time lost now won't ever come back?"

The walls are thin. Vaslav's screams bring Sasha from our room next door. He inserts himself between us, orders Vaslav to leave me alone.

It is the two of them now, my brother and my husband, hurling accusations at each other, saying what should've remained unsaid.

Sasha is an uncouth *murzik*, a brute, a talentless bungler.

Vaslav is spoilt, arrogant. Diaghilev's golden boy who thinks of no one but himself.

I sink to the floor, cover my ears, but the screams are too loud to mute.

"Why did you marry her, Sasha? To feather your own nest? To get better roles? It won't work. You cannot become who you are not. You'll always be Kotchetovsky, and no one will remember your name. "

Lunges, pushes, fists. A muddle of blows; two bodies falling to the floor, upsetting the table. The basket of roses crashes down.

I scream at both of them to stop. They do for a moment, during which I register whispers outside the door, a giggle of glee. The Russians are at each other's throats. The Russians are making another ruckus. Barbarians that we are.

Sasha brings his fingertips to his jaw, to his swelling lip, then looks at them in astonishment, as if unable to believe the sight of blood. There is a red patch under Vaslav's eye. It will soon turn into a bad bruise.

Sasha points at the scattered flowers, "Another cast-off from besotted admirers? Can the great Nijinsky not afford new flowers for his mother?"

My brother turns toward me. I do not like the steely coldness in his eyes. "Is he really worth it, Bronia?" he asks. "Can't you see he cannot stand that you are a better dancer than he is? That he will do everything to bring you down?"

I'm not a traitor anymore. Sasha is the guilty one. I'm merely stupid. *Dura!* A woman who let a man trick her.

"Do you think it's easy for me, Bronia? To see how my sister is deluding herself?"

For the first time I truly doubt that my brother loves me.

This is how Mamusia finds us when she comes back from church in her best Sunday hat, a parasol in hand. The room is strewn with trampled roses; our breaths are heavy with resentment.

I run to her; hide in her embrace, sobbing.

Mamusia's hand gently rubs the back of my neck. I press my face to the frills of her blouse, breathe in the smell of incense.

"Married women get pregnant, Vaslav," she says. "This is nobody's fault."

When I raise my head, Vaslav is pacing the room, silent, kicking whatever stands in his way—a chair; the empty flower basket, which rolls all the way to the wall. If I didn't know him so well, I might think he is considering Mamusia's words. But I the only errors Vaslav sees in himself are those of the body. A step that needs firming up, an arm raised too high or not high enough.

Mamusia gestures to Sasha to take me out of the room.

"Come, Bronia," he whispers. His cracked upper lip is still bleeding.

Before we close the door behind us, I catch my last glimpse of Vaslav. He has stopped walking and is now crouching in the corner, knees bent, face buried in his hands. I try to push away the image of Stassik that comes with a hiss of blood rising in my ears—but fail.

23.

I STAY OUT OF Vaslav's way in the days that follow. I don't want the sight of me to provoke another outburst of his rage.

Every Sunday afternoon I hear my brother through the wall that separates me from Mamusia's room: the fluster of his steps, the pounding of his hand on the table, the jingle of glass. I don't hear my name mentioned. It's the other dancers Vaslav rages against now. Their obstinate refusal to do what they are told. Or Stravinsky's pigheaded insistence on explaining to him the basics of harmony and dissonance. As if he, Vaslav Nijinsky, were a philistine who couldn't get his thick head around modern music.

Hurt, my insidious prompter, insists on keeping score. Why doesn't he come to see me? Why does he never ask how I feel? How could he believe I betrayed him?

I still hope Mamusia will end our quarrel as she used to do when we were children. Order us to apologize, embrace each other. We are brother and sister. We know each other by heart. We have been dancing partners since we were children. Vaslav knows when I'm bearing down, when my body has lost its balance. Doesn't he know when I hurt?

I don't talk to Sasha about any of it. He is trying so hard to distract me, and I do not want him to know he is failing.

In Monte Carlo I do some simple dancing, as one of the *corps*. Diaghilev has decided that since I cannot dance in *Sacre*, I won't be dancing in any key roles at all in the Parisian season. There is no need for this, but I don't question his decision. Or is it Vaslav's?

I've folded my trousers and jackets and bought a few loose dresses. A thicker one for the spring and three of light cotton for the summer. One is buttercup yellow with a pattern of tiny birds in flight. I like it the most, for it reminds me of watching swarms of swallows dive under bridges.

I still attend Cecchetti's company class, but when it ends and everyone else hurries to rehearsals, I go for slow walks. I pay attention to what happens around me: people moving in rippling waves, stopping at street curbs. I choose streets that meander, lead me toward the unexpected: a view of the sea from the far end of a terrace, a pair of tall cypresses, a crumbling wall. I collect different routes toward the same point.

Mamusia insists on a late-morning nap. She forbids me to eat at restaurants. Having persuaded our landlord to let her use the kitchen, she cooks for me. Simple meals. Chicken soup with egg drop noodles, pancakes with thick creamy sauces. Fruits she washes in boiled water. Raw carrots and radishes. Glasses of hot milk sweetened with honey, with a layer of melted butter on top.

Dr. Marcotte's voice urges me to push myself toward calm, peaceful thoughts. A mind can be trained, just like a body. "When you dance," he asked, "would you let yourself think of falling?"

Sasha likes to run his fingers over my belly, place his ear against it. He claims he hears a hum, a staccato rhythm. Kotchetovsky Junior will be a drummer? "Smile, Bronia. That's an order." Sometimes I hear him speaking with Mamusia, *sotto voce*. They are both so impatient to get back to Russia, away from aggravations. *Regular* is their favourite word. *Moderate* is another.

Sasha returns home even later than usual these days. "Do you really want to know?" he asks, before filling me in on the company gossip. Complaints multiply. A mutiny is brewing. "Nijinsky's steps" make dancers ugly, graceless. Isn't ballet about beauty? Harmony?

In Sasha's accounts the rehearsals for *Sacre* resemble scenes from a mad house. Diaghilev sticking his nose into the room only to disappear immediately. Stravinsky yelling at the pianist or at Vaslav or both. Dancers reeking of sweat, stampeding about the rehearsal room with pieces of paper on which they have scribbled their rhythm count. No one is sure whose count is right and no one dares to ask.

"Noise, Bronia. Stink. Panic."

I close my eyes, to hold on to the memory of the dance that is still alive in me. To feel the muscles of my legs and hands tingle.

"Maroussia Piltz will dance the Chosen Maiden," Sasha tells me one of these evenings.

The floor swims under my feet.

"When did you hear it?"

"Only this morning," he says, planting a light kiss on my forehead.

I know someone had to replace me and yet this is a punch in the stomach. Hurtful even after I tell myself that Vaslav has made a good choice. That Maroussia will listen to what he says. That she will not side with those who rumble against him. That she will understand how anything new must be awkward at first, for new ground cannot be broken in comfort.

"Talk to me, Bronia," Sasha mutters. My gaze veers past him, to the room we call "home." To open trunks, unopened boxes of ballet shoes—the standing order from Rome I haven't yet stopped.

When *Sacre* premieres, Mamusia will be in the audience, in the first row—her usual place. Vaslav has already given her money for a new dress. This, too, is part of the ritual. "You can sit next to me, Bronia," Mamusia has said.

Two days later Maroussia comes to see me. She makes it a proper Russian visit, with gifts: flowers for Mamusia, dried fruit for me. She asks how I feel, offers a family recipe for herbal infusion guaranteed to make my nausea go. Grated ginger with lots of honey and a spoonful of lemon juice.

"Help me, Bronia," she pleads, grabbing my hand the moment Mamusia excuses herself. Maroussia has been to three rehearsals already; soon it will be time to leave for Paris. She is lost.

We are sitting outside, in the small garden at the back of the house where we rent our rooms. Our landlady is fond of orange trees; there are two of them, heavy with fruit. "Wouldn't it be nice to have our own house one day?" Mamusia asked just the other day. "Big enough for all of us?"

Maroussia leans toward me—as if anyone could overhear her. The Chosen Maiden is too difficult for her. She doesn't have my musical ear. Her body is too open for this dance, too rounded. She manages the movements one by one, but when they are put together, they lose expressiveness. "Vaslav is so patient," she says. "But I want to run away and hide."

"Show me," I say.

"Here?"

I nod.

"Without the music?"

"Go on. Show me."

Maroussia is still not sure, but she stands up and moves to the patch of mowed grass.

I watch her shudder, lift her arms up, repeat the moves my brother has taught her. I see how Vaslav has simplified the dance for her, made it leaner.

I understand why. Maroussia is of a more slender build; she does not have my elevation, my *ballon*, and these cuts have been necessary. But watching Maroussia's diminished leaps is like watching a photograph of a painting, shades of sepia where once colours reigned.

I try to stop tears but fail.

"Am I so bad, Bronia?" Maroussia asks.

"No."

To quiet the panic in her eyes I offer a confession. I'm crying because I had to give up the Chosen Maiden, the dance I wanted most of all.

"But it's not forever," Maroussia insists. "There will be other times."

She says it with such earnest conviction that I believe her. Storms pass, I think, quarrels end. We are still young; we still have plenty of time. A year from now I'll be dancing again. The Chosen Maiden. Vaslav's new ballets. I'm just taking a break!

I feel washed through with hope, elated, weightless, even when I recall Dr. Marcotte's warning: "Expect mood swings. Your body is readjusting. It's all new territory."

Maroussia's smile is a plea. "Look at it one more time, Bronia," she asks, standing up and lifting her right knee. Her left leg is in *plié*, preparing for a jump. "See if I'm doing it right."

Maroussia never tells Vaslav that she comes to me for help and I don't tell anyone, either. In the next weeks the two of us turn into conspirators, sneaking into empty rehearsal rooms, locking the door.

She tries so hard. The leaps from side to side, sudden flights with a sideways throw of the arms; the *tours en l'air*, arms flailing above her head. She works until drops of sweat splatter on the floor, until I order her to stop for fear that she'll injure herself.

After we are done, she walks me home, up the hill, through the park. Vaslav assures her she is doing well, but she is still dreading Paris so much that when this season is over, she'll leave Ballets Russes. She will not go to Argentina with everyone else. She will not dance in the Teatro Colón. She will return to Russia, to the Mariinsky.

No, it is not because of *Sacre*.

Maroussia cannot stand the hatred, the jealousies, the coldness, the gossip. Keeping track of ever-fluid alliances, of who is speaking to whom or not. Having to look over her shoulder all the time, knowing that the smallest transgression will be reported to Diaghilev. She tells me how once when Vaslav wanted to take her for a drive in the hills, Sergey Pavlovitch stopped the cab and told her to get out.

"It won't be that much different in St. Petersburg," she admits, "but when I'm done dancing for the day, I'll be able to go home. Here I'm left to my own thoughts. You have Sasha and your mother.

"And Vaslav," she adds, though I can hear a slight hesitation in her voice. I wonder what it is that she doesn't want to say.

"Do you understand, Bronia?"

I pretend that I do.

After Paris I, too, will go to Russia. Paint the nursery, buy baby furniture. Luckily our St. Petersburg apartment has a lift.

"And then?" Maroussia asks, touching my belly, which is only just beginning to show.

"Then I'll be back dancing."

"With Ballets Russes?"

"Yes."

Maroussia, the new Chosen Maiden, nods. At least we'll both be in St. Petersburg for a while. She will come to see the new baby. Will I let my child call her "Aunt"?

I'm already in front of our house, having just said goodbye to Maroussia, when a paperboy thrusts a newspaper into my hands. "Blood-chilling accident," he yells. "Read all about it."

It is the *Excelsior*, with its endless scandals, but defeated by the boy's pleading look, I give him a coin and glance at the headline: "Isadora Duncan's children have drowned in the Seine."

The details are scarce: The stalled car; the driver getting out to hand-crank it, leaving it in gear without a parking brake. The car rolls across the boulevard Bourdon, down the embankment and into the river. The children and their nurse looking out of the car window as they roll toward the river, curious at first, unsure of what is happening, until all is lost and there is no return. Their distraught mother, a famous dancer, refuses to talk to anyone.

The paper drops to the ground. I stand in front of the house unable to move.

24.

VASLAV MEETS US AT the station in Paris. Before he left for Monte Carlo, we embraced stiffly at Mamusia's urging. No apologies, but there is a truce.

"How are you feeling?" Vaslav asks. His eyelids flutter then still.

"Good," I say.

"Won't you shake hands with Sasha, Vaslav?" Mamusia asks, and smiles when they do.

As Vaslav escorts us to our hotel, the conversation is strained but polite. Everyone in Paris, he tells us, is horrified by the accident. What a senseless tragedy. He and Diaghilev went to see Duncan. Her daughter, she said, always asked about Monsieur Nijinsky, ever since he taught her to juggle.

"How is the Théâtre des Champs-Élysées," Mamusia asks quickly. She has seen my trembling upper lip, and she wants to spare me.

"Very modern," Vaslav answers. "Far superior to the Châtelet. Some call it too German, too industrial-looking, but these are small-minded snipes at the future."

Vaslav is not looking at any of us in particular when he speaks, but he doesn't avoid anyone, either. I think him terribly tired, pale. His elegant jacket, I note, is torn at the shoulder. Mamusia is worried, too, for she asks when Diaghilev will let him take a proper holiday.

"On my way to Argentina," Vaslav answers.

He will have three weeks at sea in a first-class cabin. There will be walks on the deck, a few excursions on the way. Most of all there will be time to think about the new ballet Diaghilev has approved already. *The Legend of Joseph,* to Richard Strauss's music. For a moment my brother's voice loses all of its stiffness. "Unrestrained," he calls the music, "the least dance-like in the world, beyond all bounds of convention."

I long to ask him so many questions. Will he show me what he has done so far? Is he creating anything for me? But our truce is still fragile and I keep silent. The only consolation I allow myself is that by the time Vaslav starts rehearsals for *Joseph* I'll be dancing again.

My memory of the two weeks that follow spins a kaleidoscope of colours and angles, split and multiplied by mirrors. The brand new Théâtre des

Champs-Élysées, faced with clean white marble, feverish with anticipation of its first season, is in the centre.

I may not dance in this Paris season, but I come to the theatre faithfully. At first I go to the rehearsals for *Sacre,* but they unsettle me. The other dancers are still angular; I am already rounded. Vaslav greets me warmly, but it is Mimi Rambert, the *rytmiczka,* he depends on now. She interprets his orders for the dancers. She corrects them on his behalf. Grudgingly I admit that she is good at it, but I still find it hurtful and then feel ashamed of my own feelings. More and more often I end up wandering through the building, soaking up its elegant, modern beauty. The frescoes on the foyer walls; the auditorium with its luminous dome its surface broken by curves and straight lines; the amaranth-red seats with gilded edges, where I settle to rest.

In the last week of May, a few days before the premiere, I pass the swinging doors of the auditorium and hear Feodor's distinct voice. I knew he would be coming to Paris—his name was on the posters advertising the upcoming performance of *Boris Godunov*—but I was sure I wouldn't have to see him. *Godunov* is closing the season, two weeks after *Sacre*. By then, I thought, I would be back in Russia.

I did not anticipate such early rehearsals.

"My infatuation," I have learnt to say with a dismissive smile when anyone mentions those few Monte Carlo days of two years before. "My girlish dream, long forgotten." Even those who mean well need to be deceived. Am I not a happily married woman? Expecting a child?

With myself I am more honest. I believe in two kinds of love: one ordinary, one sacred. My ordinary love, the one I feel for Sasha, I think uncomplicated, easy. The sacred one, however, I think fragile, in need of careful tending. To keep it alive, unsullied, I have to shield my dreams of Feodor. Dreams a casual encounter with him now might topple.

Leave, I order myself, but I am already pushing the swinging door, taking a seat in the back row.

Onstage Feodor, tall and lithe, is singing Godunov's death song. His hands open up; the right one touches his heart. He sings without effort; the force that comes from inside him has no bounds. His voice is inside me. I feel his chest opening as his voice descends. I feel his lips and teeth and tongue as he forms every word. At times, when his voice rises, it seems that unseen, angelic singers are joining in, octaves above him.

I don't know how long I stay there, in the dark, listening. Time doesn't matter. I lose myself in Feodor's warm voice as it rises and falls, its supple richness and power undiminished.

This is how he still remains, imprinted on the underside of my eyelids. No casual encounters, no trivial words—*Did I sing well, Bronia? Yes. Better than in Monte Carlo? I don't want to compare*—would ever change it. Not now and not in the future.

Dreams, even the impossible ones, do not die but find their own surprising paths. Become a canvas into which I still keep weaving new, colourful threads.

25.

ON THE MORNING OF THE dress rehearsal for *Sacre* I'm in the theatre, watching the preparations. The backdrop is already secured. The musicians are tuning their instruments. The stage, I notice, has been extended forward to give the dancers extra space, and the orchestra is completely hidden underneath it.

Won't it muffle the sound? I wonder.

Since the producer's box is still empty, I get inside, sit in one of the amaranth- red armchairs, place my feet on another. Just for a few moments, I tell myself.

This is how Diaghilev finds me. He is alone, an unusual occurrence, and he is not surprised. I remind myself that in his ballet company there are many eyes and ears.

"Let's hope they like it more than *Jeux*," he says, taking a seat beside me. I quickly lower my feet to the ground.

Jeux has not been a success.

The reviews have been bad—"insignificant, shallow"—but worse than the reviews is what people say: "Nijinsky has grown too lazy to dance, giving up his greatest asset, his leap. Nijinsky wants to be original at all costs, rejecting what has made him, giving the audience nothing in return."

Hurtful words, unjust, I tell Diaghilev. *Jeux* is the best ballet I've seen so far in my life, including *Faun*. Its failure has reasons Vaslav couldn't control. Bakst's sets, the open stage, the pale grey-green garden were too huge. The dancers were lost among them. Besides, Karsavina and Schollar didn't dance with Vaslav; they opposed him. This is what destroyed what was truly brilliant: the intersecting lines, the groupings of dancers, the positions of shoulders and arms.

I speak with flair and conviction. I think I am defending Vaslav. What I don't know yet, and would not know for a long time, is that I am already casting about in my mind for the shapes of my own creations. That what I am defending to Diaghilev is my own future.

"Let's forget *Jeux*," Diaghilev interrupts. "What do you think of Piltz? Our timid Maroussia won't freeze onstage, will she? On the day of judgment?"

"Why do you think I would know?"

A shrug and a chuckle. "For a Pole you are not such a great conspirator, Bronia."

"She won't freeze," I say.

Onstage one of the carpenters securing the last boards of the floor swears and drops the hammer. He is sucking his thumb now, motioning to his companion to take over. From the orchestra pit comes the opening bassoon solo.

"Stravinsky is so nervous that he cannot get his hair to part straight," Diaghilev says. "Though he assures me that he is perfectly calm. He, too, thinks I cannot see beyond my nose."

I manage a small laugh. On the empty stage the backdrop moves. The sacred hill shakes and billows. From behind it someone shouts in anger.

The dress rehearsal may still be a few hours away, but in the corridor, after a staccato of steps, someone is already calling Sergey Pavlovitch. The journalist from *Le Figaro* has arrived.

Diaghilev's breath is forced, rasping. "I hope for a proper riot. Nothing wakes the audience better than a slap in the face," he says, lifting himself. And then he adds, "You were right, Bronia. Vaslav is no longer a boy."

From the dress rehearsal I remember *Sacre* unfolding in a perfect harmony of movement and music. Execution is smooth, flawlessly balanced; the Chosen Maiden never falters. During a celebration afterwards Vaslav is beaming. The critic from *Le Figaro* calls *Sacre* "fearless and dazzling." Stravinsky, arm over Vaslav's shoulder, announces, "If Michelangelo were alive, he would be a choreographer." When I come up to my brother to tell him how wonderful his ballet is, he turns away from everyone and gives me a warm embrace.

"The mantle shrouding classical ballet, with all its old notions of beauty and grace, has been discarded at last," I write that day in my diary. "Tomorrow will be the day of triumph!"

What I didn't want to remember then, and for a long time afterwards, is how lonely I felt, how painfully and unjustly excluded. It angered me to see Maroussia, the Chosen Maiden, flushed by the praise she heard for her dance. I did make it up to her. I threw my arms around her neck, telling her how wonderful she was. But when I saw Mimi Rambert, glass of champagne in hand, come toward me, I told Sasha that I was feeling faint and wanted to go home.

On the day of the premiere the theatre is packed. Diaghilev has given away all unsold seats. He has also made sure that the program offers a mixture of the traditional and the new. The first piece, *Les Sylphides*, has already been met with the usual applause. After *Sacre*, Vaslav and Karsavina will dance *Spectre de la Rose*. The evening will end with the wild Tatar dances from *Prince Igor*.

The day has been hot; the theatre is stuffy, the air stale. Wafts of scent irritate my nostrils. In spite of Dr. Marcotte's assurances, my sensitivity to smells has not diminished. Among expensive perfumes and pomades, I detect sweat and monthly blood.

I refuse to sit in the first row with Mamusia. I want to be as close to Vaslav as I can. To get to where he stands in the wings I take a path behind the backdrop. The floor is splattered with dried paint; the boards that secure it to the floor have been hammered sloppily, leaving nails sticking out.

Vaslav—in his practice clothes of white shirt and black pants—is standing in the passage to the left of the stage. Behind him dancers, clumsy looking in their thick, brightly coloured costumes, are warming up. A few, as if they had not heard the praises at the dress rehearsals, are casting nervous looks in my brother's direction. Others practise the shuffling steps, the jumps on flat feet, hunching their shoulders as they do so. Men adjust their false beards. One of the women crosses herself the Orthodox way; another one kneels quickly to kiss the ground.

Diaghilev walks in, a monocle at his right eye; he is not hiding his delight. "This is it, children," he announces. "Keep dancing no matter what happens." Then he mutters something into Vaslav's ear, to which my brother nods in response.

Vaslav looks calm, but I see how often he wipes the palms of his hands over his pants. As soon as Diaghilev leaves to take up his seat, my brother turns to the dancers, but I cannot hear what he says.

The three bangs on the floor are a sign from the *chef de la scène* that everyone who is not performing must clear the stage. I take a step back, deeper into the wings. A crowd has gathered there. Olga Khokhlova is waving at me to join her. Beside her a woman who looks vaguely familiar flashes a nervous, expectant smile. She is, I recall, one of Diaghilev's protégées, a rich dilettante countess ready to pay for the privilege of being part of Ballets Russes. She has been taking Cecchetti's classes. "The Hungarian," the Maestro calls her.

Angry shouts erupt as soon as the music begins. "If this is a bassoon, I'm a baboon! First listen then hiss!" When the curtain rises and the dancers appear, bent, turned in not out, stomping their feet, the riot is in full swing. "Call a doctor! Call a dentist! It is a scandal . . . a travesty . . . a sick joke . . . Where are the gendarmes?"

The musicians underneath the stage continue, but we can hardly hear them.

"*Dura publika* . . . stupid public . . . stupid public," Vaslav screams. He is standing on a chair now, his face ashen, pearly with drops of sweat; yelling out the rhythms for each of the groups. The men telling fortunes. The old woman who enters. The young girls who come from the river in single file.

"One two three four . . . one two three four five six . . ."

Vaslav's fists beat the air to keep the count. Dancers who leave the stage say with a smirk, "Didn't I tell you?" Some spit on the ground in disgust, like peasants cheated at an inn. In the audience, curses and whistles suffocate the calls for peace. Fisticuffs and cane blows erupt from all directions. Feet stomp. The lights go on and off. Diaghilev's imperious voice commands, "Let the show go on!" The music stops, resumes. *Sacre* explodes into a myriad of fragments, pieces of a broken puzzle. Stories that will change shape with each retelling.

This is how the First Tableau ends. As soon as the curtain falls, the stagehands pick up the discarded beards, hats, shoes and wipe the stage floor clean. A moment later Diaghilev arrives. "Well done, children!" he says, rubbing his hands with glee. "We have a proper riot!"

Vaslav jumps to the floor with such force that the chair falls down behind him. He gives it a puzzled look. Diaghilev approaches him, runs his hand over Vaslav's cheek, his chin, as if making sure he is still real. My brother ducks his head and walks away. Mimi Rambert hurries after him.

An old memory of Vaslav's words is elbowing its way through all this, and I mutter them like a spell: *Art is all that matters, Bronia. Everything else is distraction.*

By the Second Tableau the audience has quieted down. Quite a few people have left, declaring themselves insulted. There have been arrests. A duel will be fought in the morning over a blow.

Vaslav is back on his chair, watching, but he no longer has to shout the count. Onstage Maroussia Piltz, the Chosen Maiden, stands motionless, heels pointing out. She shudders then raises her hand. The music flows and jerks. She follows.

Her dance has been cut and diminished, but Maroussia doesn't know it. She dances well, with assurance. She has practised long enough. She leaps and swerves the way I have taught her.

Vaslav glances in my direction only once. It is a furtive look, but one I understand. The dance Vaslav sees in his mind's eye is not Maroussia's. It is mine. I long to talk to him, really talk, confess the pain of my own regrets, but I know this conversation will have to wait. As soon as *Sacre* ends, Vaslav will dash to his dressing room. For *Spectre* the rose costume must be sewn on him, become his second skin, and every moment counts.

Diaghilev was right. Nothing wakes up the audience better than a slap in the face. On that May night of 1913 Paris will belong to Nijinsky. My brother will be seen at Misia's, at the Princess de Polignac's and at Maxim's. He will drive in an open car through the Bois de Boulogne with Sergey Pavlovitch reciting Pushkin, Stravinsky will be praying loudly and Cocteau will declare himself my brother's eternal slave.

And I?

When the curtain drops, Sasha pulls me from the wings. Mamusia has come backstage, pale and shaken. Riots are not for her. She almost fainted and now has a bad headache from all the noise. "Take her home, Bronia," my husband says. His performance is next. He has to get ready.

I do.

In our hotel, Mamusia takes off her new dress and unpins her hair. The grey in it looks like tarnished silver. Her heart is still beating wildly, so I measure out thirty valerian drops for her onto a cube of sugar.

Mamusia doesn't like *Sacre*. She sighs and twitches before she confesses to her misgivings. "Is it really a ballet, Bronia?" she asks.

Her objections are predictable. Apart from the Chosen Maiden, there are no soloists. The gestures are jerky. There is no lightness to them. The music is impossible to dance to. But it is Vaslav's creation, so she admits she is old-fashioned.

"Can you explain it to me, Bronia?"

I try. Vaslav's ballet is remaking the dance, I tell her; shedding the conventions. Vaslav is discarding the old to make room for the new.

"Not all that is old needs to be discarded," Mamusia objects. Her voice is deliberate, tinged with supressed hurt.

"But this is the future," I insist.

"I hope you are wrong, Bronia." She waves her hand through the air as if she were clearing cobwebs or warding off some sadness she is not going to burden me with.

October 14, 1939

My daughter plays with the Irish girl, Fiona, who asks her endless questions and begs to be shown "ballerina steps"—whatever she means by that. Irina indulges her with clever exercises she has devised for the girl's untrained feet. Fiona is clumsy but determined, melting in the warmth of my daughter's attention. The other day, as I watched them, Irina had her pupil hold on to the banister and do pliés. *Every time my daughter bent over her, to straighten her back or loosen her at the hips, the girl giggled.*

Fiona's grandmother, who was also watching, began telling me about her son in New York. The son is her eldest; he has done well for himself and is awaiting them with great impatience. He hasn't seen his daughter for three years. A flinch of unease passed over her face when she said these last words. I also noted that she has never mentioned the girl's mother.

In my suitcase, among the documents we have brought with us, there is a manila envelope containing Levushka's writing. Every time I open the case I brush it with my fingertips, feel the bulky shape of its content—and leave it there.

Some memories are still too painful to revisit.

My dreams have always been vivid, lingering on the underside of my eyelids long after I wake up. Last night I dreamt of Feodor again, his forehead creased in a deep frown. He looked handsome but worn out, almost unkempt, his shirt collar smudged with soot.

"Have I sinned more than others, Bronia?" he asked me. "Is this why you have forgotten me?"

We were together in what looked like my last Parisian apartment, sitting at a big table strewn with papers. The smell of burnt milk wafted from the kitchen, followed by a mumble of accusing voices I could not make out.

I tried to protest, argue with Feodor, but my lips would not move. All I could do was watch him, shoulders hunched, head down, his eyes avoiding mine. How wrong it all was, I thought, how unnecessary.

It was only when Feodor left that I regained my voice. Convinced that I could still catch up with him, I ran down some strange, rickety stairs into the street, where a few steps in front of me I saw his tall figure tangled in the crowd. But then the bodies around me thickened, became all shoulders, heavy coats and fur hats, and, to my utter horror, I realized I was back in St. Petersburg, not knowing how I would ever be able to leave.

"My émigré dream," I write. "Every refugee has one."

PART FOUR:

1914–1921

1.

SASHA, NEWSPAPER IN HAND, is sitting at the carved mahogany table of our St. Petersburg apartment, so luxurious after all our travels. His shirt sleeves are rolled up, revealing his tanned arms. He smells of the duck fat he used to fry a steak I had a craving for, to Mamusia's grumbling that the kitchen wall is all splattered with grease. The steak was delicious, but now strands of meat have lodged themselves between my teeth. I rise to clear the table and get a toothpick from the kitchen, but he stops me.

"Listen to this, Bronia: 'Three hundred years of Romanov rule have brought unity and prosperity to our motherland. For the imperial family 1913 has been a year of thanksgiving pilgrimages and gratitude for Divine guidance.'"

He slaps the open newspaper with the back of his hand. "What 'Divine guidance'? Rasputin is meddling in the Winter Palace, not God. Is everyone *there* blind? Or truly insane?"

I grunt my agreement, only half listening. My body is heavy—our child is due in a month—but my thoughts are still with Ballets Russes. *Sacre* is called a "masterpiece," but Diaghilev is in debt and the Théâtre des Champs-Élysées is bankrupt. In Argentina the company sticks to the old favourites. "A strategic retreat," Diaghilev has called it, and I agree that it is painful but necessary. Before we left for St. Petersburg, Sasha and I signed a contract for January. I imagine the baby born, safe with Mamusia, while Sasha and I join Diaghilev for the season. Vaslav is there, too, rested after Argentina, maybe even with a new ballet finished already. I have shut my heart to regrets. Finally we will drop our guarded conversations, forget the still-cautious words we had exchanged when we said goodbye: "Write often. Make sure you take plenty of rest. Watch Mamusia. Don't let her work too hard."

The remnants of the steak sauce have pooled in the centre of my now-empty plate. I swipe them with my finger and lick it clean. Then I reach for Sasha's plate and stack it on mine.

By the time Diaghilev is ready to stage Vaslav's new ballet, I will have my full strength back.

Sasha keeps reading, silently, his lips moving. By the window Mamusia is folding Sasha's shirts for the maid to iron, smoothing each one as she places it on top of the pile. I am just about to go to the kitchen when Sasha stops reading the paper and gives me a startled look.

"Rasputin again?" I ask. "What have they caught him doing now?"

Sasha hands me the paper without a word, pointing to a headline: "Nijinsky Married in Buenos Aires."

"What?" I gasp. I think it must be one of Diaghilev's publicity stunts, in bad taste and completely unnecessary.

The text underneath the headline is annoyingly short: "Married to Romola de Pulszky . . . Countess de Pulszky-Lubocy-Cselfalva . . . A Hungarian heiress . . . In Buenos Aires . . . on Sept. 10, 1913. The Church of San Miguel . . ."

"It's impossible!"

Sasha is pinning the newspaper to the table, his fingers splayed like those of a scarecrow guarding a field of sunflowers.

"What's impossible, Bronia?" Mamusia asks. She has abandoned the shirts and is standing by the open window, her head tilted upward to catch the last of pale, late-September sun. There is a smile on her face. A warm, soft smile of contentment.

A telegram from Vaslav comes two days later, confirming the wedding, asking for Mamusia's blessing. Signed "Vaslav and Romola." It is followed by a letter. Vaslav is very happy. He and his bride will come to Russia as soon as possible after the end of the Argentinian trip. We'll all have a proper family Christmas.

"A shotgun wedding," Mamusia mutters. *Pod przymusem.* A game of entrapment. A conspiracy.

After Vaslav's telegram arrived, she locked herself in her room. "I don't want anything," she said when I offered to get her a sandwich or brew fresh tea. Her cries turned to sobs and then quieted altogether, into an eerie silence that scared me more than the tears. When she emerged from her room the next morning, her eyes were bloodshot and swollen as if she hadn't slept at all. She still refuses to go out, in case she meets anyone she knows. She doesn't want to be asked questions or, worse, be offered congratulations she would have to accept.

"Romola de Pulszky." She rolls the two names on her tongue, as if the sounds themselves could yield some explanation.

She recalls a tall blond young woman who came up to her in Paris, asking about Vaslav. Her assertion that she was "a member of the company," her request to see the pattern for a cushion Mamusia was embroidering for Vaslav. "I told her I had a headache," Mamusia says, "but she wouldn't leave me alone."

Romola, Mamusia says. One of *them*.

I recall the young woman at the premiere of *Sacre*. The Hungarian countess Cecchetti spoke about.

"What a woman wants, God does," Mamusia mutters on the way to the kitchen. "How can a girl from a good family marry without parental blessing? Why couldn't they return home, for a proper wedding with family and friends?"

In the kitchen pots bang; something falls on the floor there and breaks. Katyusha, the hired girl who comes to help with the cleaning, asks if she should save the pieces. They can be glued together. It is such a lovely plate.

"No," Mamusia shouts.

She returns to the living room, shaken. "Everything is falling from my hands," she says.

"Which plate was it?" I ask.

"The one with a border of purple plums and a golden rim."

Sasha emerges from our bedroom, rubbing his eyes, asking what is going on. I put my index finger on my lips. He mimes back at me: eyes and mouth wide open, hands up in an act of surrender. Mamusia sinks into the armchair, facing me. She looks at her thumb.

"Have you cut yourself?" I ask. "Let me see."

She shakes her head, sucking at the wound, but then gives in. The cut is deep, right across her thumb. I ask Sasha to bring the tin box with bandages and a bottle of permanganate solution.

The skin turns deep purple from the disinfectant. Swathed in white, the finger looks like a cocoon.

"Let's cook something simple," I tell Mamusia, tearing the end of the bandage in half, tying it into a bow.

How she has aged, I think. It is not so much the hair, streaked with grey, or the web of wrinkles around her eyes that reveals it, but her hands. They are paper-thin, with bulging veins and protruding knuckles. She is fifty-seven. A widow who was not even at her husband's funeral. One of her sons is in a mental asylum, which we all call a "sanatorium," as if Stassik were resting, gathering strength to join us. The second, most beloved, has just married without her blessing.

Still searching for an explanation, Mamusia goes to her room for Vaslav's most recent letters. The last one was mailed in Madeira. She reads it quickly to find what she is looking for: "I'm resting . . . excellent company . . . a girl with flaxen hair and blue eyes . . . she is also alone and we are often together . . . please tell Bronia to look after herself . . . your loving son."

"I didn't think it meant much," Mamusia says. "But she must have laid her traps already then."

This is what Mamusia sees: Romola on the prowl, knowing that Vaslav is hurting after his quarrels with Diaghilev. Looking for any chance to be with him alone. Slipping into his bed, most likely. Maybe even getting with child for good measure! Vaslav, too soft, too pliant, too eager to please. Flattered by the attention he is getting. He has always been like that, hasn't he? All the troubles at school—it was never his idea. It was all because he wanted other boys to accept him.

"Is it really so bad that Vaslav is married?" I interrupt, resting my hand on my pregnant belly. Perhaps he wanted it as much as she did. Why is he always the innocent one among the schemers?

"How could you even say that, Bronia?" Mamusia's eyes follow me as I walk clumsily to the table, where I pour myself a glass of water from the carafe and drink it standing up.

I have my reasons. Now that we are both married, Vaslav will understand me better. His wife will soften him, smooth what has been so awkward and tense in him for so long.

A truce will turn into peace.

Mamusia listens, but everything about her protests my words. She is shaking her head; her fingers are clenching a handkerchief.

I don't argue my side long. Mamusia will come up with her own consolations. She cannot stay angry with any of us for long, no matter how much we, her children, hurt her.

But with Sasha, later, I try to recall what we did on September 10. Did we go to the movies? See *Keys to Happiness*? Most likely, for we saw it three times. Not just because it is a film about a dancer but because it is a smashing success and this could be good for ballet. St. Petersburg might become Russian Hollywood, in need of choreographers and dancers. If anything happens to Diaghilev's Ballets Russes, we might find work here.

"And to think that was when Vaslav was getting married!" I say.

"Who would have thought!" Sasha chuckles as he undresses and puts on his pyjamas. "At least this will stop the wagging tongues."

"Will it?"

Awkward and bulky, I'm already in bed, propped on two pillows. The small of my back hurts. My feet—even after soaking in cold water—are swollen. Vaslav was no longer a boy, Diaghilev told me that day at the theatre. How did he say it? I vainly try to recall. With sadness? With relief? Is this why he didn't go to Argentina? Because they had already agreed to go their own ways? In one of Mamusia's theories Diaghilev—the great manipulator—orchestrated the whole affair himself. To get Vaslav's mind off the fact that Diaghilev took Fokine back. As our little Ptashek once predicted, that man has brought sadness to our house.

Sasha turns off the light and gets into bed beside me, placing his warm hand on my engorged belly. The baby kicks.

"What do you think, Sasha?" I ask. "Did Diaghilev know all along?"

"He knows now."

A moment later my husband is asleep. I shake him gently when he begins to snore and he turns to his side with a grunt.

2.

WHEN MY NEWLY BORN DAUGHTER is cleaned and swaddled, Mamusia places her in my arms. The baby is asleep. The tiny folds of skin around her eyes are like wrinkles. Is this how she will look as an old woman?

My tongue is coated with a bitter, metallic taste, mixed with the tinge of vinegar. I feel a chill that doesn't go away. My teeth chatter; the muscles of my legs quiver. If I move, pain sears my insides, so I keep still. I want to crawl into the safety of a mossy cave, breathe in the humid smell of fresh growth. And yet my heart turns over every time I look at my baby. I have never felt such love. Or such haunting fear.

I think of missteps, falls, sudden unexpected blows. The midwife might stumble and drop my child. A stranger might snatch my daughter from her cradle. A window might open; a basin with scalding water might overturn; a car might roll down to the Seine and sink. How can I leave her with Mamusia? The thought of joining Ballets Russes in Prague is like a terrifying curse, not a promise. To soften it I remind myself that we need the money. Vaslav has his own family now. We cannot all live on what he sends Mamusia. And Sasha cannot go alone; Diaghilev pays him half what he pays me.

I close my eyes. When I wake up, Irina is in a crib next to my bed. Mamusia is bending over her, adjusting her lace cap, cooing to her in Polish, "*Śliczności ty moje.*" My beautiful little one.

Sasha walks in holding a giant basket of white roses. As if I had just stepped offstage, having given the performance of my life.

"But I've only had a baby," I mutter.

"Only?"

My husband settles beside me on the edge of the bed. His bloodshot eyes slide over the flatness that has replaced my big belly. His breath smells faintly of vodka.

"Anyone I know?"

Sasha offers an account of those who have taken him out to toast his daughter's birth. An old friend of his from Moscow has joined the Mariinsky, where, he assured Sasha, not everyone listens to Fokine. A *régisseur* from Prince Oldenbursky's private opera, Narodni Dom, hinted at opportunities. Yes, Sasha says, Narodni is not as big or as prestigious as the Mariinsky, but before we go to Prague, he hopes to get a few engagements and, which is even more important, make connections for the future. "Just in case, Bronia," Sasha says. "It is not just the two of us anymore."

I give Mamusia a quick look and she smiles back at me—a smile that means: you were right about Sasha after all.

Telegrams fill a basket beside my bed. The one on top is from Argentina:

> Most heartfelt congratulations STOP Best wishes for the happy parents and grandmother STOP

Signed not Vaslav and Romola but *Vatsa* and *Romushka*, names transformed into endearments Mamusia repeats in a quivering voice. Diaghilev's telegram ended with "I cannot wait to see you dance again."

Through all this my daughter sleeps undisturbed.

Irina Aleksandrovna. The name I have chosen. If we had had a son, Sasha would have named him Lev. *Irina*, in Greek, means peace.

My Daughter I title my new notebook when they leave. Sasha bought it for me just before I went to the hospital. It must have been quite expensive, for it is bound in soft, navy-blue leather and rimmed with gold leaf.

> *Born on October 7. Two hundred eighty grams. Forty-six centimetres.*

I will not be left alone for long. Mamusia will come back, insisting I sleep, reminding me that I have mere three months to regain my strength. This is why it is so short, my first letter to my daughter:

> *The old world with its prejudices and hatreds is waning. The new, modern world is gaining strength. In this new world you will be a dancer, a better one than I am. Like my mother did for me, I'll smooth the path before you, make sure you have the best of teachers.*

There is such elation in these words, such buoyancy.

After I close my notebook, the image I hold on to the longest is an evening after Irina's performance, the two of us leaning over a table, talking through her joys, her fears.

—

My daughter is two months old when the *Petersburg Gazette* announces: "Nijinsky has left Diaghilev's Ballets Russes." The news makes it to the first page, but the short article that follows offers little explanations beyond "a serious disagreement over money."

I think it a storm that will have to run its course. Diaghilev is always arguing with someone over money. A "Russian quarrel," they call it in Paris. Coming to blows and then, five minutes later, drinking champagne together like the best of friends.

The Ballets Russes dancers who have come to Russia for the Christmas break tell a different story. Vaslav hasn't resigned—he has been fired. They quote Diaghilev's terse telegram: "Your services will no longer be required." Some say it is because Vaslav refused to dance before being paid what Diaghilev owed him. Others believe it is Diaghilev's revenge for Vaslav's marriage. Olga Khokhlova saw Diaghilev sitting at a table in a Parisian restaurant, staring at his plate. When she approached him, he looked at her as if she were a ghost. "Deflated," she called him, a husk of himself. "How can it be, Bronia?" she asks when she visits us, delivering a basket of gifts from the whole company—rattles, dresses, dolls, an icon of the archangel St. Michael, a large Orenburgsky shawl. "Ballets Russes without Vaslav? Who will dance *Spectre* in Prague in January?"

Vaslav's letters call it "unfortunate" disruptions. Sergey Pavlovitch is behaving like a mischievous boy, out of spite, forgetting that Nijinsky can very well work without Diaghilev. He is truly sorry not to be able to come to Russia for Christmas. He is in Budapest now, with Romola's family, considering his future. Offers of engagements arrive daily; wonderful opportunities have to be carefully weighed. The Paris Opera is one of them. Forming his own company is another. "It is difficult to commit to anything just now," he writes. "Romola is expecting."

Mamusia's jaw tenses. Her fingers clasp the fringes of her shawl.

I cannot stop myself from thinking: This is what happens, Vaslav. Married women get pregnant. It is nobody's fault.

3.

"BRONIA." I HEAR DIAGHILEV'S VOICE when I pick up the telephone a few days later. "I'm in St. Petersburg, dining at the Astoria. I must see you. Please come. With Sasha."

"The Astoria?" Sasha rolls his eyes when I repeat the invitation. It is the new, most expensive hotel in the city. A proof—if anyone needed it—that Diaghilev is not that broke.

We walk to St. Isaac's Square, through the snow, in our felt overshoes and furs, our hearts heavy with unease. Like Olga I cannot imagine a Ballets Russes without Vaslav, let alone a Ballets Russes from which Vaslav has just been fired and where Fokine is back, triumphant, ready to reinstate his rules. If Sasha and I hadn't signed the contract, we would stay in Russia and look for other work.

Sergey Pavlovitch is waiting for us in the lobby. As soon as he sees us, he walks toward us, arms outstretched.

"Bronia, my dear Bronia." He clasps me in a tight embrace. "Congratulations on your beautiful daughter!"

I am asked to stand back, told how nothing in my figure shows that I gave birth three months before. That Irina is a lucky girl to have such a wonderful and accomplished mother. That she will be proud of me when she grows up. Sasha gets a pat on the back. He, too, is a lucky husband and father. And so far still the best Moor from *Petrushka* he, Diaghilev, has seen, and he has seen many.

My husband glows with pleasure.

"Come, come," we hear as we get rid of our overboots and coats and follow our host into the dining room, where two waiters are pointing to the corner table. Beside it a bottle of champagne is cooling in the bucket of ice.

"You have always been very dear to me, Bronia. Like a daughter," Diaghilev says as the waiters bring in the dishes. On this evening nothing is too good or too expensive. Lobster, sturgeon soup, Beluga caviar. A bowl of fresh strawberries, sweet and fragrant, as if they just had been picked.

"And you are equally dear to me as an artist."

"And Vaslav?" I interrupt.

Diaghilev's face darkens. I see a tear in his eye. He doesn't wipe it when it flows down his cheek. "Vaslav didn't even find it necessary to inform me of his marriage."

Such an elegant dining room, brilliantly lit with crystal chandeliers. I hold the glass of champagne to my lips, take one sip then another. Diaghilev's eyes do not leave my face.

Vaslav has made a terrible mistake. He, Diaghilev, blames Romola for it. "This woman," he calls her, just like Mamusia does. She is cold and calculating. She has already alienated Vaslav from everybody who loves him, including his own mother. She has made him forget where his strength comes from. For "this woman" it is not art that matters the most but position and money.

Diaghilev takes my hand in his. "Bronia, I have lost Vaslav, but I cannot lose you, too. Will you promise that you and Sasha will come to Prague?"

"Is Fokine expecting us?" I cannot resist asking.

"Fokine has to do what I want," Diaghilev says. "All your roles will stay yours. Nothing will change."

"Nothing?"

"Nothing!"

"I have to think."

"Please do. I just want you to know . . ."

This is how this evening continues, until it is time to leave and Sergey Pavlovitch insists on escorting us to the lobby, where the porter brings our coats. And then, before I realize what he is doing, he bends on one knee to help me put on my felt overshoes.

"I cannot let you do that!" I protest, taking the shoes from him, passing them to Sasha. And when Diaghilev raises himself with a heavy sigh, I finally say, "All right, Sergey Pavlovitch! I will come to Prague."

In a *droshky* sleigh on our way home Sasha and I laugh at what has passed. Sasha imitates Diaghilev's praises of his "priceless Bronia." I, my head spinning from too much champagne, remind him that Diaghilev has both of us under contract. He didn't need to ask us to honour our obligations. He could have reminded us of the price of breaking them, instead. And yet he never did.

"That's true," Sasha concedes, squeezing my hand. Then with a chuckle he whispers in my ear, "Do you think that the greatest Moor of Ballets Russes should have asked the Great Charlatan for a raise?"

—

On the last night before our departure for Prague I wake up gripped by panic, clutching my empty belly and swollen breasts. Our suitcases, already packed, are standing by the bedroom door and I make sure I do not bump into them in the dark as I go to Irina's room.

The nursery is lit by a small side lamp with amber shade. The air is stuffy and heavy, a mixture of dried sour milk and pee.

The wet nurse, Olena, sleeps on a folding cot by the window. Her eyes half open when I walk in, roll and then close. A moment later she is snoring. "This is how it had to be," she said when Mamusia inquired about her own baby, given up for adoption.

I bend over the crib. My daughter is tightly wrapped in a goose-down *becik*. White, with frills around the pillow and across the front, just like the one we all had when we were babies.

There is resentment in the thought of Olena, her pink nipples my daughter's lips seek when she is hungry, the off-key lullaby she half sings, half mutters when she is nursing my baby. There is resentment in the thought of Mamusia, who cannot resist picking Irina up even if she doesn't cry. Who is terrified of drafts and keeps the curtains drawn, even though the windows are double and well sealed.

"Is it you, Bronia?" Mamusia's whisper interrupts. "Can't you sleep?"

I didn't hear her come in and this thought curdles with panic. What if someone broke in? Would I have not heard it, either? Nonsense, I tell myself, but I am already sobbing.

I don't want to cry. I don't want Olena to wake up and give me her curious look of what I sometimes take for jealousy, sometimes for contempt. I let Mamusia lead me out of the nursery to the living room, where she makes me lie down on our blue sofa, covers me with a blanket. The same blanket I remember from our childhood travels, with clusters of red and yellow circles. Bought at some bazaar from which I also remember a rainbow of spices, all lined up in burlap bags, and Stassik dipping his finger into hot paprika, licking it with anticipation, only to gag and spit it out.

"It's always like this with a new baby," Mamusia whispers. "Thank Matka Boska that Irina is healthy. Everything else will settle. You'll see."

I hold on to these words. I remind myself how each day my body returns to its old shape. Muscles succumb to the familiar routine, even feel suppler at times. An instrument that has been used in an unaccustomed way needs tuning, tightening, but it will serve me well. I'll learn to make the most of it. This is what dancers do all the time. Adjust, substitute, turn limitations into new means of expression.

"I'm here, Bronia," Mamusia whispers. "You are not leaving Irina with strangers."

How would I dance this moment?

En pointe, with prodding, insistent jabs of the feet.

4.

WHEN WE ARRIVE IN PRAGUE, Ballets Russes is in the middle of rehearsals for the 1914 season. Diaghilev is not there yet. In his absence Fokine and his wife, Vera, are wiping out all traces of the "Nijinskys' madness." Fokine will not only choreograph but he will also dance all Vaslav's roles. Mine will go to his wife.

What will I dance?

Secondary roles: Bacchante, not Ta-Hor, in *Cléopâtre*. The Street Dancer, not the Ballerina Doll, in *Petrushka*.

In the dressing rooms I am a half stranger. Many of my friends did not return, and to those who took their place I am the sister-of-you-know-who.

"*Na pochyłe drzewo każda koza skacze*," Mamusia used to say. Any goat can jump on a bent tree.

This is when a telegram arrives with unexpected but most welcome news. Vaslav is offering me and Sasha a place in his own company for the Nijinsky Season in London. A two-year contract. Eighty thousand francs a year for me, forty for Sasha, and full artistic freedom.

The truce has become a full reconciliation. We are again two halves of the same whole. Older, more mature, stronger. Better for what has passed.

"I'm not breaking my contract," I write to Diaghilev. "The terms have been broken by Fokine's decision to refuse me my customary roles. This is why I consider myself freed from my obligations."

In Paris Vaslav is waiting for us at the station, all joy at our arrival, thankful we have accepted his offer. Beside him Romola, dressed in a velvet coat, black, splashed with brown and rust chrysanthemums. It folds around her, making her look like a wrapped-up gift.

Vaslav's pretty wife, I think of her. I like the ease with which she slips her arm under mine, telling me how impatient she has been to meet me properly. "You don't remember me, do you?" she asks, but I hear no resentment in this question. A moment later, before I have time to protest, she is telling me that they are staying at the Hôtel Scribe, where they have also reserved a room for us. Everyone knows Vaslav there. Bellboys bring them gifts all the time; spoil them, really. Have I brought snapshots of Irina? Isn't it just wonderful that in five months she will a have a little cousin? That one day our children will play together?

Vaslav hasn't changed, I think, though I do note the way he slouches, as if wishing to hide from all these words. "How is Mamusia?" he asks me in a whisper tense with guilt. "Still hurt?"

I tell him not to worry—she will come around—she always does.

It is only later in the day that Vaslav gives us the details of the *Saison Nijinsky.* Eight weeks of one-hour programs at the London Palace Theatre.

Questions are already rattling in my mind. At a music hall? Hasn't Vaslav always said music halls were no places for serious artists? Hasn't he chastised Pavlova for performing on the same bill with acrobats and clowns? Didn't he tell her not to demean herself?

There is more.

The Nijinsky Season will begin on March 2, four and a half weeks from now. The three of us are the only dancers. There are no sets. In spite of this, in addition to *Faune* and *Jeux,* Vaslav has committed himself to staging *Spectre de la Rose, Carnaval* and *Les Sylphides.*

"We will dance my own versions," Vaslav says to quiet my misgivings about his legal rights to stage Ballets Russes ballets. "Not Fokine's."

I'm a child of the theatre. I do not dwell on what cannot be changed but on what can be done. In the next days, while Sasha searches for anyone who could paint our sets and alter the music scores to fit our production,

I search for dancers available at such a short notice. Since the only ones I find are in Warsaw, I have to go there for auditions and choose the best.

The new company gathers in London in mid-February, and we throw ourselves into the whirlwind of preparations. Rehearsing, training the new dancers, ordering costumes, painting the sets. Every day brings more problems. Posters arrive riddled with spelling errors. After seeing our rehearsal, the director of the Palace Theatre demands more Russian dances, and Vaslav has to fly into a rage before he backs off.

In the evenings, exhausted, we return to our hotel, to be chased by Romola's terse voice: "I've been waiting for you all day . . . you didn't come for lunch . . . you are again late for dinner . . . why are you always speaking Russian . . . are you shutting me out on purpose?"

Even Sasha, so good at diffusing tension, rolls his eyes when Romola catches my arm and screams, "I know what you are doing, Bronia. You are trying to take Vaslav away from me."

A see-saw, I remind myself. Despair and hope, down and then up. My memories of the next two weeks are still broken, made of jagging fragments that refuse to blend. First is a troubling glitter in Vaslav's eyes when he is told that the Nijinsky hour has been slotted in between a check-suited comedian thrashing around the stage on rubber legs and a fat singer of saucy refrains. Then there is the sight of my brother on the night of the premiere, sobbing in his dressing room. "What happened?" I ask, and he hands me a telegram he has just received:

> Congratulations STOP Best wishes to music hall artist STOP Anna Pavlova STOP

And then clings to me in a lingering, suffocating embrace.

One night Vaslav is screaming "Not that music!" when the orchestra plays Tchaikovsky during the interval before *Spectre*. Still screaming, he clasps his ears and throws himself on the floor. Nothing I say matters. Not when I beg him to stop. Not when I mutter that I don't know what else to do.

Terrified, I watch the theatre manager grab a jug of water and empty it over Vaslav's head, as if he were a mad dog. My brother stops screaming, rubs his eyes, stands up, his hair wet, dripping. He sees me, but there is a puzzled expression on his face, as if he expected someone else in my stead. I throw my arms around him and hold on to his wet, shivering body. "Vaslav," I mumble. "It's me, Bronia. Talk to me. Tell me what is happening."

He doesn't speak, but I feel him melt into my embrace. Slowly—too slowly, perhaps—but finally he does smile when I take a handkerchief out of my pocket, and—in my best approximation of Mamusia's voice—order him to spit into it so that I can wipe his chin.

On March 14, Vaslav and I dance *Spectre de la Rose*. He is the Spirit of a Rose; I'm the Young Girl, who has just returned from a ball. Not Nijinsky's Chosen Maiden but Fokine's dreamer.

The set is simple: an open window, an armchair where I sit. The curtain rises. I pick up a fallen rose in my hands. Vaslav glides in, his arms raised like tendrils. His movements as he circles the stage are all polished and precise, including that last leap through the open window into the void. But I know that it is just his body repeating what it has learnt so well. His soul is not there.

A moment later, backstage, I see Vaslav sitting on the floor panting, his forehead streaming with sweat. Sasha is handing him a towel and a glass of water, reminding him to sip it slowly. From the audience waves of applause reach us, followed by cries of "Encore!" Vaslav's forehead furrows.

I'm still ready to dismiss what I've seen. A weak moment, a bad day. We all have them. Even my brilliant brother. Now he will call himself a "klutz." Snap at me to stop staring at him as if he were a monkey wearing glasses.

"How was I, Bronia?" Vaslav asks. It may sound like a question, but it is a plea for reassurance.

A cold rivulet rolls down my back, soaking the waist of my ball dress. Samson? I think. A giant betrayed and blinded, his powers gone?

No one can tell you how you dance, Bronia. You must know it yourself.

The ribbons of my pointe shoes feel tight. I register it vaguely, as if my legs were not my own.

I say, "You were brilliant, Vaslav . . . as always . . . listen how they applaud."

When Romola telephones the next day to tell me that Vaslav is running a high fever and that the evening will have to be cancelled, I am relieved.

We have all worked too hard; we still have six more weeks to go; we need a day or two of rest. But then I learn that the contract Vaslav signed makes no provisions for illness or injury. The *Saison Nijinsky* has been cancelled, replaced by Miss Hetty King and her "Amazing Laughter Cure."

In the days that follow, as the Nijinsky company dissolves in debts and recriminations, I tell myself that the future is a veiled temptress, her dances slow, deceiving, each of them a tease.

Samson shook the pillars of the temple where his enemies—thinking him defeated—celebrated their shallow victory. The God of the Dance, too, will write his own ending. There will be new ballets, bold, exuberant. Beside them even *Sacre* will pale.

5.

A WEEK LATER Sasha and I take a train to St. Petersburg. When we get home, Irina gives us a wide, toothless smile, extends her hands to be picked up.

Vaslav has been generous, insisting on paying all the dancers for the whole eight weeks, so Sasha and I have enough money to rent a studio where we can practise and I can give lessons. Sasha's contacts have produced a steady stream of engagements at the Narodni Dom, at private performances, at nightclubs. Enough to keep us afloat.

I deflect Mamusia's questions about Romola and the London season. It had to be cut short, I admit, but all is well. Vaslav is happy with his wife. I don't have to do it for long. By June their daughter, Kyra, is born, and all Mamusia talks about is Vaslav's promise to bring his family to Russia for a Christmas visit.

When I'm alone with Sasha, I still cannot stop myself from dissecting the London failure. Wondering why Romola, with her prefect English, allowed Vaslav to sign such a contract. Didn't she read it? Couldn't she get a lawyer to look it over?

"You don't like her, do you?" Sasha finally asks, sucking on his meerschaum pipe. This is a new habit. The pipe's bowl is beautifully carved in the shape of a lion's head. The smoke he exhales has a nutty scent to it.

I roll this sentence in my thoughts, examine it from all sides. It is like a pebble in a shoe. Annoying at first then painful. Like all wounds, it will fester if left untreated.

"No," I admit.

Sasha shrugs off my confession. Guilt, accusations, apportioning of blame. The Nijinsky way. What's so great about it, in the end? Besides, haven't I read the news?

St. Petersburg papers report on another mysterious explosion at the railway station. Strikes, protests, marches are erupting everywhere, not just in Russia but in Germany, England, Italy.

"Passing thunderstorms," I tell my husband.

It is easy to be blinded by hope. As easy as to dismiss an account of the assassination of a European prince in a Balkan town where I have never been. Especially since I am tempted by visions of my own ballets. They are still vague, unfinished, in need of shaping and reshaping, fleshing out what has inspired them. A blinking light. A tired horse plodding along the road. A little girl skipping a rope, while her friends stand in a circle around her and watch.

A circle.

A triangle.

A pyramid.

6.

CROWDS THRONG TOWARD the square at the Winter Palace. People carry icons, flags and imperial portraits. A church bell rings. A flock of pigeons takes off in fright.

Germany has just declared war on Russia.

I lean out of our apartment window to take a better look, resting my elbows on the small cushion Mamusia keeps on the windowsill. "Look, Irushka," Sasha says, pointing at a Cossack on a horse; the Cossack's fur hat resembles the ones the elders wore in *Sacre*. "Where?" Irina asks, and Mamusia holds her up so that she can see better.

Next day we read in the newspapers that when Nicolas II appeared on the palace balcony, the people knelt on the ground and sang "God Save the

Tsar." War, the papers remind us, lifts up spirits, cleanses stagnant minds, turns discord into unity. There will be no more bickering over strikes, no more demonstrations or terrorist bombs. In the Duma all parties have vowed to defend Russia's position as a world power. Guard our unique Russian values. In the streets posters urge us to buy war bonds, at 5.5 per cent.

Everyone agrees the war will be over by Christmas.

Sasha is mobilized three weeks later. "Aleksander Kotchetovsky, 25 years old, assigned to an Artillery Unit," his papers say, but to my relief he—like many other performers—will be entertaining the troops. His recruiting sergeant asked how well he played the balalaika and an accordion and if he knew Russian folk dances and good Gypsy tunes.

On the last day of August I see Sasha off at the crowded train station. Hair cropped short, trousers tucked into his boots, my husband still looks dashing. Humming an aria from *The Merry Widow*, he anticipates campfires in the fields, army trucks turned into stage platforms, toothy grins of men sitting on their backpacks as they watch him. Men he will know how to enchant. His warm hand firmly coils around my waist, as if we were setting off to a new dance.

"Which way should I tilt my cap, Bronia?"

Sasha and I have time for tea at the station bar. At the buffet, faded paper roses stand on the beer-stained oilcloth; sandwiches are piled up in diminishing circles under the net that covers them from flies. The air smells of soot and steam.

We buy two glasses of tea and sit at a table by the window.

"This is for you," I say, and hand Sasha my gift, tucked within a linen sash.

Sasha opens it and gives off a loud whistle. Inside there is a pocket water filter and three kinds of Badmaev powders: for external injury, internal bleeding and for hunger.

"Where did you get all that!"

Diaghilev would've reminded us that whistling indoors brings bad luck, but I smile, proud of myself. At the Aleksandrovsky Market I was assured that for the soldiers the filter and powders are already the most-coveted treasures.

"What would I do without you," Sasha says, leaning forward to kiss me on the cheek. "My most practical wife!"

He has placed his hand on mine and I look at the scar on his index finger. Once, in Monte Carlo, he tried to show me how a chef he knew chopped onions. The cut was deep. The knife had touched the bone, but it healed fast and didn't even require stitches.

We talk of our future. For now the lessons and temporary engagements suffice, but we need to look for more. "Kiev?" Sasha asks. He has a good friend there who assures him that Kotchetovsky and his wife would be welcomed with open arms.

"Yes," I agree. "At least until Vaslav offers us something better."

We finish the rest of our tea in haste. I walk Sasha back to the platform, which is crowded with soldiers and their families. In one of the compartments someone is playing an accordion. Fast and very, very well.

It's all so quick in the end, a tight embrace, a kiss on the lips, hasty admonitions to write often, and then, my own slow trek back home. Alone.

7.

THE APARTMENT ALWAYS smells of laundry. When I return home from the theatre or my dancing lessons, diapers are boiling in a big vat of soapy water on the stove, or drying on strings criss-crossing the kitchen, claiming half the dining room—and Mamusia's bedroom. Thieves take anything left in the attic to dry.

In Petrograd—for this is St. Petersburg's patriotic new name, purged from all that sounds German—by mid-morning the grocery stores still sell carrots, cabbages, turnips and bony cuts of greasy meat, but they are out of bread. People are making *sukhariki*, dried bread slices that can last for months. Every time we visit Stassik Mamusia insists on bringing him something to eat, even though the director has assured her that the sanatorium, like all hospitals, has adequate supplies.

At the Mariinsky Fokine is mounting *Stenka Razin* and saluting the allies with the *Dance of the Nations*. Maroussia Piltz, who brings me this news, tells me that she is happy there. She has heard that Vaslav has reconciled with Diaghilev, and that Diaghilev invited him back to dance and choreograph for Ballets Russes. "Is it true, Bronia?" she asks, but all I can tell her is that Vaslav doesn't mention it in his letters. Maroussia is not surprised. After all the drama Vaslav is still cautious. But there is no need. Diaghilev is now besotted with Massine, a dancer from Moscow, whom he introduces everywhere as his newest star. The general verdict is that Massine has no talent.

"Once the war is over," Maroussia predicts, "you and Sasha will be back with Ballets Russes."

"Is it true that you are dancing for Diaghilev again? Choreographing, as well? What are you working on now?" I ask Vaslav in my letters, but I don't believe they make it past the censors. The ones he sends to us are short and do not answer my questions: "I'm well. I miss you all. How are you managing, Bronia? Please write more often."

I keep trying. I choose postcards over letters, for I hear that they have a better chance of getting through:

I ran into Fokine on the Nevsky. "I taught your brother and you everything you know," he said. Picture a snarl, Vaslav, curled lips, eyes like darts. "You taught us everything you knew, Mikhail Mikhailovitch," I said. "You were not the only one."

How do we manage?

I am the prima ballerina at the Narodni Dom and they will hire Sasha as soon as he returns. I also teach. Cecchetti has passed all his advanced pupils to me.

At the Narodni, I also choreograph my own short simple solos. *Poupée* on toe. *Autumn Song* barefoot. "The Nijinska ballets," the bill advertises them, rather grandly. I describe them to my brother in detail, adding that "even though I'm pleased I'm not proud. I aspire to something much better." His first ballet was *Faun*.

I do not write that our local grocer has been robbed at knifepoint or that big padlocks have appeared on doors to the woodsheds and the cellars all over the city. Or that in the house where we rent our apartment three workmen have cemented shards of broken glass to the ridge of the wall that separates our yard from the neighbouring one.

"Mamusia is healthy," I write, "Irina is growing fast. How are Kyra and Romola? Please send us their pictures."

Sasha does come home before Christmas, but not because the war has ended. My husband has been granted an extended leave.

When he walks into the room, Irina hides behind Mamusia's back.

"Come to your papa, Irushka," Sasha coaxes her that dark December afternoon. He produces a clown's red nose and puts it on, trying to make her laugh. Irina eyes him with cautious interest but stays put.

"She has to get used to you again," I tell him. "She will be all over you tomorrow."

"Did *you* miss me?" Sasha asks when Mamusia puts Irina to sleep and we are finally alone.

"Yes." I whisper, and turn my head up for Sasha to bend down and press his lips against mine.

"Show me how much."

"Shh . . ." I say, as I pull him into our bedroom, a finger on my lips. Walls are thin. I do not want Irina to wake up crying. She hasn't been sleeping well ever since Olena left after we refused her third demand for a raise.

Later, skin touching skin, hearts still thumping, we talk.

Sasha's army ensemble—a circus troupe really, as he calls it—consisted of not just dancers but also clowns, acrobats and jugglers. They performed at the southern front, behind the lines, on makeshift stages. At first their shows were all about victories and celebrations, as the Austrians were getting a beating. By November, however, they were sent to field hospitals.

"To all those pretty nurses?" I ask lightly, wagging my finger. "Should I be jealous?"

Sasha rummages through the pockets of his jacket for a packet of cigarettes. His meerschaum pipe was stolen, he says. He doesn't even know when. So were the filters I gave him. He opened the box and it was empty.

"It doesn't matter."

"No, it doesn't."

The tip of the cigarette glows with each inhale. My husband's voice is turning into a hoarse whisper.

"It's all wrong," he tells me. "Terribly wrong. At the front there is no food. For men or horses. Recruits have to wait for their rifles until another soldier is killed. Corps shrink into divisions, divisions into brigades, brigades into battalions. The tsar is a weak man who asserts himself when he shouldn't. Firing good ministers, replacing them with nincompoops. This is why field hospitals are filled with the dying.

"And we are sent to juggle flames for them," Sasha continues, his voice losing itself in his throat. "Dance the *hopak* . . ."

I hand him an ashtray and watch as he stubs out the cigarette. Krem, his favourite brand. The only words of comfort I manage are: "You won't have to go back for a long while."

In the morning we sit together over household accounts. With the war on, Vaslav, who is in Austria, cannot send Mamusia any money, so we are on our own. In addition to the rent and groceries we have to pay the girl who comes to clean. And the washerwoman. Then there are doctor's bills and the pharmacist's. Stassik's sanatorium fees. Expenses Vaslav always covered before are now ours.

We have a thousand rubles left of our savings. The Opera pays a hundred rubles a month. Lessons fetch another two hundred. We are still all right. If the rent doesn't go up.

"I'm here now," Sasha says. He reminds me that nightclubs pay a hundred rubles per evening. We can do them after the Opera ends. Ragtime, tap dance. Anything American is the rage.

He stands up to show me what we could do, but I'm faster. Ja and Jo's lessons are not forgotten. I can still brush and flap, do a roll that sounds like a galloping horse. I still remember the rhythm of a Shim Sham Shimmy.

"Do you always have to be the best, Bronia?" Sasha laughs. "Is this a Nijinsky trait?"

By January days are short and dark. To protect myself from the icy tugs of winter air I wrap my face up in scarves as I walk in the street, the silk one near my skin, the thick woollen one on the outside. When Mamusia takes Irina outside, she smears her face with a thick layer of goose fat.

The cigarette girl at the nightclub where Sasha and I dance our American ragtime number is petite. She is fond of fishnet stockings and skirts short enough to show her knees. Her lips are crimson with lipstick. She giggles every time Sasha asks her anything: "Do cigarette girls ever smoke? Can you catch fish in these stockings?"

"Lighten up, Bronia," Sasha says. "You are not jealous, are you?"

She comes by the dressing room once, when I'm there alone. Stutters when I ask her what she wants. Then leaves a packet of Krem cigarettes for Mr. Kotchetovsky. "Oh, it's—it's paid for," she stammers when I ask her how much I owe her.

In the morning Sasha slaps cologne on his freshly razored cheeks. Scrutinizes a nick on his chin. Wipes it off as if it were a smudge. The tightening inside me, the narrowing of my throat, painful and suffocating, doesn't leave.

"What's wrong now, Bronia?" Sasha asks.

On the last day of January Sasha, contrite, flowers in hand, mutters, "I was a fool, Bronia. I made a terrible mistake." Mamusia, silent and swift, retreats with Irina in her arms so that we can be alone.

"Please listen," he says.

I sit down at the table, stare at the pineapple pattern of the crochet lace tablecloth.

Sasha takes the chair beside me, rubs his eyes with the knuckles of both hands.

In the kitchen Mamusia is telling Irina to open her mouth wide, for the train will miss the tunnel. In his last postcard, from Vienna, Vaslav wrote that his daughter, Kyra, "is smiling at me when I dance."

Sasha laces fingers of his hands together. "I wasn't thinking . . . it was nothing . . . just an infatuation."

I continue to stare at the tablecloth, the pointed shapes joined by braided petals, fishnet spaces between them. The table underneath is heavy, dark. "Mahogany," Mamusia always says with pride. Vaslav paid for it when he was dancing for the Mariinsky. In spite of all Sasha and I make we had to sell his Blüthner piano. At half price, for no one wants to buy anything German.

I curse the vividness of what I see. My husband with another woman. Her fingers running through his hair, pinning him to her. His lips mouthing promises or pleas.

Sasha stirs, raises himself a few centimetres and then sits back. His voice is low, thick with guilt. "It's this damned war, Bronia. I wanted to prove to myself that I'm still alive."

I feel his thumb on the back of my hand. Tiny stroking movements, a plea.

"We have to start again, Bronia. Remember that Kiev friend I told you about?"

"Please, Bronia, look at me."

Father did not ask for forgiveness, I think. Father was never sorry for leaving us.

8.

WE HAVE SIX MONTHS TO close our Petrograd home and sell or store what we cannot take with us. In August we have to be in Kiev.

The Kiev City Theatre contract is to "stage ballets, *divertissements*, and also classical and character dances in operas." Sasha will be ballet master and *premier danseur*. I will be prima ballerina.

"Classical dances? Stage, not create?"

"It's the best thing," Sasha insists. The Kiev Theatre has pulled the right strings and extended his military leave. Our combined salaries—his double of mine—will end money worries. "No more nightclubs, Bronia!"

A clean slate, I think. A place where all is new. Unsullied.

"What will happen to Stassik with all of us so far away?" Mamusia asks when I break the news to her, having first sent Sasha and Irina for a walk.

The last time we visited Stassik at the sanatorium he was crouching in the corner, his legs skinny, yellowish, sticking out from an odd pair of trousers far too short for him. "Stassik," I called, but he didn't look up, not even when I wiped a drop of saliva from the corner of his mouth.

What more can we do for him than we already do? What can we do here that we cannot do from Kiev?

As I line up my arguments Mamusia measures out thirty valerian drops, pours them over a sugar cube. Her heart is not what it used to be, she says with a sigh. I can see her eyes take in her mahogany furniture; the doors to Vaslav's rooms; scrapbooks from the Mariinsky, from Paris, from London.

I'm twenty-four years old, I remind her; Sasha is twenty-six. We want our own ballet. We want to work together.

"In Kiev?"

I know what she is thinking. Kiev is a backwater. Kiev is where she started, forty-seven years ago, when she came to Russia with her sisters. Kiev was one of the stops on the Lukovitch tours, the one that comes with memories of giving birth to Vaslav and bringing him to a mouldy room with the stink of cabbage in the hall. If only you hadn't left the Mariinsky, Bronia, Mamusia's eyes reproach me.

"Please." I cover her hand with mine, press it down.

Mamusia nods. She is my mother. She may worry and fret, but she will do what I want.

In Kiev an apartment is awaiting us, as the contract promised. First floor, sunny, with a big kitchen and four good-sized rooms. "It is fine," I say before Mamusia has the time to comment on the faded wallpaper or what the City Theatre described as "furniture" but what looks like a collection of cast-offs and old, rickety props. The theatre is a short walk away. Mamusia can bring Irina over during the midday break.

"Look at the view," Sasha says, pointing at the gilded domes of St. Sophia. "And there is a little park right there. And a sandbox in the yard."

He does a pirouette, grinning at Irina, who first looks at him with comic seriousness and then laughs. I rise onto *demi-pointe,* put my hands on my hips and circle him.

We have such plans. We who once danced together for Diaghilev, with the best dancers in the world, now have our own ballet. We can do wonders. Some promises are like sips of champagne, bubbly, light, festive. Whirling in my head. We are man and wife. We are artists. We'll show Kiev what Russia has missed.

When Sasha and I talk ballet, Irina listens with great seriousness, her forehead furrowed as she mutters something in a private language that sounds sometimes Polish, sometimes Russian. Everything that moves fascinates her. The flow of the river, the pendulum of the wall clock, the plodding horse pulling a cart. When Mamusia arrives with her at the theatre after the morning class, she runs straight to me and her plump arms clasp my neck. I cannot believe that once, for however brief a moment, I didn't want her to be born.

"Do you think she'll be a dancer?" I ask Sasha.

"She is two years old," he says, laughing. "It's too early to know."

Mamusia agrees. Even with Vaslav she couldn't tell at this age, though he was a restless child, unable to stand still. If she looked elsewhere for a moment, Vaslav would be climbing a chair or a fence. Or hanging from a baptismal fountain, like a little monkey, as he did in Warsaw, where she took us both to be baptized.

Irina is timid. Afraid of sudden noises, big men, dogs. She is graceful, though, and her balance is good. She also likes to imitate me when I stretch. Sitting down beside me, extending her legs, bending forward.

I try to come home before Irina goes to bed, even if I have to rush back to the theatre right away. If I am late and she is already asleep, I tiptoe into her bedroom to leave a little surprise for her when she wakes up in the morning. A dried poppyseed head that will rattle softly when she shakes it, a piece of bark that looks like a bird in flight. Sometimes she wakes up. Groggy from sleep, she smiles, and I believe that in me, her artist mother bending over her bed, my daughter sees the harbingers of the life that one day can be hers.

Yes, it may be too early, but I hope she will be a dancer. I want her to live a life that is intense and all-consuming. I want her to know the elation that comes only after hours and hours of sacrifice, the pure joy—stronger than any pain—of being the very best she can be.

A new company is like a new family. Dancers—we are forty-two at the City Theatre—of varying degrees of skill and many different habits have to be welded together. Strength and harmony come after hard, patient work. In daily classes muscles have to be challenged to exceed the familiar range; in rehearsals new steps have to be learnt, absorbed into the muscles.

From the slur of bodies dancers slowly emerge. This one has an ease of limbs; that one has speed, or a spark of warmth that can be nurtured, coaxed into permanence. At home in the evening, Sasha and I together weigh their merits: who is ready for advancement, a solo; who is slacking off and needs to be warned.

A ballet master, Sasha jokes, is like a Father Confessor and a Mother

Superior rolled into one. If he had a *kopek* for every secret whispered in his ear, every tear he has had to wipe dry, we would be rich.

But dancers do not dance in a void.

Thankfully, the orchestra is excellent, unified and disciplined. And so is the chorus. But the theatre has no carpenters, no painters to build new sets and no budget for them, either.

"This is not how it is done here," the set manager, a wiry man from Galicia, tells us when we present him with detailed sketches of what we require for our first performance. Scratching his bald head, he extracts two albums from the drawer of his desk. Inside, numbered photographs show separate details of a stage set: a palace, a lake, a tree in two versions—bare for the winter and leafy for the summer. "Just write down the numbers," he says, pushing a sheet of lined paper in our direction. "Then tell me where you want each piece to stand."

We don't even ask about costumes. Or orchestra scores. We do not mention how Bakst or Benois designed sets. How their paintings not only expressed the mood for *Cléopâtre* or *Petrushka* but also framed the dancing, became one with it.

"One step at a time," Sasha says when we leave. "For now let's get the tree and the lake."

I chuckle. "Two trees. One bare, one with leaves. No palace."

Our first projects may be assigned and conventional, but *Valse Badinage* plays to a packed house and earns praise for "elegance and exceptional choreographic humour." And the administration has already given us permission to stage our own production.

On our way to the theatre we pass posters advertising Charlie Chaplin's antics in *Shanghai* and candlelight evenings with Vertynsky's ballads. Theatres are filled. And so are the nights at the Kiev Opera. The sugar factory is working at full capacity and paying salaries on time. Peasants deliver cords of firewood, cartloads of potatoes, sacks of flour. Kerchiefed women at the market where I sometimes go with Mamusia offer samples of sour cream or honey, ladling them on the palm of my hand. They call me "Sunshine" and ask where I'm from. Petrograd, I say. They don't know where it is. When I say St. Petersburg, they nod. "Winters are colder here," they say. "Remember to put on a hat, a warmer sweater, a coat."

"Petrograd stores are emptying fast of anything that can be used or bartered," Maroussia Piltz writes. "Vodka, tobacco and sugar have become safer currency than the ruble. Lines for bread form by two in the morning. Marauding soldiers who have abandoned their units are robbing passersby of anything that can be sold or eaten. At the Mariinsky the mood is despondent, but Smirnova's *arabesques* in *The Sleeping Beauty* have been phenomenal."

With Mamusia, we make up food parcels that we entrust to travelling friends, since the post is only reliable for letters. "Half for you," I write to Maroussia, "half for Stassik."

With Sasha, we are planning our new season.

When we arrived at the Kiev Theatre, ballet was considered second class. Every time an opera was interspersed with a ballet part, the conductor took a break and gave the baton to his understudy. Dancers were never invited to the foyer receptions. Already such slights are unthinkable and we are steeled for new challenges.

I know what I want: to stage the best of Ballets Russes.

Sasha agrees.

"We will order our own backdrops," he says when I shudder at the thought of the set manager and his two albums. "Reconstruct what we remember. Like we did in London, for Vaslav."

There is such elation in my memories of these days, such energy. Sasha finishes my thoughts. I slip my hand under his arm when we walk. We have always been good at making do, haven't we? We have savings. There are enough carpenters and seamstresses in Kiev. Even if the quality is not quite the same, isn't theatre about thriving on illusions?

Is this what makes me overlook the signs of danger? Looks too intense, a whisper hushed that time I walk into his dressing room in search of a missing costume. A foot moved too quickly. The little flutter of eyelids. A dancer departing with exaggerated haste.

"I'm a ballet master, Bronia. Dancers come to me all the time. I was just talking to her. I was holding her because she was crying. I was trying to calm her down."

Her. Olena. Nina. Darya.

"Please, Bronia, don't make me feel guilty over nothing."

My husband's arm is tight around mine in the memories of these moments, forcing my head against his chest. The beat of his heart is steady and regular.

Sasha is not like Father, I tell myself. The doors of our apartment do not slam. The neighbours downstairs do not bang at the ceiling. My daughter does not pee herself from fear. She will not grow up without a father.

My husband holds me until I close my eyes. Until I believe my own lie that if I remain still, nothing will change.

Our Ballets Russes evening is a sampler. "We offer you a re-creation of Nijinsky's famous roles," the program states, "modern masterpieces choreographed by Mikhail Fokine but developed and perfected by Vaslav Nijinsky, Kiev's own son."

Sasha dances Favourite Slave, Harlequin and Petrushka. I dance Cleopatra, Colombina and the Ballerina Doll.

The performances sell out and have to be extended. At the last evening of the season, Sasha and I—*corps de ballet* behind us—take the last curtain call among flowers and gifts. Backstage, dancers throw a surprise reception in our honour. One by one they come to embrace us. We are presented with a round layered cake, on which there is an inscription: "For our beloved Ballet Master and our Prima Ballerina, who have taught us all we know."

"Kotchetovsky and Nijinska raised ballet art in Kiev to new heights . . . to an international level," reviewers write. We are another milestone in Kiev's cultural life; we are Kiev's pride and joy. The invitations arrive. To gallery openings, recitals, premieres, revivals.

Kiev is not a backwater.

"You were right," I mutter in Sasha's ear. "Coming here was the best thing we could have done."

9.

ONE OF THE INVITATIONS that arrives before the opening of the new season delights me more than others: "Please come to my studio on

Fondukleievska Street, for an evening of art and conversation. If you arrive before everyone else, I can finally have you to myself for a while. Aleksandra Exter."

Exter is a painter, one of Kiev's best; her husband a well-known lawyer. We have met them both before at official receptions, events Sasha thrives at but I find draining.

Sasha calls it "another Nijinsky trait."

I am expecting a maid to open the studio door, but to my surprise our hostess greets us in person. "Come inside," she urges us, smiling. Not beautiful—that word is too fickle to describe her—but handsome. Imposing. Her thick brown hair is cropped short, like mine. The black of her dress is broken by a silk crimson flower pinned to her chest.

Aleksandra Aleksandrovna. Bronislava Fominitchna.

Aleksandra. Bronia.

The large room Aleksandra leads us to has canvasses propped against one of the walls. On the table in the corner a samovar is humming. Two uniformed maids are fussing with refreshments.

Nikolai, her husband, welcomes us as we enter. We are, he assures us, his wife's most awaited guests. Ever since they saw Ballets Russes in Paris!

It is *Schéhérazade* Aleksandra remembers most vividly; Nijinsky bursting onstage as the Favourite Slave. What energy! What total absorption in his role! "I tried to paint him," she confesses. "Or more precisely the inner force that stayed long after he left the stage."

"Tried?" I ask.

"It's not easy to paint movement and rhythm," she says, and laughs. I think her at ease with herself. Exuberant.

"Vaslav will like hearing it."

"Come," she says, leading me by the elbow to the paintings on display. "Paris, St. Petersburg, Rome, Odessa, Moscow." Cities where she has lived, each turned into a collage of impressions. "And here is Kiev," she adds, pointing to the one in the very centre. "This is where I always come back. To reflect on what I've seen."

I take a step toward the Kiev landscape, admire the fluid lines, the exploding colours. Her cities have no people in them. They make me think of music.

"For how to paint anything new otherwise?" she asks. "If you haven't yet transformed what you have seen? Don't you agree, Bronia?"

"Or how to dance anything new!"

We talk for a long while that day. Of Picasso and Matisse, Aleksandra's favourite painters, because for them a work of art is a solution to a problem, not an ornament. Of theatre sets and backdrops, which ultimately always disappoint because they are static and drama depends on movement.

Will she show me her newest paintings? Yes. One of these days. When I come back. For I will come back very soon, won't I?

I recall the feeling of regret when other guests begin to arrive, forcing me into the round of introductions, pleasantries and compliments. But I should not have underestimated our hostess. It is an evening of art and conversation, and as soon as the room fills up, Aleksandra announces the topic of tonight's discussion: the paintings of Kazimir Malevitch. Did his black square really kill art, as the critics claimed?

The evening unfolds, turns into night, with food and wine and passionate arguments. Someone has brought a guitar and plays it when we talk. "The square is incomprehensible and therefore dangerous," I recall Aleksandra saying, her voice rising above the din. "It is viewed as such because it defies expectations."

The joy I feel at all this surprises me. As if for years something had been constricted in me, something stiff and concealed, not because it was forbidden but because I didn't know what to do with it. There is such simplicity in the thoughts that come to me that evening, such power, and such relief: Transform all you have learnt. Create something new. Defy expectations.

Nothing can douse this joy. Not even a glimpse of Sasha by the refreshment table beside a pretty woman in a sequined smock and long black gloves. He is leaning toward her, whispering something in her ear. A moment later when I look at them again, they are both laughing. He raising a shot of vodka in the air, she tossing back her long curly hair.

"What were you two laughing about?" I ask Sasha later, on our way home.

"Who do you mean?"

"Thin," I say. "Foxy-looking. Long black gloves."

"Oh, her," Sasha says. "Malevitch, of course!"

"And that was so funny?"

"I found a title for his square—*Black Negroes in a Dark Cave*. Katya thought it was absolutely brilliant!"

10.

A POSTCARD FROM Vaslav arrives from Spain in the spring of 1917, delayed by a month: "I'm very well, as are Kyra and Romola. Mamusia, how are you? I'm creating a new ballet, Bronia. How is Sasha and little Irina? Loving you all. Vaslav." On the front there is a picture of a wooded hill and a palatial house with white columns.

How I loathe these postcards. So oddly formal, slipping like sand through my fingers. Each almost identical to the last, though this one at least mentions a new ballet. The censors might be happy, but I'm left with nothing except a few platitudes.

Mamusia has become an expert in scanning newspapers for any mention of Vaslav. Her eyes slide over the dispatches from the front, retreats, advances, lists of the fallen, to pluck out the tiniest bits of his news. News she can then dissect, question, enlarge or diminish:

Nijinsky has been accused of spying.
Nijinsky has been interned in Vienna as an enemy alien.
Nijinsky has not been interned, merely investigated then cleared of all suspicion.
Nijinsky is dancing in Vienna. In Budapest. In Paris.
Nijinsky is back with Ballets Russes.
Nijinsky is dancing in America.

"America," Mamusia says, is both good and bad. Good, for he is safe there. Bad, for he will soon be sailing back. Crossing the ocean in these terrible times is dangerous. Germans have submarines, torpedoes. Diaghilev is quite right to hate the water.

"Nijinsky always lands on his feet," Sasha says.

"What do you mean?"

Sasha is lifting the quilt, adjusting the pillow. I'm still undressing when I hear the bed squeak under his weight. There is a framed photograph over the bed, of the three of us as Petrushka, the Ballerina Doll and the Moor. *Petrushka* is Irina's favourite bedtime story. I've changed it a bit for her. There is no evil magician. The puppets come to life and have marvellous adventures. The Ballerina Doll creates her own dances.

The Moor becomes a champion tennis player and wins a gold medal. Petrushka dances for the King of Spain and is given a magic ring that can make him invisible.

Sasha is lying with his back toward me, his arm wrapped around his head. I switch off the light and get into bed.

His answer is a muffled, distorted murmur. I cannot make any of the words.

"Say what you mean, Sasha."

This is what he means. The whole ugly truth of it. The injustice. Vaslav, for whom we left Ballets Russes, is dancing for Diaghilev again. Vaslav, who never cares what his actions do to others. Vaslav, who thinks himself above everyone else. Vaslav is back with Ballets Russes and we are still with the Kiev Opera. Vaslav is dancing in America or Spain or wherever the hell he is, while we are stuck in Kiev.

There it is, all of it. Out in the open.

"Satisfied?"

This is not yet a quarrel, though it will become one. It will take us into dangerous ground. My jealousy against his, curling our fists into claws. Memories hurled like weapons. "Sasha is not an artist." Vaslav's voice rings in my ears. "All he cares about is applause. He will try to drag you down to his level."

Doors slam. I lie in an empty bed, sobbing.

"Don't marry a dancer," Mamusia warned me. She should've warned me not to marry a man who searches for himself in the eyes of others.

"Is the new ballet for Diaghilev," I ask Vaslav in my letters, "anything like *Sacre*? Or more like *Jeux*, with its clean lines and intricate combinations? Or is it entirely different still? Is it finished? Have you danced it in America already? How was it received?"

I send my letters to Budapest, care of Romola's mother, asking her to forward them if possible or to keep them until Vaslav comes home. I remind my brother not to worry about Russian censors. He can write freely. There is no imperial Russia anymore. At the end of February, in Petrograd, the revolution began. The tsar abdicated; we have the Provisional Government.

"I think it wonderful news," I write. "I'm not alone."

I imagine my letters piling up on his desk in the Budapest house, arranged by date. I picture Vaslav opening them one by one, smiling as he reads. A one-sided conversation, perhaps, but not less important.

The mood in Kiev is buoyant, hopeful. When a giant tree falls, smaller trees can bask in the sunlight. There are many unexplored roads. There are new directions to try out. In politics. In art.

Have you heard that the Bolsheviks have made their headquarters in Kschessinska's mansion? Turned her bedroom into a newsroom? Apparently Mathilda's giant bathtub is filled with cigarette butts, and walls of her salon have been smashed in search for her "German gold." She went to the Provisional Government, demanding to have her house back, but they just sent her over to the Soviets, who first didn't recognize her and then refused to talk to her at all. Kschessinska, being Kschessinska, decided right there that the Provisional Government will fall and the Bolsheviks will triumph. Russia's future, apparently, can be predicted by the fate of Mathilda's garish mansion!

I get letters from Maroussia from time to time. She is still at the Mariinsky, where all imperial portraits are gone, all double-headed eagles are covered with red cloth and the ushers no longer wear tailcoats. The new State Administration has replaced the old curtain (because of the imperial eagles) with the one from Fokine's Orpheus and Eurydice. It is light and white and "Greek," which—everyone agrees—is sufficiently revolutionary and new.

The theatre is freezing. They only have enough wood and coal to heat some rooms—the rehearsal rooms are a priority—so the audience sits wrapped in winter coats and hats. Former political prisoners sit in the imperial box, and each performance starts with "A Requiem for the Fallen Heroes of the Revolution." Then they sing the "Marseillaise" and only after that the performance begins.

Do you know what else Maroussia wrote? That only now she understands what you truly wanted her to dance in Sacre. *She called you a "true revolutionary" and asked me to tell you that she despises herself for being so scared then, in Paris.*

Our Kiev contract ends in a month. By the end of May, Sasha will be back in the army. The last months have not been easy. I cannot write more about it, but I think it will be good for us to be apart for a while. I know it sounds cruel of me, but Sasha will be dancing for the troops, not fighting. When he leaves, I'll take Mamusia and Irina and go to Moscow. My Kiev friend Aleksandra Exter has connections with the theatres there and the Bolshoi always needs dancers.

11.

"REUNION WITH SASHA," I call it in my diary, seven months later.

Moscow is in the Bolsheviks' hands. Posters on the walls scream: "All power to the Soviets. Peace, bread and land." The facade of the Bolshoi is swathed in red flags.

That January evening there is a knock at the door. Mamusia jumps up in alarm. Rumours make her wake up at night. Russia is burning. Drunk, marauding soldiers shoot before they think, set houses on fire. At times I find her standing by the window, peering out into the street as if she were awaiting someone. For months we have not been able to send any parcels to St. Petersburg. "Do you think they have enough food at the sanatorium?" she mutters. "Is Stassik's room warm enough?" When she sobs, when she asks me if the whole world is going mad, I put my arm around her and hold her as tightly as I can.

I walk to the door and look through the peephole. "It's Sasha," I say; quietly, for Irina is already asleep.

He is bundled up in a grey coat; his hat is off so that I would recognize him in the dim glow of a lighbulb no one has yet stolen, would know that he is not a stranger waiting for me to open the door a crack to force his way in.

"Come in," I tell him, and step back. Our conversations before he left had been so strained that I'm not sure what else to say.

He picks up his bag and walks in. The smell he brings with him is of soot and dry sweat and rancid grease. Behind me Mamusia mutters that she will heat up water for a bath. Now that she knows it is Sasha, she is terrified of what he could have dragged from the road: lice, fleas, bedbugs.

Sasha takes off his clothes, which will have to be boiled and ironed. Wraps himself in his old dressing gown, which Mamusia has dug out from somewhere, although I don't remember packing it in Kiev. He extracts a coil of thick sausage from his rucksack, a brown paper bag with *sukhariki* and a bottle of vodka. The sausage smells of juniper berries and garlic and I feel a pang of hunger, strong enough to make my head spin. Our daily rations allow us to buy a three-inch slice of bread per person. Bread that is baked hastily, from unsifted flour, with splinters of wood added for volume. I teach movement at three Moscow theatres; I have private students and take any dancing I can get at the Bolshoi. Since money loses its value from day to day, I ask to be paid in flour or potatoes or anything that can be exchanged for food. Nails. Cigarettes. Vodka.

Irina's gums bleed. She doesn't remember the taste of butter.

When his bath is ready and Sasha closes the bathroom door, I pick up Mamusia's cards, shuffle them three times and begin laying them out. The faces on the cards stare at me: jacks, kings, queens. Strange, fishy eyes, black and red. I move them around absent-mindedly, stack them in transient combinations. My hands tremble.

The bathroom doors creak open. "Let's not quarrel anymore, Bronia," Sasha says. He has shaven, his hair is moist from the bath and smells of naphtha, whose disinfecting powers Mamusia trusts. There is seriousness in his eyes, and determination.

I put the cards back into their packet, shabby and torn at the corners. I'm shivering. This apartment is always cold. There is never enough coal or firewood. Mamusia has made draft dodgers from old stockings and placed them along the windowsills and at the threshold, but it is like trying to stop a flood with a few sandbags.

I point at the chair across from me. "Sit down," I say.

The chair wobbles when Sasha sits. His voice is soft, barely audible. His hand wanders to his throat. I notice that he has not trimmed his fingernails yet. Some of them are broken; some have been chewed; but others are long and yellowed with nicotine.

"Have you deserted?" I ask.

He shakes his head. He was released. The Bolsheviks have pulled Russia out of the war. There is still no formal treaty, but a ceasefire has been already announced.

Good news?

Maybe. For it's civil war now. On his way home Sasha rode on the roof of a train. Fires are burning in every town, every village. He has seen bodies, torn by dogs or wolves or rotting in ditches. Russians against Russians. Bolsheviks against Mensheviks. Whites against Reds. Chaos, mostly chaos. Drunk soldiers topple monuments, shoot at the imperial eagles. They loot. They rape. They kill.

Mamusia brings us a plate of sausage sandwiches decorated with slices of pickled cucumbers. Delicious. We haven't eaten real sausages in weeks. The ones we can get on our ration cards are mostly ground gristle and sinews, filled out with buckwheat or millet. She has also made nettle tea, sweetened with blueberry syrup she has managed to get from somewhere, but she refuses to sit with us. "You two need to be alone," she says.

I stir the tea with a spoon, gently, trying not to clink the sides of the glass. The warmth of steaming water rises toward my lips.

"Was I right?" I ask. "Did you have an affair when we were in Kiev?"

Yes, Sasha admits, and not just one but two, though the second lasted only three days. This is not an excuse. This is the truth. He won't make excuses anymore. He won't lie. This is what he promised himself on the road, terrified that he might not find us alive. He asks to be forgiven. I don't have to answer right now. It's best if I take my time.

I, too, have a confession. When Sasha was away, Vaslav tried to get us out of Russia. He sent me a contract to dance in Spain and I managed to get exit passports for Irina, Mamusia and me, and the Spanish visas. We stayed only because the French transit visas proved impossible. In spite of all my efforts, the consul wouldn't even see me.

Sasha listens to my account with a glint of fear in his eyes. A drop of water detaches itself from his wet hair and rolls down his temple, toward his neck.

"How is Irina?" he asks.

"Growing fast. Mamusia is always letting down the hem of her skirts."

"Does she ask about me?"

"Every day."

"I've brought this for her," Sasha says. "For the birthday I missed. Her fifth."

He opens a paper parcel I haven't noticed. There is a doll inside. An expensive porcelain doll dressed in lace and velvet, with long eyelashes.

"I bought it," Sasha says quickly, before I manage to ask. "For two rubles. No one wanted it. It looked too imperial."

I take the doll in my hands. I never liked dolls as a child, but Irina is not like me. She doesn't have two brothers to play with. Her friends are imaginary, endowed with strange lives she invents for them. A few days ago Olena, her rag doll, "jumped" into a slop bucket and had to be washed and dried beside the kitchen stove. The dip and the subsequent wash dissolved her smile and her rosy cheeks. Now Olena's whole face is reddish, as if the doll had a fever, which lends itself to an elaborate play of doctor's visits, temperature taking, a "painful injection" until Olena gets better and is allowed to jump again.

The doll, I tell Sasha, imperial or not, is a perfect gift for our daughter.

"Let me see her now—please."

We go to her together. Irina is covered with my fur coat on top of the eiderdown. Her face is smooth with sleep, her hands sprawled above her head. Sasha places the doll beside her.

I imagine the morning joy. The jumps, the excitement. "Papa is here . . . Papa is here . . ."

That night Sasha wakes up screaming. He won't tell me why. He sits with his face buried in his hands, trembling, even after I cover him with a second blanket. He gasps for breath as if the air around us were poison.

His fear melts my misgivings, my own uncertainty. "I don't want us to be like we used to be," I say.

"We will start again, Bronia," he whispers. "From the very beginning."

We have been shaken, but we have survived, haven't we?

My son, my beloved Levushka, was conceived on a night soon after. Not because Sasha and I clung to each other in fear but because we both believed new beginnings were possible.

12.

WE DON'T SAY we are leaving Moscow. We are *escaping*.

Not to Petrograd, against which Maroussia warns us in one of the few letters that sometimes arrive courtesy of friends grateful for a place to sleep before they continue on their way. South, east, anywhere that borders are still porous, that ships leave ports.

> *"No one has petrol anymore, so there are few cars in the streets. We walk to the theatre and back in groups, for it is dangerous to walk alone. I've been robbed twice. The first time I lost my purse. The second time the thieves took my coat, gloves and boots."*

We are going back to Kiev.

It is August of 1918. Sasha has a new contract with the opera house. Not as good as the first. One of the dancers, Pavel Gorkin, has been appointed interim ballet master for the season, so Sasha can only be one of the principals. But this is not much of a setback. Pavel has always been more of a friend than a colleague. His wife, Nina, is an accomplished opera singer whom we both remember fondly. Besides, Sasha reminds me, his hand rubbing my still-flat stomach, Kiev is just a stopover. As soon as the war ends, we will be back with Ballets Russes.

This time in Kiev I won't be dancing. I'm three months pregnant. I've already fainted in the street three times. My gums are bleeding. My nails are covered with white patches. And I've lost a tooth. From lack of calcium, Mamusia says.

I don't mind. I will teach movement and dance just as I did in Moscow. Since I have acquired a reputation for finding choreographic solutions for actors onstage, a few theatre directors have already offered me contracts. The Young Theatre. Yiddish Kultur-Lige.

Going from Moscow to Kiev is like going abroad.

Russia is still inflamed. The Bolsheviks may be taking over more and more cities, but Mensheviks, anarchists, monarchists and other factions have not given up. The White Army is not defeated, either. The tsar, we hear, has been killed. Not just the tsar. The whole imperial family. And other Romanovs, too. Do we believe it? We believe it is possible.

Kiev is ruled by a Cossack leader, Hetman Skoropadsky. There is no revolution in Kiev; theatres are filled every night and there is plenty of food. To go there we need internal passports and permission to buy tickets. I'm glad to let my husband do it. Sasha is filled with energy. His every step bounces; his every gesture emanates strength.

The train ride is long but quite comfortable, for Sasha has managed to get us a compartment to ourselves. The windows are sticky with grime; the seats are threadbare; but I can lie down, stretch my swollen legs. Irina doesn't want to hear about Petrushka anymore, so I come up with a story about the mermaid who swims all the way to Australia, where she builds a palace out of starfish and shells. "Why are you always making them travel so far away, Bronia?" Mamusia complains jokingly.

"Do you like my story?" I ask Irina.

"Yes, yes, yes," she says, and bites her lower lip. In the past weeks she has been clinging to me. Sometimes she speaks in baby language or sucks her thumb. We haven't told her of the new baby yet, but she must have guessed something. Will she be very jealous? I wonder.

On our way to Kiev we are searched five times. The soldiers who demand to see what we have in our suitcases all have the same urgency in their voices, same stubble on their cheeks, same fingers yellowed from nicotine. It's hard to tell who they are, what authority they have, if any. It's not wise to ask.

"My wife's dancing notes," Sasha says when they, without fail, pounce on my choreographic notebooks. Demanding explanations for my drawings.

"We are dancers. This is how we write down the steps we have to learn."

It is at such moments that I most admire my husband. His answers are simple enough to be understood without raising suspicions or making him sound condescending. He interspaces his answers with subtle hints that he, too, has been in the army, understands the hardships of duty. His gifts of vodka and cigarettes are timely. He never offers too much or too little.

"What dance?"

"You know the *hopak*? These circles show the woman's steps . . . how she makes a circle around the man. Like that . . ."

How graceful Sasha is, how agile. Moving as he hums the melody these soldiers know well.

"Why don't you have such notes, then?"

"Men don't need them. We have better memory."

This, too, is an art. To dissolve suspicions, turn them into such laughter that bellies shake, eyes moisten. To make the soldiers leave, while we sigh with relief, wipe sweat off our foreheads and listen how, in the compartment next door, questions are barked, answers offered, hushed, timid, half hopeful, half apologetic—unable to hide fear.

I still wonder how much Irina understood from what was happening around us then. When I ask her now, all she offers are fragments of sensations. The rattling of train wheels, the smell of soot, the incredibly wonderful taste of a hard-boiled egg her grandmother gave her to eat. Did we manage so well to distract her? Or was her serenity the protection nature metes out to the very young?

Our new Kiev apartment is on Fondukleievska Street, a few blocks away from Aleksandra's studio. Not as big as the one we used to have but good enough. The building itself is a former palace, now abandoned, and on our way up I take a quick look at a row of spacious, well-lit rooms on the first floor that would make perfect dancing studios. Our apartment was once the servants' quarters, judging by the cheap pine frames and whitewashed walls. The kitchen is down the hall, next to it a cold-water bathroom with a copper sink and tub.

The chandelier in what will be our living room stands out. It is cast in thick wrought iron, the glass a mixture of blues, greens, yellows and dusty pink. Someone must have brought it here, salvaged or looted from downstairs. It reminds me of Bakst's designs.

I take a few steps. The floorboards squeak.

Mamusia sniffs at the air and runs her finger over the window frame, declaring the place filthy. Irina runs from one window to another to find out what she can see. "A tree," she announces, "with broken branches . . . a sandbox without sand . . . a dog peeing at the wall."

"It's so sunny," I say when Pavel, who came to fetch us from the station—with his wife, Nina, and a friend to help us carry the suitcases—asks if I like it.

We place our belongings roughly where they might go. On a makeshift table made of crates, Mamusia has put our welcoming present: a plate of cold cuts, pickles and slices of buttered bread. After Moscow days this is a feast. Sasha rummages in his knapsack and produces a bottle of vodka he has managed to save from the patrolling soldiers. He pours it generously into six glasses Nina has brought.

"To new beginnings!"

My mouth filled with food, I take a tiny sip and put the glass back. I'm queasy, and suddenly very tired. The twitch of my right eyelid announces the onset of a headache. If I don't lie down in a darkened room soon, I won't be able to stand.

Kiev is a small place. The friend who came to help with the luggage, tall, clean-shaven, his dark hair cropped almost to the skin, is Benedikt Livshits, a lawyer turned poet and a close friend of Aleksandra. "Just got out of the army," he says to explain his military looks and the fact that we are only now getting to know him. Aleksandra, who is away for a few days, has sent a basket with jams, a string of dried mushrooms, an invitation for Irina to join a children's art workshop at her studio and a thick envelope addressed to me.

The room is filled with easy laughter. Benedikt is recounting his Moscow walks with Mayakovsky. Two poets in yellow jackets, spoons in their buttonholes. "This is my first claim to everlasting fame. The second is making Marinetti throw a glass of water at me at a reading."

Irina giggles. "Marinated Marinetti," she says, and Benedikt lifts her into the air, declares her a brilliant futurist poetess and asks if he can quote her.

My daughter nods with utter seriousness.

"I have to lie down." I excuse myself, taking Aleksandra's envelope with me, waving Mamusia away when she casts me a worried look.

There are beds in the new apartment but no bedding yet. Just straw mattresses— fresh, we have been assured, with no bugs. I spread a blanket on the bed, place a pillow under my head and another under my feet.

In the living room the talk is of what has changed in our absence. At the Opera there are committees now, on programming and on dancers' rights. "Reactionary ideas don't die on their own." Pavel's voice is stern. "Art should be for the people, not for the chosen few."

Benedikt is advocating the merits of some new café on the Kreshchatik to Sasha. "You mean real coffee?" Sasha asks. "With real cream?"

In the envelope there is a small painting of Fondukleievska Street peopled with shadowy shapes, each a reflection of the other. It is signed "From Aleksandra, with hope."

I put the painting by the bed.

In the living room Irina asks, "Where has Mama gone? I want to see her."

"Mama is in the other room. She needs to rest, darling."

"Why?"

"Because she is tired."

"Why?"

And then I hear Nina, Pavel's wife, singing an aria from *Faust* about Margarita's hopeful and misguided love. And my daughter's excited request when Nina finishes: "Again! Again!"

The dream surprises me with its vividness. I'm alone in our St. Petersburg apartment, sitting on the blue sofa with a notebook on my lap, its pages covered with interlocking circles, when there is a loud knock on the door.

I know it is Feodor even before I open the door. And there he is, standing at the threshold, smiling, dressed in a white suit, a fedora in hand, just like I remember him from Monte Carlo.

I step back to let him in.

"What are you doing, Bronia?" Feodor asks, putting his arm around me, his lips touching my right temple. Cigar smoke hovers around him, and the briny whiff of the ocean.

I hand him my notebook and he examines it, turning the pages one by one, as if the next one might offer something he has not yet seen. "I don't understand any of it," he finally confesses with a mischievous smile, dropping the notebook. "I'm just a simple peasant."

I laugh. "No, you are not. You understand everything."

"Dance for me, Bronia," he says.

"The Chosen Maiden?"

"Whatever you wish."

I step to the centre of the room and raise my hands, but the composition that follows is not Vaslav's. This is my own dance, still rough and unfinished, flawed, too, but already irresistible. Even its very imperfections intrigue me.

Feodor watches me with utter concentration. "You haven't forgotten anything," he says when I finish, and then asks me to repeat the bit at the very beginning. There is something in it he would like to see again, the hints of tenderness, rendered so beautifully. "Is this what you intended, Bronia?" he asks.

13.

WHEN I THINK OF KIEV, I think of gratitude.

Aleksandra's studio is now an art school. Aprons splattered with paints hang on wooden pegs; half-finished canvasses by her students are stacked in the corner. On the floor lie boxes of charcoal sticks, cans and tubes of paint, brushes soaking in jars.

The walls are covered with elaborate collages of paintings and photographs. I recognize not just Picasso and Braque but also the Russian avant-garde: Rodchenko, Malevitch, Goncharova. Across the photograph of a stage slashed with streams of floodlights someone scribbled "Beauty is vivid rhythms."

This is where we gather every week. We, Kiev's young artists, the innovators, poets, actors, dancers, painters. We talk, we give lectures. On Russian futurism, on cubism, on the choreography of Nijinsky.

This evening Aleksandra will tell us about the week she spent in the Ukrainian village of Verbivka.

I have come alone. Sasha is at a rehearsal and promised to join me later. Our days run along different paths. He is at the opera house from morning to evening, I teach movement and choreograph stage sequences all over Kiev. Not only at the established theatres like the City Theatre but also the new ones that form and fold all the time.

"Come here, Bronia. Sit with us!"

Les Kurbas—the director of the Young Theatre—has saved me a seat, which I take with gratitude. Benedikt is sitting next to him. Both are dressed up in black tails, with red bow ties and identical black hunting boots.

"Twins?" I ask, leaning back on my seat to relieve the pressure on my growing belly.

"How about reflections?" Benedikt says, and draws an imaginary bow. Les mirrors it so flawlessly that they must have practised it for quite a while.

"Silence, please!"

This is Joseph, Aleksandra's valet, in his yellow waistcoat striped with black, announcing the beginning of the evening. Joseph—who, it is said, can assess an aspiring painter just by looking at his hands—has arranged empty easels in a circle and is standing at attention.

Aleksandra gives him a sign and he fetches the first object she wants to show us. A pillowcase embroidered with a circle of red and blue flowers, framed by green leaves. It is pinned to a corkboard Joseph carefully places on one of the easels.

Verbivka, Aleksandra tells us, is not just a village in the Poltava region but an experiment. Artisans and artists work side by side.

As she talks, Joseph fills up the easels with more pictures. One of them is a collage of petals.

This is peasant art, Aleksandra continues, ancient and traditional. It offers no scenes of village life. Yes, it refers, in a symbolic way, to the elements of nature: water, air, earth, just by using a few shapes: ovals, dots, circles. And primary colours. Pure and intense. This is minimalism—basic forms, repeated in various combinations.

Teaching and learning—the thrill of it, I think, elated. There is nowhere else I want to be but here.

The memory of this evening blends with others like it, filled with conversations I can still hear. In them the word *revolution* still carries the promise of profound transformations. Not just of Russia, we believe, but the entire world.

This is the time of boldness, of manifestoes that cannot wait.

Our beloved question is: What if?

What if we use sets not to decorate the stage but to construct it? Create an organic connection between actors and objects at rest; use light beams to join them together?

What if we stage giant spectacles in the streets? Dress up whole buildings? Move crowds in giant formations?

What if we stage Nijinsky's *Faun* with the Faun and Nymphs perched on a wooden pyramid?

What if we take dancers out of the theatre, into parks, meadows, among fallen trees? Film them dancing and then project these moving images onstage while other dancers interact with their shadows?

What if dancers were wrapped in changing lights, their naked bodies the ultimate costume that reveals the working of each muscle?

What if we changed the established order? What if we demand that the music be written after choreography, not before? Refuse to ram movement into ill-fitting music?

What if we make art into a cosmic language, an agent of spiritual transformation?

What if—in art—we *construct* life, not imitate it?

And the war? Whites? Reds? Ukrainians? Germans? Poles? Offensives? Retreats? Victory parades?

What would *you* do—the running joke goes—if you were playing ball and you learnt that the world would end in half an hour?

We would continue to play ball.

One evening at the beginning of October Sasha arrives home from the Opera fuming. Pavel, the interim ballet master, has corrected him in public. Told him not to mark the moves at the rehearsal. "You, Kotchetovsky, lack commitment," he said. In front of the *corps*! As if he were addressing a peasant!

What Sasha minds the most is the note of superiority in Pavel's voice. "Unearned," he adds, punching the palm of his hand with a fist.

Sasha has turned thirty. I think he has grown harder and stronger, but he complains that his muscles take longer to warm up. At the Opera they are staging a selection of dances from *Swan Lake, The Sleeping Princess* and *Little Hunchback Horse*. Not Pavel's choice but that of the programming committee—a decision Sasha approves. Everything around is changing, he insists when I roll my eyes. Is it so surprising that people want the reassurance of tradition?

"Give it to me," I say, extending my hands for his jacket. Mamusia has washed it only the day before, but the lapels are already smeared with face paint. I take out a handkerchief and rub at the edges. I stop myself from asking why Sasha cannot be more careful. "That is how Pavel is," I say, instead.

Sasha's voice deepens, breaking into a quaver. "I can't stand him."

"Nina complains, too," I say. A few days prior Pavel chastised her for being "too preoccupied with the shell of private life." All she did was to ask him to take the dirty plates to the kitchen after dinner. "Where did he even hear such words, Bronia?" she asked.

Sasha, his shirt sleeves rolled up, circles the room like a caged tiger. He stops at the window and looks out, toward the darkened yard where we have a woodshed. Locked with a giant padlock, the door reinforced with steel rods.

There have been no more letters from Maroussia, but those fleeing south from the revolution tell us that in Petrograd bread rations have been reduced to two slices per day. A pound of tea costs twelve hundred rubles, so people brew dried slices of carrots and beets. Everyone is terrified of the coming winter. There is no coal, no firewood. Executions are plentiful, though, we hear. Of profiteers, black marketers and counter-revolutionaries. The last category includes anyone who still has anything worth taking.

"Pavel is posturing, like a child," I tell Sasha. "Trying to find out how far he can go. Just stand firm."

I don't want to talk about Pavel. I want to talk about the upcoming production of *Oedipus Rex*, for which I've choreographed the movements of the chorus. The actors at the Young Theatre have been clay in my hands. I've taught them to move in perfect harmony, freeze in mid-step, appear to float as they emerge from shadows.

"Is this why you are never home?" Sasha asks.

I let it pass.

Sasha has stopped circling the room and picks up a newspaper. Filled with rumours and lies, he maintains, which doesn't stop him from poring over them with grim determination.

In the kitchen Irina is moaning. "Don't pull so hard, Grandma. It hurts."

"It has to hurt if you want to be beautiful," Mamusia answers with a laugh.

"No, it doesn't," Irina protests. Ever since she began her art classes in Aleksandra's studio, her voice rings with newly acquired conviction. "Green is no longer my favourite colour," she announced the other day. "Now it is blue."

I stand up and go to the kitchen. Irina is sitting on a stool, her long thick hair—so unlike mine—loose over her shoulders. Mamusia separates sections of it with her fingers and combs them one by one. There is an ease and then a tug, until all the knots are out, until Irina's hair is smooth and divided into three equal parts. I sit at the table, prop my chin on folded hands and watch as the plait grows, tight, perfectly even. Mamusia weaves in a blue ribbon, and when she is finished, she ties the endings into a perfect bow.

Irina is patient. She does not fidget or squirm. From time to time she touches the braid with her fingers, feels its thickness.

"Do you like it, Mama?" she asks.

"Your hair?"

"My blue ribbon!"

"It's very pretty," I tell her, but she frowns. Colours, my daughter tells me, are not pretty. They may be strong or weak, loud or quiet. This is what Aleksandra Aleksandrovna says.

I raise my hands in total surrender. Blue, Irina tells me, is strong but quiet. This is why she likes it.

"There you go. Finished," Mamusia says, tightening the ribbon. "You can run along now."

Irina is off to her room, skipping as she goes, and Mamusia turns toward me. "Tired? Want to lie down?"

I shake my head. "Do you want help with dinner?"

"Just talk to me."

Perched on the kitchen stool, I watch as she stirs the steaming pots. She is making sorrel soup, *bitki* in mushroom sauce, cabbage rolls with kasha. When she decides a task is simple enough for me not to mess it up, she lets me do it. Chop onions, mushrooms; peel potatoes and drop them into a pot of water. Just so, in the right order, no shortcuts, no exceptions.

Irina, Mamusia tells me, needs to have her dresses altered again: hems have to be let down. Anyuta, our hired girl, still doesn't sweep under beds. But she is clean, and good with Irina.

At the market everything is more and more expensive. Not because of shortages but because princes, grand dukes and bankers are all there, on the run from the revolution. Kiev is drowning in money. Not a single hotel room is empty. Apartments are impossible to find. Families band together to rent rooms out, making a fortune. New nightclubs open overnight. Do I know how much they charge for filleted sturgeon or Abrau champagne?

Mamusia is worried. Those who have escaped the revolution do not believe in Skoropadsky. The *hetman* will fall, they say, as soon as the German army that supports him withdraws. Ukrainian rebels are approaching fast. The name they repeat most often now is Commander Petlyura. The Bolsheviks, with their Red Army, are right behind him. Behind the Bolsheviks, the Whites.

Migratory birds, I think, all agitation, the fluttering of wings. Their Russia is not my Russia. Those who have everything don't want anything to change.

"Old Chinese curse, Bronia." Mamusia's voice interrupts my thoughts. "May you live in interesting times."

My mother's remedies are simple and straightforward.

The kitchen smells of vinegar, brine and boiled fruit. Our pantry shelves are filled with boxes, sacks, tins and jars. We have candles, matches. We have salt, flour, sugar, *sukhariki*, dried fruit. Jars with preserves are her troops, her defence. Meat fried first then covered with a layer of hot lard to preserve it. Pickled cabbage, mushrooms, cucumbers, carrots, flat beans, chunks of pumpkin. Jams, compotes, syrups. Flavoured vodkas: plum, walnut, quince.

"We have to do what we can, Bronia. Make up for what has been lost. Preserve what we have in abundance. Brace ourselves for the time of want."

Irina's face has already rounded out; the shine has returned to her hair; but I am still Mamusia's unfinished project. "Eat, Bronia, eat. Another ladle of soup. Another egg. More sauerkraut sprinkled with ground anise. More hot milk with honey." She wants me to make up for what I lost in Moscow, gather strength for what lies ahead.

Dr. Epstein, our Kiev doctor, concurs. "If you don't give the child what it needs," he has said, "it will take it from your flesh and your bones."

14.

I WRITE INCESSANTLY. On the kitchen table as I eat breakfast, in a café where I stop for a glass of tea, at rehearsals when my actor students practise the moves I have designed. I write in bed at night, with Sasha snoring beside me.

There is still little coherence to these notes. But among the reminders, prompts for discussions, thoughts to reflect upon, ideas are taking shape. The notebook has a title already—*My School of Movement*:

> *I want my dancers to be well rounded, open to possibilities. Artists, not performers.*
>
> *Like in the Imperial School, afternoons will be reserved for other subjects. Les will teach acting and drama. Benedikt will get the students to read and write poetry. Aleksandra will teach painting and stage design.*

> *I don't want to reject everything about the Imperial School. My training wasn't useless. It was restricting, but it gave me strength and flexibility. I want to keep what has been best about it, add what has been missing. Turnout, yes, but not only turnout. There are other paths of movement that need to be developed.*
>
> *The former ballroom, with its large windows and even wooden floors is perfect for rehearsals and big enough for performances.*

My notebook fills out with sketches, layouts of the rehearsal rooms, position of mirrors, barres.

> *Les, whom I admire more and more, said: "Theatre should reveal what is not visible. Theatre should create its own reality." It struck me right away that this is precisely what I want for my students. A world in which everything I teach them will open their eyes to the invisible.*

There had been no Ballets Russes school, no crèche for new artists. Vaslav had to work with reluctant dancers who never understood what he was doing.

My students will be ready for the future. Not just for Vaslav's new ballets but also for mine.

"I've never felt more alive. I wake up singing," I tell Aleksandra in her living room, where Joseph has served us tea and meringue cookies. "Do you think I'm mad?"

"You might be," she says, laughing. "Let's go."

"Where?"

"I want to see your school."

"Now?" I ask, but I'm already standing, ready to rush out of the door.

"Wait!" she says as she is ringing for Joseph. "Our coats. You are not in Monte Carlo, Bronia. It's the middle of October!"

On the way I warn her the space I have in mind is a mess, but it is only when I retrieve the key from under the loose floorboard and open the door that I see the extent of the devastation. An old, battered bathtub lies abandoned in the entrance hall, filled with broken bricks, metal rods and half-burnt papers. The former ballroom, dark because of boarded-up windows, is littered with broken furniture. White plaster dust covers the floors.

The sound of gunfire comes from the direction of the cathedral. It could be anything. A few drunk soldiers shooting pigeons or the first signs of the changing power. The Germans—everyone says so—are getting ready to pack and leave. Sealed trains filled with anything that can be moved are leaving the Kiev Station daily, heading toward Berlin. The German barracks are emptying. Once the soldiers are gone Hetman Skoropadsky's Ukraine will be history.

Am I mad?

"Let's call it our 'Kiev rule,'" Aleksandra says. "We can tell each other what we fear only once. Or better, we write it down in a letter. All the ugly, terrible, paralyzing truth of it. But then we don't mention it again. Ever."

I nod. The Kiev rule it is.

I take out a handkerchief, wet it with my spit and wipe clean a patch of the ballroom floor. Underneath the layer of plaster dust, I see intricate squares of light and dark oak.

Yes, clearing it will take a great deal of work, but the floor is not damaged. Most of the windows are still intact. Walls have been ripped open, but they, too, can be repaired, plastered over and painted. Barres and mirrors can be installed at the same time. The two chairs lying in the corner can be the school's first furniture.

This is how my School of Movement begins.

"You are not serious, are you?" Sasha asks.

It is the end of the day and we are in our bedroom, the only time we can be alone. Sasha is sitting on the edge of the bed, stretching his right leg then his left. I am standing by the small desk where I keep my notes and sketches. The desk has a hidden drawer that fascinates Irina so much I let her keep her coloured pencils in it.

"You want to return to Ballets Russes," I argue. "With what? Let's make sure we have something to offer Diaghilev after four years away. I don't want to ask for favours."

"Why not?" Sasha asks, fishing for cigarettes in the pockets of his jacket. The packet of Krems from which he extracts a cigarette, which he then softens with his fingers, is almost empty.

I manage not to cough when the smoke reaches me. My arguments are well thought out, prepared, tested in the discussions I've had with my friends.

If we go back to Diaghilev, I want to arrive with students ready to dance in Vaslav's new ballets. And I don't mean *Faun* or *Sacre*. I mean ballets that come after. The one Vaslav wrote about in the letters that manage to reach us from Vienna, and other works he is planning already. Ballets we can anticipate, prepare for.

"In our own dancing studio," I tell Sasha. "On our own stage."

I spread my drawings and plans on the desk to show him how much I have done already. Aleksandra has helped me make floor plans, promised the use of the carpentry workshop at her art school. Les and Benedikt have submitted a list of topics they would like to discuss in their classes.

"You and I would teach all dance classes," I continue. "Character dancing. Mime. Free movement."

My voice soars. Heat rises to my cheeks. The baby inside me stirs.

Sasha stands up, stubs out his cigarette but doesn't come to the desk. He is beginning to undress, opening his shirt, taking it off, folding it neatly. This is not like him, I think, but take it as a sign that he is listening. The brass buckle of his belt *clanks* when he hangs it on the back of the chair. He bends to remove his pants, one leg then another, folds the trousers along the crease. His socks are held up by black suspenders. Both socks are thinning at the toes and will soon need darning.

It is only when Sasha is in his blue-striped pyjamas—my London gift for him from before the war—that he finally approaches the desk, picks up one of the pages, glances at what I've written and reads it aloud:

"I want the art of dance to live again.

"I want senseless acrobats to become creators again.

"A creator should live only through his creation, not intoxication of the crowd."

I am very proud of these words. I want them copied on big pieces of cardboard and nailed to the school walls.

Sasha puts the paper down. His fingers are tapping the top of the desk. "Let's get out of here, Bronia," he says, his eyes locked on mine. "I've had enough of Russia. Of all this yapping about everything having to change. We should've never left Ballets Russes in the first place."

For a long moment I don't understand what he is saying. As if he were speaking a foreign language in which words may link together in phrases, but they make absolutely no sense.

Sasha repeats his plea. He wants to leave Russia. Pack what we can. Sell the rest. Someone he knows and trusts has offered to come and take a look at what we still have.

This time I do understand every word.

"Leave? Now?" I ask, pointing at my belly, the only argument I have not yet used.

"Now," Sasha says, the cigarette smoke still on his breath. While Kiev is still under German protection. Still free from the Bolsheviks. We will go to Odessa, bribe someone to let us on a ship. Like so many others have done already.

"We'll be in Budapest in a week's time, Bronia. And from there we'll go to Vienna. The baby will be born in a good private clinic. Vaslav will make sure you get the best of care. You can have your school there."

Your school. Sasha pronounces these words as if he were referring to something fanciful. A distraction to be tolerated, maybe even indulged, but a distraction nevertheless.

"We have to get out when we still can."

I stare at my husband. A dull, nauseating ache fills my head.

A sentence I once wrote in my diary comes to me: *I'm truly alive only when I lose myself in what absorbs me.*

"I can't," I say. "Not now."

For the first time in my life I am among artists who think as I do. I don't want to go anywhere. I want to be part of what is happening here. I cannot be anywhere else. I have never belonged anywhere the way I belong here, in Kiev.

These are big words, I acknowledge, solemn, but I know no other.

"So you are serious," Sasha says when I finish.

I am waiting for him to say more, but he doesn't. He walks out of the room and a moment later the water is running next door in the bathroom. He is gargling. Spitting.

Tears force their way into my eyes. I pick up Sasha's ashtray and carry it into the kitchen, where I empty it into the slop bucket and stare as the cigarette stub floats in the brackish water.

From the other end of the apartment I hear Sasha return to the bedroom, close the door. I am waiting for him to come in search of me, but he doesn't.

The kitchen is clean of daytime clutter. The last batch of Mamusia's jars are cooling on the table. One of Irina's art projects—blue triangles glued around a red circle, like petals of a flower—is lying on the table. The baby inside me kicks.

What if Sasha is right? What if it were better for Irina and the baby if we left?

At the kitchen table I argue with myself for a long time. It is not safe to stay, but it is not safe to leave, either. The whole world is at war, not just Russia.

Where else can I do as much as I can do here? Where else am I more needed?

To stop the tumbling thoughts, I stand up and go to the room where Irina and Mamusia sleep. My daughter's cot is by the window. She sleeps curled into a ball.

I kiss her warm cheeks, smooth her hair. I promise myself that tomorrow, before I leave for the theatre, I will praise her flower collage and ask her to another one, just for me.

15.

IN NOVEMBER OF 1918, after three months of rehearsals, the Young Theatre stages *Oedipus Rex.* Sasha and I go to the premiere together. On our way to the theatre the *droshky* passes a charred house, still smouldering. Around it there is a giant circle of trampled snow, dirty with ashes and soot.

Everyone is at the premiere—actors from other theatres, dancers, singers, painters. "One bomb," Sasha whispers in my ear, "and the artistic flower of Kiev will vanish in smoke."

Gallows humour, I think. Our Russian specialty.

Sasha and I have excellent seats, in the third row, but the way to them is awkward, past a bulky man who chooses not to stand up but merely swings his knees sideways to let us pass.

I'm six months gone, and I sink into my seat with gratitude, stretching my legs as far as they will go. Next to me Aleksandra, wrapped in a beautiful black shawl with white flowers woven into it, opens her arms to embrace me. She looks thinner, almost gaunt. She tells me she is painting at a frantic pace, but she cannot show me anything yet. "It's that stage I'm in, when I've lost the clarity of where I'm going," she says. "I have to see what is coming out of all this hard work. On my own."

Nina and Pavel are two seats away. Nina is motioning to Benedikt, who has finally brought his mysterious "new friend," whom we've been hearing about for weeks. She looks girlish, with a thick braid that falls over her right shoulder. I like the way she holds herself, straight but not stiff. I also like her slightly old-fashioned look. As if she stepped out of a Dostoyevsky novel. Sonya, I decide, from *Crime and Punishment.*

For Les Kurbas this is a big night. He *is* the Young Theatre, both a director and an actor. He plays Oedipus himself. For the past three days I have been barred from rehearsals. "I don't want you to scratch my eyes out if I change any of your movements, Bronia," he has told me. "I need you to see it as a whole."

Aleksandra's husband is reaching out from where he sits, to shake Sasha's hand. For a moment I consider asking if Sasha wants to switch so that they can sit next to each other, but I decide against it. "You two are apart too much," Mamusia has warned me.

"Your hair shines, Bronia," Aleksandra says. "How do you do it?"

I point at my belly. We laugh.

The lights dim. Beside me Sasha stirs. I take his hand in mine. Squeeze it gently. He bends toward me, but the curtain raises before he has time to speak.

The set is an arrangement of black and white rectangles. Among them the Greek chorus dances, watching as Oedipus quarrels with a stranger, kills him, marries a queen who bears him children. At each tragic turn of the king's fate the chorus freezes in a posture that resembles an ancient sculpture.

Les was right to keep me away from last rehearsals. For now, even as I recognize the moves I have choreographed, I no longer think of them as mine. They have become part of the ancient myth. How puny the actions of the mortals, they say. How unpredictable their consequences. How we may run away from what scares us but end up precisely where we didn't want to be.

There is a lavish reception after the performance, in the foyer of the theatre. The walls are draped with swaths of white muslin. Dancers stand motionless along them, still in their Greek-chorus chitons. I love the way their bodies intertwine into groupings. One actress, her eyes darkened with kohl, is holding a bouquet of paper carnations like a torch above her head, white flowers on dark green stems. I note how graceful her wrists are, how easy it would be to create a solo for her.

A young man with a pile of paper flyers is making rounds of the room. He looks familiar, but he is not one of Les's actors. Out of the corner of my eye I see him approach Les then Benedikt, but he makes no attempt to hand them any of his flyers.

By the time he approaches me and mutters his "Good evening, Madame Nijinska," I recognize him from the City Theatre, where I still teach. His name is Sergey Lifar and I think him more eager than talented.

"What are they?" I ask, pointing at the flyers in his hand, and he blushes before handing me one. An advertisement, it turns out to be, for a cabaret show. *The Gypsy Tears*.

"Are you in it?" I'm about to ask, when Aleksandra asks for silence. She wants to toast what we have all just witnessed: the convergence of acting, dance and painting. A manifestation of how we, artists of different media, reach similar conclusions.

"This is an evening none of us here will ever forget, Les," Aleksandra says to end. "Oedipus may have blinded himself, but our eyes are wide open. Thank you."

Les accepts these words with a low bow, pointing at his actors who have now left their spots along the wall and stand around him. All so young, so gracefully agile.

We all applaud.

The evening continues, heated, exciting. Benedikt comes up to introduce his "new friend," Tata Skachkova. Told that she reminds me of Dostoyevsky's heroine, she blushes with pleasure. Benedikt looks at her with pride, she at him with amused delight.

Tata, it turns out, has heard of my school from one of her actor friends and wants to be my student. "When will the courses start?" she asks.

"I've been warned against predicting the future." I smile, pointing at my belly. "February, perhaps?"

This is when I catch a glimpse of Sasha, alone by the refreshment table, a shot of vodka in his hands. He empties it quickly and pours himself another.

"Excuse me," I say to Benedikt and Tata.

I walk toward my husband to tell him that I'm ready to go home, but Aleksandra reaches him right before me.

"What did you think of the play, Sasha?" she asks.

He makes a vague gesture with his left hand. Then he places the empty shot glass on the table, carefully, as if it were an important figure in the game of chess.

"I'm just here with my wife," he says, his voice far too loud. "You'll have to ask her."

16.

AROUND US THE CITY IS changing hands to the sounds of rifle rounds, machine guns, cannon fire. By the middle of December Hetman

Skoropadsky has vanished. The Germans dressed him up in their uniform, bandaged his face and spirited him to Berlin. Those of his soldiers who did not escape have hidden their guns, torn off their epaulettes, insignia, badges and burnt their papers. Kiev, for now, belongs to Petlyura and his Ukrainian People's Republic, which has the support of the Poles.

Sasha is being stopped in the streets all the time. A dancer's posture can be easily mistaken for military bearing. He has an identity card declaring him Artist of the Kiev Opera, but this is flimsy protection. As a precaution he trudges through back alleys and snowdrifts. It helps that many fences have been dismantled for firewood.

When I rest my hand on my belly, I feel a tiny protrusion—a heel or an elbow—move inside it. This time there will be no clinic. Dr. Epstein advises against it. At any moment hospitals can be taken over by the wounded. Best to have him come by to check on me; then a midwife must suffice. Best not to think of breech births or umbilical cords around the baby's neck.

When Petlyura's troops entered the city, our hired girl, Anyuta, disappeared. Has she found better employment? we wonder. Been summoned home? Run away with a lover? Joined the new rulers? If so, we might soon see her in some office distributing ration cards or leading a search patrol for what she might have seen us hide.

For, like everyone else, we have hidden what is now dangerous but might soon become useful again. Tsarist rubles and imperial identity papers are pinned under the tabletop. A tin box with German marks is buried inside the bedroom wall behind the wallpaper. One with jewellery and golden coins is hidden under a loose floorboard in the kitchen.

Sasha saw the crowds in the cathedral where Petlyura was greeted, and the parade in St. Sophia's Square. "Infantry, cavalry, artillery guns pulled on carts," he says, counting them off on his fingers. "Mortars, howitzers."

We have all become experts on what can kill us.

Snow has covered the yard, the streets, the traces of the last skirmishes. If the shelling gets heavier, we will descend to the cellars, but for now the kitchen is the safest place. It is at the back of the house, out of the way of stray bullets.

Kiev wisdom, I think of it.

On the kitchen table I draw posters, announcements, lesson plans for the School of Movement. Three levels, I decide, to separate beginners from those who have already had some training and can advance faster. I wonder what I should call the morning class. Techniques of movement?

At the other end of the table Sasha is reading his newspaper. He has given up the thought of leaving. With Skoropadsky gone the chance has been lost, his eyes say. You have prevailed, Bronia.

He drinks more. A few shots of vodka every night before bed. "Best I finish it when I still can." He laughs as he points at the label Imperial on the bottle.

From Petersburg, dethroned ever since the Bolsheviks moved the government to Moscow, Maroussia no longer writes of shortages or street robberies: "At *Swan Lake*, one of the soldiers in the audience shouted at Comrade Karsavina, 'When are you going to sing?' How isolated the old ballet has been from the people!"

The baby inside me is more restless than Irina was. "Such are the times," Dr. Epstein says with a sigh. Matryona Pavlova, the midwife he has recommended, has been here already. We are under orders to always keep a vat of boiled water. We don't want typhus, do we? Or dysentery.

The page in front of me is a list of classes for the first-year students. I hand it to Sasha, who puts his newspaper away.

"No pointe work? No partnering?" he asks, his voice strung with tension. "How can they become professional dancers without it?"

"They won't be professional dancers. They will be artists."

"Of what?"

"Artists who can take what they've learnt into anything they do. New ballets, yes, but also painting, writing, theatre."

My husband sighs. "Why not have a proper dance school, Bronia? What's wrong with it?"

I've taught in Kiev long enough for the word to spread faster than I had anticipated. In the first days of the new year prospective students approach me wherever I go.

"Everyone is talking about it, Bronislava Fominitchna . . . training for new ballets . . . dancers for the Nijinsky company . . . Can this be possible? In Kiev?"

The most enterprising appear at our doorsteps and I invite them in, offer them hot bilberry tea, the only one we can still get.

So many eager faces, sparkling, hopeful. Some are dancers already, looking for different paths. Some are mere hopefuls, tempted by the rumours that I do not limit my enrolment; that I— if this can be true— even prefer those who have not been trained in classical dance.

What can we do right now, before the school opens, they ask in their eagerness, eyes sliding over my belly, urging the baby to hurry up and set me free. Clear the rooms downstairs? Sweep the floors? Chop wood?

Our apartment is filling up with art books and magazines, sheet music, fabric for costumes, folding chairs. Kolya Singayevsky, whom I have just accepted into my beginners' class, has brought green and black volumes of *Brockhouse and Ephron's Encyclopedic Dictionary*. "Take them now, please, Madame Bronia, before my mother runs out of wood and burns them."

"Madame General and her troops," Mamusia says, and laughs.

"If we get hit," Sasha warns, "we'll go up in flames."

This is how I see him in my memory from one of those January days. In his woollen jumper and thick socks, sitting on the kitchen floor, doing his stretches. Legs spread, he rolls forward, working the muscles of his inner thighs, one after another.

"A proper dance school." His voice still resonates in the silence between us. *Proper* is such a quaint word. Old, stiff. As if we were still Imperial School dancers. As if we didn't dance with Vaslav. As if we never saw *Sacre*.

Sasha rolls forward again, to put his torso flat on the floor. For a moment he looks like a marionette that has come undone, legs, arms twisted into straight angles. I'm tempted to bend toward him, massage his neck and shoulders, but something in me warns that my touch is not welcome.

Slowly he raises himself, props his torso on straight arms, flexes his feet. His eyes meet mine.

"Will you teach character dancing, Sasha?" I ask.

"Oh. So you will teach some *proper* dancing after all?"

There is hesitation on his face, but I see that he is tempted, and for a moment I'm hoping that it'll all work out.

17.

OUR KIEV APARTMENT has stoves faced with blue Delft tiles that tell a silent story. A boy sets off to try his luck in the world. He passes fields bustling with workers, windmills, copses of trees. When he comes into a town, he meets a troupe of circus artists—a clown, a ballerina, a juggler and a flame eater. Irina, who makes up her own stories now, tells me that a clown is not really a clown but a tsarevitch in disguise.

"Why did they kill the tsar?" Irina asks.

They is a general concept. *They* is vague. Indecipherable. Not *us*.

"Because they hated to be ruled by a tsar."

"Did we hate being ruled by the tsar, too?"

"Yes. But we didn't want to kill him."

Irina nods as if it all made sense, but I know that these questions will come back. There is a machine gun on Kreshchatik, silent so far, but no one trusts it to stay so and people walk past it in groups, counting on the safety of the herd. No matter how I try, I cannot shield my daughter from what will soon come.

It is a Saturday afternoon at the beginning of January. Minus forty outside, and the baby is due any moment now. This time Mamusia is certain it's a boy. "Your skin is so clear, Bronia," she says. "So smooth."

On the living room sofa, I place my swollen feet on a cushion and prop my notebook on my belly. The School of Movement has thirty-three students enrolled, eleven at each of the three levels.

Our windows are well sealed with putty and taped with wide paper strips to protect them from breaking. Firewood and coal are even more expensive, and the apartment is never warm enough. Irina is dressed in a woollen jumpsuit of multicoloured stripes Mamusia has knitted for her from whatever wool she could get. I'm wearing two sweaters, and my feet are covered with Sasha's sheepskin coat. I think of the street outside, crooked, narrow, steep. Quaint, I thought it in the summer. Hard to reach, I think of it now, even for a sleigh. A few days ago when I looked out of the front window, I saw a bloodied coat in the snow.

The snowbanks are high enough to block doors. The narrow path to the woodshed is strewn with ashes to make it less slippery. Anyuta's disappearance forced us to change the hiding place for our valuables.

Sasha has nailed down the loose floorboard in the apartment. The biscuit tin with tsarist rubles, German marks and jewellery is now buried in the woodshed under the diminishing pile of firewood. The woodshed is also where Sasha hid our old tsarist identity papers and our baptismal certificates, which we'll need if the White Army ever makes it here. The papers are pinned to a rafter, covered with a plank. We have some food there, too, a change of clothes, some candles, matches. Enough to last us for a week if we are ever cut off from the apartment and forced to run away.

Sasha swears no one has seen him do it and I'm hoping he is right. Thieves, we hear, dress up as soldiers on patrol, barge into apartments claiming to search for hidden guns and steal what they can. The victims are forced to sign papers declaring that they have just given their contribution to whoever is in power.

Sasha is getting ready to go out, polishing his shoes, spitting on the leather from time to time before buffing. His best jacket, brushed, is hanging on the chair. He will dance at a private party, for five packets of cigarettes and a pack of nails. Better than what he got a week before: a painting of a tree over a rocky gorge, cut out of its frame and rolled up. He will come home late, smelling of cigarettes, rotgut liquor and fried onions. "Papa's smell," Irina calls it, wrinkling her nose like a rabbit.

My pelvis aches as the baby presses upon it, and I grimace.

"Is the baby kicking again?" Irina asks, pushing my notebook aside to touch my belly. It fascinates her that she, too, was once small enough to fit inside me. "Is it very dark there?" she wants to know. "Can I go back in?"

"You are five years old, darling. You are too big. You wouldn't fit."

Her chin quivers; her lips curve downward. "Let's see what your dolls are up to," I say quickly.

The dolls, I learn, are asleep.

"Even Olena?"

Olena, the rag doll Mamusia has repaired so many times, no longer jumps from curtains, but prefers to have tea with Tatyana, the porcelain doll Sasha gave Irina in Moscow.

Mamusia is in the kitchen, cooking. By now the preserves are almost gone, though peasants are still selling food in the back alleys. Sasha goes with her to negotiate the price. Money sometimes but mostly barter, so the apartment is emptying out. The rosewood night table bought a tough old hen; a bunch of half-frozen carrots; potatoes darkened with decay, which have to be peeled thick for the white flesh to come out. A silver goblet Father won in a lottery when Vaslav was born bought a bag of flour, which has to be sifted for grubs, moths and nails. A wet nurse with whom Mamusia spoke wouldn't even give her a price. "We will talk when the time comes," the woman said.

What will she take? I wonder. One of the few rings I still have? Vaslav's silver candelabra? Or something more mundane but more useful? Firewood? A fur coat?

For the past week we have been eating herring, suddenly plentiful. Fried, or cooked with millet, or made into fish soup. Before it was mostly sauerkraut, in dumplings, in soups, with scraps of meat or just sprinkled with vegetable oil. Beet syrup has replaced sugar. Oatmeal and flaxseeds pounded in a heavy brass mortar have replaced flour. Applesauce substitutes for eggs. Marmalade can be made from beets and apple rinds.

Mamusia insists I get the biggest portions and is not satisfied until I lick the plate clean. "You need to eat for two," she reminds me, pouring an extra spoonful of vegetable oil on my soup plate.

I hear a knock at the front door, Mamusia's voice asking something as she opens it. A moment later she walks into the room, an opened letter in hand, her face an ashen mask.

The Psychotherapy Sanatorium at Novoznayemskaya Dacha informs the family that the patient Stanislav Nijinsky died in November 1917. A doctor's signature certifies the cause of death: "an inflammation of the liver."

"Fourteen months ago," Mamusia whispers, swaying, her hands folded across her chest. "How could I not have felt anything when it happened?"

She is still swaying while I hold her, take her to her room, where together we pray for Stassik's soul. The candle we light for him splutters at first, but then the flame catches. We stare at it in silence until the strands of molten wax begin to float down its sides.

When Mamusia stays in her room, sobbing, I distract Irina from going to her. "Do you remember Uncle Stassik?" I ask, and she assures me she does, but what she remembers are stories. The Cossack dance when he danced with Vaslav, the "Sailor Dance" when the three of us danced together. "Will I have a brother when I grow up?" she asks.

This is what I describe for Vaslav that very night, in a letter care of Romola's mother. The sad news, Mamusia's sobbing, my daughter's words. "Please let us know when this letter finds you," I conclude. "Your latest postcard came from St. Moritz. Are you there on holiday?"

I lick the edge of the envelope and seal it, thinking of the time Vaslav and I believed Stassik's miracle—coming back from the dead—was the greatest, even if he did not remember what he did in Heaven.

My son is born on Monday, January 20, 1919.

Lev Vaslav Stanislav Aleksandrovitch Kotchetovsky.

Levushka.

Have I burdened him too much with these names? Already then?

18.

LEVUSHKA WAS ONE MONTH OLD when, after two weeks of constant fire, the Bolsheviks entered Kiev. We stayed in the kitchen most of that time, sleeping there on folding cots. When the gunshots drew closer, we huddled under the table. This is where I was, holding Levushka, when I heard a thunderclap, followed by a groaning, cracking noise overhead. Plaster fell from the ceiling. From the front room came the sound of shattering glass. The explosion was so loud that I thought *our* house was hit, but it was the one next door.

Three months later Levushka still wails at the slightest noise and won't stop. Nothing calms him out of his frenzy—no amount of carrying, of rocking. Only sheer exhaustion can force him to sleep. We all walk on tiptoes, speak in whispers I find increasingly hard to hear. The ringing in my ears that began after the explosion still hasn't stopped.

This morning the wet nurse has just finished feeding him and Levushka is mercifully quiet. She's the second wet nurse already, bought with the ring Diaghilev gave me as my wedding present. The first one took Mamusia's fur coat and disappeared.

Irina is still asleep. In the bathroom where Sasha and I are getting ready for the day, Sasha is dipping his shaving brush in hot water, lathering up the soap, smearing it on his skin. As he scrapes the razor against his chin, his hand slips.

"To hell with it," he swears, as the thin line of blood thickens.

"Let me . . ."

"No!"

We haven't truly touched each other for such a long time. I miss it, the closeness in the dark, when all is mixed up, skin, hair, breaths. The time when the body hums.

"What's wrong, Sasha?"

Grunting something I cannot understand, he rummages in the drawer. Out comes a folded handkerchief, Irina's crumpled drawing, a box with odd buttons.

I consider words that come to mind, test them for safety. What can we still talk about without acrimony? Not the children, around whom Sasha is tense, impatient. He might finally have the son he always wanted, but he was far better with Irina when she was little.

"Is it Tata?" I finally ask. "Has anything happened at school?"

The School of Movement opened right after the Bolsheviks declared victory. Sasha teaches character dancing to level three students and Tata is the only one in his class without formal training, admitted at Benedikt's request. "Is she slowing everyone down?"

"Tata is fine," Sasha snaps. The piece of gauze he put over the nick on his chin has turned red. But the bleeding has stopped and now he washes quickly, under his arms, the front of his chest, splashing soapy water all over the floor. He won't wipe it up. He never does.

We do not have a hired girl anymore, I could remind him.

I don't. Water on the floor is a trivial matter, not worth talking about. But before I can say anything else, Sasha grabs his shirt and bolts out of the bathroom. A moment later I hear his raised voice in the hall: "No, I don't want a sandwich. I just want to be left alone. Is that so much to ask in this house?"

"Grom z jasnego nieba," Mamusia says, and dismisses the outburst, as Levushka—startled out of his shallow sleep—squirms and frets in her

arms. A flash of lightning out of a blue sky. Unpredictable but mercifully short.

In the school the newly replastered walls of the main rehearsal room are decorated with inscriptions: "The art of dance will live again . . . A creator should live only through his creation, not intoxication of the crowd." On a big blackboard, in Benedikt's meticulous hand, inspirations for his next poetry class:

> *If you like—*
> *I'll be furiously flesh elemental,*
> *or—changing to tones that the sunset arouses—*
> *if you like—*
> *I'll be extraordinary gentle,*
> *not a man, but—a cloud in trousers!*

The students are all bone-thin, almost gaunt. For my technique class the girls dress in hand-knitted tights and tunics, managing a flash of makeshift elegance. Gloves with fingers cut off. Leg warmers made of old scarves. A shawl turned into a wraparound skirt. The boys have all narrowed their trousers by tying them around the ankles. I use their first names, without patronymics. Pati, Anya, Kolya. They call me "Bronislava Fominitchna" or "Madame Nijinska" or simply "Madame."

Classes last from mornings till late afternoons, always ending with free discussions. All teachers take turns in leading them. The topics differ, but the overall theme is art: What does it mean to be an artist in Russia? Can art destroy the old habits of thought, sweep away the outdated, the bygone, the redundant? And if it can, where should it take us?

My students are still fighting embarrassment. They are not used to talking in front of others, but more and more they lose their shyness, and the room shimmers with excitement.

The discussions do not end when it is time to go home. At the end of the day, when I linger on the stairs leading to our apartment, I hear the din of their voices, moving from the hall into the street.

These days I circle around Sasha, watchful and unsure. He has added a relentless series of press-ups to his morning routine. There is a new look on his face; it starts with a frown and ends with staring at his folded hands. As my eyes tarry over the warn-off varnish of the stairs, the cracks in the wood, the chinks in the banister, I recall our walk to the harbour in Monte Carlo, the tears of joy when he saw me in Moscow. And yet, every step up, my thoughts grow heavier with apprehension, for I know how much a too-piercing sentence, a careless movement of the body can undo.

"Levushka will be a musician, Bronia? A concert pianist? Does the Nijinsky ambition have no end?"

As I open the door to our apartment, Irina runs up to me and grabs my hand. Her cheeks are often smudged, streaked with trails left by tears. "Will you sit next to me at supper?" she asks. Mamusia tells me that when I am away, my daughter refuses to move from the front door. And every time Levushka cries she covers her ears and shakes her head.

The first of June is a Sunday. We are all up already. I have just changed Levushka, put him back in his crib, and I go to the bathroom to drop the dirty diapers into a pail of soapy water. Sasha's shirt is lying on the floor and I pick it up, noting a red spot on the collar. At first I think it is blood from a shaving cut, but then I realize it is a smudge of red lipstick. My legs weaken.

"Who is she, Sasha?" I ask, shirt in hand, walking into the kitchen, where he is eating breakfast. Irina, holding a forkful of scrambled egg in the air, gives me a frightened look.

"Don't even start, Bronia," Sasha snarls. "It's your own fault."

"Come with me now, *kochanie*," Mamusia says, taking Irina's hand, setting her breakfast aside. Irina says something in protest, but I don't hear what.

"How is it my fault, Sasha?"

Sasha's hair is still thick, jet black. He must have trimmed it not long ago, but—and this thought comes with a pang of guilt—I don't remember when.

"Who is she, Sasha? Is she one of the students?"

My heart beats quickly; my head swims. I put my hand to it; press it against my breast, feeling its yielding softness. He couldn't have done it, I think. He wouldn't.

Sasha looks at me with such studied, detached calm. "Do you know what *I* think, Bronia?" he asks, slowly. "I think you are mad."

"You think?" I ask, and as soon as the words ring, I realize their ambiguity, and the swiftness with which Sasha latches on to it.

"Yes, Bronia. I, too, am capable of thinking."

He stands up and walks toward me. He is so close that I can see the hairs in his nostrils, the stubble on his chin. I long for something cold to put against my flaming cheeks.

"You and your whole family. You are all mad."

There is the *thump* of a falling chair, followed by the sound of fading steps. The lightning bolt of black fury runs across my spine. The memory of Father.

Later, in the evening, when I have stopped crying, I see Sasha in the yard, looking up at the bedroom window.

He is back, I think, with relief. I'm just about to part the curtain and call out to him, when Sasha turns toward the woodshed.

I watch him unlock the door and walk inside. A few moments later light flickers. The shed is almost empty by now. We are down to the last pile of birch logs, unseasoned, filling the kitchen with smoke.

What comes next is a series of movements I have only a vague recollection of. I must have raced down the stairs. Opened the back door, run into the yard. Did I want to stop him?

The shed smells of mould and mice. The flickering candle is perched on the stone ledge. Sasha is tying up the strings of his rucksack.

"What are you doing?"

He doesn't answer. The rucksack is full when he picks it up.

"What have you taken!"

Blood flushes to my cheeks. My hands shake. This is not a question. It's a scream. What are you leaving us with?

In the candlelight Sasha's face has taken on a shadowy ghostly sheen.

"Are you accusing me of stealing now?" he asks. "Can we fall any lower than that?"

He opens the rucksack and empties it on the ground. "See for yourself," he snarls, waving his tsarist passport. "I'm not taking anything that is not mine."

He points at the change of clothes, walking shoes, a paper bag with *sukhariki*, a tin of milk, a bottle of vodka. His own silver cigarette case, his own watch. Every single object an argument that establishes his innocence and my guilt.

"Don't you dare call me a thief, Bronia."

I am seething. "No, you are not a thief. You are a coward. You are running away."

Does he even hear me? He doesn't seem to, for he puts it all back into his rucksack. The clothes, the food, the cigarette case. His movements are precise, methodical. His body is taut, set on what he is about to do. As soon as the rucksack is filled and tied, Sasha puts it on and walks out of the shed. He doesn't even look up at our windows. Father, I recall, came to my room before he left to tell me that he was leaving Mamusia, not us.

I don't go to bed that night. I cry silently for a while, and when the tears dry up, I check on the children. Irina is tossing in her bed, grinding her teeth; Levushka, swaddled, is motionless like a doll. I look at them for a long while, in silence. I do not want to wake them, or Mamusia, who sleeps in the same room.

The dawn finds me at the kitchen table. The window is opened; the air is fragrant with blooming lilacs. From a distance comes a round of gunshots, followed by a flight of sparrows.

"What do I have left?" I write in my diary. "My children. My mother. My art."

19.

IN THE MONTHS THAT FOLLOW, Petlyura's army ousts the Bolsheviks, only to retreat in haste when the Red Army re-enters. We have stopped counting the victory parades, the proclamations pasted on walls or torn down. Every change of power, we have learnt, creates moments of vacuum when the impossible can happen. Borders can open to let refugees in or out; letters believed long lost can arrive.

There is no word from Sasha, but letters from Vaslav arrive in bundles, recent ones mixed with those of months before. Some were posted when he was still in America, in 1917. The latest are all in French, all in Romola's hand: "Ma chère Bronia, ma chère Maman, Are you safe and healthy? Please close the school and come to Vienna. There is enough space for you in our house. Your loving son and brother, Vaslav."

"Why is she always writing in Vaslav's name?" Mamusia asks. "Is he not even allowed to sign a letter to his own mother?" Her voice is edgy with suspicion. Ever since Sasha's departure, the line she has drawn between us—her children and grandchildren—and them—Sasha and Romola—has thickened. "Not worthy of your tears," she said on the morning I told her my husband left me. She refers to him as "Sasha of wandering eyes, of empty promises." With Irina she is gentler. "Your papa is dancing. One day he will come back."

My own thoughts, too, have hardened. Sasha's departure has freed my friends' tongues. Benedikt has seen Sasha with a pretty dancer from the Opera, his arm around her shoulders. Aleksandra has confessed to never liking Sasha much. "So shallow," she has said, and I who would have resented these words a few months before soak them up.

It is only sometimes that I waver. When I read Vaslav's request to close the school and join him, I wonder if Sasha made it to Vienna. Is this perhaps my husband's plea to make me follow him? On some mornings my hand still half expects to find him lying beside me, and when I touch my pillow, I find it wet with tears.

I don't have much time to dwell on the past, dissect what has happened. My days start at dawn and end well past midnight. In the mornings, before I leave, I help Mamusia with the children. Then I teach my classes and rehearse new ballets I have created. In the evenings, after I tuck Irina up and play with Levushka until he is ready to sleep, I work on new lectures, chart the progress of each student and design exercises that would help them improve.

I don't have time for fear, either. Not until that first pang of pain around my navel.

The pain seizes me on the stairs, on my way down to the rehearsal hall. It is so strong that I bend over and grip the railing. My stomach heaves. As the world around me darkens and swirls, I sit down and draw a few deep breaths. Eventually the pain fades to a throb and I lift myself up. But it never goes away, sharpening every time I take a deeper breath, or cough.

This is what I tell Dr. Epstein at the first chance I have. "Let me take a look," he insists, and when the examination is over, he appears worried. My appendix is inflamed. "At any other time I'd insist on an immediate operation," he tells me. "But not in the existing conditions. At least, not while we still have a choice."

Choice means that my appendix has not yet ruptured and thus it might heal by itself. *Existing conditions* means that Kiev is still a battle zone. In his hospital even the most severely wounded are put three to a bed. There are shortages not just of bandages but of disinfectant. The operating room—even if he could get me in—has become more dangerous than trying to wait it through.

"Two drops of opium if the pain gets unbearable," he says. "And let's hope for the best."

I nod.

The whole spring of 1920 is a see-saw of hope and despair. During the day I manage to teach my classes, assure Mamusia that I am getting better, but by the evening the pain is so strong that all I can do is curl in bed and clench my teeth. My thoughts torment me. What if I die? How will Mamusia manage alone with two children? With the fighting still on? So far away from Vaslav?

I shake my head, but the thoughts whirl and come back, fear and guilt twisting in long ribbons, configured and reconfigured until I fall into my shallow troubled sleep.

It is Pati who confesses to the existence of the "secret council" and its binding resolutions. Pati who crosses her arms on her chest, a shield against my protestations. "It's been a collective decision," she mutters with mischievous smile. "Neither of us has a choice."

The "secret council" has divided all the students into teams. Every morning the boys bring three buckets of water from the yard to the apartment, for since last winter when the pipes froze we have had no running water. They also chop the firewood, take out the trash and the slop pail and do all the heavy lifting for Mamusia. Kolya Singayevsky has just fetched the latest instalment of the school's academic grant: flour, millet, buckwheat, beans, salt, sugar, tobacco and matches.

The girls clean the studios downstairs, tidy up the changing room, mend the costumes, wash and dry them. And when the last class ends at night, one of the girls always stays behind, "on duty" with me.

"I don't need a nurse," I plead with Pati, as I have pleaded with Anya and Tata and others before them. "Go home, please."

"No."

She won't leave me alone. She tells me that I don't have to hide my pain from her. She knows what to do. She'll give me my medicine when I need it. At the first signs that I'm getting worse she will fetch Dr. Epstein.

I sink into bed, let Pati fuss over me—cover my feet with a blanket, get a glass of water from the kitchen, measure out the opium drops, hold the glass to my lips—even though after nine hours of teaching and rehearsing I crave solitude.

I hear Levushka whimpering in the other room then Mamusia's soothing murmurs, a Polish lullaby I remember from my own childhood: "*Aa, kotki dwa, szare bure obydwa.*" Two grey kittens who will sing my baby son to sleep, the lullaby looping, returning, for as long as it is needed.

Pati settles herself in a chair at the foot of my bed, like a peasant woman in front of her whitewashed hut. I watch her through tears, proud and ramrod straight, swaying slightly to the rhythm of her own thoughts. There is a melody to each movement. I hear it with my eyes.

The warmth that washes over me is a mixture of gratitude and elation, and with it comes the feeling of enormous strength.

A month later, in June, the pain disappears. "We are all healthy," I write to Vaslav. "Irina and Levushka are growing fast. Mamusia worries that we have no news of you. Where are you dancing now? Are you choreographing for Diaghilev again?

"The School of Movement," I continue, "is not just a school but my own dance company. The students have made tremendous progress and we are now working on a new ballet I have created. I have taught them to forget poses, positions and gestures. We do not tell stories. We enlighten, not entertain, concentrating on the essence of movement, the true material of dance . . ."

I do not tell Vaslav that I cannot leave Kiev now. He is not Sasha, I think when I lick the envelope and seal it; he will understand.

20.

IN NOVEMBER OF 1920 the School of Movement performs *Mephisto Valse, Twelfth Rhapsody* and *Samurai* at the Shevchenko Theatre. "Compositions," I call them, "explorations of movement." *Mephisto,* stark in its angles, curves and ovals, is an interplay of darkness and light.

I'm onstage with my best students: Pati, Anya and Nadia.

The tunics we wear over tights are Aleksandra's design. Made of strips of different fabrics, the treasures of Kiev attics that unfurl like multicoloured standards when we turn around. The deep red comes from Aleksandra's silk ball gown. The buttercup yellow from the linen tablecloth Mamusia got at the market for a set of tea towels. The blue from Tata's skirt. As I dance, I delight in the way it all links. Painting. Music. Movement.

My students dance as my shadows. This is our second year together. They are good. Not perfect, no, but good. Worthy of every effort. Everything is reflected in them. The long days of work. Their changing bodies. The questions we discuss in our evening sessions: Is old art dead? Is new art the answer? Will power destroy beauty?

Look, Vaslav, I whisper across the miles that separate us. I haven't thrown my gift away. True, I didn't dance the Chosen Maiden, but nothing I've lived through has been lost.

"An affront," someone shouts as the curtain falls. "A provocation."

I turn toward my students. Pati has tears in her eyes. Anya frowns and chews at her fingernails. In the wings the boys are saying something I do not hear but what sounds like a curse.

My heart is pounding; my body is covered with sweat. In the audience someone gives a loud, piercing whistle.

"Haven't we talked about it?" I remind my students as we retreat to the dressing rooms. "This is just like in Paris. This is how the old always answers the revolution in art."

—

I'm in my tiny dressing room when they come: an official delegation of workers deeply insulted by the dance they have just seen.

"Comrade Nijinska. Why do you think us unworthy of proper ballet?"

They stand on the threshold of the open door. Five young men, clean-shaven. All muscular, but only the tallest one has a good posture. The rest are tense and awkward.

The stage manager who has brought them flashes an uneasy look in my direction before vanishing. The Bolsheviks have been in power for five months now. Workers and Red Army soldiers fill up theatres and concert halls. If art is for the people, people have the right to approve it or disapprove.

"Please, come inside," I say. I'm still in my tunic, my face still grey with paint.

They walk in, tugging on the jackets of their ill-fitting suits, smelling of cigarette smoke mixed with something. Tar? Grease? Dressed the way they would've dressed for church, I think, which could be either a compliment or a reproach.

The tallest one, their spokesman, holds his head high. His hair is cropped short. "Why, Comrade Nijinska?" he repeats his question in a stern, demanding voice. His hands are big, his fingers yellowed from nicotine.

"Unworthy?" I ask. "What makes you think that I consider you unworthy?"

The bewilderment in my voice sounds genuine enough to take them aback. They all begin to speak at once. "Why are you not dancing for us the way you once danced for the former tsar? Like a proper ballerina. In a beautiful dress. With these shoes." Here they bunch their fingers together and bend their wrists, to imitate dancing on pointe. "And the stage? So empty! Why there is no scenery, no trees, no lake, no mountains? Are we the workers not good enough for you artists? Not worthy of your effort?"

These are accusations, yes, but also real questions.

"Why should I dance for you the same way I danced for the tsar?" I ask back, raising my hand quickly to stop protests before they hear me out. I address them as comrades. I choose words they understand. "Are your lives like the life of the tsar? Did you grow up in a palace? With all his riches? Then why would you like me to dance for you the way I danced for him?"

They stop talking. They are looking at me. No, they are not yet convinced, but they don't reject what I say, either. So I continue.

The tsar's world, I tell them, was filled with glitter and ceremony. The tsar's ballet—*Swan Lake, The Sleeping Beauty*—was like that, too. Beautiful? Yes. Like a ball gown, like expensive jewels. But this world is gone now. So why dance in the old way?

I pause. I know they are listening. I see it in their eyes, their arching eyebrows, the way they lean slightly forward. They're still not convinced, but no longer offended, either.

For now, this is all I need.

"Have you seen porcelain dolls?" I ask. "Beautiful but so easy to break. Costing more than you make in a month. Did your sisters play with such dolls? Do your daughters play with them?"

I pause. Their smiles are sheepish. The very thought of their sisters or daughters playing with porcelain dolls may be tempting, but it is also frivolous. Perhaps even shameful.

"I don't want to be a doll dressed up in borrowed clothes. Like you, I didn't grow up in a palace. And I'm not dancing for the tsar. I'm dancing for you. The old world is gone. Shouldn't we all be allowed to create a new one?"

I pause again and wait. The break is short. I still have to change my makeup and put on a new costume. My students must also be getting anxious. I've promised to come to their dressing room as soon as I'm ready, to reassure them.

"Comrade Nijinska is right," the tallest worker announces with authority. "We've been blind."

One by one they thank me and shake my hand. They say their names. Comrade Tovarov, Kuzmin, Vargas. "We are glad we came to talk to you, Comrade Nijinska . . . you've opened our eyes . . . now we'll tell the others."

When they are gone, I put on my samurai costume. Into this one Aleksandra wove wide shafts of deep reds, yellows, and purples. I add shadowy lines to my face, making it fierce, relentless. In this dance of jutting triangles I'm a warrior, a samurai; filled with fury at being trapped, taken for dead.

The stage manager knocks at the door. He wants to learn what happened.

I smile.

"We have new converts to modern dance," I say.

21.

AFTER THE NEW YEAR, when classes resume, Anya is absent from the morning class.

Before I have time to ask, Kolya Singayevsky, who lives in the same building, a floor below Anya, stands up. In a trembling voice he describes the telltale noises that woke him at night: banging, heavy steps, things falling to the floor. The search went on for at least two hours. When it was over, he looked out of the window, but it was too dark to see anything. All he heard was the motor starting and an army jeep driving away.

I motion to him to speak louder. I don't want to miss a single word.

He ran upstairs to Anya's apartment. Her mother was crying. The place looked awful. Books on the floor; papers strewn everywhere. Broken glass in the kitchen. Bags of flour and millet emptied over the counter.

They confiscated some letters, Anya's mother told him. A few books. Ordered Anya to put on a coat. Her mother didn't even have the time to slip her a toothbrush before they took her away.

They? The CheKa. All-Russian Extraordinary Commission for Combatting Counter-Revolution and Sabotage.

I leave Pati in charge of the morning practice and rush to the CheKa headquarters. The guard at the door refuses to let me in.

This is when I remember the art commissar. A few months before he praised me for the school's exemplary work, gave me the academic grant. Perhaps he will have more luck finding out what has happened.

Anya Vorobyeva, my student, I explain my request to the secretary, a thin, gaunt woman in a green uniform. Arrested at night.

The secretary gives me a sharp look of disapproval. "Comrade Commissar is too busy to see anyone," she says, and turns away.

"I'll wait," I say to the clattering of typewriter keys.

I sit down on the rickety chair by the window. The room smells sour and ashy. The round tin plate on the secretary's desk is overflowing with cigarette butts. People come in, leave; some join me in waiting. No one talks. Soldiers deliver packages. A priest who arrives a few moments after me is told to go home. He obeys.

As minutes turn to hours I consider what could have caused Anya's arrest. A denunciation by a jealous neighbour hoping to get her family's apartment? A scorned suitor? A former family servant holding a grudge? Whatever it is, I'll need to find out whom to bribe and whom to ask for help. Aleksandra? Benedikt? Pavel, who has just been made director of the Kiev Opera? Les has seen him drinking vodka with the art commissar.

Three hours later, the doors to the commissar's room open and the secretary motions at me to go inside. The floor squeaks under my feet. The commissar looks at me as if he is seeing me for the first time. "What's it about?" he asks, running his hand through his short-cropped hair.

"Vorobyeva," I say, "is one of my students. She has been arrested. I would like to know why."

The commissar raises his eyebrows. "Vorobyeva is a state criminal," he says, pointing at a thick file in front of him.

"What has she done?"

"She has made statements against the Soviet state."

"What statements? When? To whom?"

My questions thrash like fish yanked out of water. The look I get is clear: in this room I am not the one to ask but to answer.

"Do you sympathize with Vorobyeva's statements, Comrade Nijinska?"

"I'm not aware of any statements she has made against the state."

"Perhaps you are not aware of many other things. Perhaps you should pay more attention to what your students say."

It is all like a nightmare. My legs are leaden, my flesh crawls. I have a terrifying thought that my presence in this room might make matters worse. That I might say something that can be used against Anya.

"How old are your children, Comrade Nijinska? You have a girl and a boy, am I right? Has their father come back?"

My heart tightens. Dark spots skid across my field of vision. In the room next door a telephone begins to ring, but no one picks it up.

"Go home, Comrade Nijinska. When we want to talk to you, we will send for you."

It is noon, but the streets are deserted. I pass by what used to be a café, now boarded up with planks and plastered with posters. On one of them a hobbled boot is crushing a Fabergé egg. On another a solider with a red star on his helmet is reaching for a small, fear-stricken child, alone amid the rubble.

I turn into our street. The snow is piled against the buildings, leaving only a narrow path for pedestrians. It has been sprinkled with ashes, to make it less slippery. My cheeks are numb with cold.

Mamusia is waiting for me downstairs in the hall, Levushka holding on to her skirt. When my son sees me, he extends his hands toward me. In three weeks he will be two years old. He is not as good with words as Irina was at his age, but he says *Baba*, *Mama*, *Rina* and knows how to ask for more food. I pick him up and kiss his smooth cheek, but my lips must be cold, for he squirms in my arms.

Mamusia is fighting tears. She clasps my arm and whispers, "Have you thought what would happen to us if you didn't come back?"

The search begins at one in the morning, an hour after we turn out the light, as if someone was watching the house. Mamusia holds Irina. I pick up screaming Levushka, who refuses to calm down. One of the soldiers empties the contents of his cot onto the floor. The quilt, the mattress, the blanket.

They work with grim precision, checking for what must be the favourite hiding places. Loose boards. False wardrobe bottoms. The underside of tables. One of them orders me to undress my son. He wants to see what I might have hidden in his diapers.

They take my choreographic notes and all the school records, but they don't go the woodshed.

An omission or a sign that this is just a warning?

22.

ANYA HAS BEEN RELEASED, but she hasn't come back to school. Kolya has not seen her, either. Her mother, he tells me when he comes by before school to help Mamusia with heavier lifting, didn't even open the door when he went to their apartment. Just told him to please not come again.

Is this a sign, too?

I do receive a summons, to the CheKa headquarters. My interrogator looks barely twenty. I do not know who he is or how to address him. My work, he informs me, has been examined. I dwell too much on bourgeois experimentations. I forget that here a class struggle going on, that nothing is free from ideological meaning.

My file is on the desk. Three thick bundles, one of them opened, revealing my choreographic notes and a thin volume of Mayakovsky's poems, a gift from Benedikt I hadn't even noticed was missing.

The interrogator is seated behind the desk, in his Red Army tunic without insignia. He picks up the book, leafs through it, puts it back. The reddened skin of his hands is a sign of old frostbite.

"The Soviet state," he says, "supports the artists, but the artists have duties, too. They have to support the state."

"I—"

He doesn't let me finish.

"Nothing stays the same, Comrade Nijinska. You of all people should know that what is innovative today, tomorrow becomes old and reactionary."

From underneath my notes he retrieves a few loose pages and reads: "'Bronislava Nijinska has told us that we should be ambitious and strive to be the best we can.'"

He stops and looks at me. "Is this what you teach your students, Comrade Nijinska?"

I nod, wondering if these are Anya's words, the transcript of her interrogation. Is this the real reason I am here?

He shakes his head as if I have disappointed him. "This is dangerous elitism," he announces. "Trickery meant to cut off the working class from your art."

What follows is a well-rehearsed lecture: "Art—" he pronounces the word in an arch, unnatural voice "—has nothing to do with personal ambition. Art must serve the people. Art is to be like bread—nourishing, accessible to everyone, not just a chosen few. Those who cling to the ways of the past, to their old privileges, are cowards, afraid of the future.

"Think about it, Comrade Nijinska. You are an intelligent woman."

He rises from his chair when he says it. I, too, stand up, wondering if I am free to leave. "One last thing before you go," he says. "Do you know where your husband is now? Are you perhaps, planning to join him?"

—

I don't go home right away. I do not want Mamusia to see my agitation. I want to be able to tell her convincingly that it was all a misunderstanding, that I answered a few questions and now all is fine.

The small park a few streets away from our house was stripped of trees during the last winter. In the flowerbed someone has planted cabbages and turnips.

I sit on a bench beside a tree stump and take out my diary:

You don't talk about art. You talk about power. You shut me in a cage and demand the songs of a free bird. Soon there will be no more songs left. How can we be somebody's property? No matter how well you feed me, free hungry life is still better.

My hand is shaking; letters come crooked, misshapen:

We are the creators. We change the world through art. Why can't you let us do it? There are so few of us left.

I write for a long time, and when I finish, I tear the written pages out of my notebook, strike a match and set them on fire.

A week later my students and I are in the middle of rehearsal for a new choreographic sketch when two Red Guards arrive. Two young women in uniform, determined to make themselves look older. One is sniffling from a cold; the other is eyeing the inscriptions on the wall.

"Is this the School of Movement?" the guard with a cold asks, a note of disappointment in her voice, as if she were expecting to catch us marching in groups to a military beat, or practising for street protests.

"Yes."

"Are you the teacher, Comrade? Then you have to step outside."

In the corridor the guard opens her leather bag and takes out a piece of paper. Before I have the time to examine it, her companion extracts a hammer from her and nails the order, stamped and signed by the art commissar, to the school's door. The School of Movement has been closed.

A neighbour's cat slinks over and begins to twine around my ankles. I wonder how it got inside.

"Why?"

This is a pointless question. The guards point at the order and leave. I shoo the cat out, close the door and return to the dance hall.

My students are gathering around me. Is it true? their eyes ask. Where will we go now? What will become of us?

I clear my throat.

Words come slowly, cracked with pain. I thank them for all they've been for me. I tell them that they have danced my visions, made them real. That we have been artists together. That I'll never forget it.

I pause and wipe tears off my cheeks. Pati is kneeling on the floor, hunched, face against her knees. Someone behind her is sobbing. The boys stand motionless, staring at the floor. When I finish, Kolya punches the wall with his fist. I don't hear the punch, but I see how fast his hand stains with blood.

23.

IN MY ESCAPE DREAM a CheKa patrol stops us in the Kiev Station just before the train arrives. Men in long black leather coats cock their guns. Irina and Levushka hide behind me. I can feel their hands clasp my skirt. Mamusia is staring at me, her lips moving in prayer.

"Papers," one of the men barks.

I take out my papers. My identity card, permission to travel. I hand them to him.

"What is it?" he asks.

He is shoving the papers in front of my eyes. The pages are all blank.

If I don't wake up then screaming, the dream continues. I see Mamusia pushed aside. I see Irina and Levushka sobbing, marched away from us, their tear-stricken faces turning toward me.

I, too, am marched into a small room, where another CheKa man is already waiting for me. He calls me a "saboteur, a traitor, the enemy of the people." He orders me to take of my shoes and examines them. "Are you smuggling diamonds in the heels of your shoes?" he asks.

I shake my head.

"Confess," he yells. "If you want to see your children ever again."

I'm walked to the back of the station. A soldier whistles. He has blackened teeth; a little ball of brown spit hangs in the corner of his mouth. The tip of his gun glitters in the sun. I notice all these details with such hunger, such terrible regret.

There will be an explosion, a thunder, then nothing. My body will be one of many left to rot in a muddy ditch.

My children, abandoned, will roam Russia like hungry dogs, rummaging in the garbage for scraps of food. Or be killed, executed for the crime of being old enough to be considered tainted, "deprived" by me. Or maybe, mercifully, taken into some orphanage. Told to forget who they have been, for from now on the Soviet state will be their mother and father.

Then a wave of darkness descends and there are no more thoughts.

"We are going to join Vaslav," I tell Mamusia.

She doesn't know that among the lasts batch of letters was one from Romola's mother, dated a year ago: "Vaslav is seriously ill. He needs his family with him. Come," she writes. "I offer you my house."

I did not show it to Mamusia, not wanting to worry her with old news. I alone wrote to Romola's mother, explained that her letter was held at the border and has only now reached us. "Vaslav must have recovered by now," I replied, "so please pass on our news to him."

I did not show Mamusia another letter, either, this one delivered by an Austrian pilot who had landed in Kiev in the first week of March. It was from Romola, addressed to me and written—to my surprise—entirely in Russian:

> *Your brother, Bronia, is mentally ill. The doctors believe it is imperative for his recovery that your family be here with him. I earnestly request that you immediately come with your mother and your children to be with Vaslav.*

I read this letter again and again, worried by then but still wondering what it meant. Why was it in Russian? Why was Romola not writing in French, as she always did? Was she trying to give me means to apply for an exit passport?

The pilot who brought the letter didn't know anything about Vaslav Nijinsky. He had only delivered Red Cross supplies for the Kiev hospital. But—on his way back—he offered to smuggle me and the children to Vienna.

"And my mother?" I asked.

His plane was small, he said, one engine. He could take me and the children. My mother must stay behind.

I refused.

"How can we leave now?" Mamusia asks.

I know what she is thinking. In Bolshevik Kiev we need written permissions to buy train tickets or stay in a hotel. Not everything can be forged. The CheKa patrols, it is rumoured, do not take bribes. Smugglers and profiteers or anyone suspected of being an enemy of the people are shot on the spot.

There is an art of escape. You start with your best, most reliable friends. The only ones you tell of your plans. They'll connect you with others you can trust. They will help you sell what you can to pay for your escape. They will keep silent.

Packing is of utmost importance. Soft bundles, small enough to wear over your shoulders, are best. The ones easiest to reach should be filled with little objects that can be given as bribes or exchanged for food. A silver chain. An embroidered tablecloth. A roll of ribbon. A sash with buttons. Money has to be separated, sewn into clothes. All kinds of money, just in case. Tsarist rubles, German and Polish marks.

"How are we going to get to Vienna?" Mamusia asks.

We are sitting together on the sofa, knees touching. I can feel her body tremble. I make my voice sound casual and assured. I've made excellent contacts. I have found a guide who has done this many times before.

Volotchisk is the closest town to the Polish border. A trusted friend has forged a paper testifying that the State Dramatic Theatre is sending me on an "official mission" to Volotchisk to inspect the facilities for planned guest appearances. The guide will smuggle Mamusia and the children into the same train. Then pass us on to another guide, who will take us over the border, to Poland.

It is May. We don't need any winter clothes.

Mamusia nods.

That night she doesn't sleep. I can hear her in the kitchen, drying slices of bread, meat, apples. The smell is soothing, almost festive. I, too, am awake, lying in the dark. The ticking of the clock is relentless. I feel an urge to get up, run, right now, without waiting.

The children must sense something is happening, for they both sleep lightly. Levushka cries in his sleep. At two and a half he is like Vaslav: impossible to keep still. Anything is good to climb on. A couch. A table. Irina is eight and I've told her that we are going on a trip. "To Papa?" she asked. I lifted her face and looked her in the eyes. "We'll see."

In these last days I've been looking at the apartment with the eyes of those who will come in after we are gone. It has to become mute, cleaned of anything that might hurt anyone who has helped us. I've burnt any papers I cannot take with me. Bills, receipts, letters, postcards, books bearing inscriptions from our friends. Anything with a name or address on it.

My diaries of the past five years are the hardest to part with. Seven notebooks of my thoughts, plans, dreams. They have to be ripped apart, burnt slowly, a few pages at a time, so that I don't choke the fire and fill the kitchen with thick, suffocating smoke.

There are no passenger trains from Kiev to Volotchisk. The freight train we take stops at all stations.

The train is dusty and dark, with just a little light flickering through the wooden slats. We sit on bundled newspapers that are being delivered on the way. Every time the train stops the doors open and someone gets in to take a few bundles. The CheKa sentries come in to check the papers.

Since I'm the only one with permission to travel, as soon the train approaches a station, Mamusia and the children have to hide. Their hiding place is in the darkest corner of the car, behind bundled newspapers. I don't ask how my mother keeps the children quiet. I know Dr. Epstein has given her some tonics. In between stations, when I check on the children, they are both asleep, their bodies soft, fluid. Levushka never wakes. Irina sometimes opens her eyes and gives me an absent look.

This is how we arrive in Volotchisk, ten miles or so from the border, a small town where everyone knows everyone else and where strangers won't be able to hide for long.

"Go now," the guide says. "Come back in three hours."

I carry Levushka, who is beginning to wake up, whimpering, asking for a drink. I give him a sip of sweetened tea. Irina is walking on her own, silent, holding Mamusia's hand, sucking on a slice of dried bread. We go to the theatre, where I present my letter and conduct my inspection, while they wait for me in the main entrance hall, out of sight.

When we return to the station, our guide puts us on another train, to Proscurov, the town on the Polish border. Another guide will find us there.

How?

"Stand in front of the movie theatre. Look at the posters."

This is the art of escape. A chain of friends and strangers you trust. With all you've got.

The border is a stream between two steep banks. There is a path that takes us there, through the forest.

It is broad daylight.

"Can the guards not see us?" I point at two soldiers who are lying on the grassy slope. They have put their guns aside. One is whistling a simple tune. Another one begins to sing.

My heart is pounding. Irina is walking right behind me. I've told her that we are going on a long hike. She wants to know where but doesn't ask any more questions. Not after the guide yelled at her to be quiet.

"We are too far," the guide says, dismissing my fear. He is taller than I am but not stronger. I hide my dancer's strength carefully and let him carry Levushka and three of our bundles. Trust is conditional. So are greed and betrayal. In this border town we are strangers with no papers and many possessions.

I have strapped three bundles to my back. Mamusia has done the same. She walks behind Irina. I can hear her panting breath.

This is our second attempt. Last night we came to the same spot, sat down and waited. "What are we waiting for?" I asked, but the guide just put his finger on his lips. After an hour or so he rose and said we had to go back. "Is anything wrong?" I asked. He didn't answer.

I'm agonizing over my choice of guides. The farmer with whom we have stayed the past four nights also offered to take us through. "I know the commander," he said. "You pay me, and they will let you over the border. No need to wade the stream."

I didn't choose the farmer. I'm walking behind the man who came up to me as I was staring at the movie poster. Paid what he asked. Up front.

"A long hard walk," I told Irina before we set off, just as I told her last night. "But you cannot complain or cry. It's too dangerous."

I can see her face darken and freeze, but she walks silently, determined not to be a burden. She is wearing her leather sandals, socks, a blue cotton dress. Blue is still her favourite colour.

The path we are taking leads us through thick shrubberies. The stream is below us.

"Stay here," the guide says, handing Levushka to me.

The guide will walk to the sentry hut. If he comes out and waves a white handkerchief, we are to walk down to the stream and start crossing it with the children. "As quickly as you can," he says. "Leave your luggage here. I'll bring it when you are on the other side."

"And if you do not wave?" I ask.

"Then you'll have to turn back."

From where we sit on a patch of grass, hidden by a thick honeysuckle bush, I can see the sentry hut into which our guide has disappeared. If it doesn't work this time, either, I've decided to take the farmer up on his promise. But then the door opens and the guide emerges, waving a white handkerchief.

Mamusia crosses herself.

We leave half our bundles behind and begin to descend to the stream.

Twenty steps? Thirty. Steep at times. Irina stumbles. Mamusia walks sideways, trying not to slip on the grass. She is slow, cautious. "Go ahead, Bronia, go," she mutters when I stop.

I wonder what will come first. A shout? The swish of a bullet? But the soldiers, who must see us by now, pay us no heed. One is rolling a cigarette. Another is rummaging in his backpack.

Levushka is heavy in my arms. He is no longer asleep. I wonder if he can sense the fear around him. And if he does, what it will do to him. Where will it go?

By the time we reach the stream, the guide is already there, waiting. "Let's go," he says, and picks Irina up. I can see her stiffen.

"That's all right," I tell my daughter. I carry Levushka. Mamusia is behind me now, her breath heavier.

The guide, with Irina on his back, steps into the water. I follow.

"The stream is shallow here," the guide assures me, but after a few steps water is up to my waist. I can feel Levushka's fingers dig into my neck.

Still, we make it to the other side in a few minutes.

I step out of the water and put Levushka down. My sandals are filled with sand. I am wet, but the day is warm and I feel a wave of relief.

And then, behind me, sharp whistles are followed by peals of loud, jeering laughter. I turn and see that Mamusia is still on the other shore. She has stepped into the water. She is holding her skirt up, but she is not moving.

"Come," I call. "Hurry!"

She doesn't hear me, or if she does, her legs do not obey, for she is standing in one place, the water reaching her knees.

"Hurry up," I scream, but she doesn't move.

The guide is swearing, cursing us all. If we get into trouble now, we have only ourselves to blame.

I don't have much time to consider the danger of turning back, leaving the children alone on the Polish side. I place Levushka in Irina's arms, tell her not to let him wander off. "Do you understand?" I ask.

She nods.

I rush back into the stream and wade to the Russian side. When I get to Mamusia, she is still rooted to the spot. "I can't walk," she mumbles. "My legs are not moving."

Nothing I say helps. Not my assurances that the water is shallow enough, that the children are waiting for us. Her teeth are chattering. When I grab her hand, she pulls me back so hard that I almost fall.

"Get going, woman," the guide barks. He is right beside me, towering over us, grabbing Mamusia's other hand. Together we drag her with us, step by agonizing step. The soldiers are having a good time watching. "You don't like to wet your bum, Matushka?" one of them shouts.

It may only be a few minutes, but they stretch into infinity. The children alone on the Polish shore, both of them crying. A step, another one then one more, and then, at last, we are all on the other side.

Soaking wet, with half our luggage—but alive.

October 15, 1939

Yesterday at dinner one of the ship's officers came up to our table. His name is Michael Ritter and he is an engineer. I could see he was drawn to my daughter, her quiet elegance and her voice, which when she speaks English has a lovely tinge of French underneath. From the little I could understand of their conversation, Mr. Ritter talked mostly about pistons, pressure valves, cylinders and the electric current. Once he even began drawing something on a piece of paper, some elaborate construction at which Irina marvelled with an absorption I did not anticipate. As a result, later today my daughter will get a tour of the ship's insides.

I worry about her, wonder why at twenty-six she is still alone. Did I burden my children too much? Dwarf them with my dreams? Make them believe they have disappointed me?

The fleeting romances Irina had at the companies she danced with never amounted to anything serious. If Mamusia knew why, she never betrayed Irina's confidence. Though I am certain she did warn her not to marry a dancer.

Let her be, I tell myself. She will find her own way.

In the ship's smoking room, where I settle today to escape the growing chill of the mornings, I open a packet of studio portraits I have brought with me. The publicist of the Australian tour has asked me for a few suitable ones. I quickly select the two most recent and put them aside. Then I add an older one, which is still my favourite. Man Ray took it, in Paris, in the fall of 1921.

There is the scent of cigarette smoke in my memory of this picture, the sensation of smoke filling my lungs, and, still not quite accustomed as I was to this new habit, a surge of dizzy energy. I am at some noisy party Diaghilev took me to, his new choreographer for Ballets Russes. A young woman in a tight, glittering dress sings a street ballad about a sailor who found his girlfriend in the arms of a clown. I sneak out onto a balcony. Below me the city is awash in light. After the thick, sticky darkness of Kiev nights, such brightness still astonishes me. And the abundance of food. Pyramids of cheeses, charcuterie, *cuts of meat piled up in shop windows. Jars of jams. Mountains of apples.*

When I turn around, I see Diaghilev standing in the balcony door, framed by the subdued light of the room. His suit is too tight, its shoulders sprinkled with flakes of dandruff. His black eyes are fixed on me. "Man Ray wishes to take your portrait, Bronia," he says. It is an honour, his eyes insist, a distinction, which he has secured for me. He, the great Diaghilev, is making sure his new choreographer, his "returned Bronia," meets all the right *people.*

Emmanuel Radnitzky cut letters from his name until only Man Ray was left. Like me he believes in discarding what is no longer necessary.

Two days later, in his Montparnasse studio on rue Campagne-Première—really a small, cramped apartment, its washroom converted into a darkroom—Man Ray spreads objects on a wooden tray and asks me to pick one that strikes my fancy. I choose a giant comb that looks like the wooden rakes peasants in Russia use in the fields. He gives me a black wig with dishevelled strands of hair sticking out and sticks this prickly comb in it like a trophy. Then he blackens the sides of my face, leaving one white stripe in the middle. Around my lips he paints a gaping mouth with two pointed fangs and an arrow that leads from my right eye down my nose. Finally, he drapes a black shawl over my shoulders.

"Don't move," he repeats, lighting or switching off lamps, approaching me, only to step back right away. As I stand there alone in the changing light, I become aware of the wave of rot escaping his darkroom, a whiff of perfume, the smell of soot doused with water. I stand motionless for a long time. Long enough for the muscles of my face to tense.

The photograph that arrives a few days later is a portrait of a woman with her painted mouth disfigured by a grin, her eyes wide open. She has seen what others have been spared.

"There is so little of you in it, Bronia," Mamusia says.

She is wrong.

PART FIVE:

1921–1932

1.

"FOLLOW ME," the nurse at the Steinhof Asylum says, putting on a side table a pile of blankets she has been carrying. She is small and wiry, her arms strong, her movements precise.

Out of the corner of my eye I can see Mamusia's lips tighten. She casts a nervous look at the gleaming dome of St. Leopold Church, dedicated to a saint who stayed away from the trappings of glory.

In a long black and white tiled corridor that leads to Vaslav's room the odour of ammonia drowns all other smells. Patients stop us as we walk by, trying to grab our hands. A thin man with hollow cheeks, an empty sleeve where his right arm should be pinned to his caftan, mutters, "Allow plants to be mute. Focus. Focus. Focus."

Mamusia walks so fast that I almost have to run to keep up with her. When Romola picked us up at the Vienna Station, Mamusia embraced and kissed her. The talk was of hope. Of yanking Vaslav out of "his catatonic stupor." Of the necessary agitation, which seeing his mother and sister after seven years would surely bring. In the commotion of collecting luggage, getting the children into the car, I even saw Mamusia slip her hand under Romola's arm. Wiping away tears at the news that she had a third granddaughter now, year-old Tamara, named after Karsavina. But later, at the Hotel Bristol, after Romola left for her own hotel, Mamusia turned to me, bewildered: "No proper home? Only hotel suites? With two small daughters? What kind of a life is that? What kind of a family?"

The nurse tells us to wait. "Just to be on the safe side," she says, before stepping into his room. I don't ask her what she fears. I don't want to know. Besides, the door opens right away.

"Come on in," she says.

Mamusia walks in ahead of me, calling Vaslav's name with forced cheerfulness. Chastising him for giving us such a fright. "What lies are they telling me, Vaslav? You are not that ill, are you? There is no need to hide here any longer. Get ready. Bronia and I, we've come to take you home!"

Then I see him.

Vaslav, his back perfectly straight, is sitting on his bed; wearing a simple white shirt and black pants, as if resting after practice. But the moment that he should've jumped from the bed to embrace us has already passed. He doesn't even turn his head in our direction. Only his fingers show any signs of life. He is pulling the flap of skin between his index finger and his thumb. My knees weaken under me.

The room is stark, with just a white iron bed and a small metal table screwed to the floor. Walls, painted white, are thin enough to let in the voices from the corridor. Thick metal bars protect the window.

"Vatsa, Vatsushka, look at me!" Mamusia calls my brother by his childhood names. She embraces him, kisses his face, smooths his hair.

"Vaslav!" I echo softly, willing him to turn his head toward me. Catatonic stupor? Romola's sister, Tessa, who brought us here in a cab, was more blunt: "Be forewarned," she said to me as I was opening the car door. "It's like talking to a corpse."

"We have come all the way from Russia," Mamusia pleads, waving at me to join her. "Aren't you happy to see us?"

"They all send their greetings," I tell my brother. "The greatest artists of Russia. Karsavina, Pavlova, Stravinsky, Bakst. And Diaghilev, too. Sergey Pavlovitch needs you back. Without you, Vaslav, there is no Ballets Russes."

Minutes pass, five, ten, twenty; our voices grow hoarse and teary. Each breath is harder to take than the one before, and even harder to release. By now even my brother's hands have stopped moving.

"Remember, Vaslav? The "Sailor Dance" . . . the snowman we made in Kiev . . . Ptashek . . . how tame it was."

Mamusia raises herself up and rings for the nurse. A vein in her temple pulsates. She demands to see the doctor in charge. She wants to know what is being done for her son. Her voice is a shriek, piercing.

"You must calm down," the nurse insists.

"Is this what you are doing to him?" Mamusia asks. "Keeping him calm? What are you drugging my son with?"

She keeps talking, as if silence had to be beaten into surrender. Nervous breakdown? Yes. She can see why. Working too hard, not eating properly. Everyone around him just making demands. Wasn't Vaslav smearing his body with poisonous greasepaint day after day? Has anyone even thought of it? And does anyone here speak Russian? Or Polish? No? So how can they ever understand what her son might want to tell them!

My mother, who only a few weeks ago stood terrified at a stream, unable to cross it, is charging ahead.

And I? I'm fighting a childhood memory of St. Petersburg's winter market. Frozen animal carcasses perched on the piles of snow.

There is one perplexing moment of this long day that I keep returning to, year after year. Mamusia is still somewhere in the hospital building, demanding to see yet another doctor, and I'm with Vaslav, outside. I've pushed his wheelchair to a small bower where there is an empty bench and where we can be alone.

I may have lost all hope he hears what I say, but I cannot stay silent, either. So I tell my brother about Kiev. About my own ballets without plots, without stories to tell. Ballets in which groups move together as one, in which dancers' bodies form structures that transform themselves into new forms, in which only the essence of the dance is left.

"Warriors, Vaslav. Marching crowds. Parades. Demons haunting the living souls . . . The ballets I have constructed. For myself. For my students."

What happens next looks like a miracle.

My brother stands up, his hands extended as if he were preparing to lead me in our next *pas de deux*. "A ballet is never constructed, Bronia," he corrects me in his familiar, chiding voice. "A ballet must be created."

"Vaslav," I cry out, my hands reaching for him.

But he is already sinking back into the wheelchair, his body limp, his eyes unseeing. And I will forever wonder what I've been offered. A farewell or a promise?

2.

THIS IS WHAT Romola tells me that May.

There had been odd, uncomfortable moments for some time. During the American *tournée* Vaslav dived into the hotel pool and stayed underwater so long that she thought he had drowned. After he emerged, gasping for breath, blue in the face, gagging and spitting, he refused to tell her why he kept her terrified for so long.

"This man," he said a few days later, pointing at a bulky man in a black suit. "I've seen him before." His whispers were frantic, insisting that he was being followed. In every theatre where he was to dance, *they* were lurking in the wings, leaving nails on the stage, setting traps, trying to kill him. He told her that he wanted to go back to Russia. Live like a peasant, till the land. Just like Tolstoy had taught him. That he believed in justice. For a while it meant giving up his own roles to lesser dancers and taking theirs, instead. Infuriating the audience.

"Tell me about the war, *femmka*," he asked, for this is how he called Romola, the French word for wife, made to sound Russian.

She did. She read to him the newspaper accounts of the rat-infested trenches. Of machine guns that mowed down the advancing men. Of soldiers trapped in spirals of barbed wire, bodies left rotting in the muddy fields. She read to him the names and ages of the dead. Twenty . . . twenty-two . . . twenty-three . . . Seventeen. Sixteen. "Too young to even enlist," she had said. "These are still children. Is anyone even paying attention?"

She thought of this moment a few weeks later, on their holiday in St. Moritz, when Vaslav put a large crucifix around his neck. The servants came to her, distraught, to tell her that Master was stopping people in the street. "Go to church," he screamed. "Pray for the sins of men against other men and Your Creator." When she asked him why he was doing it, he looked at her with bewilderment. "Didn't you say *no one* was paying attention?"

Vaslav was an artist, she reminded herself. A genius. So much more sensitive than ordinary men. She knew it when she married him, didn't she?

She tried to overlook his rages, his feverish drive to exert himself, his accusations that she, his wife, didn't understand what he felt; that she thought with her mind, not her heart. She ignored his refusal to sit with them at meals after he had seen Kyra eat a steak. She didn't mind that he locked himself in his room. "I'm working," he'd yell when she knocked, and when he opened the door, his lips were curled with disgust.

"Do you want me to go on, Bronia?" Romola stood up in agitation, wrung her hands, took a few steps toward the window then away from it.

"Yes," I said. I wanted to know everything.

There was that evening at the Suvretta House, in January of 1919. It was Vaslav's first public performance after returning from America. A "recital," Romola called it. Much anticipated by the best of society.

"*Crème de la crème*," she said. Otto Khan came from New York, people from Covent Garden, from the Paris Opera. Her mother's friends from Vienna.

They rented the ballroom. Vaslav had ordered his costumes. He was practising in secret, in his room. He didn't tell Romola what he would dance or even what music he wanted the pianist to play. On the day of the performance he had been nervous all day, and she worried, but then, he was always tense before a performance, wasn't he? He needed to transform himself, become one with his dance. So she didn't ask, and after a while Vaslav did calm down. Even told her that his dance would be about creation. About what was happening in an artist's head when he created ballets. "This will be the day of my marriage with God," he also said. She puzzled over that, but then, Vaslav's French was often odd and hard to understand. She was used to guessing what he really wanted to say.

The Suvretta House ballroom had filled up. People came not just from St. Moritz but also from the villages around. Skiers, holiday makers, friends. Her mother came, her stepfather. Those who had not seen Vaslav dance before listened to those who had. The great Nijinsky, the genius, the living miracle of dance, the man who had danced for the tsar, for the kaiser, for the queens and kings of Europe, would now dance for *them*.

The lights of the giant chandeliers dimmed. The conversations died down. The pianist sat down at the grand piano to a wave of applause. The *scène* remained empty for a long while, but not long enough to cause concern. And then Vaslav appeared in a costume of white silk bordered with black, and white sandals on his feet.

So beautiful, Romola thought, muscular, yet slender, too. With his long neck and catlike eyes. A panther? Half tamed, half wild. Ready to saunter into the darkness if startled. Or bare his teeth and fight. Mesmerized, she watched him walk up to the pianist, whisper his instructions. When the music began, a Chopin prelude, he picked up a chair and sat down, facing the audience.

He didn't move.

The music continued then ended. A chair behind her creaked then another. A man in front of her cleared his throat. Someone coughed. There were whispers, too. Romola's mother looked at her as if it were all her fault. Made that regal gesture of hers, as if she could command the waves.

Vaslav didn't move.

Is that what happens in an artist's mind? Romola asked herself. Such absolute stillness? For so long?

He continued sitting, staring at the audience, oblivious to the twitches of unease. As if the people who had come to watch Nijinsky dance were the ones onstage, performing for *him*. The pianist waited then repeated the prelude again.

Vaslav didn't move.

"I tried to guess what was happening," Romola said. Was it one of his dark moods? Or was it a new, daring choreography we just couldn't understand? Like the people who booed and screamed when he showed them *Sacre*. The people Vaslav called "*dura publika*," stupid audience. Didn't they scream "Call the doctor" and "Call the dentist" then? Didn't they think themselves cheated? While he, Vaslav Nijinsky, was showing them the truest, the most prescient vision of the future?

Who knows the meanders of an artist's soul during the act of creation? Is stillness important? Is the absence of movement also part of the dance?

Who were they to disturb him?

But she could not bear it in the end. What if he was frozen with fright? What if he needed her help? She gathered all her courage and stood. Walked up to him. "Won't you dance something, Vaslav?" she asked in a whisper. "Maybe from *Les Sylphides*?"

He looked at her with such hatred, such rage. His lips raised, his teeth bared. A wild beast, ready to tear her to shreds. "How dare you disturb me!" he yelled. "I'm not an automaton. I'll dance when I'm ready."

She went back to her seat, wiping tears from her face. That's it, she decided. I'm taking Vaslav home.

But just then, as if he had been waiting for these very thoughts, Vaslav began to move. He stretched his arms, raised his hands, as if protecting himself from a blow. He reached upward and then folded his hands in a prayer, all in perfect harmony with the music.

This was pure beauty, she thought. Simple. Straightforward. So much more powerful after the long wait. Too long, she would tell him later, when they are alone. Necessary, yes, but maybe if he would shorten it next time. Or maybe she wouldn't tell him anything. He was the artist. She was merely his wife. Her role was to praise, to encourage, to support. No, she would not criticize.

She watched, unable to take her eyes off him. They all watched.

For by then Vaslav had begun a merry dance, a madcap diversion that made the audience laugh. And when that, too, stopped, he turned his face to them, a sad Petrushka face. His body grew limp. He staggered, almost fell. Yes, she thought, Petrushka, abandoned by his magician. Gathering strength. Growing in power. For when he stood firm again, he was unfurling lengths and lengths of black and white fabric, a wavering sea of ripples that settled and grew still, in the shape of a giant cross. Vaslav, his arms opened wide, stood at the head of this cross, like a crucified Jesus.

Then Vaslav began to speak. His sentences were short and simple. There had been a war. Terrible, bloody. Millions of men, young men, died. Some were children, too young to enlist. Their bodies are still rotting in the muddy fields. These men will not have children. They will not write new music. Create new ballets. Paint new pictures. "I'll dance that war for you now," he said. "The war that you *didn't* prevent or stop. The war *you* are responsible for."

And he danced, fast as lightning, leaping into the air, hovering over the stage, as brilliant as ever but also broken and maimed. The stage may have been empty, but when he danced, they all saw the trenches and the fields. Broken, stiff bodies visible under a layer of mud. He, soaring over them, stricken with horror, was their conscience. He was dancing the graven images of their own mortal sins.

This, Romola thought, humbled, is what happens in the artist's head.

When Vaslav stopped, there was silence first then applause. More and more bold. With cries of "Encore!" With cheers.

Vaslav bowed and straightened up, his face sweaty and flushed. He was breathing heard. His white silk costume was torn at places, smudged with black streaks.

He shook his head. There would be no encores.

A wise decision, she thought.

There was a reception afterwards. Vaslav had changed into his dark blue suit by then and joined her. She made sure he drank plenty of water. Brought him some slivers of apples, a piece of an orange to eat. A few chunks of dark chocolate.

Vaslav seemed pleased at first. Relieved that it was over. Smiled when she told him how much he had moved them all. Bowed even, his hand over his heart, as if he were still onstage. But the odd moments continued. A woman came up to tell him how much she liked his dancing. "You, Madame, move in a way that excites me very much," he said, and then put his finger over his lips as if he had just told her a secret she was to keep to herself. "Please look," he also said, lifting his foot, and she, Romola, noted with trepidation that he was still wearing the white sandals. His foot was bleeding, and blood was what he wanted everyone to see. Those standing near recoiled.

"I don't like blood, either," Vaslav told them. "This is why I don't like wars."

In the car on their way home Vaslav was no longer sure of himself. "I wanted them to see what they've done," he told her. "How many men had to die before they would look? Do you think they understood?"

"Yes," Romola said. "They did."

The weeks that followed were tense, unpredictable. Vaslav would come to the breakfast table in the morning, joke with Kyra, make her laugh with a silly song about a small green bridge. It was in Polish, but he would explain how the bridge bends when people walk on it and would tickle Kyra until she squirmed with laughter. Then, suddenly, he would grow serious, run to his room and lock the door behind him.

She, Romola, knew that he was writing, for she peeked through the keyhole and saw him hunched over his desk. Then he walked around the room, and she again thought of a panther, a caged one, no longer roaming free. Sometimes he played the piano, loudly, all night. Stravinsky's

Sacre, *Petrushka*, *Firebird*. And then Richard Strauss. The same pieces over and over again.

She fetched a doctor to examine him. Dr. Greiber talked to Vaslav every day. Got him to form free associations, hoping for clues they might reveal. Vaslav was writing poems then, in Russian, and Romola asked him to translate them for the doctor. "More babble than poems," Dr. Greiber told her. "Something about God and Mother Earth, or just the same word written over and over again." Vaslav also showed the doctor some of his drawings. They were of eyes, big and small, watching him, or of rings made of smaller circles. A few depicted what he called his "inventions": a bridge that would connect Europe and America, a pen that would never run out of ink.

"A nervous breakdown," the doctor said. Vaslav was an artist; it was not surprising that he was highly strung and sensitive. He needed to be left alone. Romola should place him in a sanatorium and leave for a while. Let him get over this crisis.

But how could she? Leave him? At night Vaslav cried in her arms. Said no one could understand him. Said he was all alone, for everyone had betrayed him. "It's my soul that is sick," he said, "not my body. I want to dance. To play music. Compose ballets. Love everyone."

This was the hardest to bear. Seeing Vaslav like that, a frightened little boy who wanted to be held, calmed down, told that all would be fine in the end.

"I'll kill myself," he said.

"I don't want my heart to stop," he said.

He laughed.

He cried.

He told her she was his beloved wife.

He pushed her away and said she was a wanton woman, a traitor and a whore who was scheming with the doctor behind his back. Betraying him, like everyone else.

He wanted to have a son with her. He wanted to teach his son to dance.

"I didn't want to leave him, Bronia," Romola said. "Was I wrong?"

The day the ambulance came to take him to hospital, Vaslav locked himself in the room and wouldn't open the door for five long hours. He yelled and raged at the servants. He had a big knife with him. "To sharpen the pencils," he shouted through the locked door when she asked why he needed it. "So that I can write."

They finally broke down the door and took him away.

He looked so frightened, she said, when they marched him down the stairs. Not a panther but a tortured cat chased into a corner.

From then on it was hospital rooms, doctors, nurses. Sometimes he seemed to get better. He was talking, drawing, playing the piano and billiards. A few times he asked for art books, looked at Dürer's drawings for hours. He refused to speak French but spoke German, instead. Just a few simple sentences, for his German was never good. Then he told her that he wanted to create ballets with Strauss's music.

But on other days he would just stay in bed and not move. Or repeat every word anyone said to him. Or smash the furniture in his room. Or smear the walls with crayons or food or excrement. He had nightmares, too, and visions in which he was Christ being led to crucifixion. He began seeing people who weren't there. He heard music, or a tennis ball bouncing back and forth. He cried. He called for his mother. He held his breath until he got red in the face. Ate too much or nothing at all. Called himself a "tired little horse," a "poor abandoned monkey." Attacked other patients, pushed them, tried to scare them with grimaces and leaps. Grabbed Romola's stepfather by the throat and started to choke him.

"I asked you to come, Bronia. Didn't you get my letter?"

3.

"TO MY RETURNED BRONIA," Diaghilev's telegram begins when he wires me the money for a ticket to Paris. "Come at once. I need you to choreograph for the London season." White orchids are delivered to the Bristol Hotel. Tougher than they may look to someone who doesn't know them.

It is the end of July, 1921. When Sergey Pavlovitch arrives to fetch me from the Gare de Lyon, I think him changed, aged, worn down. His face is puffed, sweaty with exertion and summer heat; the silver lock of his hair is plastered stiff to his forehead with greasy hair paste. Once I thought he resembled a bulldog. Now he is more of a sea lion. His movements are slow and forced: a body at odds with gravity. Seeing me on the platform, he opens his arms. I stumble into his embrace, tight, almost crushing. His frock coat smells of flowery cologne and sweat.

"How is he, Bronia?" I hear a muffled gasp. When I lift my head and look up, his cheeks are streaked with tears.

At the Steinhof Dr. Wagner had shown me a few pages with my brother's writing, and I remembered them now:

> *Diaghilev hit me with his cane because I wanted to leave him . . . I pushed him on a street in Paris because I wanted to show him that I was not afraid of him . . . Diaghilev reminds me of a wicked old woman when he moves his two false front teeth.*

"What did they quarrel about?" Dr. Wagner had asked. "Art," I had answered. "Diaghilev could not always see my brother's genius."

"What do the doctors say, Bronia?"

My eyes, too, fill with tears as I recount Dr. Wagner's words. Catatonic stupor has a predictable course. Mood swings and unpredictable actions come first, followed by depression and muscular rigidity. The stupor can last for hours, days or weeks. When it ends, as it eventually will, Vaslav might rage, scream, run around in a frenzy. Smash furniture, stab himself with any sharp object he can get hold of, strike others. Then the cycle begins again.

Sergey Pavlovitch gives me his handkerchief to dry my eyes. Then he takes it back and wipes his own face. "I wanted to go to Vaslav as soon as I heard," he says. "But *she* wouldn't let me. Said she would have me arrested if I tried to come. That all the doctors had been warned."

A monocle on a silken string is dangling on his chest. He picks at it carelessly, smearing the glass with his fingers.

She. Romola. "Like a block of ice, Bronia, this woman. All money and lawyers. Vaslav has never been like that. For him it was only art. With her it is what I owe him. What I have *not* done for him. What I have appropriated as mine. Has she told you that I haven't paid him for his last performance? Has she?"

I follow his lips as he speaks, a new habit, more and more necessary to make up for what I can no longer hear. Parched, I notice, the corners reddened. His two false teeth in the front do wobble when he touches them with his tongue.

"No wonder Vaslav had a breakdown! An artist locked with this half-baked aristocrat . . . deprived of cultured society."

Around us the platform is emptying. A porter is hovering a few steps away, eyeing my two frayed suitcases with an expectant smile. Sergey Pavlovitch waves him to approach.

"Did you tell the doctor Vaslav is a genius?" he inquires as we walk to the waiting cab, the porter deftly following in our footsteps.

"He knew that."

"Did he ask you anything?"

"Yes."

"What about?"

"Mother. Father. You."

"Me? What about me? Did the doctor know who I was?"

"The Tsar of Art."

"Is that what he called me?"

"No. That's what I said."

The Tsar of Art is breathing with difficulty, stopping a few times as we walk, leaning on his cane. Outside, the porter deposits my suitcases by the waiting cab, smiles at the coins Sergey Pavlovitch places in his open hand and salutes before turning back and walking away.

The cabbie must know where he is taking us, for the car begins to move as soon as Diaghilev gets inside. I scan the streets I haven't seen for seven years, scars of the Great War still visible. A captured German cannon on display, gaps along the grand boulevards where trees have been cut for firewood. Beggars, limbless, in worn-out army uniforms, standing at street corners. A man whose face is half covered with a metal mask. Two young women in mourning, one holding a little boy's hand.

"You blame me, too, Bronia, don't you?" Diaghilev asks.

The temptation of blame, I call it in my thoughts. Who betrayed whom first . . . who turned away . . . who dragged whom into that marriage . . . who was spending whose money . . . who fired whom . . . with what cruel words . . .

By the time I left Vienna, accusations were flying unchecked. Romola accusing Mamusia of pushing Vaslav too hard when he was a child.

"Making him feel guilty every time he lay down to rest!" Mamusia telling Romola that all she ever wanted was Vaslav's fame and money. "A thief," Mamusia called her. "A brigand." My children huddled, trying to weave these incomprehensible moments into their already incomprehensible worlds. "Is Aunt Romola a tsarina?" Irina had asked. "Will the Bolsheviks kill us all?"

I was alone, packing, when Romola stormed into my hotel room, dragging Kyra by the hand. Demanding to know where I was going and when I would be back.

"Paris. Then right away to London," I said, looking at my niece, who was pulling her hand from her mother's, complaining that she was squeezing it too hard. "I'll be back when the season ends."

"To Diaghilev, Bronia? That beast? That monster? After what he has done to Vaslav?"

"Where is Irina, Maman?" Kyra interrupted, her hand, freed, pounding on her mother's thigh. "You promised I could play with her."

I bent over Kyra, glad of the shield of her presence, explaining that Irina and Levushka had gone with their grandmother for a walk. That they would be back soon. Kyra frowned and stretched her right leg, flexing her foot. Her dark hair was cut just the way Mamusia cut ours when we were little. Straight over our eyebrows. She had Vaslav's eyes, almond-shaped, fiery. And his way of titling his head. "Tatakaboy can fly," she told me when I saw her for the first time. "Tatakaboy" is what she called her father.

"Is dancing more important than your own brother, Bronia?" Romola asked in an icy tone. In her tight-fitting flapper dress, her Cartier earrings, fishnet gloves, she looked like an actress ready for a grand finale. From her purse she extracted the telegram to Vaslav the whole of Paris once talked about, her ultimate evidence of Diaghilev's guilt:

> Monsieur Diaghilev considers that by missing a performance at Rio and refusing to dance in the ballet *Carnaval* you broke your contract STOP He will not therefore require your further services STOP

Blood rose to my head. I grasped the frame of the bed to steady myself as I let out my own accusations. How dare she blame me for her own meddling? Why didn't she stop Vaslav from hurting Mamusia and Diaghilev with a hasty marriage? Why did she make Vaslav refuse to dance in Rio? And does she forget that Diaghilev hired Vaslav back? So why can't I work for him? Has she not told Mamusia she would not pay our bills?

"So this is why you came from Russia, Bronia?" Romola seethed. "For Vaslav's money?"

It got worse. Slights real or imagined followed, dragged out, waved in triumph: how we, Vaslav's mother and sister, never accepted her because she wasn't Polish or Russian. How we wanted Vaslav to ourselves. His money. His connections. His fame.

Romola could understand our whispers. Romola wasn't stupid.

They all wanted her to divorce Vaslav. Her mother, her stepfather. The Hungarian authorities when the war began. Leave him, they said. He is an enemy— he is a madman—he is finished—he will be nothing to you but a burden. Yes, she could've abandoned him. Taken her daughters and left. She could've married again.

This is when I caught sight of Kyra, her head lowered, staring at the tip of her sandal. Romola did not stop, but I no longer listened.

"Shall we go and look for Irina?" I asked my niece, wiping my eyes with the heel of my hand. "She cannot be too far."

Kyra nodded, but she was still staring at her shoe. Before I had the time to take her out of the room, Romola snatched her daughter's hand from mine. "I should've known! You've always been jealous of him."

"Not in front of a child, please," I said, trying to keep my voice steady.

"Why not? Let my daughter hear what kind of family her genius father comes from."

A knock on the door ended this tirade. Kyra's nurse, holding baby Tamara in her arms, poked her head inside the room, asking if she was needed. Romola announced that they were just leaving. "For there is nothing else to say, is there?"

I watched them go. Romola slowly, in defiance. Kyra running out, without looking back. A wave of nausea rose to my throat. Black flecks appeared in front of my eyes.

When the doors closed, I sank to the floor. There was a wet spot on the carpet where Kyra had stood. I wiped it with my hand and raised the fingers to my nose. They smelled of pee.

To calm down before Mamusia returned with the children, I rose from the floor, washed my hands at the sink and opened the window. The afternoon was warm, though windy. I spotted them at the street corner, Mamusia holding Levushka's hand, Irina skipping in front of them in her blue dress and white socks. She looked up and, seeing me in the window, waved and pointed at something in her hand—what would later turn out to be a wooden carving of a peacock with a broken tail.

"Look, Mama! Look what we have found!"

No, I, Diaghilev's "returned Bronia," don't want to talk about blame on my first evening back in Paris.

I want to talk of what still matters. Of that miraculous instant at the Steinhof Asylum when the right words managed to bring my brother back. Of Kiev, the new ballets I created there, in which dance was stripped of all frills, of all that obscures movement, leaving only the essence of dance.

"It never pays to look back, Bronia," Diaghilev says. "You know what happened to Orpheus."

I don't listen to him. Not for the first time.

4.

IN LONDON I STAY AT A small but comfortable hotel near Leicester Square. I begin each morning with stretching exercises and a run-through of my body to check current points of weakness, identify and work through any stiffness or pain. My feet have bloodied, red patches, calluses that never go away, throbbing bunions, but my belly is as taut as it was before I had my children. In front of the wardrobe mirror I do a few simple gestures, a slow pirouette, a *plié*. A friendly mirror, I think it, reflecting back to me a body scarred but strong. An instrument. Fine tuned. Reliable. Solid.

In the hotel restaurant, decorated with hunting scenes of men in red jackets on horseback, hounds ready to take off, I eat a small breakfast. An egg. Roasted tomato. No toast. No butter. A cup of hot, sweet tea. The waiter, who knows by now not to offer milk, brings slices of lemon on a separate dessert plate. And three spoonfuls of jam. Strawberry, black-currant, quince. No marmalade.

This is the only quiet time in my day. I always bring a notebook and my cigarettes. After the last bit of jam, I record the events of the previous day and light the first cigarette. This is still a new pleasure but already irresistible. Holding a cigarette in my fingers, softening the tobacco inside, feeling it the way women used to feel chickens at the markets of my childhood. Placing it in my amber-tipped holder. Lighting it and then waiting for the crackling of burning paper and the caress of the first inhale.

At the Alhambra Theatre I teach the company class, audition new dancers, run daily rehearsals. Since I also dance the Lilac Fairy, I have to find the time for my own practice. Mamusia is in Vienna with the children, at the Central Pension, where the proprietor is kind enough to wait for his money until I get paid. Her letters always start with the news of the children. They both wake up at night crying. Irina is asking when I'll be back. Levushka loves chasing pigeons. Every time Mamusia gives him crumbs for the birds, he eats them. My son also uses feminine endings when he speaks of himself in Russian: "*Ya byla,*" not "*Ya byl.*" This is not a surprise. He is growing up among women.

The letters all end with Romola:

> *She has found her goal in life, and this is to speak in Vaslav's name. She has taken all that was his . . . She has destroyed him . . . She has severed all his ties with anyone from his past . . . She has placed herself between him and me . . . She has turned the doctors against me. I'm not welcome at my son's side.*

My mother's fury, I think, is her flimsy shield against despair.

To distract her, I fill my letters back with company news. Diaghilev's stepmother died in Russia. So did two of his nephews. Olga Khokhlova, our old friend from Monte Carlo, is now-fashionable Madame Picasso, the mother of Paulo, with a chauffeur, two maids and a nanny, and asks me to pass on her warmest greetings. Karsavina is in London, a diplomat's wife, but she no longer dances for Diaghilev. Pavlova is touring the world with her own company. Fokine got out of Russia and is now in Sweden. Such is, I write, the *new* Ballets Russes.

In this new Ballets Russes I'm La Nijinska, the sister of you-know-who. One who can recall every ballet she has ever seen, including every step of Petipa's choreography. The dancers I work with, new and old, are my colleagues but not my friends. I don't stand with them during breaks. I excuse myself from late-evening drinks in the pub. I dread questions about Vaslav or Russia, the platitudes I would have to offer in reply.

At such moments I miss my Kiev students the most. The easy closeness borne out of simple joys. The roster of duties so gladly assumed. Chopping wood. Clearing the snow. Finding paint for the sets, fabric for costumes or just a few discarded boards that would give us a few hours of warmth.

Ever since that first evening in Paris, Diaghilev and I have been arguing. The "returned Bronia" still cannot get over the fact that her first assignment as choreographer for Ballets Russes, the most modern and experimental Western dance company, is *The Sleeping Beauty*. Renamed *The Sleeping Princess,* for, as Diaghilev quips, beauties are plentiful, but thanks to the revolution the supply of princesses has dwindled.

"Isn't that precisely what we opposed at the Mariinsky?" I argue. "Petipa's tired old tricks?"

"The Russia we opposed, Bronia," Diaghilev says, "has been murdered. And it was not all bad! We need to remind the world of that!"

"What about the new Russia, which the Bolsheviks are killing right now!" I don't give up. "Why don't we stage new Russian ballets?"

But since the Tsar of Art always believes he is right, I'm in London dusting off imperial glitter. "Only the best, Bronia," Diaghilev assures me. Best soloists, best costumes, best sets. Olga Spessivtseva! Vera Trefilova! Lubov Egorova! Stravinsky is reorchestrating Tchaikovsky's music. Lev Bakst is working on the sets and costumes.

"Choreography by Bronislava Nijinska," Diaghilev put in his first ad, but I protested. I didn't wish anyone to think that this is all I'm capable of. Finally, we agreed on "Choreography by Petipa with additional dances by Bronislava Nijinska."

For the past few weeks, at Diaghilev's urging, newspapers carry articles on Imperial School training. Russian dancers, I read, were pampered by the tsar, chaperoned to and from performances in gilded carriages, fed chocolates by imperial hands. Now Diaghilev is offering England a slice of that old Russia lost to them forever.

"Nostalgia sells, Bronia" is Diaghilev's crowning argument. This is said with a wink and followed by assurances that he is not giving up *real* ballets or modern music. He just needs the money to stage them.

And I? I have a family to feed.

We are in the third week of rehearsals when Diaghilev brings me Sasha's letter; hands it to me with two fingers, teasingly. "Smeared with marital guilt, I presume?" he says, and I think I might've told him too much. "Or just a case of general Russian malaise? In a rather shabby envelope, if I may be the judge." He takes a sniff at it, adding, "Sasha darling is smoking cheap cigarettes."

I tear the flap, recoiling at the memory of him in the woodshed on Fondukleievska Street, packing his rucksack, turning away from me.

There is a single page inside the envelope, covered in Sasha's neat, even handwriting. Dainty, almost, I think, like lace. He saw my name in the paper in an article on the Ballets Russes's much-awaited London season: "Madame Nijinska, newly arrived from Russia, has rejoined the company." This is how he knew where to look for me.

> *I'm sorry it all went so terribly wrong. I want to see you, Bronia. I want to see the children. We had so many wonderful years together. When I think of our quarrel in Kiev, now it seems to me incomprehensible. Did we really—in the middle of all this mayhem—fight over whether Levushka will be a concert pianist?*

"Good news?" Diaghilev asks. "All things considered?"

I'm grateful for the lack of sarcasm in his voice. And for his hand on my shoulder, a gentle, soothing pat.

"Yes," I say, slowly. "All things considered."

I arrive at the hotel on Cranbourn Street unsure of my own feelings. He has left you, I remind myself. He has not written. You don't even know where he has been. But when I glimpse him in the lobby, tall and slim, pacing nervously back and forth, holding a bouquet of flowers, I feel the old anger thinning. Letters got lost in the war. Perhaps he did write and thinks it is me who has not answered. We have two children together. I have no right to keep him away from them.

Sasha stops when he sees me; his face lightens up with joy I cannot doubt. A moment later he hurries toward me, kisses my hand, hands me the flowers. Red roses, long-stemmed, awkward to hold.

I wish the children were with me. Imagine Levushka's tight, sweaty grip, Irina biting her upper lip. This is your father, I would say. He has come to see you.

"Do they ask about me?"

"Yes."

Sasha doesn't take his eyes off me. It is a misty October evening; wet London chill lingers in the bones. My coat is grey, shapeless and too loose, one of Romola's cast-off gifts I cannot yet afford to replace.

"You haven't changed, Bronia. Your hair is still short."

Behind me the hotel door opens, letting in a draft of cold air.

I take a step away from the door. Sasha moves forward, but when I stop, he doesn't, crushing into the flowers I hold.

"Shall we eat something?" Sasha asks. "You must be hungry. After the whole day at the theatre."

"Very hungry."

"I thought you would be," Sasha says, gesturing at the hotel restaurant. I follow as he walks. He stops by the wooden lectern. He has made a reservation he informs the hostess. The name is Kotchetovsky.

Sasha's English has always been good, but now it is even more fluid, assured. Has he been here, in London, all these years? Like Irina, he has an ear for languages, an ability to imitate accents with great ease. I will tell her that.

The hostess points at the coat rack. Seeing the flowers in my hands, she bends under the table and produces a glass vase to relieve me of my burden. Sasha helps me with the coat. Before leaving the theatre I had put on the good blouse I keep there to wear with my slacks—Diaghilev's gift for when he needs my presence at some late supper with a balletomane or benefactor. The blouse is quite becoming, with a collar of shimmering fabric. Diaghilev, like Mamusia, believes in the power of an artistic appearance.

And I? I do not want Sasha to think that without him I have let myself go.

The hotel restaurant is quite dark, lit only by weak ceiling lamps. The tables are covered with crimson tablecloths. A waitress mumbles something I cannot hear and hands us two thick folders with menus. She is wearing a white apron, and a lace headpiece like an old-fashioned St. Petersburg maid.

"She asked if we want a drink," Sasha says.

"Wine," I say. "White."

"French," Sasha tells the waitress. "Dry."

The chair is soft, well padded. After the whole day of rehearsing, I welcome its soothing comfort.

Sasha leans back and I see his lips move. "You have to speak louder," I say, pointing at my right ear, reminding him of that shelling in Kiev when a mortar hit the house next door. The din in my ear has never gone away, though it dampens only some frequencies, as if someone cut off parts of sounds, blurring them. I have to guess what I do not hear. It gets worse when I'm tired or when there is noise around me.

Sasha remembers the shelling but not its consequences. "Your hearing wasn't so bad then, was it?" he asks.

"Let's not talk about it anymore," I say. "We are all scarred."

He nods.

We have so many good memories of London, Sasha reminds me. The restaurants where we used to escape from the others, complaining about English food. Carrots and peas boiled tasteless, thick salty gravy on thin slices of beef. Bread that resembled cotton wool.

Good beer, though, I agree. Decent wines. Like the one we are drinking now. Nicely chilled, clear, with an aftertaste of sun-soaked grapes.

"Do you have photos of the children?" Sasha asks.

I reach into my purse for the small pocket-sized album I always carry with me. As Sasha flips through the pages, I describe what he is seeing, fill in the missing details: Irina just after we arrived in Vienna. That big bow in her hair is blue. Her dress is white. Mamusia made it for her from my old one. Here Irina is in her dancing costume, at the barre. Mamusia is teaching her. In the old Russia she would now be preparing for the entrance exams at the Imperial Ballet School. Taking advance classes. Fretting over her weaknesses.

"Is this my son?" Sasha asks, looking at Levushka in a sailor's suit. "But he is already a man!"

I tell him that Irina wants to know if she resembles Papa or me.

"And what do you say?"

"That she laughs just like her father."

Levushka's questions are simpler. "Papa?" he asks, pointing at men in the street. Especially when they wear military coats with shining buttons, wield a gun and look important.

"May I have it?" Sasha asks, choosing a photograph of the two of them playing in a Warsaw park right before leaving for Vienna.

I nod and take another sip of wine, thinking that I should eat something, but the food is slow coming.

During our last weeks in Kiev, I tell Sasha, to amuse Levushka Irina "mounted" ballets for the two of them, drawing scenes in makeshift notebooks Mamusia made for her from scraps of paper, binding them in the middle with a thread. In Levushka's favourite one the "Whites" and the "Reds" were fighting a rather haphazard and chaotic battle. But since Levushka got bored quickly, Irina made him jump and unfurl banners she had fashioned herself. One said, "Death to the enemies of the people."

"My daughter? A Bolshevik?" Sasha laughs and I laugh, too. Children play with what they see and hear, don't they?

That evening we eat shepherd's pie. We drink far too much wine. We share a bowl of trifle, which—Sasha declares—is just about the only dessert worth having in London.

We reshape our stories of the past. I of escape. He of departure.

"I wrote to you from Odessa, Bronia. Begging you to join me. For two weeks, I practically lived at the station. I scouted the platforms, met every train that came from Kiev. Ran after every woman who resembled you. I had a connection who promised to take the three of us—four if your mother wished to go, too—on a boat to Constantinople. I waited in vain."

Sasha's leg finds mine under the table. Just a touch at first, but then, slowly a persistent presence.

"I wonder what he wants, Bronia," Diaghilev said as I was leaving the theatre to come here. "To get back into Ballets Russes or just your bed?"

"I didn't get your letters," I tell Sasha, but I don't point out that in 1919, when he left, the front was running right through Kiev. That frantic crowds waited at the station, storming the trains. That Levushka was weak and colicky. That I needed a wet nurse to keep him alive. That Irina had nightmares. I don't mention my school, my students, my ballets, either. I believe that there will be time for straightening it all out.

"I did write, Bronia. I did wait. You must believe me. Only, when I knew you wouldn't be coming, I went. To Sevastopol, through Constantinople to Paris."

Sasha speaks loud enough for me to hear him, ignoring the disapproving looks from other tables. "Don't mind them," he says. "We are foreigners. We are expected to create an outrage. Even if it's a small one."

Under the table his hand is caressing my knee.

I take another sip of wine. I close my eyes. He is still my husband, I think. My children still have a father.

The next day Sasha comes to the theatre while I'm teaching the company class, giving corrections to one of the newly hired dancer. I order a short break and walk up to Sasha. "I can't see you now," I say, making a gesture that includes the dancers at the barre, the rushing stagehands, the wardrobe attendants.

"I know." He grins. "I'm off. Just wanted to see La Nijinska in her full splendour."

I wave him away.

On Sunday, my free day, Sasha and I go for a walk to Hyde Park. Like Paris, London has not escaped the scars of the Great War. Men with artificial legs limp by. Veterans at street stalls sell jewellery made from copper shells. Pendants, necklaces, time capsules. "Made in the trenches," the handwritten signs say.

"For you," Sasha says, picking a piece of crystal locked in a copper tube.

Sasha looks somber, subdued. He tells me that the day before he was trying to buy some toys and clothes to send to the children and realized he didn't know what they liked. He could not answer the shop assistant's simplest questions. How tall Levushka is. What is Irina's favourite colour.

Blue, I tell him. Levushka is forty inches—tall for his age.

We walk toward the Serpentine, where the ducks swim by the shore. I wish I'd brought some breakfast toast with me to give them.

Dancing is so haphazard, Sasha says, so much the matter of chance. He has made many mistakes. In Paris he is barely making any money in vaudeville shows. Threatening his limbs every night. "Yesterday when I saw you at the Alhambra, Bronia," he says wistfully. "All those young dancers looking up to you! This is what I need."

"Having young dancers look up to you?" I tease.

"You know what I mean," he says with a laugh, and squeezes my hand.

If nothing else works out for him in Europe, Sasha continues, he will have to go to America. New York or Chicago. Maybe to Hollywood. Character dancers, he has heard, are in short supply there. For now, he needs to return to Paris, to the shows he has committed to. He is quite popular on the Apache dance circuit. A neckerchief, a cap, he says of his costume, tight-fitting shirt, fitted pants. Back bends are tricky. Mock slaps and punches. He has to throw his partner to the ground.

"Remember the ragtime number we danced in St. Petersburg?" he asks.

"A hundred rubles a night? How can I forget?"

We stop. The ducks have given up on us, eyeing better prospects: two brothers in grey coats, with bulky paper bags, their governess or nanny staying on the path, rocking a big pram. The smaller of the boys bends over the water and empties the whole bag at once. "What are you doing, silly?" his brother shouts.

We sit on the bench and I fish in my purse for my cigarette case with the last two Sobranie "cocktails," the old imperial brand. I have been saving them for a special occasion.

Sasha whistles with appreciation. "Where did you get them?" he asks.

"Olga Picasso's welcome gift." I chuckle, cigarette in hand, and watch as he bends toward me, to light it. There is a dark shadow of stubble over his upper lip and chin.

I believe that we have to start repairing us somewhere, and starting with our bodies is the safest way.

We make love that afternoon. In Sasha's hotel room, which is small and shabby, with blankets rough from frequent washing, and a small basin in the corner, with scalding water in one tap and ice cold in the other.

We search for what we still remember. The smooth, velvet skin on his belly, the ticklish spot under my ribs. The white lines where the surgeon once cut the skin to set broken bones: on my shin, on his ankle. We take the measure of the last two years. What is stronger, what weakened. What has changed and what feels the same.

The soothing, warm spasms of pleasure.

Afterwards, we lie close, covered with sheets and blankets, warming each other. He tickles me under my chin, just as he once used to, to make me laugh.

"What was his name?" he asks.

"Whose name?"

"The dancer you were correcting."

"Patrick. He isn't that good, but he has the hunger to excel. And he can project warmth onstage. He reminds me of one of my Kiev students."

"Aha. I asked and I got the answer."

"What answer?"

"Nothing. You are right. He's not that good yet."

"You are not jealous, are you?"

"Jealous? Of that little boy?" Sasha laughs, banging his fists on his chest. "Me? Tarzan?"

I laugh, too.

Sasha rolls to the side and rummages for his cigarettes. We smoke together, sitting up, propped against the pillows. And then he says, "I want to be with you, like we used to be. I want us to work together again. Will you think about it while I am in Paris? Ask Diaghilev if he would have me back?"

I tell him that I will.

5.

THE NOVEMBER PREMIERE of *The Sleeping Princess* is a series of mishaps. Falling sets, broken machinery. Then come the reviews: "derivative . . . nostalgic . . . London expects more from Ballets Russes and Monsieur Diaghilev's once-so-innovative vision." Whatever praises there are go to individual dancers—to Trefilova, to Spessivtseva—although my choreography of the "Dance of the Three Ivans" is called "particularly inventive and daring."

Diaghilev urges us all not to lose faith. We have been in worse scrapes and come through. Forget the critics. Think of the audience. Ballet doesn't always have to break new ground. What's wrong with just giving people an evening of true pleasure? Showing London the Russia we grew up in?

Worse than bad reviews is the fact that the shows are not selling out. Diaghilev sneaks in and out of the Alhambra to avoid creditors. The dancers whisper that we might not get paid.

In his last letter Sasha promised to come back as soon as he gets a few free days. He has also written to the children, sent them toys. He tells me he hasn't heard back from them yet, but it has only been two weeks, so he will be patient.

One day in the first week of December, I'm standing in the theatre lobby during a break in the rehearsal, smoking a cigarette I've craved since the morning. I am wondering where I will find the money to pay our Vienna bills and whether I should mention any of it to Sasha.

The young woman who walks into the lobby looks like a dancer in search of work or lessons. A bit awkward for a dancer, though, I decide, for she moves with some hesitation, carrying a folded raincoat on her arm.

She comes up straight to me.

"Madame Nijinska?" she asks, and I take in the red lipstick, piercing black eyes and thick curly hair. A "Gypsy look," we called it in Russia.

"Yes," I say.

She is English. Her Russian is very bad. Her French is better. Her name is Celia Goodman. She is a dancer. *Corps de ballet* in a small company whose name means nothing to me.

"I don't know what to do," she says, and drops the arm with the folded coat to reveal her protruding belly. Fifth month, I think, still not quite sure what it has to do with me. She says something more, but I cannot make out the words. Something about having to see me. Is she apologizing? For what?

"Sasha didn't tell you?" she finally asks, squinting as if it strained her to pronounce his name. "I thought he wouldn't. I thought it would be best if I came to see you myself."

She took a train from Paris yesterday then the ferry and another train. She came straight from the station.

"His child?" I say, looking down at her belly, my cheeks flushing as though I were the one responsible.

She nods.

Celia Goodman makes no claims on Sasha. She knew he was married when she met him. But he has told her his wife left him and stayed behind in Russia, so she thought it was all right.

My hand begins to quiver.

Sasha, she continues, has prospects in New York. Someone has promised him an engagement on Broadway. Also teaching and dancing in Chicago and Cleveland. He asked her to go with him. Her baby—their baby—would be born in America. But lately Sasha has been talking of staying in Europe, of being asked to rejoin Ballets Russes. He didn't tell her about coming to London to see me. But she figured it out. Her mother saw me dancing the Lilac Fairy. Her mother lives in London.

Celia Goodman watches me with nervous caution as she speaks. What has Sasha told her about me? I wonder. That I am a Fury? A jealous wife likely to scratch her eyes out?

"What do you want from me?" I ask.

She cocks her head. "Are you and Sasha together again?"

"What did he say?"

He is Sasha. He didn't tell her much: That it will work itself out. That he will not abandon her.

The rehearsal room door opens; a head pops out. I'm needed inside.

"It *will* work itself out," I say. "But I need to go now."

"Y-yes," she stammers. "Of course."

I'm tempted to end my marriage with a telegram, in the way of Diaghilev: *Applying for divorce. Marry your fiancée. Take her to America. Bronia.* Eleven words, not counting the address. But in the end I write Sasha a letter. Short, straightforward, amounting to the same thing.

He telephones me at my hotel two days later, his voice a mixture of astonishment and pain. As if it were all my fault.

"When did you intend to tell me?" I ask.

The gasp for air is followed by excuses, explanations, reasons. He made a mistake. He was lonely. He thought I was never going to leave Kiev. He thought he would never see his children again.

Milkweed seeds, I think, little white parachutes, anchoring themselves anywhere they can.

"Why didn't you tell me, Sasha?"

"I meant to."

"When?"

"As soon as I was sure you would listen."

He is still talking when I put the receiver down and light a cigarette. Blow smoke up into the air.

What do I feel? Hurt. Jealousy. Anger. But something else, too. Relief. An echo of that moment on the border. Water still sloshing around my shins, my sandals sinking into the sandy bank. Mamusia's hand still gripping mine. The moment I know that the four of us have made it to the Polish side. Alive.

6.

BY FEBRUARY OF 1922 it looks as if Ballets Russes might become history. After 115 performances, the Alhambra takes Diaghilev to court for unpaid debts.

Diaghilev has not come to rehearsals for the past few days, so when I spot him alone in a cheap restaurant, I walk in determined to find out the extent of our troubles. I expect he might resent my presence, but he waves as soon as he sees me. "Come, come, Bronia," he yells, causing the other patrons to jump and give us looks.

"How much?" I ask, thinking of my own unpaid Vienna bills, the shoes the children have outgrown.

"Thousands," he says. "Of pounds." If it were German marks, he would be laughing. The dollar is now worth 320 marks, while merely a year ago it was eighty-four.

"A pity, then, that we are in England, Sergey Pavlovitch," I say as I sit down at his table. He still smells of almond blossoms and dry sweat. The shoulders of his black frock coat are still sprinkled with white flecks of dandruff.

That one sentence brings forth a tirade. The English, cool as cucumbers. Unable to appreciate the pearls he is throwing in front of them. Mumbling as if they had mouths filled with bliny. Only the devil understands them.

"They lined up all night for *Spectre*. They loved *Petrushka*," I say.

He gives me a hard stare. I hold his gaze. He sighs.

"Always contradicting me, Bronia," he says.

"Not always. Only when you need it."

Diaghilev orders the cheapest dish on the menu, a shepherd's pie. No wine. No beer. When the plate arrives, white cloud of mashed potatoes covering the slimy minced meat underneath, he looks at it with disgust. "More water," he calls to the waiter, who hurries over with a pitcher.

I order a small salad. I, too, ask for water to drink.

"You'll soon hear many vicious things about me," Diaghilev says.

"True things?"

"Some of them."

He plunges his fork into his shepherd's pie. His hands are trembling. "Not enough nutmeg," he says.

"You haven't even tried it yet."

"Believe me."

"I always do in the end."

"This is not going to be pretty this time."

"I never cared for pretty. Remember how we quarrelled when you wanted me to dye my hair red? You said I was 'too solid. Too real.'"

"Would La Nijinska ever let me forget?"

He laughs. A hearty laugh I do not expect from him. Not now. Not after he has outlined the extent of the disaster about to be revealed. There are lawsuits pending. The costumes and the sets will be impounded for unpaid bills after the last performance, making it impossible to show *The Sleeping Princess* in Paris. There is to be a ban on performing in London for at least three years.

"Let's not talk of it anymore," Diaghilev says. "What will you do when it all collapses?"

"Go back to Vienna. My mother needs me."

Mamusia's letters describe increasingly bitter visits to the Steinhof Asylum: "I cannot restrain myself seeing how much wrong has been done to Vaslav . . . The doctors won't see me, Bronia . . . Vaslav has thrown a chair at me . . . It smashed to pieces against the wall."

"What have I done now?" Diaghilev asks, handing me a handkerchief to wipe my eyes.

"It is not always about you, Sergey Pavlovitch."

"How disappointing! You are not crying over that good-for-nothing husband of yours, are you?"

"No."

"You know I still feel responsible for that marriage. After all, I gave you away to him. Shall I congratulate the two of you on a glorious reunion?"

"Let's not talk about that, either."

He gives me a piercing look. "Then let's get the cheapest wine to toast our glorious and not-so-glorious defeats."

When a bottle arrives, Diaghilev makes a big show of tasting the wine and pronouncing it vile enough for our purpose. Medicine is never supposed to taste good, is it?

We talk of the new child dancer Diaghilev has found, Alicia Marks, who has the makings of a great ballerina and whom he wants me to see. We talk of Kschessinska, who has finally married one of her grand dukes, in Cannes. Her sumptuous mansion on Trotsky Square may be Bolshevik headquarters, but Mathilda the Great is now a real Romanov princess, still giving her famous parties and charming her newly acquired, if quite a bit tarnished, relatives.

"Should I finally ask her if there really was a secret tunnel connecting her house with the Winter Palace, Bronia?"

"Yes."

"Before or after I ask her for a loan?"

"Before!"

At the Alhambra, *The Sleeping Princess* will run for one more week. Four more times I will put on my Lilac Fairy costume: the bulky skirt, the royal coat, the wig of golden locks and a small crown. I'll smear greasepaint on my cheeks, draw black lines over my eyes to make them look bigger. "But not too big," Diaghilev's remembered voice will caution, words I've repeated so many times to my dancers. "Only the first few rows will see your face, Bronia. For the rest of them it will be a blur. It's with your dancing that you have to captivate them, not with your makeup."

His plate empty, my salad finished, Diaghilev dives into his pocket to pay for our meal. "I'll walk you to your hotel," he says, heaving himself up with a deep sigh and a squint.

We make our slow way through the half-empty street on this cold, misty evening. A car passes by slowly, feeling its way through fog.

Other pedestrians appear out of the fog for a few moments and disappear again.

Diaghilev's voice is punctuated by the tapping of his cane on the pavement.

"Remember what Vasily likes to say, Bronia? Master Diaghilev doesn't have a penny, but his intelligence is worth a fortune.

"I still have friends in Paris.

"You are still my choreographer, Bronia. Think big. Think bold.

"We will bring back *Faun*. Remind these philistines in their moth-infested fineries who we really are. Then maybe *Sacre* again? Or no—no, we need something new."

And then, as we stand in front of my hotel door, Diaghilev's hand extends toward me, smooths my cheek. Do I remind him of Vaslav? And if I do, does it hurt or please him?

"Last-minute rescues have always been my specialty, Bronia," he says before turning away and melting into the fog.

I recall his words a few days later when the news breaks that Diaghilev has escaped to Paris like a thief; before the last performance, without paying his hotel bill. He has borrowed the money for his passage from the mother of one of the British dancers. He is in Paris now, at Misia Sert's apartment, hiding from creditors. No more wages will be paid.

After the last performance, with the Alhambra stagehands keeping guard at the dressing room doors so that we can't steal the costumes or anything else of value, I collect my practice clothes, my shoes, my makeup tubes.

I go back to Vienna, also on borrowed money, to Mamusia and the children. Back to nightclub dance numbers, the prospect of some dancing lessons.

This is where a telegram from Diaghilev finds me:

Miracles do happen STOP We are saved STOP Come to Monte Carlo at once STOP

7.

THE MIRACULOUS ARRANGEMENT with the Théâtre de Monte-Carlo means that Ballets Russes has a permanent home and a permanent subsidy. "All paid by the Casino profits," Diaghilev tells me at the Café de Paris, where he holds court every afternoon. There is money for new ballets. There is money for workshops. For travel. There is money for old debts.

I bring Mamusia and the children from Vienna. Soon we are well settled. We are renting a spacious apartment in a Beausoleil villa a few minutes' walk from the opera house. Irina has started school and continues her dance lessons with Mamusia. Levushka no longer wakes up screaming. I throw myself into work.

I am in the midst of rehearsing a new ballet to Stravinsky's music, when Kolya Singayevsky, one of my Kiev students, arrives at the opera house, a tattered suitcase in hand. I barely recognize him at first. A wetland bird, I thought him in Kiev, slightly awkward, with long, wobbly legs. He looks slightly more balanced now.

"I didn't know where to go . . . I—I don't know anyone else . . ." Kolya stammers.

He left Kiev seven months after we did. Got on a train to Odessa then snuck onto a west-bound ship, where he hid among coils of rope until the ship was at sea. To pay his way he gutted fish in the ship kitchen. Got off in Varna with a Russian family he befriended, who took him to Paris. There he learnt that I was in Monte Carlo with Ballets Russes.

"Did Papa tell you where we live now?" Levushka asks Kolya when I bring him home that day. After I refused to talk to him, Sasha showed up in Vienna, hoping Mamusia would help him change my mind. She wouldn't, but he did spend a whole day with the children, and in Levushka's memory this day shines with an untarnished glow. The Prater, a puppet show, a ride on the Ferris wheel.

Levushka frowns when Kolya tells him that he read about his mama in the papers. And that no, there was nothing in the papers about him or Irina. Not even about his famous collection of shells.

"Shh," Irina says. "Let Kolya speak." At nine she is tall for her age and graceful, so much prettier than I ever was.

"'Nikolay Nikolaevitch' to you," I insist, but Kolya protests. To my children, he is not Nikolay Nikolaevitch. Unless I want to make him feel like a stranger.

"Kolya," then. Weighed by stories of a Kiev that no longer resembles the city I fled. The Young Theatre has been closed. Aleksandra Exter is in Moscow, teaching colour and composition. Anya is in St. Petersburg, asking about me.

"You've spoilt us for any other life," Kolya tells me, after wolfing down Mamusia's borscht and more *bitki* than I've cared to count.

I still get letters from Kiev. The stiff, official ones that have to be read as though written in cipher and the more candid ones smuggled through the still-porous borders. "No one can replace you. No one can teach us what we really want to learn," Pati has written. She is dancing at the Kiev Opera and hating every day of it. Benedikt and Tata ask my forgiveness "if some of us stop writing. If you were here, you would understand."

Too many have left, I read between the lines. Too much has ended.

I persuade Diaghilev to see Kolya dance.

"How many more reasons do you require?" he asks, after enumerating Singayevsky's shortcomings. Heavy bearing. No spark in his dancing. Poor turnout. To be fair, some fluidity, perhaps. With tutoring, Kolya might be a notch above *corps*, but only in limited capacity. "Do you want him out of guilt, Bronia?"

I shake my head. "No guilt."

"Then what?"

"Kolya was one of my students, Sergey Pavlovitch. He needs to start somewhere. I'm the only one he knows."

"May I suggest accounting? Or sweeping the floor before you as you walk?"

"Humour me, please."

"Handsome Singayevsky," Diaghilev says with a chuckle, rolling the words on his tongue. "Head over heels in love with you, of course. Nice to know that even La Nijinska is not immune to earthly temptations."

I think this utter nonsense. I say so.

"Come on, Bronia. You can't be that blind!"

We pull and push often these days, my visions, my intuition wrestling against his. I want to give Kolya a chance. Diaghilev wants to hire Sergey

Lifar, another Kiev student of mine who has shown up, and whom I think utterly devoid of talent.

A trade.

"Oh, just take your Kolya! Only, don't let him leach on to you for nothing." His hands are rubbing as if he has just closed a deal. I know what's coming. Another Russian joke. The sign that no revolution can break the Russian spirit.

"How do you deal with mice in the Kremlin?"

I play along, feign anticipation, laugh when the punchline arrives.

"Put up a sign saying Collective Farm. Then half the mice will starve and the rest will run away."

8.

SUNDAYS ARE THE ONLY DAY I'm home. Over breakfast we talk about what has happened during the week. I mostly stick to the funny stories of slips and mishaps, which my children love: how the sets went missing, only to turn up in the wrong ballet; how a ballerina was carried offstage by a distracted partner just when she was supposed to dance her own solo.

Then the children take their turns. Irina performs a routine she has worked on during the week. Mamusia designs it so that it is simple enough but also varied, so that all muscle groups get developed.

Levushka watches but always refuses to try.

At three Vaslav danced the *hopak* in the children's performance. Levushka is almost four. Instead of dance lessons, he wants a bicycle and he wants to play soccer. "All these rough games," Mamusia says with a grimace. "They interfere with the body's harmony." Once a boy on the beach teased him. "Jump, Nijinsky," the boy said, and Levushka flew at him with fists.

While Irina dances, I never correct her. When she finishes her routine, I feel her legs, her joints, her back. I look for the strengthening muscles, the evidence of her progress. I praise what I like. Her precision. Her grace.

She smiles, visibly relieved.

Levushka is jealous of our intimacy. He presses his body to my side, demands we look at his drawing of seashells. He is still too young for school so Mamusia takes him to the beach; to the Oceanographic Museum, where she devises clever little games for him. "Can you spot a red flag on this ship?" she asks in front of a painting. My son goes along with it most of the time, but once he told her that she was old enough to spot things for herself, without his help.

"Why don't you sit down," I tell Mamusia. "Rest."

She is so small, so birdlike, always in motion. Working far too hard. We have a hired girl who comes once a week to do the heavy cleaning, but the rest Mamusia manages by herself. "I have to keep busy," she says, dismissing my concern. She wants to be so tired in the evening that she will fall asleep without thinking. "Not to give vultures a chance," she says, meaning the circling thoughts, their sharp beaks.

I know when the pursuit is too close, for then I find her at the kitchen table, waiting for me to come home, no matter how late it gets. I know her laments by heart: Stassik dying alone, thinking himself abandoned, betrayed; Vaslav, beloved of the gods, snatched away, a prisoner of his own mind, pushing her away with fury; her two sisters gone, their graves somewhere she can never visit. So much lost, destroyed. How to live with such burdens, Bronia?

I hold her, smooth her grey hair, plaited then coiled into a bun, smaller with each year.

I wait for her sobbing to stop. I offer small, tested pleasures. Chocolates. Madeleines. Strawberry pastry. I love to watch her eat. Small, dainty forkfuls, the guilty licks of the tines. I dip into the memories I know she craves. The exquisite beauty of Vaslav's dancing. The thankful words of those he moved and inspired.

"What would I do without you?" I ask.

9.

"THINK OF MARRIAGE, BRONIA," Diaghilev tells me. "Think of a wedding."

A Russian wedding. Bright, colourful. Dances that make the audience want to jump out of their seats. After "that imperial *merde*, 'The Sleeping

Bitch,'" we need a spectacular success. "You were right, Bronia. Aristocrats are former people. Empty, glittering shells. The soul of Russia—just like Tolstoy taught us—is the peasant."

The Monte Carlo contract has buoyed Diaghilev's spirits. "All those mediocre souls who thought me finished." And he chuckles, flanked by his adoring golden boys who mirror his every move. Patrick, who has renamed himself Anton Dolin. Diaghilev's new secretary, Boris Kochno, and Sergey Lifar—or "Serge," as he calls himself now—still newly hired and thus not as sure of himself as I remember him from Kiev. All three flexing their muscles, eyeing one another with murderous jealousy, registering every sign of Diaghilev's favour. An elegant kid leather wallet, a well-thumbed copy of *Death in Venice*, an invitation to tea, a trip to the museum. Then there are the transient ones. Appearing, bewildered, dazzled for a day or two, only to disappear without a trace.

Boys, not men. Pliant and grateful. Vaslav's pallid, disappointing shadows.

"Diaghilev's court," the other dancers call them. It *is* a court, with intrigues and petty hatreds. And Sergey Pavlovitch, the all-powerful emperor, keeps them all in check. No golden boy ever truly knows where he is and where he is heading. Up or down? In or out?

I'm a choreographer, I tell myself. I place dancers onstage. I move them around in and out of music. The only tensions that matter to me are in my art. I won't be drawn into intrigues.

A ballet set to Stravinsky's *Les Noces* has been in the works for almost ten years. Vaslav was to choreograph it once, but Stravinsky kept changing the music, adding more and more instruments or voices to the chorus.

Now, Diaghilev announces, the score is finished.

Igor Stravinsky plays it for me himself, in Monte Carlo where Diaghilev summons him with a telegram and a first-class train ticket. "Just the piano," Stravinsky warns, without the chorus, without the orchestra. Sometimes he refers to the work as a cantata, sometimes an oratorio. The singing will be entirely in Russian.

To make sure I hear everything, I sit close to the piano and shut my eyes. Even stripped down the music grips me with its overwhelming sadness. Unrelenting, I think it, as it sweeps me into its current.

After the last note ends, Stravinsky stands up and leans over the piano. His eyes, from underneath his thick glasses, pin me with a questioning look. We are not exactly friends. "Igor Feodorovitch . . . Bronislava Fominitchna," we address each other. I think him a great artist but a slippery man, ready to change his mind when it suits him. For him I'm Vaslav's sister, commanding some of the Nijinsky touch but unfeminine, devoid of charm.

"Could you please play it again, Igor Feodorovitch?" I ask.

I want to be sure of the images that float toward me. For I already know that my quarrels will not be with Stravinsky but with Diaghilev.

"This is how I see it, Bronia. The girls coming in with the comb to comb the bride's hair at the wedding."

"No. We don't need the comb. All we need is the idea of the comb."

"A wedding cart?"

"No cart. Circling of the arms is enough."

"I see whitewashed huts, Bronia. Wicker fences, clay pots drying on them. Sunflowers, watermelons. Women with kerchiefs over their hair, embroidered, rich, sparkling. This is a beautiful Russian wedding. A feast of colours."

"We are not at a folklore festival, Sergey Pavlovitch. We are in a real village. Colours are expensive for a peasant. There is little time in the day for frills. And even less money."

"Joy, then?"

"What joy? The bride is leaving her parents to go with a man who has been chosen for her. To her future family she is an extra pair of hands. She has to say goodbye to her mother and to her youth. And the groom? How can he rejoice? Seeing for the first time a girl who will be his wife? Not sure if he even likes her?"

"Look at these costumes I've commissioned, Bronia. Look at these sets. Beautiful like Easter ornaments. Like paintings decorating the whitewashed walls."

"These heavy long robes? Boots on heavy heels? Yes, they are magnificent, Sergey Pavlovitch. Suitable, perhaps, for some grand Russian opera, but completely impossible for any ballet. They don't respond to Stravinsky's music. They have nothing in common with the way I see *Les Noces.*"

"Stravinsky liked them. I've already told Natalia Goncharova that I've approved them."

"Didn't you tear up Picasso's first sketches for *Parade*? Tell him to come up with something more suitable? Can't you ask Goncharova to redesign hers?"

A sigh. A shrug. A grunt. A flash of cold anger. I'm not just contrary and pigheaded. I need to be reined in. Reminded who I am.

"I shall not let you direct *Les Noces,* Bronia."

"Fine."

And then, after months of such bickering: "What did you say the other day, Bronia? All we need is fragments? Abstractions? What would you do with the story, then?"

"Replace it with pure choreography. Get rid of all the ostentation, make the complex visible through what remains simple."

"Like Nijinsky in *Sacre*?"

So much is hiding in these words. Absence, its shooting pain. Memories of the soaring god who has abandoned us both. Left us longing for what might have been.

"No, Sergey Pavlovitch," I say quietly. "Like Nijinska after *Sacre*."

My victory is a surprise to me.

No interference. No compromises. No restrictions. Goncharova will design new costumes according to my specifications. I can choose my own dancers. I can have as many rehearsals as I need. Diaghilev will watch, but he will not object to anything.

Les Noces is mine.

In May, two weeks before the premiere of *Les Noces*, Ballets Russes arrives in Paris for the final round of rehearsals at Théâtre de la Gaîté-Lyrique.

This is where Romola finds me.

I leave the rehearsal hall, feeling faint with fear. The last time I called the Steinhof the secretary informed me curtly that Dr. Wagner had no time to talk to me.

"Vaslav . . ." I ask, unable to finish my question.

"Vaslav is here," Romola says, clutching at my hand as if we'd never quarrelled. "In Paris."

I sink into the nearest chair, willing my heart to calm down, as I listen to Romola's explanations. The Steinhof doctors cannot be trusted. They are isolating Vaslav on purpose, to keep him from making progress. Vaslav is their most famous patient and they don't want to lose him.

"This is it, Bronia. It's decided. My mother took the girls to live with her and I'm taking care of Vaslav myself."

From her purse she retrieves a stack of calling cards and hands me one: "Romola and Vaslav Nijinsky. 10, rue du Conseiller-Collington. Paris." The apartment is not that grand but big enough for the two of them, the attendants she hired and a very capable nurse. Now she wants many visitors. But not just anybody. Vaslav has to spend time with other artists.

"He has to come here," she says, pointing at the rehearsal hall. Talk to Diaghilev, listen to music, watch other dancers. "I want him to see *Les Noces*."

Rue du Conseiller-Collington is a quiet street, close to the Bois de Boulogne. The chestnut tree in front of number 10 is in full bloom. Perhaps Romola is right, I think as I ring the bell. Perhaps this is what Vaslav needs. Hadn't I once seen my brother snap out of his stupor? Heard him tell me that ballets had to be created?

Romola answers the door herself, takes the box of strawberry pastries I have brought and embraces me. I follow her inside.

My brother is standing by the window.

"Vaslav!" I exclaim, and rush toward him, my arms outstretched.

"*Ne me touche pas*," he says in French, his eyes sliding down to my feet.

I don't touch him.

"You mustn't mind," Romola tells me. Vaslav says it to everyone. She is the only one he allows to come near him. But in time he will get used to me again. "Isn't it true, Vaslav, dear? Am I right?"

Romola talks incessantly. Points at photographs that line the walls, as if she were talking to a small child. "See, this is you, Vaslav, dancing in *Petrushka*. And this is Bronia. She is your sister. She, too, is a dancer. And a choreographer. She works for Ballets Russes. And now she has come to see you."

Vaslav trails Romola as she moves around the room, echoing her gestures as if it were all mockery. As if at any moment he might wink at me. Say something in Russian or Polish only the two of us would understand.

"Can you leave me alone with my brother?" I ask.

My sister-in-law hesitates.

"Please!"

When Romola leaves—though I know she is next door listening—I begin to talk. I suppose my voice is shaky—plaintive, perhaps—but it doesn't break.

"Mamusia is well, Vaslav. She will come to see you soon," I begin. "She thinks and talks of you all the time."

Vaslav is smiling now, but his is an odd smile. Every so often he moistens his lips with the tip of his tongue, a gesture he performs with great concentration. He looks at me without recognition or curiosity. I might as well not be there at all.

I speak more quickly, louder. I tell him how *Les Noces* is taking shape, describe groupings of dancers onstage, moving together. Dancers' bodies, I say, become entangled in heaps, are woven together like ornaments. Sometimes I turn them into a perfectly straight line, sometimes a pyramid. Men and women dance the same steps. No one is supporting anyone. In my ballet *en pointe* steps evoke hardness, lives pierced by fate.

As I speak, my brother rocks back and forth. Sometimes he smiles or frowns; sometimes his hand twitches. The hope I've had for coaxing him out of himself is seeping away.

When I begin to sob, Romola rushes into the room, and I steel myself for her reproaches. How can I forget that he needs to be kept calm and cheerful?

But there are no reproaches. Just a hasty retreat to a room next door, a glass of cold water the nurse brings, a lit cigarette Romola hands me—that I smoke with hasty greed.

No, there is no real peace between us. We both have our *pretensje*, the Polish word I evoke often, for no other quite reflects this shaky ladder of claims and grudges, accusations and regrets.

But we are in it together.

Diaghilev, once a conniving charlatan, has become Romola's most eagerly awaited guest. He not only brings dancers to see Vaslav but also takes Vaslav out to concerts and performances, arranging for the orchestra to greet my brother with the music of *Spectre, Petrushka, Sacre* and *Jeux*. He worries him as one worries a tender tooth, for the slightest flicker of comprehension: a twitching muscle, a shudder or a few words that can be later repeated all over Paris.

"Come, Vaslav, get a grip. Stop being lazy. I need you to dance for me!"

"I cannot dance because I'm mad."

But far more frequent are the voices of pity:

Have you seen Nijinsky? Short . . . haggard . . . in this tattered coat . . .

Have you seen his face? Grey . . . flabby . . . empty . . .

When he goes down the stairs, Diaghilev has to support him for he, Nijinsky, would fall.

I'm deaf in one ear, I soothe myself. I don't have to hear any of it.

On June 13, 1923, *Les Noces* premieres at Théâtre de la Gaîté-Lyrique. It will be followed by *Petrushka*, in which I dance the Ballerina Doll.

Still in my role as choreographer, I gather my dancers for one last time.

"Forget lightness," I tell them. "Forget grace.

"You are closing what used to be opened. You are letting jumps yield to gravity. The earth is pulling you . . . you are piercing the ground with your toes. This ballet is about heaviness, about the force that keeps you down. Bodies bent under the weight of toil. Fate. Forces bigger than yourself."

They stand around me, shoulders touching. Dancers with whom I've worked so hard for the past months. From whom I demanded absolute perfection, not just in the precision of their steps but in every detail. Eyes, elbows, knees lining up. The symmetry of circling arms.

Ours is such a fine balance of belief and doubt, hope and fear. Theatre is all about illusion. Dancers have to believe in my vision, but I have to believe in it even more. The moment doubt creeps in, the whole structure falls apart.

I know my own strength by now. I've been tested and I did not break. But do they know theirs?

My speech finished, I send them off to prepare, and this is when Kolya comes up to me. Vaslav and Romola—he calls her "Madame Nijinsky" with a quick gasp, as if it were a sacrilege he cannot condone—are waiting for me in Diaghilev's box. Do I have a moment to see them right now?

Kolya is not dancing in *Les Noces*, though he is cast in *Petrushka*. A notch above *corps*, just like Diaghilev predicted, in spite of my tutoring and Kolya's relentless diligence. It would be cruel to make him believe he could be more. I've already suggested other opportunities but have only succeeded in making him even more determined. I find him in the rehearsal room before the company class begins and see him stay behind when everyone else leaves.

As I enter Diaghilev's box, my heart tightens. Vaslav is seated with his back to the door, staring at the curtain. I note his smart-looking suit, white kid gloves, polished shoes. Romola raises to greet me, but Vaslav doesn't even turn toward me.

I speak his name. I ask him how he has been. Tell him how much I want to know what he thinks of my new ballet.

"Created, Vaslav," I say. "Not constructed."

He doesn't seem to hear.

When I finally stand to leave, Romola follows me into the corridor. "No more visitors, Bronia," she tells me, leaning toward my good ear. She has had enough of all those second-rate dancers coming and prancing in front of Vaslav. Casting for some sign of his approval. Just to be able to say: "Nijinsky saw me. Nijinsky smiled when I danced."

"People are mean," Romola says, her hand clutching mine. Vaslav is sensitive to all negative thoughts. He can sense disapproval. Gossip. Malice. No wonder he has started to raise his hands over his head as if to protect himself from blows.

I close my eyes, breathe deep, order tears to stop.

Have I heard that both white and sweet chestnut can cure mental anguish? Romola asks. So does crabapple if it is taken daily. This is what she will try with Vaslav. And if this does not work, she will take him to Lourdes in the summer.

"*Tonący brzytwy się chwyta*," Mamusia will say. A drowning man will clutch at a razor blade.

I'm relieved to see Kolya running toward us. "Madame Bronia," he gasps. "You are needed backstage. Right now!"

I follow him quickly, imagining the worst. A last-minute injury? Whose? A broken piece of the set? But as soon as we are out of Romola's sight, Kolya stops and turns toward me, smiling. "We don't have to rush," he says.

I look at him, his boyish grin. So pleased with himself.

"Was I wrong to think you needed rescuing?" he asks.

"No," I say, a wave of warmth washing over me. It has been so long since anyone watched over me like that.

—

I view *Les Noces* from the wings, as my dancers morph into images I first saw in my mind and have laboured so hard to make real. The women crouching, placing their heads in a straight line, offering themselves in sacrifice. The men thumping the floor with dull force.

They are magnificent. If anyone doubted me during rehearsals, these doubts have now melted into the dance and the music. They are me and I am them. Our minds twined, until the applause claims us, until the curtain calls.

As soon as the last of the applause dies out, I hurry to my dressing room, past all those who come backstage to congratulate me; put on the costume of the Ballerina Doll and slip into Fokine's old steps.

When the evening ends and I can finally lock the door of my dressing room, I am too tired to think. The room is filled with flowers, cards, notes and telegrams from friends and strangers.

A small bouquet of violets is placed beside my makeup tubes. A note scribbled in pencil on a scrap of lined paper torn from a notebook is propped against it: "I'm offering you my sacred love. If you don't want it, just toss it away." It is signed Kolya Singayevsky.

I think of a puppy. Folds of loose skin, needle teeth, wobbly feet.

But there is another image that pushes itself forward. The Kiev winter. The stove with Dutch tiles. The path between two banks of snow. Kolya pulling a sleigh piled up with the school supplies: flour, buckwheat, millet, lard. And rolls of grey cotton fabric from which there will be enough leftovers to make Levushka's first little pair of pants.

The most sumptuous party to celebrate the success of *Les Noces* takes place on *Macheral Joffre*, the barge floating on the Seine. Gerald and Sarah Murphy, our fashionable Parisian hosts, ordered a great laurel wreath to hang from the ceiling with the inscription "Les Noces—Hommage" in golden letters. I—its choreographer—go there reluctantly, have champagne at the bar, and leave before dinner is served.

"You should've stayed, Bronia," Olga Picasso gushes to me later. "It was magnificent. The best party in years."

My old friend means banquet tables set with pale blue china, soothed by candlelight. A pyramid of toys adorning the centre of each table, instead of flowers.

She means Stravinsky, at dawn, drunk with champagne and his success, sprinting the length of the room and leaping through the laurel wreath, crashing into the wall. She means Misia Sert at the piano, playing *Prélude à l'Après-midi d'un Faune*; and Serge Lifar dancing the Faun and snatching the shawl from her shoulders.

The faun is dead—or mad? Long live the faun?

Yes, perhaps I should've stayed. But I so much dislike it when we artists become mere mortals again.

10.

KOLYA AND I are married a year and a half later, in October of 1924, in Berlin, where one US dollar is worth just over four billion German marks. "Remind me to keep all my debts in Germany from now on," Diaghilev says.

I am still his choreographer. I've proven myself, not just with *Les Noces* but also with *Les Biches* and *Le Train Bleu*, though I've failed to convince him to let me revive my Kiev ballets. Too abstract, Diaghilev tells me, too foreign even for him. "Why are you insisting on turning a ballet into a symphony, Bronia? Who would want to watch it?"

Kolya, who in spite of Mamusia's efforts has not put on any weight, wears a black frock coat. I choose a simple mauve dress and a matching hat. Diaghilev gives me away, as he did when I married Sasha, but now I'm older and wiser, thirty-three to Kolya's twenty-nine.

"Your father was younger than I was," Mamusia says.

"Is that a warning?" I ask.

She shakes her head. "No. Kolya is different." She means solid, reliable, persistent. Refusing all flamboyance. Kolya's eyes are not trained on himself. Or on other women.

"I loved you already then," Kolya told me about the Kiev years. He saw me in the Kiev Opera, when I was still dancing there with Sasha. He recalled a rehearsal he was allowed to watch, during which I, dressed in simple black practice clothes, stood in the thick beam of light, and he thought me—like this light—ethereal, woven out of particles that could at any moment rearrange themselves and make me vanish.

The first time he said it I laughed. I was not an apparition, I told him. I was solid, earthbound. I was made of heavy clay, not glass. "I know that now," Kolya replied with a smile that suggested he was still convinced of his own vision.

Irina and Levushka are dressed in sailor suits. Irina's is white, Levushka's navy blue. Hers has a pleated skirt, his short trousers. They are both wearing white knee socks and shiny brown shoes. I watch them running about the room, carefree, excited with some game of theirs. Hide-and-seek? Tag? When Irina spills redcurrant juice on her white skirt, Mamusia sprinkles the stain with salt. "It will be invisible now," she says hopefully.

"Can I become invisible?" Levushka asks, and then sobs until Kolya tells him that it would not be such a good idea, even if it were possible. Why? "Because people would forget all about you!"

Among the telegrams from Paris, two stand out. The first is from Aleksandra Exter, who has just left Russia with her husband and who is looking forward to continuing our Kiev talks. Her gift to us, a drawing, is waiting for our return. The second is from Romola. Terse, with best wishes for a lifetime of happiness, signed *Vatsa and Romushka*.

"I don't understand your choice," she had said. "And neither can Vaslav."

Yes, it is surprising how quickly you can get used to being loved.

Good, I think of the years that follow, fruitful.

I leave Ballets Russes. I form my own company: Théâtre Chorégraphique Nijinska, with Kolya as my general manager and assistant. It folds, but not before we show our abstract ballets in England and France, performing at the Paris Opera and the Grand Palais. I rejoin Ballets Russes to choreograph a modern version of *Romeo and Juliet*, which—to Diaghilev's delight—causes a surrealist protest. Then I choreograph for the Teatro Colón in Buenos Aires, for Ida Rubinstein, for Anna Pavlova, for the Paris Opera.

The scrapbooks Kolya maintains with diligent passion fill up with praises:

She likes strong movement and she likes it danced big . . . a modern choreographer of rare quality . . . Noble, fierce, simple, fresh, thrilling.

11.

IT IS RIGHT after Kolya and I return to Paris from Argentina that I catch a sight of Mamusia putting on two pairs of thick stockings.

"Are you cold?" I ask. "In the middle of summer?"

"It's my rheumatism," she says. "The doctor told me to keep my legs warm."

"Let me see."

"There is nothing to see, Bronia."

I make her take off the stockings. The sharp smell, she tells me, is of viper venom salve. It helps the circulation.

The reddened spot at the bottom of her foot doesn't hurt. She doesn't know what caused it. A pebble in her shoe, perhaps. It'll heal in no time. No, she doesn't need to rest. Do I want her to sit and do nothing all day? No, she doesn't want more help. The cleaning lady is trouble enough. Besides, haven't I always assured her that she is the true *gospodyni,* the mistress of this house? That I earn the money, but she runs the house the way she sees fit?

"Let's talk of more important things, Bronia. Let's talk of the children."

During the Argentinian engagement I saw the children only once, when Kolya and I came to Paris for the Christmas break. Otherwise I got letters. Mamusia and Irina wrote detailed reports on everything from the cost of school books to a new arrangement of the living room furniture. Levushka mostly asked questions: Have I seen a crocodile? Does Kolya swim in the ocean? When are we coming back?

I am in negotiations with Ida Rubinstein for the 1928–29 season. Mamusia is pleased with Rubinstein's offer. Not only will I be based in Paris again, but I'll also be paid double what I got in Argentina and finally able to pay off the debts my defunct dance company still owes. But Mamusia is against Ida's offer to hire Irina for the *corps.* "She is only fifteen. Let her finish school first, Bronia," she tells me. When I agree, she confides her worries about Levushka. He is a good child but cannot be relied upon. Always losing things. That fountain pen Kolya gave him for Christmas is gone. Why did he even take it to school?

In moments like that it is not hard to dismiss a reddened spot on the foot, a few drops of pus on the stocking, a wound that refuses to heal.

After all, Mamusia's voice reasons with my lingering unease, she is seventy-two. Is it so strange that at the end of the day she is tired or thirsty? Or that on her feet, her poor dancer's feet, toenails are darkening, growing thicker, harder and harder to trim? Isn't it the dancer's lot? The instrument once ruthlessly overused never forgives.

"Something is always the matter, Bronia . . . if you wake up and nothing hurts, it means you are dead."

I still reproach myself. I let Mamusia work too hard. I believed her assurances. I didn't guess the extent of her pain until that terrible day when the doctor told me that in diabetic patients gangrene never heals. That my mother's choice is amputation or death.

A few weeks after Mamusia's operation, Diaghilev comes to visit, loaded with presents for Pani Nijinska and "the children." If he is still allowed to call them "children," that is.

In the hall he hands me his scarf, his top hat. He takes off his gloves. He looks more worn down since I last saw him, but his hands are still beautifully kept, fingernails buffed, filed into perfect rounded circles.

"How is she?" Diaghilev asks.

The operation has been successful. The stump is healing well. She is still in pain, however, and worried about how she will manage with a prosthesis. The doctor is hopeful the new drug will prevent other such mishaps.

"Ida Rubinstein's company, Bronia?" he manages to say before we step into the living room. "After all your Argentinian triumphs? Why on earth would you work for a self-obsessed amateur?"

I have forgotten how quickly he can make me bristle.

Or forgive him, I think a moment later when I watch him hurry toward Mamusia, reclining on a chaise-longue we have bought for her.

"My dear Pani Nijinska, you look just like Madame Récamier in David's painting!"

He presents her with a basket of pink roses, passes on best wishes from everyone in Paris and settles himself at Mamusia's side. A moment later I see both of them lost in the conversation on ignored first symptoms and narrow escapes.

Irina has baked a chiffon cake, according to Mamusia's instructions. Levushka has put on his best suit. At ten he is taller than his sister and has Sasha's mischievous smile. Yesterday when I went to his room to say good-night he threw his hands around me and pressed his head to my chest. "Is anything the matter?" I asked. "No," he muttered. "Everything is fine."

Kolya opens a bottle of white wine. Mamusia—defying the doctor's orders—asks for a glass. I nod my permission. It's just this once. We don't have guests that often.

With Mamusia still too weak to protest, I have reorganized the home to free her from most tiring tasks. A housekeeper comes every day. So does a nurse. And whenever I have to stay at the theatre in the afternoons or evenings, Kolya goes home to keep her company, keep an eye on the children. "Make her laugh," I always remind him before he leaves.

"God's will, Sergey Pavlovitch . . . we all have our crosses to bear."

"Your strength has always inspired me, Pani Nijinska."

Mamusia's face is flushed with wine or memories or both. Diaghilev adjusts his monocle. They sigh in unison. They agree on the wisdom of the old Chinese curse "May you live in interesting times." In a Parisian court Marie Rasputin sued Prince Felix Yusupov for the murder of her father. Symon Petlyura, whose victory parade we witnessed in Kiev, was assassinated here in Paris, on rue Racine. In Berlin a woman fished alive out of a canal still claims to be the tsar's daughter, miraculously saved.

I think: how good we all are at not mentioning what hurts us the most!

After what my brother's new doctor refers to as the "Parisian disaster," Vaslav is in Switzerland, in the Bellevue Sanatorium, where no visits are allowed until he settles. Before the Bellevue attendants arrived to escort him there, I saw him punch a wall until his bloodied fist made a hole in it. Then there was that night when Kolya and I rushed to rue du Conseiller-Collington to pacify the concierge, who threatened to call the gendarmes. Vaslav, we were told, had just torn a window from its frame.

Kolya's voice weaves itself into these thoughts. He wants to tell us a joke he has heard. A Russian merchant arrives in Berlin on business, gets drunk at a station bar and boards a train back to Moscow. "Not worth going to Germany," he tells his friends. "They are all drunks there."

My husband is not the best storyteller. He repeats the punchline twice, as if we didn't get it. But he makes us all laugh.

Diaghilev takes out his cigarette case, offers it around.

"May I have one, too, Sergey Pavlovitch," Levushka asks, still chuckling.

"Levushka, please," Mamusia pleads. Irina rolls her eyes. I warn my son not to be cheeky.

Diaghilev gives Levushka a long look, as if he only just noticed his existence. "What do you want to be when you grow up, young man? A dancer?" he asks.

"No!"

"Oh," Diaghilev says, taken aback, not by the answer itself but by its sudden, unexpected harshness. "Did you know, Bronia?" he asks, turning to me.

"Yes," I say.

"And you don't mind?"

"No," I lie.

When it is time to leave, Diaghilev kisses Mamusia's hand and tells her that mothers like her make this world bearable. She calls him an "incorrigible flatterer." "You meant *irresistible*, didn't you?" he asks.

In the hall, when I give him back his hat, scarf and gloves, he asks me if I will consider choreographing for him again.

"It depends what you offer," I say.

He rolls his eyes in mock exasperation. He lifts my hand to his lips. This is when I notice red pinpricks on his wrist. What is he injecting himself with? I wonder. Morphine? Cocaine?

I stand in the doors as he walks toward the elevator, hat in hand. The metal doors open and he disappears inside.

Eight months later he will be dead.

12.

AFTER THE OPERATION Mamusia's health improves steadily. Her doctor's faith in insulin has proven well placed. Still, I insist she take a proper summer rest, without any duties. At first she visits with friends who live by the sea, but as soon as I pay the last of my debts, I make her take proper spa cures. Irina has finished school and dances in the ballet companies I run, in Paris and on tours. And for a while, during his summer break, Levushka has no choice but to come with us to rehearsals and on summer tours.

It is Kolya who, when Levushka turns twelve, suggests sending him to the Vitiaz Russian summer camp in Laffrey. For a whole month his days will be structured. There will be mountain excursions and swimming. There will be history talks and singalong evenings around a bonfire. His Russian will improve.

"You'll like it," I assure my frowning son, who calls himself "Léon" at school and doesn't like to speak Russian. "And if you don't, we'll come and bring you back home."

Levushka returns from the camp on a windy afternoon at the end of August. Litter is blowing along the pavements; the gusts are threatening the hats of passersby. When he spots me waiting at the Gare de Lyon, he jumps out of the train with graceful agility, stands still to adjust the epaulettes of his blue uniform and then shades his eyes with his hand, even though the day is not particularly sunny. Just like Vaslav on the day of his entrance exam.

"Mama! Mama!" Levushka shouts, as if I could've missed him. He runs into my outstretched arms, smelling of soot and harsh soap. As we walk arm in arm, he leans sideways, so that his hips and mine bump playfully. He is taller than me already, tanned, and there is new sturdiness to him, a sheen of that different life lived away from home.

In the street the wind is lifting his words and tossing them at my feet. "It was swell," Levushka repeats, waving to friends who pass by, flanked by their own parents and siblings. "How right you were to say I'd love it." In the taxi home he talks of the long mountain hikes, racing to reach the summit ahead of everyone else. "You should've seen it, Mama. The view from up there." And I imagine the rocky top of a mountain, the circle of arms he and his friends have made, their breaths mingling as they sing.

Later, at home, after we have finished the dinner Mamusia prepared with Irina's help, Levushka tells us how the senior Vitiaz boys tended to the picture of the slain tsarevitch. It was on display in the main hall, on a side table, he says, surrounded with fresh flowers, which all the boys took turns to arrange. "Why didn't you ever tell me, Mama?" my son asks. "Why didn't I know?"

I'm slicing the walnut cake—Levushka's favourite. "You knew that they were all killed," I say, offering him a thick slice on a plate. The cake is smeared with cherry jam, sprinkled with powdered sugar and decorated with balls of whipped cream. My hand must've trembled, for the cake topples to its side and the cream touches the edge of the plate.

Levushka is shaking his head. "Not killed but murdered," he corrects me. Yes, he knew that. And what Irina has told him about the jewels the grand duchesses sewed into their dresses. Diamonds and sapphires that deflected the first bullets. Others, however—the true Vitiaz boys—knew so much more: How the house where the tsar was kept was called the "House of Special Purpose." How the Bolshevik who killed the tsar was named Yakov Yurovsky, and he can never find peace. And how Tsarevitch Aleksei took all his humiliations, his pain, his suffering with such saintly resignation, with such utter acceptance of his fate.

Like Tsarevitch Dmitri before him . . .

I look at my son's face, lit with a fiery eagerness I don't recognize, his jaw clenching at the injustice of it all. I want to warn Levushka against such feelings. Tell him that everything that looks too simple must have been distorted. That he has to be cautious, vigilant. That wanting to belong could be a dangerous feeling.

But then I recall Mamusia's warnings to me, to Vaslav, all useless in the end, and merely extend my hand with the plate of mangled cake. Levushka takes my offering, swipes the splattered whipped cream and licks his finger clean. This is when I first notice a pinkish spot on his wrist, round, whiter in the centre.

It is Kolya who turns the conversation to less swampy grounds. The taste of sausages roasted over fire, the best way to heal blisters after hiking, the songs Levushka has learnt.

The evening melts, turns mellow. We urge Mamusia to rest, not to undo the benefits of her water cure, while Irina helps me clean up. When the table is clear and the dishes are done, Irina brings out their old childhood favourite, the Stomachion puzzle.

"Remember how many shapes we used to make out of it?" she asks, taking the triangles out of the tattered box.

"Let's have a contest," Levushka says.

"Oh, yes," Irina agrees. "Let's."

We all work in silence for a while. Mamusia puts together a mushroom, which both Irina and Levushka dismiss as simple. I manage a tree, Kolya a frog that I think quite deft. But then I see that Irina has constructed a figure of an old woman holding an umbrella and Levushka a clown standing on his hands.

"Look at this!" Kolya exclaims. "I give up."

"I can't do any better, either," I say. "The children win."

Irina and Levushka exchange a knowing look and barely manage to stifle a laugh. Mamusia thinks they've clearly been up to something, but they laugh even more and declare themselves absolutely innocent of any mischief.

"What do *you* think?" they ask Kolya.

Kolya lifts his hands in mock surrender. He won't take sides. Not he. Especially not against their grandmother.

"Come on, Kolya," Levushka teases him. "Where is your Russian courage?"

"Am I that dangerous?" Mamusia asks.

I lean back in my chair. Before I agreed to marry Kolya, I warned him I didn't want any more children. He said that once we became his family, he would never want any other.

Declaring the need to celebrate Levushka's return, my husband dashes to the kitchen then emerges with a bottle of cherry brandy and four glasses.

"What about me?" Levushka asks.

Kolya looks at me and I nod, making a sign with my fingers to indicate a little bit. "I'll get his glass," I say, glad to be able to stand up and move.

We toast Levushka's return, make plans for the future. Levushka has to work harder this year than he did the year before, both at his *lycée* and at the music conservatory. His piano teacher demands far more regular practice. I have offers from Vienna, from Berlin, and they all include Kolya and Irina.

The cherry brandy spreads warmth inside my stomach. Mamusia declares it far superior to the Carlsbad waters. Levushka drinks his in one gulp. Kolya tells him that brandy is not lemonade, that he should've warmed it in his hand first. "So can I have another one?" Levushka asks. "For practice?"

"Aren't you really clever?" Irina asks.

Levushka makes a funny face. "Don't spoil my élan," he moans. "Come on, Mama, just one more."

"Sorry," I say, shaking my head. "Next time you'll know."

Only crumbs remain from Mamusia's walnut cake. Kolya is picking them one by one, slipping them into his mouth.

The wind has quieted down by then. Warm August air comes through the open window, mixed with the fumes of passing cars. In the street children are screaming with joy. I draw the curtains but leave the window open. They billow from time to time, like sails or white flags.

Kolya, who likes to keep records of all we do, draws the shapes of our creations on a piece of paper, with our names underneath and a note that the first prize in the Stomachion contest on that twenty-eighth day of August in 1931 went to Irina and Levushka. Everyone else conceded defeat.

When Levushka is in bed, I knock on his door. "Come in, Mama," he says, even though he couldn't have known it was me.

He is lying down, his hands straight along his body. Almost young man's hands, I think, looking at his thickened fingers. Soon he will insist I, too, call him "Léon," not "Levushka."

I sit beside him on the edge of his bed, smelling the freshly starched linen. He has on blue-striped pyjamas, Mamusia's Christmas gift. I run my hand through his hair, dark, thick, unruly, cropped short before the camp but now almost back to his usual length. I touch his still-smooth cheek, tanned and free from pimples. And then I raise his right hand up to take a closer look at the round pinkish spot.

"What's that?" I ask.

"Nothing."

"A cigarette burn?"

He nods.

"Was it an accident?"

Levushka removes his hand from mine, covering the burn with his sleeve. "Don't worry about me so much, Mama," he says. "I'm fine."

13.

A FEW MONTHS LATER, in the spring of 1932, I am in Berlin with Kolya, working with Max Reinhardt, choreographing sequences for his theatrical productions. At my request, in addition to Irina Max has also hired Vaslav's elder daughter, Kyra, who has just turned eighteen. Only Levushka has stayed in Paris with Mamusia.

At the end of this long day, in our hotel room, Kolya has just opened a bottle of wine, filled two glasses, and is lying on the carpet, leaning on his elbow, his dressing gown opened. Time has sharpened his face, given him a distinguished air. "You look like a movie star," I tease him sometimes, and he runs his palm over his hair, or reaches forward to catch my hand and pull me toward him. For a kiss, a caress, lovemaking. For whatever I'm willing to give.

As the wine breathes, I'm smoking a cigarette, going over the day's work.

The rehearsals are going well, but I have had another tense encounter with Kyra. After I told her to try harder, she threw herself to the floor and began to scream: "Why are you always picking on me?"

I still remember her from Vienna, a little girl with a gap between her front teeth, eyeing us with suspicion, her new family. She has Vaslav's eyes, I thought then, the same almond shape, the same dark intensity. "If only she were a boy," Romola said then, managing to make her voice both wistful and angry.

"What does Kyra mind so much?" I ask Kolya, who lifts himself up from the floor and hands me one of the glasses. "A dancer who cannot take corrections? She should've heard her father yelling at me when he thought *I* was slacking off."

The wine, warmed up, is thick, soothing. I return to the rehearsal; parse the memories of Kyra's dancing, the force of her accusations.

"It's not your fault, Bronia," Kolya says.

He is wrong.

I am picking on her. I cannot help myself. She has Vaslav's posture; the same line of the neck; the same thick, powerful thighs. Even the absent smile on her lips as she stands in preparation is the same. But when she begins to dance, all she can manage is an imitation.

A deft forger, I think her, and she knows that.

The last sip of wine has lost its taste. My stomach feels hollow; my head spins. I put the glass aside and take a last drag of the cigarette. From the open window comes the smell of something burning. Rubber? Trash?

A letter from Mamusia has just arrived from Paris. Her script is neat and even, each letter beautifully shaped. She is feeling well. The nurse comes every day even though there is no need. The price of eggs has gone up again. Levushka's Vitiaz friends come around all the time and once she allowed him to go out with them. She won't do it again, though, for he is not practising his piano long enough. Ludmila Schollar came by, with a *kulebyaka* pie, from Pyshman's, dripping with butter, just like the ones we used to have in St. Petersburg.

And I, with my teacher's eye that should've spotted all false gestures, all masked imperfections, miss the only sentence in the letter that should alarm me:

When you have a bit of free time, Bronia, could you buy me some Doppelherz tonic for the heart?

When we get home from Berlin, Mamusia looks small and withered. Her lips are parched, her throat hoarse. The nurse tells me that she has had no appetite.

"What have you had for breakfast?" I ask her.

She doesn't want to talk about herself. She is worried about Levushka. He has a note from the teacher he won't show her.

Levushka rolls his eyes with impatience. He loves his grandma, but at thirteen love doesn't mean acceptance. Why does she always smell like a pharmacy? Why won't she let him go out with his friends? What is she always so afraid of?

I give my son a warning look.

The note from his teacher turns out to be about a fight he has got into and I brace myself for a tense afternoon. "I hate school," Levushka has told Kolya. To me he complains that the teachers pick on him because he is Russian.

"What happened?" I ask.

It was not even a fight. A boy pushed him and called him a "coward," so he pushed him back. No, he won't tell me the name of the boy. He is not a tattletale. His lips are sealed. End of interrogation.

"You have to sign the note," he tells me.

I send him to his room. "In two hours I want to see your homework. If everything is in order, I will sign the note."

"What do you expect, Bronia?" Kolya says when Levushka leaves. "He is a boy." My son's last composition, he also points out, merited a different note from his French teacher: "Léon has a keen and highly original imagination and true sensitivity to words that should be nurtured."

"Kolya is right," Mamusia mutters.

"You are all the same," Irina announces. "You always spoil him."

"Wait until you have children," Mamusia says.

A few days later, in the evening when I wash the stump of Mamusia's leg, soothing the reddened skin with cool water, she calls me "*Moja pociecha.*" My comfort. The inexplicable yearnings of the missing limb bewilder her. The itch that demands scratching, the tingling of toes no longer there. "How is that possible, Bronia?" she asks. Then she knocks on her head with her knuckles and says, "What is going on in there?"

"You two both always talk at once," Kolya says.

"It's more efficient that way," I say, defending our private language, the stream of words half Polish, half Russian. Good for the accounts of everyday troubles, mine of the theatre, hers of the home. A surly dancer, too sure of himself. A new maid who doesn't dust under the beds. Torn costumes. A coat that needs alterations. Bedbugs in the hotel. A mouse in the kitchen. Again? Again!

"Like a Gypsy," Mamusia whispers. Not a warning anymore, just a statement, worn out with repetitions. She has no more warnings for me. Not even a wrinkling of her nose when I light another cigarette. I try to coax her out of this calm she buries herself in. It is too thick, too dense, too much like a shroud.

As we often do, we talk about Vaslav. He is still strong. He requires two attendants to dress or feed him. He has smashed another chair. This is how he lets us know that he still feels pain.

Romola is in Hollywood now, an aspiring actress giving interviews on how she danced with Vaslav in St. Petersburg before the Tsar of All the

Russias, her husband's intimate friend. How Grand Duke Dmitri welcomed her as one of the tsar's household. How she danced not just for the tsar but for other crowned heads, all over the world. And how fleeting it all was, for she only cared about artists: musicians, sculptors, painters and dancers.

"And they believe this nonsense? In Hollywood?" Mamusia chuckles, and I'm so grateful to hear her laugh.

A week later, on Friday morning her eyes bother her, so I draw the curtains. There is a single shaft of light shooting through them, though, where the two edges of fabric don't quite meet. The air is crowded with motes.

The day passes quietly. In the living room Kolya is adding up our accounts. Levushka is at school. When he comes back, mercifully without any notes from the teacher, we all eat *salade niçoise*, without anchovies but with extra capers. Irina helps me clean up before she goes out in the evening for a walk with her friends, then to the movies. My level-headed daughter. The child I don't have to worry about.

Levushka has gone to his room. Last time I checked on him he was writing something—making sure he covered the page with his elbow when I approached. He must have finished by now, for he is playing his guitar. The chords are breaking down, again and again, ending too abruptly.

"Levushka is just like Vaslav," Mamusia tells me. "He needs a lot of patience."

I sit by her bed. It creaks and squeaks.

She reaches out a trembling finger toward the water jug. "I'm thirsty," she says. I support her head. Hold a glass to her lips. The back of her neck is sweaty, hot, like that of a feverish child.

She takes a sip. Then she lies back, deflated and waxy against the pillow.

Irina walks into the room, in her blue dress, her hair bobbed and waved. Onstage and in the rehearsal room I look at her with my teacher's eye. Shoulders too tense, legs too weak. Good technique, though, excellent turnout. It is her stage presence that bothers me. There is something fundamental lacking, something I'm trying to break for her into smaller, manageable fragments she can tackle.

At home I ban such thoughts.

At home I am only her mother.

"How is your leg today, Grandma?" Irina asks, bending over Mamusia to give her a kiss on the cheek. "Does it hurt?" *Are you sure you want me to go?* my daughter's eyes ask.

"No," Mamusia mutters, and we both wave Irina away, making her promise to enjoy herself. "Have some nice treat," I say, sliding a few bills into her pocket.

I try to make this into an ordinary day. All of it. Irina blowing me a kiss before she disappears. Kolya knocking on Levushka's door, reminding him not to leave his homework for the last minute.

For supper we have leftover rabbit stew with mustard sauce. Kolya opens a bottle of red wine. I eat quickly and take a small plate to Mamusia.

She doesn't want to eat. She is not hungry. No, not even a tiny bit.

I give in and put the plate aside.

"And to think that I didn't want you to be born," Mamusia whispers.

I have to lean toward her to hear.

The day she knew she was pregnant with me—knew from the sharp smell of sweat, the queasy feeling in the morning—she was terrified. Stassik and Vaslav were still so small; the money was so tight. "I didn't think I had enough strength for another baby, Bronia," she whispers. She tells me how she pounded her belly with her fists. And when that didn't work, how she climbed on the kitchen table and jumped. Hard, on the floor. Not like a dancer but like a sack of coals, with a *thump*, with her heart going up to her throat. How she waited for a spasm of the womb, a gush of blood. How she wanted to shake me out before my time.

When it didn't happen, she intended to jump again, but then Vaslav screamed and she ran to soothe him. He was teething then, running a fever. She lifted him up from his cot and carried him until he fell asleep. "He saved you," she mutters, tears falling down her cheek. "For me. So that I wouldn't be alone. As if he knew you'd be the only one left."

The wrinkles on her face make a complex maze of connections. Her eyes are watery, red rimmed. She licks her parched lips. Without her false teeth her face looks sunken, hollowed. I gently wipe a drop of pus from the reddened corner of her mouth. There is a sweet smell about her, lingering over her hair, her mouth.

I put my hands under her shoulders. I pull her toward me, so small in my arms, so fragile. I hold her for a long, long while, until I feel her impatient wiggle. Only then do I lower her back on the pillows.

Once she falls asleep I go to the living room. Kolya lifts his head from over the accounts he has been adding up. I reach for a cigarette, fit it into the holder, and he lights it for me.

I take a deep drag, exhale the smoke.

I can feel my face burning. Do I already know Mamusia will die soon? Or is it her story that has shaken me? The thought of her whose love I breathe in like air not wanting me once, just as I didn't want Irina to be born that day in Monte Carlo?

I smoke the cigarette until the very end, remove it from the holder and extinguish the stub in the ashtray Kolya has pushed toward me.

"Make yourself indispensable," Diaghilev told Boris Kochno when he took him on as his secretary and lover. Kolya, my manager and my assistant, keeps track of our income, expenses and losses. He sorts through newspaper clippings that arrive every month, decides which ones to use for promotion. He arranges photographs in albums: files brochures, theatre programs, drawings, notes, letters I receive.

I watch him when he works, assessing the levels of his patience. It appears bottomless. Sometimes I catch him look at me with the same bewildered happiness I saw on the day I agreed to marry him, when I could not predict either the shape of our life together or that anything Kolya did could truly hurt me.

On Saturday morning Mamusia wakes up gasping for breath. "Is Stassik home already," she asks. "Is he still cross with me?"

"No," I tell her.

"Where am I, Bronia?"

"You are with me," I say.

"In St. Petersburg!"

She smiles with great eagerness, tries to raise herself in bed on her elbows. "Open the windows, Bronia," she orders. "I want to see the monkeys in the Summer Garden? Can we go there?"

I want to lift her in my arms and carry her outside, her poor, hurting, maimed dancer's body, so small, so shrivelled by illness. Carry her past the street to the parkette, where she could lie under a tree, and smell the earth and grass.

"Good girl, Bronia," she says, "You have washed the windows the way I taught you."

We call the doctor, who immediately takes her to the hospital. I'm by her side when her heart gives out. *July 23, 1932—6:30 p.m.* This is all I manage to write that day in my diary.

October 16, 1939

The proximity of New York has whipped up bouts of nervous energy. Passengers gather in clusters at all hours to trade rumours. One of the flyers slipped under our cabin door promises a farewell dinner. Another is a reminder that on arrival "passengers disembark at Chelsea Piers, North River (Foot of 18th Street)."

I cannot sleep. Beside me Kolya twitches and groans; his mouth freezes in a wordless scream. When he shivers, I put my hand on his shoulder and shake him gently. Enough to break the bad dream but not enough to wake him.

The luminous hands of our alarm clock point to one o'clock. Five hours before dawn. My suitcase is propped open on a stand and my hand knows where to look for what I want.

The smoking room is a few steps away from our cabin, empty but for two men lost in conversation, paying no heed to me. I settle in the farthest corner and will myself to open the manila envelope.

Levushka's handwriting is as neat as I remember it. He must have copied these pages many times, until they pleased him:

> My sister knows how to make herself invisible. She plaits some twigs and leaves into her braid and wraps herself in it. Then she walks into a room and no one sees her, but she can hear and see everyone.
>
> She is older and knows many things, not just the wonderful ones, like how to make soap bubbles float, but also scary. She knows that *they* are listening, because *they* are making loud, crackling noises that make my ears pop. She also knows when

they are sending their spies who disguise themselves so that I would think they are my friends.

"You have to make yourself disappear, too," she tells me, and walks away.

I try to plait twigs and leaves into my hair, but it is too short and whatever I put in it falls to the ground. "This is all wrong," I tell myself. "I have to find my own magic."

It is not easy. When I splash myself with well water, it only makes my clothes cling to my body like a second skin. So I smear my face with ashes and soot. But people only notice me more and Grandma gets really cross. "Change your clothes, you urchin, and wash your face and hands!" she tells me. Then I try to wrap myself in a cloak, like a magician in a circus, but people just ask me if I'm cold. I try magic incantations, too—abracadabra . . . hocus pocus . . . czary mary . . . mene tekel fares—but nothing happens, even when I press my fists into my eyes until they hurt.

In the end, when I give up trying and begin to cry, my sister comes back. I don't see her for she has made herself invisible, but she speaks to me, and so I know she is close by. "I'll help you," she says, and wraps her arms around me.

"Am I invisible, now?" I ask.

"Look at the floor," she says.

I look at the spot my sister is pointing at and I see that we do not cast any shadow.

PART SIX:

1938–1939

1.

FEODOR'S GRAVE AT THE Batignolles Cemetery is made of brown granite topped with an Orthodox cross. "Chaliapin, the son of the Russian earth," the inscription says. "Born February 13, 1873, in Kazan. Died April 12, 1938, in Paris."

The grave is still covered with flowers. Three young women standing in front of it eyed me quickly before making room. They look like sisters, slim, dressed in tight-fitting coats with fur-trimmed collars, their blond hair fashionably waved. One of them is holding a bouquet of red roses. Another is adjusting the flowers, carelessly, for—having hurt her finger on a thorn—she holds it to the air and then sucks on it. Her companions giggle.

Among the flowers that cover the grave I see theatre programs and music scores. Fans have left opera glasses, keys, Russian *kopek* coins, and carefully calligraphed notes: "Thank you for beautiful memories . . . please sing a prayer for my soul to our Lord in Heaven."

My eyes lift to the pattern the darker flecks of granite make on the cross.

The news of his death reached me in Warsaw, at Teatr Wielki, during a rehearsal of *The Legend of Cracow*. I knew he was ill, but he had been ill before. In 1934 when I was in Hollywood choreographing *Midsummer Night's Dream*, Feodor's son, Boris, told me of a fainting incident in London. Followed by another one in Berlin. And yet in the end Feodor always recovered.

On that April day in Warsaw, when Kolya burst into the hall, newspaper in hand, I stopped the rehearsal.

Chaliapin's death was not even first-page news. The short obituary sounded stiff, official: "One of the best bass singers in the world . . . Warsaw had a chance to hear him a few years ago in his signature role of Boris Godunov."

Kolya walked to the pianist, bent over her and whispered something. A moment later she began to play the "Song of the Volga Boatmen."

I let the dancers go early that day. I bought flowers from an old woman in front of the theatre who reminded me of the sellers at the Kiev Market. "Picked today," she said, pointing at the tin bucket at her feet: daffodils, tulips, hyacinths. April flowers. Blue, red, yellow.

I chose every one of them myself, rejecting even the tiniest blemish, the slightest hint of fading. The woman smacked her lips with appreciation and carefully tied the bouquet with a white ribbon.

"For a special occasion?" she asked.

I nodded.

If I had been in Paris then, I would have taken my flowers to the Orthodox church on rue Daru, where Feodor's coffin stood on a catafalque surrounded by burning candles and where his grieving friends gathered to mourn him. In Warsaw I put my solitary bouquet by the entrance of Teatr Wielki, where Feodor had sung. I could not think of any other place.

2.

WE MOVED INTO this corner apartment on avenue des Ternes after my Polish contract was terminated. As Parisian apartments go, this one is quite spacious and pleasant, with a large living room and two bedrooms. The windows are tall, with white shutters. We have no balcony, but the apartment comes with a maid's room in the attic, ideal for storage. Kolya has promised to put up shelves in there.

Irina is sitting by the window, her eyes fixed on the street below. She has extended her right leg and is flexing her foot. She did not join me in my morning practice.

I ask her how she slept.

"I slept," she answers. Her face is perfectly oval, skin translucent like in old portraits. When I was a girl, Mamusia told me she drank vinegar to have pallor like this.

"Where is Kolya?" I ask my daughter. When I woke up, his side of the bed was empty already.

"Out."

"Did he even have breakfast?"

"Two fried eggs."

I sit at the dining table strewn with newspapers—French, English and Russian because émigré papers, my husband likes to remind me, reprint stories from various sources. "It is as if no one remembered the last war," Kolya says. "As if we were mad enough to go through another."

The headlines support my husband's fears. Countries are being devoured by other countries. In Paris refugees arrive in waves. German Jews, Spaniards, Austrians, Czechs. The Nazis vow to eliminate all degenerates, social parasites, inverts who love other men, and those who've lost their minds.

Like Stassik, who is dead. Like Vaslav, who is still alive.

I move the newspapers aside, push away an empty glass. "It's only wine," Kolya says when I complain he is drinking too much. Alcohol makes him stiffer, more meticulous in the way he sorts through the folders of reviews, notes, theatre programs to be included in what he calls "La Nijinska archives."

He wants to make sure nothing more is lost.

The other day I found him patiently gluing together a teacup Irina had dropped on the kitchen floor. "In Japan," he told me, "artists repairing broken cups fill the cracks with gold. The broken fragment is what makes them beautiful."

"Do you want some tea?" I ask.

Kolya has left the samovar on and it is bubbling hot on the sideboard. Tea glasses are out there, too, in silver-plated holders almost the same as the ones we had in Kiev.

Irina doesn't want tea, so I pour tea essence into one glass, dilute it with hot water from the samovar, add two spoonfuls of sugar and a slice of lemon. Like Mamusia, I believe tea in a glass tastes better.

Holder in hand, I walk to the window to see what has caught my daughter's attention. The day is cool, but this is Parisian winter so people wear light coats. A small boy is shovelling coal into a tin bucket, while an older boy is carrying another one into the cellar. Their faces are smeared with soot. They work fast, with the well-rehearsed movements of brothers who don't quite know where one begins and another ends. The pile of coal diminishes quickly.

I close my eyes. When I open them, the boys outside have stopped working. The older one whispers something in his brother's ear. A joke, perhaps, for the younger one bursts out laughing.

Irina stands up and walks away from the window. By the ottoman, she picks up some invisible speck from the floor. She is bending from the hips, on straight legs, which is good. Today she is limping, though. A slight limp, but I worry. What undiscovered damage is still there inside?

"Don't cry so much, Bronia," Kolya still begs me, but I turn away and cry even more.

I take the last few sips of tea, watching how my daughter begins stretching the arm that was broken in five places. It has healed well, but my daughter fears that her body, once maimed, will always betray her. Muscles will defy her at the most important moments. When movement should flow, she'll become rigid. I stop myself from reminding her how such restrictions of the body can be turned into a dancer's strength. How Anna Pavlova used her thin ankles to make herself look fragile and ethereal. How Alicia Markova overcame her weak, buckling knees. Instead I note silently that Irina is massaging her arm the way I've taught her, in round, even motions.

"Did Kolya say anything about coming to the studio today?" I ask.

"Only that he'll be back before the first class."

The studio we rent is a short walk away. I run a small professional class every morning at ten then coach select dancers, most of them American who came here to perfect their technique. Kolya is my assistant. After Kiev I had not anticipated much joy from teaching, but shaping young bodies has seduced me again. I love to catch the first glimpses of true independence of spirit, readiness to extend beyond technique.

In Paris I have a reputation for dramatic tension of movements, unlike Kschessinska, who in her studio stresses ballerina grace and the old Imperial Ballet School technique. I have no shortage of students, but a week ago I lost yet another American dancer, who decided to go back home. It is a pity for this particular one—Margaret Owen—was showing great promise, without the arrogance to destroy it.

The American girls call Kolya "Monsieur Sin." They find Singayevsky too hard to remember or pronounce. Sometimes they laugh at his manner, which is, I admit, very Russian. "Madame wishes you to take your place at the barre . . . Madame wants you to concentrate more, please." To American ears *formal* means merely stiff.

"Will you come with me to the studio, in case he is late?" I ask my daughter as I pick up my bag, checking if I have everything: keys, cigarettes, lighter.

Irina shakes her head. "Kolya won't be late."

Downstairs I stop by the concierge to pick up today's mail: a letter from the bank, which I put aside for Kolya, and a postcard. Alicia Markova is in New York, where her Giselle, which I coached her in, has been a stunning success. She will be dancing in Paris soon and hopes we can meet—if we are still in France, that is.

My Kiev friends and students no longer dare to write. We who have left Russia have become "traitors of the Motherland." All contact with us is forbidden. So is modern art. In the last wave of purges Benedikt Livshits and Les Kurbas were arrested and executed by firing squad.

Outside our building, the two boys have finished their chore and are gone. The coal is in the cellar; the pavement has been swept. Only a black, sooty shadow marks the spot where they worked.

I quicken my pace.

In front of the studio's door, Kolya is waiting for me, looking as if a sudden gust of wind might knock him over. The tips of his fingernails are blackened. I know he wants me to ask him where he has been all morning, but I cannot make the words *Levushka's grave* pass through my throat.

3.

A PACKAGE WITH American stamps arrives a few weeks later; it is addressed to Irina. She opens it quickly, to extract a thin brochure and a letter. The brochure advertises the Kotchetovsky Ballet School, located at 3407 Milam Street in Houston.

Sasha's American dream.

The one-page biography lists Aleksander Kotchetovsky's debut at seventeen in Moscow, his leaving the Imperial Theatres at the age of twenty-two and joining the Diaghilev Ballet Company as a solo dancer. Then come engagements at the Vienna Opera, the Paramount Theatres in New York, the McVickers Theater in Chicago. There is a glowing thank-you from Gene Kelly for "teaching me to dance." Not a word about the Nijinsky 1914 season in London. Poor marketing sense? Or a deliberate desire to cut himself off from the Nijinsky experiments his audience would clearly not like?

"As a teacher and choreographer of Ballet and Character, Mr. Kotchetovsky ranks as one of the best in the entire world."

Letter in hand, Irina casts a glance in my direction. "I asked Papa to send it to me," she says.

I wonder why she feels the need for this explanation. Have I not always encouraged my children to write to their father? Sasha—to his credit—has always written back, mostly with funny accounts of his American exploits. At first the mighty town of Houston didn't like the idea of men in tights "prancing and cavorting onstage." They tried to scare him off, denounced him for demoralizing American youth, but he persevered. Now he can say that he has re-created the best of Russia in Texas, where the art of dancing is cherished. "The great thing about America," he once wrote, "is that it doesn't need a revolution to change."

In the studio photograph printed in the brochure Sasha's hair is cropped, flattened with pomade, without a spot of grey. A half-smile lingers on his lips. He still looks handsome, self-assured, untroubled. Dancing through life, I think, picking up the most becoming roles, discarding them when he is done.

He didn't marry Miss Goodman. He went to America alone.

Before leaving he got drunk and came to see me. We were both in Paris and he must have just finished an engagement, for he was still in costume, a kerchief around his neck, the underarms of his too-tight jacket stained with after-dance, foxy sweat.

Such is my last memory of him: Sasha wobbly on his feet, with vodka on his breath, listing his regrets. Marrying me cost him his place in history books. His name was scratched from the annals of Ballets Russes, where by now he would've been a star.

Kolya, who has already won in the game of arithmetical advantage—the total of hours he's been with me is greater than the hours I ever was with Sasha—is still jealous of him. "He will have his name in history books," he declares. "Of Houston."

"Do you want me to read what Papa writes?" Irina asks.

I don't like the trembling in her voice, but I nod.

"'Dearest daughter,'" she reads slowly, trying to keep her voice steady. "'Thank you for your last letter. It has given me a lot of pleasure.'"

The Kotchetovsky Ballet School, I hear, has waiting lists. The students are causing a sensation. Sasha still dances: his mazurka and *hopak* are unequalled. Houston doesn't have enough of the Russian spirit. Gene Kelly's endorsement is still doing wonders. What a man, what an actor, what class.

Irina's lips begin to quiver; her eyes blink. Red-rimmed eyes, with bloodshot whites, from another sleepless night. The letter ends with Sasha's warm greetings to me and Kolya, followed by admonitions to write more often. As if nothing has happened.

"Why does he always write the same things?" my daughter asks, tossing the letter aside. The envelope and the pamphlet follow. Levushka would have demanded to see the stamps, in search of something rare. A mistake, a forgery.

"Read between the lines," I tell Irina, "the way we read Russian papers. Your father wants you to be proud of him. My father did the same and I, too, cried over it."

But my daughter doesn't want my consolations. "When a letter comes," she says, wiping her eyes, "I always hope that this time Papa will at least mention Levushka."

I rub her back when she sobs then wrap my arms around her and hold her tight. I recall a Kiev day, in winter, when I helped Mamusia dress the children for a walk. The tight felt shoes that made walking so hard, the coats with buttoned-up collars, the scarves I tied far too firmly. My nail scratched Irina's chin, drawing blood. I licked my finger and wiped it clean.

"Does it hurt?" I asked, mortified at my clumsiness.

"No," she said.

How do you tell your child not to be too obedient? Too tame?

"You know what I've just remembered?" I murmur.

She looks at me silently when I conjure up Levushka at four, in Monte Carlo. Diaghilev leaning over him, lifting his chin with his finger. "Do you know who I am, little boy?" A nod, bright and determined, is followed by my son's crystal voice chiming, "You are big, fat Diaghilev!" The Tsar of Art turns to me, his voice suddenly unsure, dropping to a whisper: "Am I really that fat, Bronia? Be honest! Tell me!"

Laughter. A magic trick of the mind.

4.

HAD I NOT BEEN OUSTED from the Polish Ballet, I would be in New York now, at the World's Fair, for the April premiere of *The Legend of Cracow*.

"The greatest exhibition in history," newspapers call it, "the miracle of tomorrow, the dawn of the modern electric era." The Westinghouse Time Capsule, buried in the Fair ground, will be opened in 6939. Levushka would have found this fascinating. "Just think, Mama," he would've gasped, though I cannot guess which of the buried items he would have approved of the most. The Mickey Mouse watch? The kewpie doll? The copies of *Life* magazine?

In Kolya's archives *The Legend of Cracow* has accumulated a bulky folder of reviews. At the Exposition in Paris, the ballet was a sensation, and I, its choreographer, received a gold medal.

But that was not enough, in the end, to protect me from intrigues.

I picture my Warsaw dancers in New York, getting ready to return to Poland. I wonder what they will dance in September.

Kolya tells me we should still go to Warsaw for a few days, collect my papers, my choreographic notes, a myriad of things I left behind, believing I was just going for a vacation. We still have good friends there, heartbroken by what had happened. And so are my dancers, who assure me that I made true artists out of them. But I hate the thought of such a journey. Not only because travelling through Germany, even in transit, fills me with dread but because I cannot get over the sneakiness with which I was dismissed. The management of Teatr Wielki didn't have the decency to inform me that my contract was terminated, let alone to provide me with reasons.

These are the thoughts that rattle in my head when our telephone gives a loud, sharp ring. Kolya, who usually answers it, is reading a magazine, so I pick up the receiver.

"Vaslav is making incredible progress, Bronia," Romola's voice booms, making me hold the receiver away even from my bad ear. "His hands are completely healed. He is no longer picking at his fingers."

"Are you still in Münsingen?" I ask.

"No. We are in St. Moritz. We are taking a short vacation before the last round of treatments. Vaslav loves it here. Tomorrow we will go on a hike to a waterfall."

Since last June, at the Münsingen Mental Asylum, Dr. Müller has been giving Vaslav insulin shocks. This is the latest of all the miraculous cures "guaranteed" to bring my brother back.

Before the shocks Romola swore by Émile Coué and his autosuggestion, which involved repeating upon awakening: "Day by day, in every way, I'm getting better and better." Simple, my sister-in-law conceded, but able to reverse any illness of body or mind. Still before, there had been "these incredible herbs doctors don't want you to know about"; a monk who laid his hands on Vaslav's head; a visit to Lourdes; and a seance in Paris, where Diaghilev's ghost told Romola that she would soon see Vaslav onstage again.

"Your sister-in-law is making a serious mistake," Dr. Binswanger, who took care of Vaslav before Romola transferred him to Münsingen, told me in July, before the treatment began. "It's like trying to fix a Swiss watch with a hammer."

I still tried to be hopeful then. Insulin helped Mamusia, I reasoned. It made her last years bearable. New drugs have more uses than doctors might have anticipated. But when I saw Vaslav after that first shock-induced coma, he mumbled some incoherent words and wouldn't stop shivering. He didn't recognize me. He didn't recognize Romola, either.

What has happened since has confirmed Dr. Binswanger's misgivings. From Romola's clipped reports, I get glimpses of Müller's methods. If there is no coma after the first shock, he just doubles the dose or triples it. So far the first seven months of treatment have resulted in nothing more than a few outbursts of uncontrollable rage.

"I told you so," Romola now insists. "You who have lost faith in his recovery. You do not believe Nijinsky will dance again. You who ask too many questions . . . contact doctors behind my back . . . seek second opinions . . . break the magic circle of faith . . . deny your brother his last chance to have a full life. You, Bronia, with your dark thoughts, always expecting the worst."

I clench my hands. Let my fingers dig into the palms; bite my lips, hard, until I taste blood. It hurts to know that Madame Romola Nijinsky is the sole custodian of my brother's life.

"Is Kolya in the room, Bronia?"

"Yes."

"How can you bear the sight of him after what happened?"

This is not a question I want to discuss. Especially not with Romola.

"Are you still there, Bronia?"

Our Parisian telephone has a long cord. I can take the phone with me to the sofa, put it on the floor. Cover it with a pillow if I wish not to see it.

"Yes. I'm here."

"We go for long walks, Bronia. Visit friends. Kyra is coming to stay with us for a few days."

I can see Romola in one of her silk dressing gowns, black, with some Chinese embroidery, open to reveal her breasts. Holding the telephone to her ear, her eyes rolling in exasperation. Kyra, who tries so hard to cut herself off from her mother, does it in the same way. Movements that link families, I think. Bounce off each other. If we could see, in fast motion, a film of the people we descended from, what odd dance would we see?

"Kyra will only tire Vaslav." Romola rattles on. "He cannot stand her fidgeting. And her spoilt son is always screaming. Vaslav won't be able to rest as he is resting now. We've just come back from a walk."

I should end this conversation right here. Stop the flow of Romola's self-absorbed nonsense, but I'm forever harbouring hope that she might reveal something I should know.

"End it," Kolya mouths, imitating putting the receiver down. "You don't have to talk to her."

He never knew the real Vaslav. He can never understand that even this exchange—painful, almost ridiculous in its predictability—is a gate to my brother, who can no longer reach out to me in any other way.

From the receiver I hear Romola's quick, chirping words: "Vaslav has just come in and is calling me, Bronia. We have to go. Today is such a beautiful, peaceful day."

I let my hand drop. A sentence comes to me, fragments of Vaslav's diary—another publishing venture of Romola, the self-appointed keeper of Vaslav's memory: *I hate mountains. They hide the view. I want to see far, far away. I do not want to be shut in.*

"What did she want this time?" Kolya asks, removing the receiver from my clenched fingers.

"There will be one more treatment," I say as I walk toward the bedroom. "At the end of May."

5.

TEN YEARS HAVE PASSED since Sergey Pavlovitch Diaghilev died in Venice, an anniversary his last besotted golden boy, Serge Lifar, celebrates with the Ballets Russes de Diaghilev Exhibition at the Palais du Louvre.

"I want to go alone," I tell Kolya, and he nods, too quickly perhaps.

I am not fond of ballet frozen, put on display. I dislike limp, lifeless curtains, scenery dragged out of storage and placed in spaces too small and too bright, all of it covered by glass, untouchable. Like photographs of dancers—mere aids to memory—pale reflections of their magic. I would so much prefer to hold the old costumes in my hand, for they at least keep the memory of the dancers' bodies, buried in the wrinkles, in the spots that have stretched. Sweat stays in them, too, long after the dance has ended; works on the fibres, loosens them, makes colours leak out.

Lifar calls the exhibition his "humble attempt to pay an artist's debt." The man who, after delivering his sentences, however trivial, scrutinizes the faces around for the signs of applause, wants to record *his* gratitude to Diaghilev, who told him: "You, Serge, will be a second Nijinsky when you grow up."

As director of the Paris Opera Ballet, Lifar is a man considered well suited for such claims. No one will point out his glaring omissions or question his judgments. Why there is so little about *Sacre* and *Faun*? Nothing about *Jeux*? I won't even mention my *Les Noces* or *Les Biches*.

Is this how we all remember? So little beyond ourselves?

Don't dwell on it, Bronia, I order myself. *This is not what art is about.*

In the exhibition program, slim and surprisingly unglamorous, a few printed memories try to evoke Diaghilev's power: "That prince of the theatre, that Tsar of Art . . . that noble Russian spirit who lived for the miracles he performed . . . With him it was all the tumult of the heart."

What would he, Sergey Diaghilev, make of us now? His orphaned, estranged children, still consumed by jealousy, still fighting among ourselves. Who is more important? Whose claim to him is greater? Who has taken more than his or her share? Characters from a play that has ended its run, I think, in search of another magician who would give them a new life. Fodder for the journalists who descend here, sniffing for stories.

The new Ballets Russes—reincarnated after Diaghilev's death—has now split into two rival companies, locked in acrimony, suing each other for the rights to ballets, scenery, music.

By the glass cabinet with a few costumes from *Sacre*, Igor Stravinsky, in solemn widower's black, surrounded by journalists, offers his recollections "of the night Paris laughed at art." In his voice I hear notes of self-righteous malice, as if *he* didn't put down Vaslav's choreography every time he thought it might hurt his music.

"Remember those cries of derision—'Call the doctor . . . Call the dentist'? Diaghilev was right when he said that the miracles of creation never perish," he tells journalists now, and coughs into his handkerchief, flinching. "I, Igor Stravinsky, have had the privilege to work with the best and the brightest."

I make a note to inquire about his health after this commotion is over.

I, too, am asked about my Ballets Russes days. "Not just as a dancer, Madame Nijinska, but also its only female choreographer . . . Memories, reflections."

"Diaghilev was a demanding teacher," I say, "assured of his vision. Ready to fight for what he believed."

One of the journalists asks if I would agree with a statement that the first years of Ballets Russes were "the days of civilized, uncensored pleasures when we still believed in a permanent, peaceful age."

"I do." I keep my reservations to myself.

Another asks if I have any regrets.

Yes.

That Diaghilev and I couldn't have worked together longer. But I wanted to try my own luck. Develop my own ideas. Work on more abstract dances, like my experimental ballet concertos.

Diaghilev would've stopped me: *Don't look back, Bronia. Remember Orpheus.*

Journalists, ballet critics, photographers might scramble to hear better, but they really hope for stories less generous, bloodier, stained with resentment and pain. They want to hear of lingering jealousy and crushing disappointment. The antics of Diaghilev's former lovers always make for a good entertainment. Lifar and Kochno at each other's throats over who would tend to Diaghilev's body. Lifar challenging Massine to a duel in Central Park. Nijinsky's madness.

"Not too good," Igor Stravinsky tells me when I inquire of his health a few moments later. It's been a bad year. "God has His inscrutable plans."

He, too, lost a child, and then his wife. Pain he doesn't have to tell me about, does he?

No. We all keep tabs on what is happening to us all. Good and bad.

He thinks God is testing him, to make him stronger.

I think life is a rigged deal I have to fight against until my last breath.

He has been in a sanatorium. He is still weak. The doctors are still worried. That much he can tell me. And that he has been asked to lecture at Harvard and will go to America shortly. "Change of climate," he says. "An old, tested cure."

"How do *you* manage, Bronislava Fominitchna?" he asks.

"I manage."

"And Irina?"

"She is afraid to dance again."

"Let her be. She'll come around. She is still young."

"Yes."

There is a pause, a sigh. "I need to tell you something," he says.

For a moment I think he is going to drag out some old Diaghilev grievance. This or that betrayal, a flurry of telegrams over who owns what, who promised what to whom and did not deliver.

But it is Vaslav Stravinsky needs to talk about.

Vaslav, who, when he was going to dance in America, in 1916, asked Stravinsky and his wife, Katya, to take care of Kyra. Said he didn't want to drag a three-year-old across the ocean with the war on. "Please, Igor Feodorovitch," Vaslav begged him, but he refused. He thought Kyra a spoilt child. He didn't want the responsibility. Katya was already feeling ill. "I thought Vaslav would understand," he says. "But he just stood there when I told him I wouldn't do it and then began to cry."

I quickly extend my hand and touch his. Nothing else is expected. Nothing else can be offered.

A woman I don't recognize is approaching. Young, with smartly bobbed black hair, a colourful shawl draped over her petite shoulders. "Maestro!" she exclaims, smiling with such radiance, extending her hands. "How I hoped to see you here."

Maestro straightens up; his owl face is all smiles.

We all have our consolations.

I'm just about to leave the Palais du Louvre when Serge Lifar stops me.

"What wonderful news from Münsingen, Madame Nijinska."

He is leaning forward, high on his own importance and the yarns of gossip he so likes to spin. How Diaghilev never cared for any of my ballets, that this is why I left Ballets Russes. I hear that at Misia Sert's famous parties he entertains the guests with impersonations of Vaslav.

I stiffen and step back. "What news?"

"The insulin treatment. The miraculous recovery!"

I must've looked at him as if he had lost his mind, for he pushes himself upright.

"I spoke with Madame Romola just the other day. Are you saying she is wrong? Do you have other news?"

I mutter something about my sister-in-law meaning well, being entitled to her opinions, and about the wisdom of being cautious with stories that generate unfounded hopes.

Do I sound harsh? Suspicious?

When I still went to confession, the priest once warned me against bitterness. It hushed God's voice, he said. Like acid, it ate into the shield that protected the soul from the sin of despair.

"Tell me, Father," I asked, "where does bitterness end and knowledge begin?"

6.

BY JUNE OF 1939 Paris is getting nervous, unsure of itself. "Too many strangers," people mutter. "The strays of the world are flocking here. As if we could take them all."

At times of trouble compassion is reserved for one's own.

"Let's get out of France, Bronia," Kolya tells me. We are at the studio, where he has returned after a whole afternoon of exploring some mysterious "possibilities."

"To go where?" I ask.

"London."

As I gather my teaching notes and pick up my dance bag, Kolya tells me that *Bullet in the Ballet*—a comedy-thriller featuring a fictitious Russian ballet company, which we both read some time ago and liked—will be turned into a film. A British producer is in Paris right now, looking for dancers and a choreographer for all the ballet scenes. Filming will start in mid-September, in London, so they need someone quickly.

"There is no serious competition," Kolya continues, with growing eagerness. Massine has an engagement in New York. Fokine is there already. Besides, would anyone be better suited than La Nijinska? They would be lucky to get me. And Irina, too. She could dance the Ballerina Doll, couldn't she? This is not onstage. There are retakes. She won't object to that!

"I've looked at the script," Kolya says, handing me a booklet with drawings of Petrushka, the Ballerina Doll and the Moor on the cover. "It's a light comedy."

It also pays a pittance as engagements go, but it is welcome nevertheless. Kolya doesn't have to spell it out for me. As political tension increases, our Nansen passports look more and more flimsy. We are stateless, without protection. One glance at the map readily confirms that England is safer than France if war breaks out.

I sigh and pick up the script. "It's quite funny," Kolya pleads.

He shouldn't worry. I have never opposed laughter.

Kolya has read enough of the script to tell me that, like the book, it revolves around a detective summoned to solve a series of murders that plague a Russian ballet company performing in London. The company is just like Ballets Russes. Everyone recalls the imperial grandeur with which nothing ever compares. British dancers change their names to make them sound Russian. The victim is always the dancer who dances Petrushka.

As Kolya speaks, I can already see dancing sequences I could devise: spoofs involving Petrushka dying too early, ahead of the music; the Moor quarrelling with the orchestra; dancers and musicians missing their cues, appearing too early or too late.

It'll not be hard.

I'll meet with the producer, I tell Kolya.

In this world preparing for war, one of the newest restrictions forbids telephone calls to and from hotels, so Kolya has to become a messenger. He will go to the Hôtel Scribe right away, make an appointment for tomorrow. No time to lose. As soon as the word spreads, there will be others, less suitable but perhaps more ruthless.

It is only later that day, when Kolya comes back with the news of a lunch meeting set up for Sunday, that the possibility of leaving Paris truly hits me. It will be worse than leaving Russia, I think. Too much has happened here. Too much is buried in the ground.

On Sunday morning I tell Kolya I'll meet him in front of the Hôtel Scribe at one. I need time alone, I say. I want to soak Paris in, I think, hide it under my skin.

My husband nods and leans to kiss my lips.

I turn my face away.

"I'm expecting an offer today," Kolya says, cheerfully, to mask the tensing of his jaw. "Who else could be better than you? By the end of August, we'll be in London."

I go to rue Daru first, to the Orthodox church, where—in the small courtyard and on the steps leading to the front door—Russian beggars murmur their pleas: "Give to the former member of the intelligentsia . . . to an unemployed victim of new labour laws." Noses are reddened from too much vodka. Here and there a torn uniform coat is fastened with a safety pin. One of the beggars offers to recall the street signs on the Nevsky Prospekt for me: "On both sides and in the right order."

I give alms as long as my coins last, but I distrust the quagmire of nostalgia. I feel no outrage hearing that this or that former grand duchess embroiders linen or makes hats, or is forced to sweep her own floors.

They are alive.

In the vestibule, still mostly empty since the liturgy won't begin for another hour, I buy seven candles and step inside, past the red columns with gilded tops. It always strikes me how small this church is, how densely filled with painted mosaics and holy icons, and how quietly solemn.

I walk to the centre, where Levushka's coffin once stood. I cross myself the Polish Catholic way. Not out of defiance but of habit. The words of old prayers I mutter to myself are also Polish. This is the only way I know how to soothe the souls of my dead: Levushka, Mamusia, Stassik, Father, Feodor, Sergey Pavlovitch. And of Vaslav, even though he is still alive. I feel as if a monster followed in my footsteps and devoured all I cared about. First places and things, and then, not having enough, people.

When I finish my prayers, I light my seven candles, place them in front of the icon of the Virgin Mary. I ask for forgiveness for being so terse with Kolya, for turning away from him at night. For refusing to put my hand on his shoulder when he sobs. I beg for more time.

Opposite the church is a small corner café—À la Ville de Petrograd. I don't usually go there, for it is too crowded and too gaudy, but today I make an exception.

The only free table is the one below the print of Tsar Nicholas on a horse and a *troika* of horses galloping madly through a snow-covered field. The tablecloth is red, the napkins bright yellow. On the shelf beside me a tiny samovar made of china rubs shoulders with ducks and painted lacquer boxes.

The waitress is young, flustered by the constant calls for her attention. The kerchief she has draped over her shoulders is frayed but still colourful, blue and green, the peacock colours.

I ask for a glass of samovar tea and *vatroushka,* Russian cheesecake.

"I recommend quince preserves," the waitress says. Her Russian is from here already; she burrs when she pronounces the Russian *r*.

"What is your name?" I ask.

"Tanya . . . Tanya Petrovna," she adds quickly.

She has a job, which in France now—when each month labour laws impose new restrictions on hiring foreigners—is nothing to sneer at. Were her parents allowed to become French citizens? This is much more likely if she has a brother. Girls are of no help with the French authorities. Little boys, after all, could be future soldiers of France. For a moment I imagine her at the Vitiaz summer camp. With Levushka. She is his age; he would have been twenty by now.

"Thank you, Tanya." I smile and watch her disappear into the kitchen, from which smells of dried mushrooms and smoked fish waft.

I light a cigarette. The first drag goes right to my head. I close my eyes and feel myself swaying a bit. But when I take another hit off the cigarette, the dizziness passes.

Tanya brings me my glass of tea with a slice of lemon and cubes of sugar on the side. *Vatroushka* is served warm with a dollop of whipped cream. Before the dessert gets cold, I take one last drag and flick the cigarette down, stub it inside the heavy ashtray.

The sugar cubes dissolve as I stir the tea. Lemon lightens its colour, adds the delicate sour note to it. Then I hold my hands over the steaming water for a few seconds. It's an old habit, from Kiev winter days when every sliver of warmth had to be captured.

"What is Stalin doing?" I hear two men at the table near me. "He is killing and killing. And what is Hitler doing? He is studying at Stalin's university. His diploma is almost ready."

Kolya is waiting for me in front of the Hôtel Scribe, walking to and fro along the pavement. From this distance he looks even slimmer and more trim, taking as little space as possible. Like the man in Hans Christian Andersen's tale who is being replaced by his shadow. When

Kolya sees me, his long, drawn face lightens and he waves, as if I could have missed him.

"I'm not late, Kolya, am I?"

It can be construed as a question—a hint of apology, even.

"No . . . you are not late. We have time."

His eyes are fast, assessing; the eyes of a man who has always had to watch out for himself. He slips his hand under my arm, holds on to my elbow, and we walk together into the carpeted lobby. Husband and wife.

Mr. Load is dwarfish, short and plump, but carefully dressed. I note a well-fitting suit, gold cuffs. There is a gap between his two front teeth. We shake hands. His is warm and moist with sweat. He has already chosen the table for us, by the window. He recommends rabbit. And vichyssoise.

"I'm not that hungry," I say. "No soup for me. Just rabbit."

I sink into the chair, my legs hurting from the long walk. The right foot—the one I injured in Argentina—is more tender. Pain pulsates upward, toward my shin.

We chat for a while. London, Paris, differences in weather, habits.

Mr. Load has a black leather briefcase beside him, but he makes no attempt to open it. He has a few questions, if I don't mind.

I've been a freelancer long enough. I know not to appear overly eager. Yes, I have read both the book and the script. I'm impressed how the script preserved the book's humour. Nevajno, the choreographer, is an especially nice touch. His symbolic ballet danced by shirts alone is particularly well conceived. Red shirts angry, brown shirts making speeches. *Corps de ballet* with bandages round their mouths. All in a constructivist setting with a big airplane upstairs and prison downstairs.

In the film we could have whole dance sequences flashing as Nevajno spins his visions to the director.

Mr. Load nods, visibly pleased. "As I expected, Madame Nijinska has no shortage of brilliant ideas."

I slip in more details and anecdotes that might be used in the film. Have I not seen the best of dancers perform *Petrushka*? Nijinsky, Massine. Have I not danced the Ballerina role beside Vaslav? "Diaghilev's favourite dancers," I tell Mr. Load as he jots notes in jerky script, "wore white ducks, blazers, straw boaters."

Kolya touches my elbow, a sign that I'm overdoing it, a hint to let him take over, not to be too forceful. His eyes warn me: you don't want to be seen as inflexible and too ambitious, insisting on your own vision.

I take a deep breath, longing for a cigarette, for which I'll have to wait until we finish eating. Two waiters bring our food. Rabbit for me and Mr. Load, duck for Kolya.

I look around. Unlike the café on rue Daru, there are mostly women here, in fashionable small hats, black veils draped over their foreheads. Their perfume wafts in the air. Coco Chanel has conquered Paris again.

Should I have worn my hat?

I take a few bites, praise his having suggested the rabbit, which is indeed excellent, its grainy mustard sauce compensating for the mildness of the meat.

Mr. Load lifts his fork in the air. This is the announcement time. My name, he says, came up in a conversation with Mr. Nakhimoff, who is the number-one choice for director.

I smile. Nakhimoff is Russian. He has already made a film about Pavlova, which I liked. That he is the preferred director bodes well for the project.

"I'm flattered," I say.

"Nakhimoff is right," Mr. Load continues, in between rabbit morsels, which he carefully smears with the creamy sauce first. "You, Madame, will be perfect choreographing the ballet scenes. Coaching the actors to adopt the authentic Russian mannerisms. Perhaps even dancing yourself?"

"I don't dance anymore. I am a choreographer, a teacher . . . The younger generation needs to take over . . . have its chance to shine."

I take the opportunity to mention Irina. Let Mr. Load picture the credits: with Irina Nijinska as the Ballerina Doll.

"Yes," Mr. Load mutters. Mr. Nakhimoff would be delighted. "We have an agreement, then, do we?"

Beside me Kolya sinks deeper into his chair, relieved. I'm glad I can excuse myself from negotiating the details. The offer—it's not hard to tell from an embarrassed grin on Mr. Load's face—won't be generous. He knows we cannot afford to mind. We know he knows.

We choose our desserts: stewed pears, *crème brûlée*. Coffee arrives, and with it the permission to smoke. As the tip of the cigarette roasts over the flame, I inhale its smoky promise, relishing the sound too faint for my damaged hearing but still clear in my memory: the crackle of the burning leaves.

"You must be so happy with the latest news from Switzerland. Vaslav Nijinsky's miraculous treatment! A promise of his return!" Mr. Load has read it in the bulletin the Nijinsky Foundation puts out every month.

Are we that gullible? Or that desperate for good news?

Kolya tenses beside me, ready to jump in, to shield me, but I am faster with my warnings. Vaslav is almost fifty. He hasn't danced for over twenty years. Even if he recovered completely right now . . .

Mr. Load nods, reluctant, not hiding his disappointment. A miraculous return of Vaslav Nijinsky—the ultimate Petrushka—would've been a great coup for the film's publicity.

I rise from my chair, plead another pressing engagement, even though Mr. Load has already opened his briefcase and extracted the contract. "My husband will take care of the business details," I say hurriedly. "And I can promise you my answer very soon."

Kolya gives me a pleading look: Do not do anything to spoil this. Go, but do not say anything else.

I smile, extend my hand to Mr. Load, who, too, rises and—in an awkward gesture he must have observed but rarely practised—kisses the top of my hand.

"It is a fine script," I say. "And Mr. Nakhimoff's participation bodes well."

I leave without turning back, quickly, diving into my handbag for the package of Gitanes I bought in the morning. I extract one cigarette, roll it between my thumb and forefinger, disappointed already, for it feels dry and will be stale. The street vendor must have slipped me his oldest pack.

7.

THIS CONVERSATION IS costing the Nijinsky Foundation a small fortune, though it must be nothing compared with the professional fees, insulin treatments, private nurse and first-class room and board—which

I presume have taken at least seven thousand francs. Dr. Müller's "expertise" does not come cheap, either.

"Have you read the papers, Bronia?" Romola's voice is always high-pitched, but now it is soaring on something more potent than her usual gin and tonic. Morphine or cocaine? Injected or snorted? Or is it another instalment of love?

"The Great Nijinsky dances again in a Swiss insane asylum. A triumph of modern medicine," the headlines shout. The *Paris Match* photographs reveal that my once handsome, lithe brother has turned into a short, portly man; his ill-fitting suit—I cannot but notice—looks even worse when contrasted with Romola's sleek Chanel dress.

"Yes, Bronia, Vaslav is completely recovered."

The papers describe a hospital hall crowded with journalists and photographers. Romola enters with Vaslav, her hand firmly under his arm. Serge Lifar—"a dear friend and Nijinsky's disciple"—is right behind them. "The long-awaited moment is near," Lifar is quoted saying, pointing at the barre.

The photographs that accompany the reports tell a different story. It is Lifar who dances, and Vaslav stares at him with a sad, lopsided smile, before bowing to him then kneeling to feel Lifar's calf. Only then comes the miracle shot: Vaslav in the air, in a middle of what must have been an awkward jump but what a caption describes as "Nijinsky's famous *entrechat* in which no other dancer has rivalled him thus far.

"Monsieur Lifar declares it the most beautiful moment of his life. 'To be able to awaken the God of the Dance when so many others—no doubt more worthy than I am—have failed.'"

Fame is like carrion, I think. It'll always draw out the hyenas.

"Can you hear me, Bronia? Are you still smoking that cigarette? Vaslav can't stand when people smoke."

This is a picture Romola insists I see: Vaslav eating lunch in the hotel dining room; taking a nap on the balcony, which has views of the mountains. Vaslav in a beige woollen sweater listening to a radio broadcast. Shuddering when he hears Hitler's speech, turning the dial right away in search of announcers with slow, measured voices. BBC is his favourite.

When I put the receiver down, I must look agitated, for Irina is watching me with narrowed eyes. There is so much of Mamusia in her. The daintiness of her features. The swiftness of her movements.

"Aunt Romola, the Goddess of the Dance?" she asks.

I nod and close my eyes to stop tears.

8.

WE ARE LUCKY. I can read it in the eyes of the clerk at the British embassy, where we've come to apply for our British visas. He is in his early thirties, clean and polished, sure of his own relevance.

"What will you be doing in London, Madame Nijinska?" he asks.

Kolya is at my side, ready to repeat a question I may not hear. In defiance of warm June days, he has put on his double-breasted striped suit of grey wool. There is a whiff of brilliantine about him, almond blossoms, the same scent Diaghilev favoured.

The desk in the room we have been led into is almost empty apart from the writing pad and a thick file, tied with a ribbon. I wonder if it contains everything the British know about us. Or it is just there to intimidate.

The contract of my engagement is in the clerk's hands. I repeat exactly what it specifies, careful not to diverge from any of the points: "Choreograph ballet sequences for the film. Hire dancers for the sequences approved by the director and producer. Conduct rehearsals." Spartan, as I suspected it would be, with a whole list of restrictions. I must comply with the director's vision. I cannot break the contract without penalty, but the producers can terminate it at any time and for any reason without compensation.

Irina will be questioned next, separately, for at twenty-six she is no longer my dependant. Thanks to Kolya's insistence, the contract includes her as one of the film dancers. On our way to the embassy I made her recount her credentials: debuted with Olga Spessivtseva in London; ballerina with Ida Rubinstein's company, with La Théâtre Chorégraphique Nijinska, with the Polish Ballet. Irina repeated it all after me, but on her lips these words did not sound like accomplishments.

"Your passports, please."

Kolya, fedora on his lap, dives into his breast pocket and hands the clerk our Nansen passports. In France they always elicit comments. We are chastised for "sticking" to them, refusing to become French—as if it were possible for all of us—clinging to the dream of the imperial Russia we have lost. In addition, Russians with Soviet passports despise us for having accepted that we would never go back.

Here in the British embassy our stateless status is not a disadvantage. In British eyes France is growing more red, closer to the Soviets. Refusing to become French is considered a sign of prudence.

Kolya and I are questioned about our Kiev years. How did we leave Russia? Do we have family there? Are we in touch with anyone still?

We fled. Kolya's two sisters live there. No one has been in touch for the past six years.

The clerk has an annoying habit of not lifting his eyes from his writing pad when he asks his questions, and then, like a pupil caught daydreaming, jerking his head up and looking straight at us. I meet his eyes, wondering what our faces reveal. Desperation? Fear?

The lineups at the embassy doors grow longer every day. Parisian railway stations team with "tourists" who head for the cheapest hotels and try to locate anyone who could get them out of France. Britain is second on the list of desirable destinations, after the United States. The English Channel may look trivial on the map, but it is an obstacle that can buy time.

"Go back to the waiting room, please," the clerk says. "We'll call you."

The waiting room is crowded but subdued. I scan the faces, looking for anyone I might know. Men are all in suits, hats in hand; women in summer dresses, with light jackets thrown over their shoulders or folded over their arms. A mother and father with two small children have placed themselves in the corner. The boys are sitting on their parents' laps. The older one is quiet, but his brother is whimpering. The father, on whose knees he sits, moves his leg up and down. The boy is clearly not impressed with this lame imitation of a trotting horse. An elderly woman—a grandmother, perhaps—rummages in her bag then produces a well-loved teddy bear. The boy shakes his head and hides his face on his father's chest.

Irina joins us half an hour later, smiling at me with reassurance. She looks fresh and almost girlish in her crepe de chine yellow dress. It must be the white collar that does it, and the absence of lipstick. A young man standing by the door is looking at her. She must notice his interest, but nothing about her indicates that. When she danced at the Polish Ballet,

I often saw her talking with one of the dancers from the *corps*—Yurek. I tried not to pin any hopes on these sightings. I thought she would tell me herself if it ever became serious. She didn't.

"They've asked me about my father," Irina says. "I told him he is in America."

Kolya is pacing the room, his hat in his hand. I stand with Irina by the window.

From time to time a name is called. All eyes follow the ones who hurry out of the waiting room, disappear in the corridors. No one comes back, so it is hard to know what the verdicts are. From what we hear most applications are refused, but these are all rumours, unconfirmed. Many of the dancers we know have been hired by Massine for the September Metropolitan Opera production and are applying for American visas. Others swear that Portuguese visas are easiest to obtain.

"Monsieur Rosenberg!"

There is a commotion by the window. The children are put on the floor and the whole family follows the father out of the waiting room. Without the teddy bear, I notice, for the toy is lying under the chair. I move to pick it up, but before I reach it, the grandmother returns and retrieves it. We exchange a quick look. Hers of relief, mine of understanding.

"Madame Nijinska!"

This is when I know that another escape has begun. Our British visas, we learn, will be ready in two weeks' time. They will be valid for six weeks.

Six weeks make a month and a half. If not a salvation, then it is at least a reprieve. The film may take longer than six weeks, or some other choreographing engagements might arise in the meantime. Mimi Rambert is running a ballet company in London, Tamara Karsavina is there, too. We are luckier than many. The name Nijinsky still opens doors.

Now we have to empty the Parisian apartment, fold up our affairs here. It would be easier to think of this departure as temporary, but it would also be foolish.

We take a cab back home.

The taxi driver speaks all the time, a long monologue, unperturbed by our silence. He knows we are foreigners—our accents always betray us—and will not argue with his assessment of where the world's troubles come from. He announces that the German aggression has to be curtailed. Germany is insatiable and will never show any pity to the weak. France should've helped Franco when it could, stopping him from aligning himself with Hitler and Mussolini. He likes Mussolini, though. "Fascism is not Nazism. Besides, Mussolini made the trains run on time."

I listen, offering a noncommittal murmur here and there to keep the cabbie talking. It's important to know what others think. As important as keeping our own thoughts secrets. Loose words travel along unpredictable paths.

9.

IRINA IS SITTING ON THE FLOOR, surrounded by empty boxes marked TAKE WITH US, or BURN, or TRASH. Most of the bigger boxes have friends' names on them. Lifar has offered space in the locker room at the Paris Opera. A big question mark beside this offer is Kolya's or Irina's concession to my misgivings.

Nina Youshkevitch, an old friend who lives just outside Paris, will store all the scrapbooks, folders and costumes from my years with Ballets Russes, Teatro Colón, the Ida Rubinstein Company and Teatr Wielki. She has a large house and doesn't mind holding my archives for the time being. "I don't know for how long," I warned her on the phone. She answered with a question: "Do we ever know, Bronia?"

Kolya has persuaded our concierge to let us keep the maid's room in the attic after we move out. This is where the costumes from my own original ballets *Le Guignol* and *On the Road* will go. My husband has already sprinkled them with pepper and wrapped them in tulle. They are not the ones we used in the performance. Aleksandra Exter, my old Kiev friend who, too, has fled to Paris, re-created them for me, after the originals were impounded for someone else's debts.

Théâtre Chorégraphique Nijinska didn't have Diaghilev's ruthlessness in marshalling support, or Ida Rubinstein's inexhaustible inheritance. We didn't know how to navigate stock market crashes or protect ourselves from cheaters. Mamusia would have reminded me that I chose this fate myself, against her warnings. And I would have sighed, impatient, and pointed out to her that the security she cherished had its own shackles, no less painfully tight.

"Not there," Irina tells me when, trying to help, I put newspaper clippings about my staging of *Hamlet* in the wrong pile.

Irina also reminds me that we'll need to go shopping. There have been blackouts in England. We need batteries, candles, matches, vacuum-packed coffee, rolls of black paper. Stockings, too. And good shoes. Lace-up leather brogues. "They are building another bomb shelter," our concierge said when I asked her about the jackhammer noises in the street. Cars are leaving Paris for the country. The Louvre is packing up is treasures.

"My winter coat is still fine," I say, clapping my hands to kill a fluttering moth. "But we should get you one. Better here than in England."

My daughter nods. Trunks and suitcases are lined up in the dining room, open, to get rid of the smell of mildew. Moths are a sign to look over the woollens, assess the damage already done. Mamusia used to toss a handful of cloves into the storage boxes. I never asked her if it worked.

"Mothballs, too," Irina says. "I'll make a list."

Irina has put on weight, not much yet enough to make her features rounded, lovelier. Her body is no longer an instrument but a harbour. She doesn't do her morning routine anymore. If I remind her—which I try not to—she dutifully goes through the positions, but that's all. If I leave before she is finished, she doesn't continue. "Please, Bronia. Don't push her too hard," Kolya pleads.

But when we talk about things practical, straightforward, manageable, something begins to shift between us. Irina grows and I diminish. She stands on solid ground and I begin to quiver.

"Look, Mama." Irina's chuckle brings me back.

I walk up to her and she hands me an old drawing. Kolya's attempt to preserve the shapes of the Stomachion figures the children had once made, the memory of my amazement at their deftness. "You never guessed then, did you?" she asks.

"Guessed what?"

Instead of answering, Irina hands me a copy of a magazine with one of the pages marked by a folded corner. I open it to see two familiar figures: the old woman with an umbrella and a man doing a handstand. Two winning entries for a contest my children fooled us with.

"It was my idea, not Levushka's," Irina confesses. "Though I wanted to confess right away and he refused."

10.

PEOPLE HAVE BEEN MAKING inquiries with Madame Clavette, the concierge. There was a woman she describes as stoutly and matronly looking. Then another one, younger, with red hair and a foreign accent. Russian? I ask, but Madame Clavette is not sure.

The Russian-émigré papers Kolya reads have just reported that another CheKa spy has been uncovered in Paris, and another White officer kidnapped. A joke is making the rounds: "Christ has risen!" the Russian ambassador hears on Easter Sunday. "I know," he replies. "I've already been informed."

My unease must be palpable, for Madame Clavette says with a huff, "But, Madame, she merely heard you were leaving France and she was inquiring about the lease." The huff means: how touchy and finicky these Russians are. As if the whole world was filled with spies and traitors.

"They, too, will learn," Mamusia used to say.

As my hearing deteriorates, my sense of smell sharpens. In the entrance hall where we stand talking there is a whiff of tar and of the whetstone Monsieur Clavette uses to sharpen his knives. There is a whiff of the cat piss Madame Clavette has not yet washed away.

The cobbler next door is hammering away. I like him, a man who understands feet. Knows how they age, grow calluses, deform the shoes that used to fit like a glove. A man who evens up worn-out heels, changes soles, can make a pair of shoes to measure. A good shoemaker is always a dancer's friend.

"How is Monsieur Miron?" I ask.

Madame Clavette is always ready for gossip. "Sick with a bad cough for the second week . . . his son in the army was supposed to visit, but his leave was revoked . . . the war must be closer than they say . . . and how are you holding up, Madame Nijinska?"

I've forgotten to touch my cheeks with rouge. Nothing like a bit of stagecraft to stop unwanted questions. Darkness of thoughts is best dispelled one tiny movement at a time. If one is skipped, omitted, the whole structure will collapse.

As my heart tightens, I murmur something about having to rush off on my urgent errand, and walk into the street.

The side street leading to the St-Ouen gate is lined with funeral stores. Flowers, wreaths, headstones, *monuments funéraires*. I buy two votive candles in glass containers: green for Mamusia, amber for Levushka. I'll not leave any flowers this time for they'll wilt right away in the summer heat. Instead I'll pay the caretaker to plant daffodils every spring we are away and chrysanthemums every fall.

I have come here alone, in spite of Kolya's pleading looks.

The cemetery office is right behind the gate, where the word *Pax* is carved in stone on both sides. This is where I go first, while grief is still manageable.

There are only women in the office. Men, especially young ones, are getting more and more scarce. Three of the women are whispering over an open newspaper, pointing at something in the lower corner. The fourth one, the youngest, seeing me enter, detaches herself from them and asks how she can be of help. She is pretty in a French way, slim, dark-haired, confident in her movements. There is an engagement ring on her finger. Not too expensive but tasteful.

My business is easy enough. To pay for the two plots and for the caretaker. "For how long, Madame?" the clerk asks. Her breath smells of mint.

It's a simple question I should've anticipated, but all I can say is that I have no idea when I might be back. Wars and revolutions make short shrift of such arrangements. In Russia Stassik's grave must be long gone, his body forced to make room for newer dead.

"I have seventy-five hundred francs with me," I say.

The young woman at the counter doesn't seem surprised. Obviously I am not the first one with such a vague request.

She is not a balletomane. She asks me twice how to spell Nijinsky. "Is it a Russian name?" she inquires, and I nod. Russian, Polish—they're the same to her and I don't want to answer too many questions.

The formalities are over fast. The plot is mine until 1947, a date abstract but distant enough to offer some protection. I'm relieved the receipt is a small piece of paper. I'll give it to Irina to put it with other documents we'll take with us to London: Certificates of births and death. School transcripts. Records of employments. Expired passports and identity cards proving who we once were.

The grave where Mamusia and Levushka are buried bears evidence of Kolya's visits. A rosebush growing by the side of the tomb has been recently pruned, the gravel path leading to it raked clean. The votive lights are all clustered together, ready to be lit.

The headstone is simple, without ornaments, the way I wanted it:

Eleanora Nijinska 1856–1932, Lev Nijinsky-Kotchetovsky 1919–1935

"You blame me, don't you?" Kolya said after the funeral, lowering his head. "And every day I wish I had died instead of him."

The wooden bench beside the grave is old, worn by many seasons. I sit down, blink and wipe the wet from my eyes.

I pray in Polish: *Wieczne odpoczywanie* . . . eternal rest grant them, O Lord.

I've steeled myself for this visit with my strategy of containment. This is your time to grieve and hurt. Do it and then stop. But it is not that simple.

I hold the memory of my son in my body. The lankiness of his arms in mine. The prickly stubble of his cropped hair. The ease with which the smudge of soot on his cheek gives in when I wipe it away with my hand.

Moments hang heavy. Black flecks float in front of my eyes.

When it is time to leave, I walk away along the tree-lined alley that leads me back to the gate. For a long while afterwards I have a clear sense of life going on without me, as if a glass pane separated me from reality.

I do not resent its protection. It's better than the searing pain of the past four years.

October 17, 1939

Sudden death is merciless in its betrayals. Nothing left behind, however petty, is spared, saved from spying eyes. Before I die, I hope to have the time to go through what I still possess, separate the truly important from the worthless and the misleading. Destroy the trails that lead where I do not wish to be followed.

The next few hours before dawn are all I have left of solitude.

Apart from the polished pages, the manila envelope contains scores of half-finished notes, copied passages, variations of the same paragraph. There is a whole page scribbled with different versions of my son's name: Lev Vaslav Stanislav Aleksandrovitch . . . Léon . . . Nijinsky . . . Kotchetovsky.

In the year 2000, long-range, all-seeing machines will allow travellers to see what is happening at home. Radio will allow to hear any voice anywhere on earth, or sea. There will be special centres for these long-distance seeing calls. Transporting photographs and films through the air will also be possible in an instant.

As you can see, life in the year 2000 will be truly worth living.

Why do I have to study music? Why is it not enough that I know how to play?

I don't want to be a musician. We don't have people who like art now. Why do we want to do art if nobody needs it? This is what I've asked Mama, but all she ever says is that all artists have doubts. She refuses to accept that I'm not an artist.

—

"You faggot," Vova yelled after me and J-P. "And your fancy boy."

I turned back. I walked to him, grabbed his collar. He was panting, glaring at me. His face was bruised, scratched. A blob of saliva gathered in the corner of his mouth.

"What did you say?" I asked.

"Faggot."

I punched him again and broke his nose.

I'm not afraid of death. It's just a moment. A blink.

I didn't go to school today but sat at a bistro and ordered a coffee. As I was lighting my cigarette, I noticed a woman staring at me as if she recognized me from somewhere. She must've been very beautiful once, and her bold glances came from that part of her which was how she looked then and not now. I liked that, so I smiled back and she moved toward me and asked me for a light.

I lit a match and she bent over with her cigarette. "I'm Kiki," she said.

"Kiki," I repeated, stupidly.

"What's your name?" she asked.

"Léon," I said.

"I like to talk," she warned me. "So if you don't, just get up and run away. I'll pay for your coffee."

"It's all right."

"Do you want to hear what I did during the war?"

"Yes."

"I worked in a factory where they repaired soldiers' shoes."

"How did they do it?"

She told me that the shoes came from the dead soldiers. At the factory they had to be dipped in oil, so that they softened, and put on wooden trees where they were hammered back into shape.

"This is what I did," she said.

"Hammered them?" I asked.

"No, silly. I was just a child, younger than you are now. I was putting them on wooden trees."

"How old were you?" I asked, but she said it was not my business to ask a woman's age. Then she took my hand, lifted it up and looked at the scars and the cigarette burn.

"What's that?" she asked.

"Nothing," I said.

"Are you feeling sorry for yourself?"

"No."

She was not that talkative at all, but as I was about to leave, she told me that she had been to America. "Don't ever go there," she said. "It's not the way it is in the movies."

There is no more time left. Lighting another cigarette, I begin writing the hardest words of all . . .

It is September 4, 1935. Wednesday. We are in Deauville, and this is the last day of our Normandy vacation after my London season. Normandy was Levushka's choice.

For the past week we've been driving around the countryside, through ancient villages with their stone churches and thatched-roof cottages so beautifully topped with rows of wildflowers. We've eaten at *auberges*—fish soup, mussels, lamb raised on these salty marshlands, clearing our palates with Calvados and apple ice cream.

We've walked along the beach from Villers-sur-Mer all the way to Haulgate, at low tide, along the crumbling limestone cliffs, past the Black Cows—giant pieces of limestone that have fallen off and rolled toward the sea.

We've sat sunning on the beach; watched a cormorant drying its wings, seagulls feasting on mussels. We've cleared seaweed from limestone boulders, looking for fossils, hoping to find dinosaur teeth.

This morning, at our Deauville hotel, we have an early breakfast of croissants with apple jam and café au lait, for the tea the hotel serves is undrinkable.

Levushka sits with us at the table. Irina is still upstairs. "Why is your sister taking so long?" I ask him.

"Why would I know?"

"Sometimes you two can be worse than a ballet company," I say.

The day before, Irina and Levushka quarrelled. He had dropped his wet swim trunks on the floor and left them there, and the floor underneath turned visibly lighter. Irina called him a "slob," careless not just with his things but also hers. Levushka told her that she was "bossy," always telling him what to do. "Just because you only think of yourself," she shot back.

This is so unlike Irina, I thought, always the one to smooth all sharp edges.

Levushka must have been thinking the same, for he asked, "Has something bitten you all of a sudden?"

"Yes. You!"

I interrupted this bickering, reminding them that we were returning to Paris tomorrow. Why spoil the last evening of our holiday?

"Why are you always taking his side?" Irina asked.

It was Kolya who managed to defuse this silly quarrel. First he declared the floor perfectly fine. We were in a seaside hotel, after all, where the floor should be able to withstand a pair of wet trunks. Before Irina could protest that he, too, was taking her brother's side, Kolya remembered a Russian joke about a pet parrot:

The parrot has disappeared. Its owner runs to the CheKa. "Why would you come to us?" they ask. "We don't busy ourselves with runaway parrots."

"Someone will bring it soon, Comrade Commander," the man says. "I just wanted to declare that I don't share its opinions."

I was the only one to laugh.

"What's so funny about it?" Levushka asked, his tilted head the only indication Kolya was in for a teasing.

"It's the CheKa," Kolya began to explain in earnest, until he realized Levushka was pulling his leg and chased him around the room.

—

As we wait for Irina, who is taking forever to come down, Kolya scans the newspaper. "'Growing discontent in Germany,'" he reads to us, 'massive demonstrations. Belgium has just recognized the Soviet Union, a stamp of approval for Stalin. In France, Croix de Feu is calling for national renewal and demonstrations to promote French values. Military discipline is one of them.'

"It this the only choice we have?" Kolya sighs, folding the newspaper. "Either this or Communists?"

My son puts another thick layer of apple jam on his croissant then takes a big bite. Brown pastry flakes scatter on the tablecloth all around him.

Irina finally appears, dressed in her favourite blue dress, with a matching jacket. I'm about to tell her that it will all get wrinkled in the car but stop myself.

"Anything left for me?" Irina asks.

Kolya waves for the waiter to bring us more coffee. We also order more croissants. And half a grapefruit each.

"Have you seen my yellow blouse, Mama?" Irina asks, casting a quick look at Levushka, who is picking at the croissant flakes, arranging them in small islands then scattering them with one flick of his fingers. "I couldn't find it anywhere."

"It might be in my suitcase," I say, before she manages to say something about messy brothers who never grow up.

Kolya picks up another newspaper, but I take it away from him.

"Let's not talk about politics," I say. "Big or small."

Before we set off, Kolya and Levushka unfold the road map, chart the Shell stations on our way and calculate the distance: two hundred kilometres to Paris. We will drive through Tournedos then Évreux. Our car, bought with my Hollywood honorarium, is a Buick sedan. It can go ninety kilometres an hour, but we won't go that fast.

"So that bicycles can pass Kolya?" Levushka asks with a mock grimace.

"Yes," I say.

The packing is easy. Two suitcases, one for me and Kolya, one for the children. Levushka also has a backpack. It is made of cowhide, covered with brown matted fur.

When the suitcases are in the trunk, Kolya makes us pose for photographs. Me in front of the car, in my travel clothes: a pair of dark brown trousers and a green blouse. Irina and Levushka leaning on the hood, making faces, their hands clasped. "Do you want to sit beside me?" Kolya asks Levushka, who wants to get his *carte rose* as soon as he turns eighteen.

"Later, when we get closer to Paris," Levushka says. "Now I'll sit with Irina in the back."

The quarrel is obviously over. They are friends again.

Kolya is just about to tell us to get into the car when Levushka announces that he has to go back to the hotel room. He has forgotten something. "What is it?" I ask, but he walks away, his hairy knapsack in hand.

"Should I go with him?" I ask Kolya. "He needs to get the key."

Kolya shakes his head, which means that I'm fussing. "He is seventeen. He can get a key to the room by himself."

"All right," I say, and light a cigarette. We are not in a great hurry, and Irina doesn't like when I smoke in the car. It makes her nauseous, she says.

Kolya is poring over the map again. The road back is pretty straightforward, but he likes to plan the stops. On our way here we had lunch in Évreux. The restaurant looked nice from the outside, but *tarte aux pommes* turned out to be the only decent thing we ordered. This time Kolya is determined we choose more carefully. Take *Michelin*'s recommendation.

My thoughts drift to upcoming engagements. In London I met with Alicia Markova, whose career I've watched carefully ever since her Ballets Russes days. In my choreographer's notebook her name is marked with three asterisks—for rapidity, delicacy, lightness. "How I'd love to work with you," Alicia said. "Would you consider it?"

"All good," Kolya says. He has made a show of opening the hood up, touching something there, though we all know the car doesn't need tinkering. Not this one.

The clouds are low, blue-grey.

"Is it going to rain?" I ask Kolya.

He points to a strip of pale light stretched along the horizon. Like a satin ribbon. In the morning the forecast promised a sunny day with partial clouds. Although since then, on the radio, he has heard that we might expect some rain.

Kolya follows the weather the same way he follows politics, assessing each shift of an ever-evolving story. As forecasts change, contradict themselves, he draws my attention to what he calls the "extremes." Isn't this summer the hottest we remember? This winter the mildest? Have I heard of such flooding before? Or such erratic pressure, rising and falling without as much as a warning?

"Even if it rains, we are not made of sugar," I tell him. "We won't dissolve."

When Levushka is back—there have been no problems; he got what he wanted; no, he won't tell us what it was—we take our seats. The car smells of plastic and gasoline. This is what makes Irina nauseous, I think, not the cigarette smoke.

We leave Deauville in high spirits. The road takes us past apple orchards, half-timbered houses with wood stacked for the winter, herds of cows grazing on meadows. The first drops of rain fall on the windshield.

"Don't go so fast, Kolya," I say.

He slows down.

In the back of the car Irina and Levushka talk in low voices. I cannot hear what they say, but I relish the easy flow of their conversation and occasional laughter.

"Auberge de Bretagne," Kolya says. This is where we should stop to eat. Ten kilometres past Évreux. It is a *Michelin* recommendation.

Any opposition?

None.

"Remember my Kiev *Mephisto?*" I ask Kolya. "I am thinking of staging it again."

"Good," Kolya says. "It was your best."

"Diaghilev said it was too hermetic."

"Diaghilev only liked ideas that he could claim as his own."

"I don't want a straightforward revival," I tell Kolya. "I want a memory transformed."

He nods, and I slip into that dreamy state that always precedes creation, when everything around me feeds into my vision. The poplar trees on both sides of the road flicker as we pass, just the way I want the dancers to come in and out of the audience's field of vision. The sprawling house we are driving by reminds me to explore all the sides of the stage, not just the centre.

This is when I feel the swerve of the car. Hear the screech of brakes followed by Kolya's jarring scream.

For a moment the world turns black.

I do not have a clear memory of what happens next. There is a moment of stillness when nothing is yet final. The rest I am not sure about. Not anymore. There must have been a moment when I got out of the car, saw its front maimed by the tree trunk. A moment when I opened the back door, saw my children. The unnatural contortions of their bodies.

I remember the screaming, which must have been mine. Kolya's arms enclosing me, suffocating. My arms pushing him away. "You drove too fast," I yell. "Why?"

I remember hearing Irina's raspy breath. I remember bending over Levushka, beseeching him to open his eyes, look at me.

I remember the blood, the silence, the stillness that is no longer filled with hope.

At the Évreux hospital where the ambulance has taken us the nurse gives me an injection and mutters some kind words I cannot hear. When I am able to stand up without shaking, I ask to be taken to Irina's bedside. I sit there and stare at her bandaged head, her arm in a cast; her breath is laboured, uncertain.

The red spot on her forehead grows. Her eyelids twitch.

"Look at me," I plead.

I pray. I bargain with God, Matka Boska, the Universe. The dull pain in my chest grows. My mouth and throat are dry. Anger washes over me. No—not anger. Rage.

Why?

An hour, a day, a week.

Cards. Telegrams. Newspaper headlines. Flowers. Baskets, wreaths, bouquets.

Words. So many words.

I remember the emptiness. The sticky days when all I do is stare out of the window, or walk a few steps, only to fall on my knees and sob. Time when I retrace the moments of that day, imagine us leaving earlier or later, stopping for lunch in Tournedos, taking another route. Imagine myself not closing my eyes to think of *Mephisto* but instead telling Kolya to slow down, to watch out, to be more careful. Until we pass that bend in the road, that tree; until we pass Évreux. Until we all arrive in Paris, safe.

On such days I hide deep inside myself, refuse to talk, move, eat. Stillness is my only temptation, a lure of numbness. I could stare at the wall until I die. I could hide in the corridors of my own mind. It would be easy. I would not hurt.

"Please, look at me, Bronia," Kolya begs. "Please don't go after him."

I remember wondering whom he means. My brother or my son? Madness or death?

And then I remember a doctor bending over me, telling me that my daughter has come out of the coma. "She needs you," he says, and stillness is no longer possible. I'm picking up her limp hand, covering it with kisses. Preparing myself to answer the question her parched lips will whisper.

"Levushka?"

Many newspapers wrote about the accident. In France, England, Germany, Monte Carlo. After the funeral, Kolya arranged the clippings in a black scrapbook with Levushka's photograph on the front page. And then, with red ink, he underlined all the mistakes.

Levushka was seventeen, not "sixteen." Levushka didn't "dance in his mother's studio." Levushka's parents were not, as one French paper claimed, "Madame Romola Nijinsky and her husband Léon Kotchetovsky."

Kolya painstakingly corrects all these errors. But to me they are strangely soothing. Each is like a hole in a woollen shawl. Small at first, but if I press my finger into it, it will grow bigger, wider. And if there are enough of them, the shawl will disappear.

I never hoped that writing would relieve me from grief. The notebooks I have filled are an offering for those I loved and lost. I have made space for the dead in my heart. This is where I will keep coming to touch them, stroke them, soothe them with my stories. So they will let me go on living.

I put down my pen, close my notebook and head for the deck.

Dawn has lightened the grey sky. The air is chilly. Gulls circle over the ship, a sign that land is close. They are dipping and wheeling over me, diving for fish or scraps.

Irina won't go with us to Australia. If Kolya and I do sail to Sydney with de Basil, Irina will go to Houston, to Sasha. Teach at his ballet school; wait until we come back. "It's not because of the accident," she has told me. "I've never been good enough. You've always known it."

"There is only one La Nijinska," she added.

Old dreams. Heaps of regrets.

When I sat by her hospital bed in Évreux, unhinged by grief and fear, I soothed myself with a vow that if she, too, died, I would climb into bed like my own grandmother once did, turn to the wall and wait for my own end.

I swallow the lump in my throat, breathe in the briny smell of the ocean. I think of Diaghilev, with his utter terror of any open water. Of his nervous half-smile when he watched Vaslav swim in the Lido. Of his relief when my brother, in his striped swimming costume, ran toward us, cold, dripping, splashing us with water he managed to carry in his cupped hands. "Come on, Serge, you coward. Come with me."

Will I find the strength for another struggle? After all I have lost?

Kolya is a few steps away from me, his face dense and heavy with waiting. I see his chest heave; I note a pulse throb in his throat. Don't blame me, Bronia, his eyes plead. If I could give my life for Levushka's, I would.

Harsh winters strengthen trees. The ring that forms through a time of stress is stronger than the ones formed in milder times. The Chosen Maiden, my brother once told me, is a warrior, not a dying swan. She dances to make life possible again.

This is an old memory, but Vaslav's voice remains urgent: Are you ready, Bronia?

I nod.

I step forward and raise my hand.

Acknowledgments

I came across Bronislava (Bronia) Nijinska's *Early Memoirs* by chance and instantly became smitten by her voice. The pages of *Early Memoirs* sparkle with recollections of her life as a young dancer, her complex and influential relationship with her brilliant brother Vaslav and her struggle to hold her own in the ballet world as an artist and a woman. The *Memoirs* end in August of 1914, and I still mourn the fact that the planned sequel never progressed beyond an outline and a few fragments.

Inspired by this captivating voice, I explored the Bronislava Nijinska Collection at the Library of Congress in Washington, D.C., a treasure trove of diaries, choreographic notes, correspondence, photographs and scrapbooks filled with reviews, interviews and theatre programs. *The Chosen Maiden* emerged out of these documents, and I like to think of it as archival fantasy, a fictional blend of facts and imagination.

I have many people to thank for their help.

My heartfelt gratitude goes to the staff and friends at the Library of Congress: Zbigniew Kantorosinski, Kevin LaVine, Natasha Nikitina, Agata Tajchert, Erika Kalvaitiene, Marina Melnikova and Luba Taubvurtzel, who helped me navigate the collection and decipher handwritten Russian documents.

Many people generously shared with me their love and deep knowledge of modern ballet. I'm particularly indebted to Carol Bishop Gwyn, Katherine Barber and Marjorie Fielding. I also owe enormous gratitude to dancers and choreographers who let me observe how they work and experience the world of dance, especially to Veronica Tennant, Piotr

Stanczyk, Caroline Niklas-Gordon and—in Poland—Krzysztof Pastor and Dominika Krysztoforska.

Jeff Prince, Anna Maria Jaroszynska, Anna Fishzon, Elizabeth Boone, Monika Caputa, Victoria Rachynska, Pia Kleber, Ann Lawson, Paul Brehl and Christopher Reynolds offered expert help, hospitality and guidance every time I needed it. Ophélie Lachaux was the perfect guide to the Théâtre des Champs-Élysées. Lisa Quoresimo shared with me her professional insights into the impact of Chaliapin's legendary voice.

Shaena Lambert, Zbyszek Stachniak and Carol Bishop Gwyn read early versions of *The Chosen Maiden* and offered just the right amount of encouragement to keep me going. Lara Hinchberger, my perfect editor, helped me shape the final versions of the novel. Helen Heller has been the best of agents.

Thank you!

xxx

Here are the books I found invaluable as I worked on *The Chosen Maiden*. All are excellent reads for those wishing to linger in Bronislava Nijinska's world for a while longer:

Bronislava Nijinska, *Early Memoirs*. Vaslav Nijinsky, *The Diary of Vaslav Nijinsky.* Romola Nijinsky, *Nijinsky* and *The Last Years of Nijinsky*. Feodor Chaliapin, *An Autobiography as Told to Maxim Gorky.* Tamara Karsavina, *Theatre Street: the Reminiscences of Tamara Karsavina.* Michel Fokine, *Memoirs of a Ballet Master.* Lydia Sokolova, *Dancing for Diaghilev*. H.S.H. The Princess Romanovsky-Krassinky, *Dancing in Petersburg: The Memoirs of Mathilde Kschessinska*. Lynn Garafola's *Diaghilev's Ballets Russes,* as well as her articles on Bronislava Nijinska, especially "An Amazon of the Avant-Garde: Bronislava Nijinska in Revolutionary Russia," published in *Dance Research.* The biographies of Vaslav Nijinsky by Richard Buckle, Lucy Moore, Vera Krasovskaya and Peter Ostwald. Sjeng Scheijen's *Diaghilev. A Life*. Kevin Kopelson's *The Queer Afterlife of Vaslav Nijinsky.*

EVA STACHNIAK was born in Wrocław, Poland and emigrated to Canada in 1981. She is the award-winning and internationally bestselling author of five novels. *The Winter Palace* was a *Globe and Mail* Best Book of the Year and a *Washington Post* Notable Fiction Book. She holds a PhD in literature from McGill University. She lives in Toronto.

www.evastachniak.com

Behind every great ruler lies a betrayal.
Immerse yourself in the world of Catherine the Great in Eva Stachniak's #1 bestselling novel.

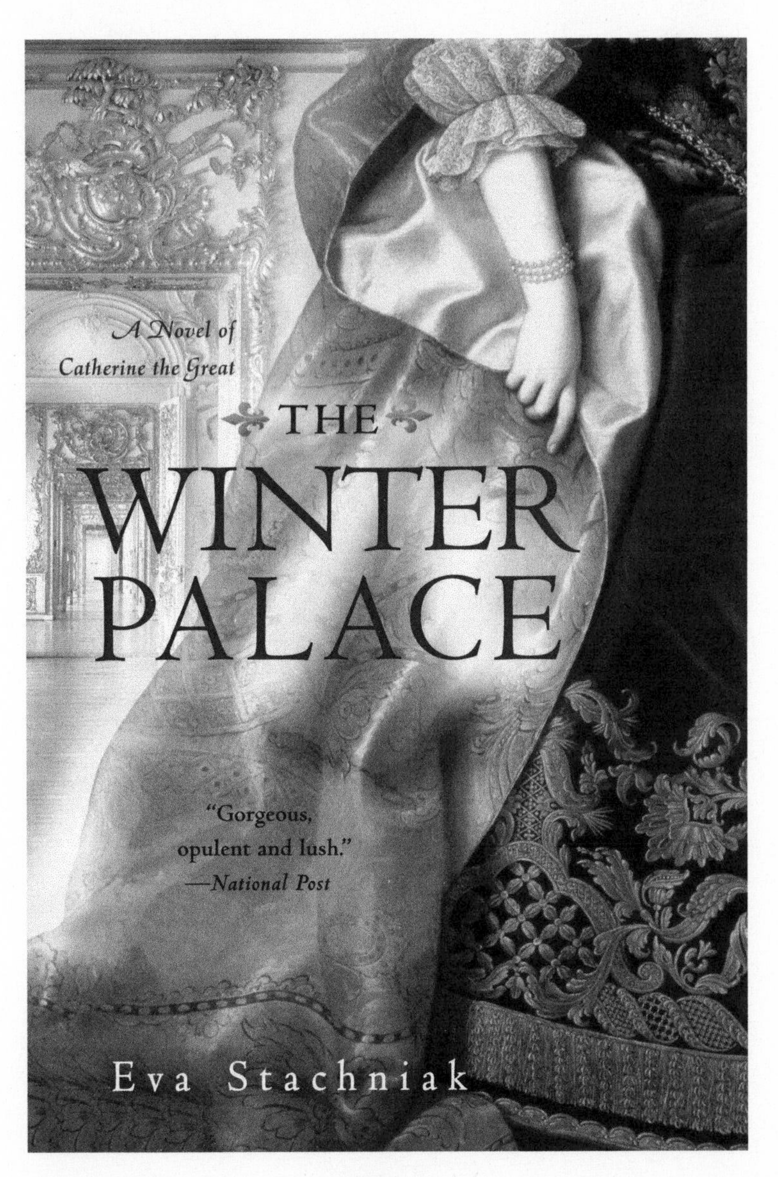

Revisit the splendor and deception of Catherine the Great's court in this stunning follow-up to *The Winter Palace*.